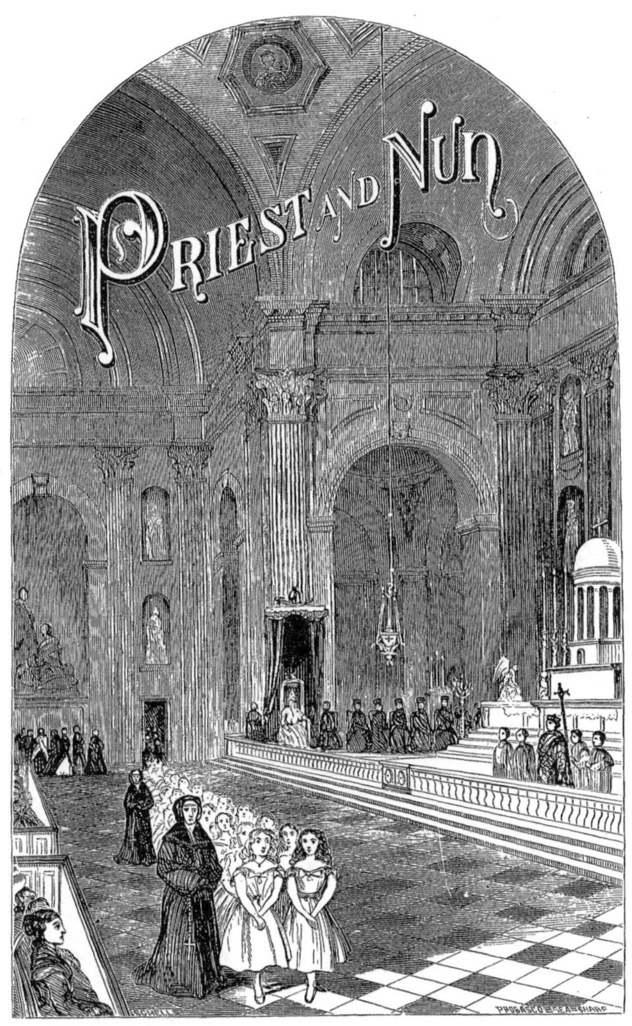

CRITTENDEN & McKINNEY,
Philadelphia.

D. E. FISK & Co.,
Springfield, Mass.

PRIEST AND NUN.

BY

MRS. JULIA MCNAIR WRIGHT,

AUTHOR OF

"ALMOST A NUN," "SHOE BINDERS OF NEW YORK," "NEW YORK NEEDLE-WOMAN," NEW YORK BIBLE-WOMAN," ETC., ETC.

WITH A

Valuable Appendix by the Publishers.

TWELFTH THOUSAND.

"Say is it wise,
Or right, or safe, for some chance good to-day,
To dare the vengeance of to-morrow's skies?
Be wiser, thou dear land, my native home;
Do always good, do good that good may come.
The path of duty plain before thee lies:
Break, break the spells of the enchantress, Rome!"

PHILADELPHIA:
CRITTENDEN & McKINNEY, 1308 CHESTNUT STREET.

SPRINGFIELD, MASS.
D. E. FISK & CO.

Entered according to Act of Congress, in the year 1869, by
CRITTENDEN & McKINNEY,
In the Clerk's Office of the District Court for the Eastern District of Pennsylvania

Westcott & Thomson,
Stereotypers, Philada.

NOTE BY THE AUTHOR.

THIS book stands firmly on facts. It contains no statements that can be traversed. We send it forth as presenting some faint picture of Romanism as it is to-day in these United States.

NOTE BY THE PUBLISHERS.

WE send this book out with the confident assurance that it will interest its readers, and in the firm belief that it will be productive of great good, not only in the United States, but in England; having pleasure in announcing an arrangement with Messrs. *Hodder & Stoughton, of London*, for its contemporaneous issue in the two countries.

Providentially, when we had nearly finished the stereotyping of the work, the senior member of that firm, being on a business tour in this country, called upon us, and, after an examination of the proof-sheets submitted to him, was so fully impressed with the excellence of the book, and with its peculiar adaptation to the present exigency of the times in England as well as here, that he readily negotiated with us for a duplicate set of stereotype plates, and for electrotypes of the fine wood-cuts with which it is illustrated; very honorably, also, contracting to allow us a royalty on sales effected, although not legally protected by any international copyright law.

NOTE TO SECOND EDITION. OCTOBER 15, 1869.

The publishers are happy to acknowledge the great favor with which "PRIEST AND NUN" has been received by the public, and to announce that the book has met with such rare success as to demand the printing of a *second three thousand in just two months from the date of first issue.*

CONTENTS.

PART FIRST.

SHOWING HOW ROME NOURISHED AND BROUGHT UP CHILDREN.

PART SECOND.

SHOWING THE MANNER OF ROME'S CHILDREN.

PART THIRD.

SHOWING HOW ROME'S CHILDREN REBELLED AGAINST HER.

LIST OF ILLUSTRATIONS.

PART FIRST.

SHOWING HOW ROME NOURISHED AND BROUGHT UP CHILDREN.

PRIEST AND NUN.

CHAPTER I.

CONSECRATION OF THE CHILDREN.

"The cloister—where, above all other places, the deceitful heart seems to learn the art of calling evil, good, and good, evil."—R. J. BRECKINRIDGE, D.D.

ON a bright, warm Sabbath in April three girls are to be consecrated, with others, to the Virgin. The families to which these girls belong are by no means common people. They have wealth, social position and what is called education. They pride themselves on their reputable birth, high breeding and descent from "good families." They do not trace their ancestral line back to Adam, for that any poor sinner may do, and by his very sinfulness prove his paternity. The roots of their family tree take hold on the Conquest; they had once a little "de" in the family, and they speak with infinite satisfaction of Norman blood. They belong to highly respectable society—in short, to the very *crême de la crême* of American city life—and are not to be set aside as nobodies because they become perverts to Rome.

Rome says she *tolerates* and *loves* her dear Protestant children—she longs to take and cherish them in her maternal bosom—and the history of these two families may illustrate the sincerity of her professed loving regard. A majority of these households—once unhappy heretics in Rome's estimation—have been artfully drawn within the fold of "the only true Church," and, with the love and zeal common to proselytes, the works of their spiritual Mother they do. Not content with dedicating their children to the Lord, like devout Papists they would also consecrate them to the Virgin Mary.

These two families reside in two fine brick houses that face each other on one of the "best" streets of the city.

Let us enter one of these homes. It is a well-appointed house indeed, with marble steps and portico, square hall of entrance with marble and stained glass in plenty, broad inner hall and staircase furnished in the highest style of the upholsterer's art, and through this we will pass up to a large front room. This can be done much more easily than you could find your way through the involved relationships of the family here abiding. This front room is occupied by the two daughters of the house—two of the three girls introduced to us at the opening of the chapter. It is a charming apartment—the bed high overarched with canopy of crimson silk, the mirror reaching from floor to ceiling, the toilette-table perfect in its various appliances. On the toilette-table lay a box from the milliner's, holding discord all unsuspected, and on the bed are carefully displayed the shining, undisturbed folds of two dresses of white alpaca with satin pipings.

In opposite corners of this room are the duplicate emblems of this family's creed. In each, suspended by a heavy gilt cord, hangs an oval frame of choice workmanship, this frame filled with black velvet, and the velvet serving as a rich relief to the pearl crucifix fastened upon it. Beneath this framed crucifix stands a rosewood table with a top of sandal-wood mosaic; on the table a breviary bound in scarlet, an open dish of fragrant hot-house flowers, a rosary whose beads —strange fate!—were cut from lava flung from the fiery heart of Vesuvius, and most precious of all, a vial of water dipped from the Tiber and blessed by the Pope. The furnishings of these two corners did not differ save in the embroidery upon two small chairs and footstools before the tables. As we shall learn from the satin paper-box which came from "Mrs. Deane, Fashionable Milliner," if the corners had differed trouble would have sprung therefrom.

The apartment is provided with two dressing-rooms. A tidy lady's maid, in waiting, has placed a chair in front of the mirror and stands behind it, brush and comb in hand, ready to begin her work whenever a subject shall present herself. And now, almost simultaneously, from each dressing-room walks a girl of fourteen.

They are pretty creatures, with their faces fresh from the bath, their damp hair falling over plump white necks, their slippered feet peeping from the lace, tucks and cambric of their skirts. The girl with curly, auburn hair steps the quicker and seats herself in the chair before the mirror. The brown-haired damsel shrugs her shoulders and looks about for a book. The maid hands her a dressing-sacque and a small red volume, whereupon she establishes herself on a hassock and begins to study as if she had no other object in life.

"Give me my Catechism too, Lucy," says miss in the chair; "I'm sure I've forgotten every solitary word of it. Do you know yours, Grace?"

"Don't bother me, Adelaide," replies Grace, with indifference, though it would have been shorter to say "yes" or "no."

Adelaide now addressed her maid: "Lucy, how many times do you suppose you have said the 'Hail Mary?'"

"Oh my, miss, a million at least; it's just tacked on to everything. As, of course, is proper."

"Grace, I wonder what Lilly means to wear!"

"Oh, clothes," said Grace, rattling over question and answer. "This tiresome Catechism slips out of my mind so fast."

"I'm sure I've learned it fifty times perfectly. Lucy, put on my shoes before you do Grace's hair. Mind, Lucy, that you put our white shoes in the bag; it would be *dreadful* to get there without them."

"Not half so dreadful as not to know what we are to do or say," said Grace.

"Yes it would," persisted Adelaide; "the idea of getting up there before all the folks in the cathedral with black shoes on! Why I wouldn't for a kingdom; I had rather not be consecrated. I'll tell you what I *would* do. Father Murphy 'd just have to wait until Lucy ran after the shoes!"

Grace opened her eyes and the maid was horrified at this astounding assertion. Adelaide was delighted with the effect of her remarks. She tossed her well-curled head and reiterated, "I certainly *would*, and if he didn't wait I'd turn heretic and join the Methodists."

"You'll have to confess that, Adelaide Grant."

"Bah!" said Adelaide, ungenteelly, resigning her

chair in favor of Grace. "I'll confess just what I please."

"But you know what the Catechism says: If we conceal a thing at confession we 'commit great sin by telling a lie to the Holy Ghost, and make our confession nothing worth.'"

"Pooh, pooh, pooh!" cried Adelaide, gayly spinning about on one toe until her skirts stood out like those of a "fate lady." "Why, Gracie, do you suppose the Catechism means all it says?"

"Of course it does," replied Grace, sedately, submitting to have her hair curiously braided by the skillful Lucy.

Meanwhile, we are sorry to say that although it was Sabbath, and she on the eve of taking part in a religious act, our Adelaide pirouetted about the room, practicing the last new airs and graces learned from her dancing-master, and, in her present ballet costume, much to her own satisfaction.

"For shame, Adelaide!" said the serious Grace; "you had better be saying your prayers."

"Oh, *they're* all done!" cried the flippant child. "I did them all up before I got out of bed this morning."

"Miss Grace always says hers devoutly at her *prie-Dieu*," said Lucy.

"Ah, yes; but I'm afraid I'll wear out my *prie-*

Dieu. I would not spend another three months working one for a fortune. I made so many mistakes that Sister Cecelia was as cross as two sticks."

"A Sister cross!" cried Lucy.

"To be sure; they're *folks* like the rest of us, and why not let them have the satisfaction of getting cross?" and Adelaide danced into the dress her maid was holding out to her, while Grace quietly put on her own. "Do you think," cried Adelaide, with the air of one asking information of deep interest, "that these dresses are as handsome as the ones we wore at confirmation last year?"

"Why, yes," replied Lucy, weighing the matter carefully.

"Grace, what do you suppose there will be for us to do—in church I mean—next year? Last year was confirmation; this year is consecration; what next?"

"You might take the veil," suggested the unwary Lucy.

Adelaide threw up her hands and uttered a queer little exclamation; then, preserving the tragic attitude, flew to the mirror: "Grace, as sure as you're alive, this is just the way Madame Virginie acted in Athalie the other night. I believe I was born for an actress. If there's nothing to do in the church next year, I think I'll go on the stage."

"Oh, Miss Adelaide, you'll never be dressed if you will not keep still; do let me put on your sash;" and Lucy opened the luckless box on the table and took out two rolls of rich ribbon.

The quick-eyed girls uttered an exclamation, and each laid hold of the satin sash. "I'll have this," said Grace, in her incisive way.

"No, Grace Kemp, I must have it. The satin is mine."

"Your mother thought them alike. Miss Adelaide; this watered ribbon is handsomer," cried Lucy.

"Not with satin shoes and pipings. I'll have the satin. Do give it up, Grace."

"You always want me to give it up!" exclaimed Grace, "but this time I shall not. I'm a month older than you, and I have as much right to the satin sash as you have."

"Miss Adelaide, you will be late to the cathedral," interposed Lucy. "*Wouldn't* you let me put on this watered ribbon?—I'm sure it's a beauty."

"No, not if I never go there; I tell you I won't wear that thing!" cried Adelaide, stamping her foot.

"Not dressed yet, girls? why, what is the matter?" said a lady who now entered the room. She was like Adelaide in features and complexion, a little faded by her forty years; a very precise and finished woman of the world, whose eyes were mild and of a light hazel, and whose chin retreated just a very little.

"Why didn't you buy our sashes alike?" cried Adelaide, rudely.

"The sashes, ma'am—they both want the satin one," explained Lucy.

"How very careless of Madame Barry!" said Mrs. Kemp, taking a sash in either white, jeweled hand, and looking uncertainly at the two girls.

"I think, ma'am, that you'll have to send for another," said Grace, coolly, "for neither of us will wear that one."

"But this is Sunday morning, my child, and madame's store is shut. Adelaide, my dear, let Grace have the sash she wants."

"I'll stay home from church first," said Adelaide.

"Grace, I'm sure you will not mind; let Adelaide have this satin ribbon to oblige me, my love."

"I'm for ever asked to give up to Adelaide. I have as good a right to my own way as she."

"That is true. Adelaide, what will Sister Cecelia say if you are late, for a silly quarrel? I wish she were here to manage you."

"I don't care what she says, and I sha'n't be managed by anybody," retorted Adelaide.

Mrs. Kemp looked from one girl to the other in despair, and then at the clock. But now Lucy turned to Grace:

"I'm sure, miss, when you are so well prepared, and know all your questions, and you such a favorite of Father Murphy, and you to be consecrated to our Blessed Lady, you will not quarrel with your sister about a bit of sash, who knows not nearly so much religion as you do, nor can say her prayers and her questions to equal you. You might set her a good example, miss, as a child of our Blessed Lady should."

This was but a disjointed exhortation to be sure, but Grace had had time to change her mind. She held out her hand for the despised sash.

"Thank you, Grace!" says Mrs. Kemp, quite relieved. "Now, daughter Adelaide, I hope you're satisfied."

"I always am satisfied when I have my own way," replied Adelaide, unabashed.

"Indeed, Miss Grace," said Lucy, "you're a true child of our Lady, and I don't misdoubt you'll be like your holy aunt,—our—mother of the Immaculate Heart of Mary."

"Yes, yes," cried Adelaide, her sash now properly bowed, "do let us see how you would look, Grace;" and catching up a cambric kerchief she pulled it about her sister's face, and wrapped a black veil above it, after the fashion of a nun's headgear. "Gracious, child, you look like the 'Mother' to the life!"

"Oh, Miss Adelaide, your sister's hair!—you will have it mussed so I must do it over!" cried Lucy.

"Let me alone, Adelaide; how silly you are!" said Grace.

"Adelaide, pray act like a lady," remonstrated the mother.

After all this folly and bustle consuming the morning of the day claimed by the Creator as his own, Mrs. Kemp, Grace and Adelaide were ready to set out for the cathedral, Lucy following with the satchel containing white wreaths for the girls' heads and white shoes for their feet.

Much did Lucy think of the rite in which her young ladies were to participate. To her simple mind it was something that should lift them out of their common life and make them sacred, as were the treasures of old laid up in the ark of God.

As for the girls, they were troubled with no such serious reflections. Adelaide, being dressed to her taste, was in exuberant spirits, while Grace walked with more than her usual dignity and self-consciousness, for to herself she seemed the centre of the little ceremony—we had almost written comedy—which was to be performed before the admiring throng in the cathedral.

But now that we have Grace and Adelaide safely started toward the cathedral, we must go back a little in point of time and see what has been going on in the "fine brick house" opposite Mr. Kemp's. This house was the home of Judge Schuyler.

Lilly Schuyler was being dressed in a white costume, even more rich and elaborate than that of her youthful neighbors. She was a delicate-looking girl, with hair of the palest flaxen hue, shining and soft, and curling about her neck. She had the large, dreamy eyes, the transparent complexion and the mobile mouth of an enthusiast, looking more like the ideal of angel or fairy on a painter's canvas than a veritable being of flesh and blood. Yet there were two or three lines and touches of expression on her face that showed she might be resolute as impressionable. Her room looked almost as much like a little chapel or oratory as a young girl's apartment. Besides the crucifix, holy water, flowers and *prie-Dieu*, where she might properly say her prayers, there was a shrine sacred to the Virgin Mary, whereon stood a large doll dressed in white silk, with a spangled blonde cloak, a small silver diadem on its head, Lilly's best chain and locket about its neck, and her one jewel, a small diamond pin, shining on its unstirring bosom. This image was our Blessed Lady, patroness, not only of Lilly Schuyler, but of the Holy Church, and chosen by our Father of Rome as the patroness of America—said America being yet but a sprawling heretical infant, yet expected by our aforesaid Father to grow up as a good many other infants have done, to zealous and obedient popish manhood.

About Lilly's room hung twelve small paintings, the twelve stations which hang in churches and are preached about in Lent. There was also hung opposite her bed a fine oil-painting of Our Lady of Seven Sorrows.

There was another lady in Lilly's room, who seemed more truly sorrowful than the Lady who held the heart with seven arrows in it in the picture. The living lady sat by a window looking into the street, one hand lying listlessly in her lap, the other holding a handkerchief, wherewith she now and then wiped the tears that rolled silently down her cheeks. This lady was Lilly's mother, and Lilly and her maid frequently glanced toward her—the maid, Hannah, with eyes of respectful commiseration, Lilly with mingled anxiety and obstinacy.

Lilly passively submitted to be dressed, giving no heed to the matter at all; unlike Grace and Adelaide, she was occupied entirely with the *religious* part of the morning exercises; her little hands told over her rosary, while her lips moved rapidly, and one moment she looked at the crucifix and the next at the shrine of the Virgin. Glancing often at her mother, various emotions contended in her face as she saw that mother's grief.

"How bad your ma do feel, Miss Lilly!" said Hannah under her breath.

Lilly sighed and looked at her Virgin.

"She's breaking her heart, Miss Lilly, and you all the child she has. Don't you do it, miss."

"Hush, Hannah. Am I dressed? Well, then, you may go and wait for me in the hall."

Thus Lilly was left alone with her mother. She stole up to her and touched her arm: "I am all dressed, mother."

There was no response.

"Won't you look at me?" asked Lilly, tremulously.

The lady turned and gazed with tearful eyes at the little white-robed figure by her side.

"Lilly," she said, "you will break my heart."

"What, mother! just by being consecrated to the Virgin?"

"No, but this is only one step among the many that shall take you from me for ever."

"No, mother!" cried Lilly, clasping her hands and her eyes growing radiant in her enthusiasm; "you

Lilly and her Mother.

Priest and Nun. Page 24.

shall come with me; you shall come into the true Church, where father and I are. This makes me more ready to go, so that you will come too, mother."

"No," said Mrs. Schuyler, "I shall never turn in my trouble to that Church which has separated me from my child—that Church which has taken from me my dearest treasure. Child as you are, Lilly, do you belong to me any more? Have not priests and nuns come between you and your mother? After all these years, when you have been my one thought, do you not go to those whom you call your Mother and your Sisters, and trust them instead of me, and follow their counsel to disobey me, and leave me lonely that you may spend your time with them? And so it will be until I am a lonely old woman, without a daughter or a comfort in all the world."

Lilly was weeping too. "I *do* love you mother; I do trust you. I will not leave you alone in the world," she sobbed.

"Yes, Lilly, and this very moment there is one of your nuns waiting for you in the parlor, to take you to a ceremony which I think both idle and wicked, and from which I have besought you to turn."

"But father allows me, mother," said Lilly.

"Yes, Father Murphy is setting against me both husband and child. He tells you, Lilly—for whom I have lived and hoped these fourteen years—that I am a heretic and unfit to guide you, and he counsels your father to take you from my influence;" and the excited and unhappy woman bowed her face to her lap and wept bitterly.

"Miss Lilly," said Hannah at the door, "Saint Cecelia says you must come or you will be late."

"Good-bye, mother," said Lilly, and getting no reply, kissed the back of her mother's bowed neck, and then with a humble reverence to Our Lady's shrine, as if passing a royal presence, Lilly left the room.

Saint Cecelia was a small, shriveled, clear-voiced woman, in coarse black dress, broad black apron reaching to the hem of her gown, a rosary at her waist, a kerchief about her colorless face and a black hood on her head, her whole garb being unsuggestive of the saintly, except to prejudiced minds.

"What is my dear child crying about?" asked the nun.

"Mother feels so dreadfully," gasped Lilly.

"You must not mind *that*," said the Sister as they left the house; "this may help to your mother's conversion."

"She mourns so that you are all taking me away from her," said Lilly, sadly.

"If she were a good Catholic, and not a heretic, she would rejoice over that; we must mortify the desires and affections of the flesh," said the sympathetic Sister.

"She said I am breaking her heart," cried Lilly; "and oh, Saint Cecelia, suppose I am—suppose my dear mother should die?"

"Then I dare say that our prayers would cause her to die in the Holy Catholic faith; and of course you know, dear child, that it is better to die a Catholic than to live a heretic."

On went the child in white and delicate array, beside the Sister in rough black garb, thus symbolizing the course of Rome's proselyte, from the first fair allurements to the days of living death. Saint Cecelia, with her crucifix held between her clasped hands, tranquilly pursued her way; but Lilly constantly wiped her flowing tears with her small morsel of pocket handkerchief.

"My dear child," said the calm monotone of Saint Cecelia, "it would be well to cease crying; some one meeting us may suppose this gracious privilege of consecration an unwilling sacrifice, or judge that our gracious Mother the Church is unable to comfort her children."

Lilly obediently gave her distressed face a final wipe with her wet handkerchief, yet pressed her small hand to her fluttering heart, and caught a sobbing breath every now and then.

"My dear child," said Saint Cecelia, regarding the sad, sensitive, flower-like face as calmly as one would regard some wet pebble in the bed of any little brook, "this all comes of your not being confirmed. If you had done right and come to the arms of the Church, she would have supplied to you the place of any mother whatsoever, and, safe in her embrace, you could not have so rebelliously wept over the grief of any heretic."

"But she is *my mother*," gasped Lilly, piteously.

"Do you know what our Holy Church says?" replied the nun: "He that loveth father or mother more than me is not worthy of me."

But they were nearing the lofty front of St. Joseph the Just, and Saint Cecelia saw that her little charge must be soothed; so she said: "It is not unlikely that your prayers, vows, offerings, penances and other acts of religion will be blessed to the conversion of your mother. Think, dear child, of your joy at saving your mother's soul! You are now to be given to our Blessed Lady, and you must beset her with prayers night and day for your mother's good. You cannot serve our Lady too well. For myself, I set apart the first day of every month as a day of prayer and praise to Mary."

Herein our zealous nun exceeded and anticipated our Father the Pope, who had not then ordered the eighth day of December as a Festival of Obligation in honor of the Virgin.

And now they entered the vestry, and there were Grace and Adelaide duly wreathed and in the requisite white gaiters, and there were about twenty other girls of equal age; and now they were placed in order by the Sisters, and with slow steps and bent heads, a white-clad procession, upon whose footsteps hung the nuns, as clouds hang sometimes where bars of white moonlight have broken through, they stole to the sound of soft organ music through the grand entrance door of St. Joseph the Just.

(I suppose you have all read the story of the Minotaur and the Labyrinth of Crete.)

The ceremony of consecration was but a small affair in itself, the preparations and dressing being the greater part. There were some questions, music and prayers, and then these girls were supposed to have been placed under the especial patronage of the Virgin, sure of her protection and intercession, and forming perhaps some sort of juvenile sodality vowed to Mariolatry—a polite and modern form of paganism.

The service over, Saint Cecelia took Lilly home. The girl was a charge too precious to have less than the most watchful care. "Saint Cecelia, what shall I do to-day?" asked the girl, meekly.

"Fast, my child, until evening. Spend two hours in adoration of our Blessed Virgin and be punctual at vespers."

Oh, crafty Sister! Fast until evening? There would be then no dinner with her mother. Two hours of adoration at our Lady's shrine? The young heart would then be strengthened against that mother's sad reproachful face. Early at vespers, and lost the evening hour when mother and child might sit together in the gathering twilight.

Sister Cecelia had one crowning merit—she wrote a most beautiful hand. She formed English, French and German script like the fairest specimens of copper-plate. Before her humble girlhood two paths of life had opened—to be a writing-mistress in schools and private families, or to bring herself and her talent into the convent. Deciding to take vows and the veil, she at once became a *saint.* Oh, short and broad and easy road to heaven—a garb, a promise, a fixed routine of living; and lo! a portal, said of salvation, opened wide. If we might but be *sure* it is one of the pearl portals opening on the golden street of God's city, and not that back door on the under side of a hill which Bunyan saw in vision!

As in duty bound, when at so little sacrifice of her loneliness and poverty Sister Cecelia had from the Church at once her daily living and her saintship, she served that Church with ardor. We can give no better definition of this nun than that we find in "The Constitutions and Declarations of the Jesuits," published in France in 1762. "One ought to permit himself to be conducted and directed as if a corpse, which is moved as any one wills; or as the cane in an old man's hand, which serves any end for which the owner employs it, and upon whatever side he chooses to turn it."

Sister Cecelia lived, moved, wrote (copies), spoke, thought, for the Church. Her even, gliding step, her cold, steady eye, her monotone running in set form, "My dear child, thus and so," as clear, as even and as unexpressive as endless repetitions of E flat in the treble, with never another note struck between, were all the outward tokens of her passive, unreasoning, unstirred inner life.

Lilly bade her adviser "good-morning" and went up alone to her room. The bell for dinner was ringing, but she was bent on fasting and two hours of "adoration."

"Please come to dinner, Miss Lilly, your ma says," called Hannah at Lilly's locked door.

"Tell mamma that I am to fast to-day," cried Lilly, clearly. She was already kneeling on a little cushion before the marble table that held "Our Lady."

Hannah gave Miss Lilly's message to Mrs. Schuyler. The lady made no reply, but left her food untasted on her plate, and sat, her head resting on her hand, at her lonely board. Judge Schuyler had been invited to dine with Father Murphy and one or two other Romanists of high authority. The judge, a new and valuable convert, was treated with great respect by these ghostly fathers; indeed the judge had been invited to visit Archbishop Hughes, and had received from Rome the picture of a famous cardinal set in gold. Mrs. Schuyler, being a misguided heretic, did not feel any less lonely in her large dining-room because the husband, who should have sat opposite her, was dining with Father Murphy, and because the daughter, who should have been beside her, was fasting by order of Saint Cecelia. Indeed, we think she was only the more lonely and sad as she thought of these causes of her desertion, and saw the gulf between herself and her kindred growing wider every hour.

Presently she rang a bell: "Take the dinner away, Henry; I do not want anything to-day," she said, and then went up to her parlor: but the parlor was as lonely as the dining-room. She looked across the street. Mr. Kemp was just coming from his front door, with a cigar in his mouth, drawing on his gloves for a cheerful Sunday stroll. He nodded at her as he saw her pale face at her window. Mr. Kemp was her brother.

"Yes," sighed Mrs. Schuyler, apostrophizing her brother's retreating figure, "it seems as if our family were under some especial curse: first *you* went over to Rome, then my husband, and, as if I were not wretched enough, they have taken away my child. They have taken away my child, and what have I more?" It was as if she lifted up the doleful cry of Micah, following his captured gods.

Mrs. Schuyler's friends called her "a lovely woman," "an amiable woman." She was also undeniably a weak woman; even to her child she had never dared speak strong, earnest words for the religion she professed; she had never knelt with that child to pray, never questioned as to the state of her heart toward God, never besought her to embrace the Saviour. When she saw that child thrown among popish influences and companions, she dared not interfere because those companions were relatives. When the child was sent to a convent-school—the act was the father's—the mother ventured a faint remonstrance, and like other weak women could but resort to tears. Had this mother but been able to firmly fulfill a mother's duties, perchance no one could ever have come between her and her child, but closely together they might have walked toward heaven.

CHAPTER II.

WHY THEY WERE ROME'S CHILDREN.

LILLY had come back from vespers, and now had a little time to devote to her mother. Judge Schuyler had also got home. He was always affable and gentlemanly. To-day he had had both wine and flattery with Father Murphy; had been at the cathedral to see his daughter consecrated, and told his wife it was a charming sight, very touching and suggestive, and she should have been there to witness it.

"You cannot expect religion in Protestant girls, Maria," said the judge, putting on the slippers Henry had brought him and unfolding his Sunday paper; "they have nothing to provoke it. Protestantism is dull and dry—utterly barren of all that would move the youthful heart or stir the imagination."

Mrs. Schuyler was silent; she had been a Protestant girl, and perchance had merited this present accusation.

"Of course, Maria," continued the judge, searching for the report of Saturday afternoon's interesting case, "you will admit the testimony of facts. 'By their fruits ye shall know them;' isn't that the doctrine? Well, where do you find such fruits as in the Romish Church? Just look at whole communities of men and women wholly devoted to doing good. In what other denomination are children so well cared for and instructed? What other Church is so zealous for proselytes? I'm convinced, Maria, that there is but one true Church, and that is— Ah here is Davis' speech; just listen to it, Maria; it was as complete a thing as I've heard for a year."

Mrs. Schuyler had meditated asking Lilly to read a chapter of the Bible to her, but she could not suggest that Davis' speech was not the best possible Sabbath reading, or that herself and Lilly might be better employed than in listening to it.

Meanwhile, just across the street, Grace and Adelaide had the parlor to themselves; Adelaide lying on a sofa, reposing after the fatigues of attending vespers, and Grace looking into the street.

"Gracie, what in the world are you looking out of the window so long for?" demanded Adelaide; "*has* anybody passed along this stupid street for half an hour?"

"I don't know—I'm thinking," replied Grace.

"I believe you spend half your time thinking. What's on your mind now?"

"I was thinking of a little book Annie Mott has; it is called, 'Why am I a Presbyterian?'"

Adelaide burst into a fit of laughter: "If that isn't *too* absurd. Who cares why any one is a Presbyterian? They are a dull, stiff set, very much like the Methodists and Baptists and all other heretics. I shouldn't think any one could write a primer about *that.*"

"But this was not a primer: it was a good-sized book, nicely bound. Annie's uncle gave it to her for learning the Catechism."

"The reward was as stupid as the task," said Adelaide. "He should have given her a hundred dollars. I've seen Annie's Catechism. Oh, it is *fearful!*—worse than ours. But, Gracie, you must be badly off for something to think of, if you spend your ideas on Annie's silly book."

"Oh, it had set me thinking why am I a Catholic?"

Adelaide laughed louder and longer than before. "Why is anybody a Catholic?" she cried.

"Yes," returned Grace, seriously, "why is anybody anything?"

"I should think your poor head would ache trying to unravel such nonsense, Grace!" exclaimed the lively Adelaide. "Let me enlighten your ignorance at once. Here: 'Why was your mother a Catholic? Lay it to Aunt Robart.' 'Why is my mother a

Catholic? Ditto.' 'Why is father a Catholic. He's a politician, and wanted votes.' 'Why is Uncle Schuyler a Catholic? Because he was too busy to do his own religion, and Father Murphy was quite willing to do it for him.' 'Why is Lilly a Catholic? Referred to Aunt Robart again.' 'Why are you and I Catholics? Because our mothers are.' 'Why is everybody a Catholic? Because they are not heretics.' 'Why is anybody a heretic? Because they are not Catholics.' There, my dear Gracie, I have cleared all that matter up. Dear me! you seem quite astonished."

Grace was indeed astonished at Adelaide's summary way of disposing of her rapidly-put queries.

"Why, Adelaide," she said in a puzzled way, "your talk sounds more like brother Richard than just you. I'm afraid you'll get to be one of those people who don't believe in anything."

"Believe, *believe!* yes I do. I believe everything that's told me, even when I *know* it isn't true. Father Murphy told me at confession only yesterday that young girls had no right to reason or think for themselves, but just trust to the Church, and, of course, I'm not going to bother myself thinking after that."

"I shall," said Grace, independently. "If you can't think, you might just as well be a wax doll."

"By no means," replied Adelaide; "for then you couldn't have the pleasure of dressing or eating, and there's a deal of pleasure in those things, Grace, and —there's the supper-bell."

All this family were to be seen at supper—Mr. Kemp, Mrs. Kemp, Richard, a youth of twenty-two, half-brother to Grace, and these two girls. The young man occupied one side of the table. Grace and Adelaide were opposite him.

"What! ready to eat again?" cried Richard, lifting both hands at his opposites. "Consecration does not seem to have etherealized you particularly."

"Nobody expected it to," said Adelaide, but Grace was silent, for she felt that the rite ought to be worth something.

"Then nobody was disappointed," pursued Richard. "I had the pleasure of coming home just behind your troop of white-robed neophytes. Your Sisters were intent on your appearance before heretical eyes. My Adelaide was absorbed wholly in the vanities of her own array. Grace, with puzzled face, was engaged in solving some mighty Why? The Shannon girls were bickering, as they always are. Mary Ralph looked black as a thunder-cloud because her dress was spotted, and poor little Lilly was evidently the modern Iphigenia."

"Why, Rick, were you near us? I didn't know

it," said Adelaide, regarding with eyes of sincere affection a quivering amber mould of jelly on its crystal dish.

"I saw Father Murphy leaving the cathedral, and I had a mind to tell him to take Shannon, Ralph and company back and consecrate them over 'again,'" rattled on Richard.

Mrs. Kemp half smiled. It was her policy never to frown at word or deed of her step-children; but Mr. Kemp suggested to Richard the propriety of guarding his tongue a little better.

"There's no need of that, sir, until I run for Congress," replied the irrepressible young man.

One might suppose that Mr. Kemp would have been mortally offended at this palpable hit, but, on the contrary, he smiled. He regarded his politico-religious manœuvres as worthy a Machiavelli, and Machiavelli was his demigod.

We have stumbled upon the very middle of a long (and strong) chain of circumstances. The beginning of this chain lies as far away as when the present Mrs. Kemp was a little girl. A pair of very foolish parents had three daughters. The parents were nominal members of a Protestant communion. Though it is a communion which has good schools of its own, these very foolish parents—we call them this *par excellence*, feeling quite sure that besides them there were never any others—sent their daughters to a convent to school. They had *heard* it was a most excellent, thorough, well-disciplined school, so they sent the three girls there until school-days were ended. The three girls came home and were shortly after married. The eldest daughter married Mr. Robart, the second Mr. Grant, and the third Mr. Kemp, a widower. The first two ladies were left widows—the third died, leaving Grace, her daughter. After a year or two of mourning, Mrs. Grant married Mr. Kemp, and became step-mother of her niece Grace, and of Richard, the child of Mr. Kemp's first marriage. Mrs. Robart, being rich and childless, went over to the faith wherein she had been educated at school, and entered a holy order, her fortune and decided abilities making her very welcome. Sister Margaret Robart's first step was to confirm the Romish *inclinings* Mrs. Kemp had gained at the convent. Her next was to convert Mr. Kemp, to do which, as spiritual motives would not avail, she used political. Of course the children were swept along in this strong current setting toward Rome, and not the children only:—Margaret Robart had read the character of Mr. Kemp's brother-in-law, Judge Schuyler, and he too was carried into the true Church.

Sister Margaret lived in the odor of sanctity, and grew in favor daily. She was chosen Superior of her order, the Mother of the Convent of the Immaculate Heart of Mary. Her other honors lay shining before her. Thus, you see, from the educational theories of those parents, now asleep in their graves, Rome was edified by a Mother of the Convent of the Immaculate Heart, etc., by two mothers of families—for Grace's mother had died in the one infallible Church—by a politician well before the public eye, and by a judge upon the bench in the honorable court of a very honorable city. Besides all this, from these parents' school choice came young Richard, sneering at nearly everything, and Mrs. Schuyler breaking her heart, and, Lilly!—well, we shall see what of Lilly.

These many conversions were in days before "Ritualism was predisposing the Protestant world to regard with merited consideration the exalted and venerable rites of the holy Catholic faith." *

We have heard Adelaide wondering "what there would be next to do." This craving for excitement is well understood and constantly met in the Romish Church; the youthful mind is kept in a continual whirl. Instead of the calm gravity, dignity and clear reasoning of Protestantism, such youths as Adelaide see in religion a rush of holy days, white dresses, emblems, processions and the like. The next "excitement" for our girls was not

* Catholic Standard.

supposed to be primarily of a religious sort—it was the grand yearly exhibition of the Conventual School of the Immaculate Heart of Mary.

"Exhibition, exhibition!" was now the cry of the girls from morning until night.

"Indeed, Miss Adelaide," remonstrated Lucy, "I do not believe you have said your prayers for a week."

"Oh yes, I have, Lucy. I rattle them off whenever I think of them; but you've no idea how much time it takes to prepare for exhibition. I'm learning a dozen of things for that, and of course I have no time to go over ever so many prayers."

"But what will Father Murphy say when he hears that at confession?"

"Oh, I'll get them all said before that. Yesterday, while we were waiting for the dessert, I said the Confiteor and 'Blessed be the Hours,' and to-day I shall do the Act of Contrition and those other ones. I'll get them done, never fear."

With Grace it was different; she was ambitious, and intensely anxious to make a good display of herself at the examination and exhibition. She would for a day or two be as negligent of devotional exercises as Adelaide; then, seized with one of her often-recurring fits of spiritual uneasiness, she would be constant in her worship before her shrine in the bedroom.

Grace and Adelaide loved each other sincerely, but there was a sort of rivalry between them that made each jealous and watchful lest the other should do or have something better than herself. This peculiarity had been fostered by Mrs. Kemp's nervous anxiety lest she should seem to discriminate between her daughter and step-daughter. Her chief ambition was to fill acceptably, and to the admiration of all the family friends, the difficult position of third wife, and when any dispute arose between the girls, she besought, with perfect impartiality, first one and then the other to yield. Generally Grace yielded, but managed to have the best of the bargain still.

At this exhibition, Grace, as the pupil having the most self-possession and elegance of manner, was to open the evening on the part of the pupils with a salutatory address in French.

This threw Adelaide into high excitement. Grace speak a piece and she have none! She would never go near the school again! she should keep her room; she would speak to nobody if she could not speak in public as well as Grace!

Mrs. Kemp, finding it impossible to placate the offended power, consulted with Sister Cecelia and with Sister Saint Sophia, the principal teacher, and it was arranged that Adelaide should recite a poem, called "Our Blessed Lady."

Grace was to write her salutation, and expended much time upon it. When she sent it in for correction it was quietly rewritten by Sister Lorette, a nun from Paris.

"Why," cried Grace, "there's hardly a word of mine left!"

"Yours was very good for your age, but, of course, a Parisienne like Sister Lorette can do it much better. We shall have a large audience, and we want the French exercises of the very best. Sister Lorette can compose it, I will copy it and you can speak it, which you will do better than any one. Very likely the audience will want the paper handed around," said Sister Cecelia.

"But on the scheme for the evening it is put 'French salutation, *composed* and spoken by Grace Kemp!'"

"It is virtually yours; the *ideas* are all as you had them."

"But the French is not mine!" cried Grace, "and it is a real humbug. I won't have my name put to it, if it is not mine."

"If Mother Robart thinks best you will."

"No, I shall not; it is telling lies!" cried Grace, angrily.

This language was reported to Father Murphy, Director and Confessor of the Convent, and Grace was called to account.

"They wanted me to help *deceive*," said Grace, scornfully. Grace from earliest childhood had been a worshiper of truth. It was a love predicating her outgrowing Rome, and Father Murphy regarded to with suspicion.

"Such things are not called *falsehoods*. They are expedient, and a child of your age should obey and not question. This which Saint Cecelia proposes is *not* a lie, and you insult her by calling it so," said the priest.

"It is not *truth*," said Grace, boldly.

The matter was settled by having Grace write the composition and Saint Lorette correct it, while Grace was to ask pardon of Saint Cecelia and do penance by fasting on bread and water, and spending two hours of play-time in the chapel at her prayers. Said Father Murphy to his pupil: "You, Grace, *know* the most religion, but Adelaide *acts* the most. She obeys *unquestioningly*. She does not set up her own opinion. In religion *obedience*, and not wisdom, is the thing acceptable."

"Grace," said Adelaide one evening when the girls were alone in the parlor, "I've been fairly frightened to death by that algebra examination, but I see now how it is to be done. Do you notice that for three mornings in our 'general review' we have had the same examples? Sister means to have us perfect in them, and then give them to us on examination."

Grace wondered if that were "deception," but did not say so, for she had just been doing penance for too free an expression of opinion.

Richard was sitting on the balcony, and here put his head into the window: "Adelaide, how far along are you in algebra?"

"Oh, most through. You needn't ask me any questions though, Rick."

"How do you like equations?"

"Equations; what are they?"

"Algebraic equations, child; how do you like them?"

"Oh, I haven't got to them yet."

"Why, yes we *have*," cried Grace, impatiently—"ever so long ago, Adelaide. The example you had on the board to-day was an equation."

"Well," said Adelaide, triumphantly, "I don't know a thing about them. I didn't know that until Sister worked it out for me."

"Adelaide Grant! and Sister Saint Sophia has marked you *nine* on the rolls, and that is nearly perfect," cried Grace.

"Well, what of that? They mark all the scholars

eight or nine, so their friends will like the school and send them back. They wouldn't put down poor marks. Who do you suppose is to get the French prize?"

"Who?" cried Grace, eagerly.

"Nannie Graves! She is about the poorest one there is. She can't talk ten words right, and she always blunders in reading, and her exercise is worse than mine; but her father is a rich Protestant, and he is very particular about her learning French, so she gets the prize to make him send her back."

"It's too bad," cried Grace, bitterly; "all the prizes go to Protestant girls!"

"Yes, that is to make them come back and bring more; they know we'll come, anyway," said Adelaide.

A few days before this exhibition the two girls came home in great glee. They rushed into the parlor, where their mother sat dressed for the evening, and Richard was resting after his day of office-work.

"We've been to a wedding!" cried the girls.

"Horrors!" exclaimed their mother; "not in cambric dresses?"

"Oh, it was in the convent chapel; Mother Robart had us all in," said Grace.

"I do like weddings!" cried Adelaide. "Rick, get married, please, so we can have a grand wedding to go to, and father will get us white silks; do, Rick."

"Nonsense!" ventured Mrs. Kemp. "Lilly will not be old enough this five years." A match between Lilly and Richard was her darling hope.

"Lilly!" repeated Richard, scornfully.

"Why not?" laughed Mrs. Kemp. "She is a little girl now, but by the time you are ready to settle down, she will be one of the most beautiful and accomplished young ladies in the city."

"She's a regular little Papist!" said Richard, hotly.

"Girls," said Mrs. Kemp, quickly, "go and dress. Lucy is waiting for you. Put on your check silks and blue sashes." The girls ran off, and Mrs. Kemp, looking full at her step-son, said, "So am I a Papist, Richard."

"I beg ten million pardons, you jewel of a mother!" said Richard.

"And it *should* be in your eyes an advantage," said Mrs. Kemp, loftily.

"Doubtless, it does admirably for father, as he says he is one himself, but for myself, being none, I do not want my wife to be."

"But why not?" persisted Mrs. Kemp.

"I should offend you," said Richard.

"I proclaim an amnesty beforehand; let me hear your objections."

"Well, then, I don't want a wife who is under the control of a priest—who makes known to her confessor my private affairs, applies to him for direction rather than to me, and lays open to him my deepest confidences. I do not want a wife belonging to a Church which tells her, 'A wife may gamble, and take for that purpose the money of her husband.' * I think Rome comes between the most sacred relationships. See, for instance, Lilly. Until maturity, at least, a mother is supposed to be a child's nearest friend. In a mother the child should confide. The mother's wishes should be its guidance. A good mother is, next to God, a child's nearest and wisest friend. But Lilly is made to deceive and cast off her mother. She is forced to withdraw from her, to treat her coldly, to disobey her, to break her heart. Never was there a better and gentler woman than Aunt Schuyler; and it makes me indignant to see her trampled on and wounded in her tenderest love. Don't talk to me of Lilly. I think of some bit of Scripture I've read: 'If they do these things in a green tree, what shall be done in a dry?' If Lilly at fourteen is priest-led enough to forsake her mother, there would be no hope of her husband's being more than a secondary consideration to her when she comes to marry."

* Chap. du Larcin, tr. 1, No. 13. Quoted by Sauvestre.

"But, son Richard, you forget that the priest is not to be looked on as mere man. In the confessional he is in the place of God, and to be so considered."

"When I marry," said Richard, "I shall choose a woman who will go to God, if she wants to go at all, without any flesh-and-blood medium. You know," he added, "you promised me an amnesty, and you must not be offended at anything I have said. I don't even hint at you. I think, as I before remarked, that you are a jewel, and permit me to escort you down to dinner."

The bell was ringing. He offered Mrs. Kemp his arm, and they went together to the dining-room. Grace and Adelaide rushed in after them with unbecoming haste, but it was not dinner they were eager for: "Mother, mother! you needn't think we will wear our blue silks nor white tarletan. Lilly is going to have a lovely new silk and a white lace overdress, and we mean to have new pink silks. You must get them early in the morning, so we can have them made. We won't go without them."

"Oh, girls, girls! some other time I'll think about it."

"No—promise now," cried the two.

"Bless me! let us have dinner in peace," said Mr. Kemp.

"Make one more charge, girls, and you are victorious!

> 'Charge, Chester, charge!
> On, Stanley, on!'"

cried Richard.

"Mother, the dresses! pink silk! white trimmings!" shouted the girls, laughing extravagantly.

"Give them the dresses. I wonder if all girls of their age are so wild and untrained?" said Mr. Kemp.

"We can behave splendid now, we have what we want. We were only trying to get the dresses," said Grace, coolly.

After tea the conversation very naturally turned upon the marriage the girls had that afternoon witnessed.

"Who were the parties?" asked Mrs. Kemp.

"The lady had been educated at the Immaculate Heart of Mary," said Grace. "She was one of the first pupils. Her parents are Protestants: the gentleman is a Spaniard from Porto Rico. The lady's parents would not let her marry him because he was a Catholic. They left her home yesterday, and are to sail for Porto Rico next week."

"They are rich," said Adelaide. "The lady gave Father Murphy an alb trimmed with elegant lace; and the bridegroom presented the statue of the Virgin with a gold chain, a perfect beauty."

"It was a stolen marriage, then—a runaway bride, in fact?" remarked Richard.

"I suppose the lady was of age, and certainly her parents were very bigoted to refuse consent because the gentleman was a Roman Catholic," said Mrs. Kemp.

"She has property in her own right. She confessed to Father Murphy this morning. Father Douay was there and several others, and the bride and groom knelt at the altar and received the sacrament," explained Grace.

"What a good thing it was that she had been to the convent, so that when her parents were so cruel to her, and would not let her marry whom she liked, she had a place to come and be married!" said Adelaide.

"What a pity," observed Richard, "that her parents had not considered, before they sent her to the convent, whether they were willing to relinquish all claim upon her obedience!"

The evening of the exhibition came. A choir of girls dressed in white opened the entertainment by singing, "Mother of Angels, hail!"

Grace's salutatory was much applauded.

Adelaide was highly satisfied with her recitation of "Our Blessed Lady." There was a composition written by Sister Saint Sophia on "The Order of the

Little Sisters of the Poor," but avowedly the production of the pupil who read it.

The music of the evening was good.

Copy-books were handed about, and Sister Cecelia's writing highly lauded. The drawings of the pupils, carefully retouched by Sister Anna, made a fair display. Lilly was very lovely in two tableaux called the "Young Devotee" and the "White Veil." Her mother, with tearful eyes and heavy heart, beheld the girl enrapt in her acting of these scenes.

An important part of the ceremonies of the evening was a presentation from the pupils to the convent chapel of a velvet altar-cloth, embroidered with gold, which was duly accepted and "blessed" by Father Murphy.

A poem in honor of St. Joseph the Just was recited, and there was a conversation on confirmation between five girls, in which the fifth girl is convinced and converted from *atheistic* errors, said errors being in very truth not at all atheism, but pure Protestantism. It would never do, you know, *openly* to attack Protestantism, but every right-minded person will consent to a refutation of *atheism.*

Thus the affair passed over, and there was a vacation of two weeks, during which the Abbess gave all her dear pupils a strawberry fête in the convent-garden.

"Rick," said Grace, "our examination and exhibition was a real farce. It was just surface. Sometimes, Rick, I wish so much for teachers who could go deep into things and satisfy me, and tell me the *why*. Most of the girls like the way we are taught, because they have no trouble *thinking or studying*, but that is not what I want. Saint Cecelia would say it was arrogance or infidelity in me, I suppose. I don't dare to say it to any one but you."

CHAPTER III.

BEAUTIFUL INSTITUTION FOR THE CHILDREN.

FATHER MURPHY was walking down Great street. Truly to-day he was a goodly sight to see; florid and stout, and well dressed, his gown reaching nearly to his feet, his hat bedecked with a heavy silk tassel, his eyes cast down, his gloved hands clasped behind him. He was to-day—as, indeed, almost every day—looking after his flock. Father Murphy was not a priest given to books or acts of religion. He had taken in book-learning enough at the College of Holy Joseph before he was in orders. He could inculcate the importance of "acts of religion," and of course he was supposed to do the proper amount of fasting and praying. I know well that he *watched* and *preyed* continually—in fact, there are many kinds of modern Levites, and Father Murphy was a Levite in whom there was *much guile.*

"The Church," said Father Murphy to the Reverend Father Douay, "is a temporal and a spiritual kingdom: therefore her servants must look after both temporal and spiritual interests. Very few men have a call to look after both these branches of interest. My vocation is to wait upon the temporal wants of the Church, which I think the more important of the two. Money is the life-blood of the Church." Agreeably to this indication of his principles, Father Murphy peregrinated the city each day, looking after his flock. When I tell you his eyes were cast down, I do not mean to suggest that he saw only the ground; on the contrary, he saw everything and everybody that passed. I have studied the private orders of the Holy Brotherhood of Jesuits, and never have found any rule that forbids them to look a person in the eye fully and frankly; yet such a law must be implied somewhere, as it is constantly followed. Thus walking and looking down, Father Murphy saw on the other side of the street, one block distant, Michael Shinn coming up. His reverence managed to meet him. Michael, several rods off, saw the inevitable result and trembled. Michael Shinn was the owner of a livery stable, and long was the train of carriages that flowed from that stable to the cathedral, and thence to the cemetery, on occasions of burial for the faithful. Father Murphy might be Herod, and Michael Shinn Tyre and Sidon, "who desired peace with him because their country was nourished by the king's country."

About two feet from Michael, Father Murphy all at once recognized him. Until that moment he had not seemed to notice him; and the burly owner of hacks and horses was beginning to breathe freer, in a vain hope of being served as the priest in the parable served the wounded man on the road to Jericho.

Father Murphy had the deep mellow tones of a man who always eats good dinners and is never contradicted. He stopped short, and said, "Good-day, Michael!"

"Good-day, your riv'rence," said Mr. Shinn.

"You were not at Church last Sunday?"

"I was not, your riv'rence," said Michael, meekly.

"Nor at mass the first of the month; and you have not taken communion for two months."

"Your riv'rence is right," said Michael, sighing.

"I have not seen you at confession; and you are behind in your Church dues," said Father Murphy, continuing the list of his sheep's shortcomings.

"That is true, your honor," said Michael, with great self-abnegation.

Father Murphy struck off on a new theme, still in the same mellow tones: "You let carriages, Michael, and get orders for all the cathedral funerals?"

"Yes, your riv'rence."

"And that is your best source of profit?"

"That I'll not be denying, sir."

"I shall keep it in mind. Don't let me miss you again; and the matter of dues?"

"It will be me duty and pleasure to make it right to the Church, taking sorrow to meself for me neglect," explained Michael, quickly.

"I shall keep an eye on you, Michael. The riches and vanities of this world are leading you from your duty to the Church;" and, so saying, Father Murphy passed on. The connection between Michael Shinn's delinquencies and the letting carriages to funerals may not be patent to persons of slow powers of observation, but it was very plain to Michael.

On went Father Murphy, and turned up a stairway leading to Judge Schuyler's office. The clerks were all very busy in the outer room—mounted on high stools and bending over their desks. The scratch of pens, the rustling of paper and the untimely fall of a pencil were the only sounds that stirred the air. The stove was fireless, the day being warm, and the open hearth was resigned to ashes, apple cores and cigar stumps. The office-boy ushered Father Murphy into the judge's private room, an inner sanctum where the great man was supposed to be very busy. Having provided employment for all his clerks, he had opened a ponderous tome, lighted a cigar, and was meditating upon a very "nice point."

Father Murphy's visit was not unprecedented, and the boy knew perfectly well that the priest was free to the private room. When he entered that receptacle of sofas, easy-chairs and library, the judge greeted him right cordially, and closing the huge volume of legal lore, turned cheerfully to his conscience keeper. The reins wherewith Rome guided this proselyte were silken, and he hardly felt them. Judge Schuyler gave his priestly adviser a chair and a cigar.

They discussed the weather.

The weather was found to be agreeable and healthful.

The judge unlocked his secretaire and produced wine-glasses and a dusty bottle; the bottle, held to the light, looked ruddy as a carbuncle. Father Murphy and the judge probably admired carbuncles, for they regarded the bottle approbatively. The judge called himself a very temperate man. He had never been intoxicated in his life. He despised porter and hated brandy, but he said wine was a fit drink for a gentleman—good for the health and useful to the brain. He placed a glass of wine at the priest's elbow. The visitor nodded: "I feel free to drink what is convenient of wine," said Father Murphy, "as the Scripture tells us it was given to make glad the heart of man—it is also recommended for his stomach."

Father Murphy made it a point to quote Scripture to the judge. He did not say that he felt free to use olive oil because it is given to make a man's face to shine. It was Father Murphy's policy to instruct this new son of the Church at all times, and he continued: "Protestants, as you will observe, are of those who strain at a gnat and swallow a camel. Wine, dancing, a hand at whist are gnats they choke over, while they make no difficulty of the sacrilege of giving the Eucharistic wine to the people, despising the Holy Virgin and the blessed saints, and dying unconfessed and without extreme unction."

The judge bowed assent, as he always did.

"Now," said Father Murphy, benevolently, "I regard Protestants as lost sheep of the house of Israel. I feel compelled to bring them back to that fold from which they went out. In so doing I shall, as the Apostle James says, save a soul from death and cover a multitude of sins. I welcome all such returning sheep with open arms;" and Father Murphy took a sip of wine, and mildly regarded the judge who was one of these same returned sheep.

"Of all things," said Father Murphy, "one of the most surprising is the way the Protestants regard our convents and sisterhoods. On these particular institutions of our Church they fall with full fury. They abuse and deride them in a way that is perfectly amazing, especially when we see what a benefit these very institutions are to Protestants—what an unrivaled opportunity for educating their daughters. Why, sir, just see how this works," cried Father Murphy, taking another sip of wine and joining the tips of his forefingers, as if thereby to point a moral to his theme: "Here's a poor orphan child. Shall it be thrown upon the community as a beggar? No, the convent is open to it, and it is for ever taken care of. Here's a young woman, friendless and homeless; she goes to the convent; she joins a sisterhood and is devoted to good works, is a benefit to society. Here's a refractory girl; her parents can do nothing with her; send her to a convent; of course a Mother Superior, who has trained hundreds of girls, and has given her life to nothing else, is far more capable of training this girl than her own mother would have been. Everything in the convent gently coerces the pupil to right. The parents can be easy about their girl. From the hour they give her to the convent she is perfectly safe."

The judge nodded again. He had a girl of his own, but he knew far more about hunting up precedents than about bringing up girls. He could give a decision in court with much more force and clearness than he could upon any of the educational systems of the day.

"Here again," continued Father Murphy, charmingly ignoring the fact that he was very plainly putting the judge's own case. "Here is a family of wealth and position. They have, we'll say, an only girl—sensitive, lovely, retiring. They need not feel that their death will throw her upon a cold and scheming world—that her life may be lonely and untended. The convent opens its arms to her orphan state. The Church is an immortal mother: for the child of the Church is provided a safe home, tender mother and sisters, occupation, refined society, good works. Her hours of illness find no hired nurses, but tender sisters. She has no business cares; no commercial crisis can throw her out of home and support. Ah," added the good Father, with unction, "it is a beautiful institution—a beautiful institution, worthy of the only True Church."

The matter thus fairly set before Judge Schuyler, he quite agreed with his priest. In the light that morning thrown upon it the convent did look a very beautiful institution indeed. All that his faint-hearted wife could say in a year on the contrary side would be but as small dust in the balance against the view he had gained from the reverend Father. In fact, that very evening Mrs. Schuyler ventured to say, "I wish you would send Lilly to a different school. She is hardly at home with me at all. The

Sisters contrive to keep her every day until tea-time."

"Why, what do they find?" asked the judge.

"Oh, new music or fancy-work or a sick person or an orphan-house to visit."

"Of course, you wish her to be accomplished and charitable?" said the judge.

"Yes, but these are things she could learn with her mother," said poor Mrs. Schuyler.

"Mothers must not be selfish," said her husband. "I'm sure Lilly could not be in a better school."

"But," said Mrs. Schuyler, desperately, "suppose it all ends in Lilly's taking the veil?"

"Worse things might happen," said the judge, coolly. "She would then have a safe and quiet life before her, and be out of the reach of sharpers and fortune-hunters."

Mrs. Schuyler groaned, "Entirely in their hands, I should think;"—but she groaned it to herself.

It was about six o'clock now—almost dinner-time —and Lilly came in from school.

"How late you are, Lilly!" said her mother, as the girl, newly curled and furnished with fresh frills and kerchief by the faithful Hannah, came into the parlor.

"I went to the cathedral, mother, to see some dear little babies baptized. Poor little wee things, mother, they looked so funny compared to Father Murphy, One was four days old, and the other a week."

"Poor little creatures! What a dreadful thing to take them out at that age!" cried Mrs. Schuyler.

"Oh but, mother, it was to be *baptized.* Suppose they should die very soon—"

"They are much more likely to after such an absurd exposure," interrupted Mrs. Schuyler.

"Yes, but *now* they will be saved. If they had died unbaptized, their poor little souls would wander shivering around—well, around *somewhere*—for ever. Sister Saint Cecelia told me so."

"And do you believe *that?*" asked Mrs. Schuyler.

"Of course; Saint Cecelia always speaks the truth."

"Well, Lilly, you have two dear little brothers who died unbaptized."

"Oh, mother!" cried Lilly, horrified. "How *could* you let them?"

"They died suddenly when quite small infants. If they had lived, very likely they would have been baptized. But I do not suppose that the souls of those dear babes are shivering about *somewhere. I* believe they are in heaven with Jesus, who said, 'Suffer little children.'"

Judge Schuyler was making impatient movements. His two lost boys were sore subjects to him.

"But, mother, Saint Cecelia says unbaptized babes *cannot* get into heaven; they *cannot* be saved," said Lilly, weeping at the dreadful thought of her brothers.

"*I* think," said Mrs. Schuyler, "that it is the blood of Jesus and the renewing of the Holy Ghost, and not baptismal waters, that take children into heaven. Go, Lilly, ask your father if Saint Cecelia is right, and our two dear boys are lost because they were not baptized."

This was a very artful thing of Mrs. Schuyler, quite unprecedented. The judge winced, as Lilly, who considered him the wisest of men, drew near his chair with appealing eyes.

"I'm surprised, Lilly, that Sister Cecelia should have told you anything of the kind. I am sure she would not had she understood the circumstances of the case. It was quite useless to say such a thing to *you*. You know, Lilly, that in our Church there is a great mass of ignorant people who are not easily reached and brought up to their duty. They would entirely neglect the needful rite of baptism if they were not *forced* to attend to it by being told that their infants were lost if dying unbaptized."

"But," said Lilly, with wide, open, honest eyes, "they either *are* lost or *are not*, and if they are not it is a lie to say they are!"

"Lilly," said the judge, uneasily, "you are too young to argue on this kind of questions. Very likely *some* infants are lost by want of baptism—children of very wicked parents, for instance; but I am quite sure that *my* children unbaptized are quite as safe as the youngsters you saw at the cathedral to-day," said the judge, with dignity.

The judge resumed his paper; Lilly went over to look at her mother's embroidery. "You see, Lilly," said her mother, "that you are not to believe implicitly all that your Church tells you."

"But, mother, Saint Cecelia says that the Church *cannot* be wrong."

"Then, you are not to believe all your father tells you?"

"Oh, mother, father knows everything!" cried Lilly, and stopped confounded. The poor child was in a "sea of troubles."

"Maria," said the judge, shortly, "don't try to unsettle the child."

Is this a very happy family? It might have been had not Popery been introduced to disturb its peace.

As Lilly was discussing baptism at home, Father Murphy was going to his own house from the cathedral. He had in his pocket the baptismal fees, though the feeble mother of the week-old infant was doing her own work, being too poor to hire help, and the other babe had but two changes of raiment.

The rich judge's dinner-hour was the poor man's supper-time, and Father Murphy met Ann Mora going home to tea. Ann was one of his lambs, and the reverend Father stopped her: "Ann, where are you going to school now?"

"To the free school," faltered Ann, curtseying low.

"And why have you left the parochial school?"

"Father says we are too poor, sir. It cost fifty cents the month for me, and twenty-five cents for Pat, and wages is low, your reverence; and mother don't get much washing in; and it took all she could lay by for dues, your reverence, and so they sent us to free school, please."

"Very well," said Father Murphy, sternly, "I suppose your father is home now. I'll go in with you." How poor Ann's heart fluttered! But down the side street and up the narrow stairs panted the portly Father, and was led into the room where Mora, his wife and boy sat at supper. Father Murphy had better suppers by far on days of *entire abstinence.*

"Oh, your reverence!" quavered Mrs. Mora, "will you take a chair, sir?" and she rubbed the best one with her apron.

"I cannot sit down under this roof!" said Father Murphy, with indignation in eye and tone. "John Mora, you have periled the souls of your children by sending them to Protestant free schools."

"Oh, your reverence," said John Mora, meekly, "I could not stand under the price of the other."

"Then let them bide at home until you can."

"Times gets harder every year," said John, a very shrewd-looking fellow, "and I want the childer eddicated, as I've always heard say this is a free country, and by eddication a fair chance of people rose above their first station. I'm looking up for my childer, sir."

"Why not look up for yourself?"

"I've no eddication, your honor's reverence."

"Perhaps the day will come, John, when our Father, the Pope, can give land and place and fortune to the faithful without education. Too much education is apt to turn the heads of the masses."

Father Murphy had cast out a baited line, and watched to see if it was bitten.

"Eh, your reverence?" said John Mora, looking up quickly.

"I say, John, that our Father, his Holiness, is rightful head of all lands, and he may one day here distribute to his faithful those rewards which they will use for the benefit of the Church."

"Belike," said John, his face flashing into interest, and pushing back from the table.

"You had best be faithful to your Church, John."

"I will that, your reverence."

"Then take your children from those heretical schools. Don't let them go there another day. It may do for Protestants to send their children out of their own schools, and say others won't change their faith. I tell you, John, if your children go to those heretical schools, they will suck in as much of these notions of liberty and free speech and Bible poison as will cut them loose from the Church and drift them into perdition. Protestants may count on them just as surely as *we* may count on nine-tenths of the Protestant children sent to our schools."

"I'll mind, your reverence," said John Mora.

"To send Roman Catholic children to Protestant schools," cried Father Murphy, "is an unnatural crime, as cruel as murder. Children so sent will be devils in perdition!" * and Father Murphy brought down his fist on Mrs. Mora's frail tea-table to the table's evident peril.

"My children shall come back to your parochial school, your reverence, to-morrow," said John Mora.

* "The Catholics who send their children to Protestant schools have inevitably before them companionship with fiends."—*Catholic Universe*, Philadelphia.

"See that they do," said Father Murphy.

Under this storm of priestly wrath, Mrs. Mora was cowering and crying. Ann and Pat had fled to opposite corners of the room, and shook as in an ague. John Mora was reduced to intense humility. Father Murphy regarded them in silence. His countenance cleared. He spread out his hands: "Benedicite!"

It was as the sun returning after a tempest.

The family revived.

Father Murphy departed.

"John," said Mrs. Mora, "I'll not get a new bonnet. Mine's done for four years. It may do five."

"We'll do without that corner cupboard," said John.

"I'll mend up Pat's old trowsers again," said Mrs. Mora.

"I want new trowsers," whined Pat.

"Hold your tongue, and don't be a heretic!" said his father.

After tea, Mrs. Mora got a worn-out pair of plaid pantaloons, and taking Pat's gray trowsers, she cut out the four patches of three colors that already ornamented them, taking out a good margin with each, and set in four plaid patches. Meantime, Pat sat and snuffled.

"They'll hold out two months if you're careful,

and the patches are all alike," said his mother, consolingly.

"Great oaks from little acorns grow." From these four plaid patches, and the ignominy of wearing them, added to the tyranny of being kept half an hour a day longer in school, we date Pat Mora's lapse from Romanism.

The next day Lilly at school revived the question of baptism with Saint Cecelia, and reported the conversation at home. Saint Cecelia saw that she had made a false step: "My dear child," said the Sister, "of course you desire the salvation of those infants greatly."

"Oh, indeed, I do!" cried Lilly.

"We do not know the limits of heavenly goodness," said Saint Cecelia. "We know that the Blessed Virgin is merciful, and she is your patroness, and that Saint Peter keeps the keys of heaven. Perhaps, if you are a *very* good Catholic, and *do a great deal* for the Church, you may purchase the salvation of your brothers. Who can tell?"

"Oh, *do* you think so, Saint Cecelia?" cried Lilly.

"And," said Saint Cecelia, "it is not right to let our good deeds be known. Kept secret, they are more acceptable to heaven, as perfume shut up in a box does not waste itself. You had better not mention the matter at home;" and so Saint Cecelia of the

"Beautiful Institution" taught our Lilly to render honor and confidence to her parents. But Saint Cecelia saw it was time to distract Lilly's mind. "I am going to visit the parochial school, and you may come with me," she said.

"Let me go, too!" cried Adelaide, who stood near.

"And me!" cried Grace.

"Sister Grace," said the nun, mildly, "your French composition is not ready. Sister Adelaide, your embroidery must be picked out; your moss rose is crooked, and your violet is not shaded right."

Grace, fond of study, cheerfully attacked the French composition; but Adelaide pouted, knocked down her embroidery-frame, and cried, "Hateful stuff! You make a pet of Lilly. She is your favorite, you know she is!"

"Sister Adelaide," said Saint Cecelia, quite unruffled, "we are going to have a procession and a festival to honor the Assumption of the Blessed Virgin. You may choose your own part, my dear child;" and, on hearing this, Adelaide's spirit floated tranquilly into sunshine.

Lilly went to the parochial school.

"Why is Ann Mora at the foot of her class?" asked the nun.

"She has been absent a month going to a heretic school," said the lay sister who was teaching.

Lilly saw a boy weeping in a corner. Ever sympathetic, she went to him: "What is the matter, boy?"

It was Pat Mora, who blubbered out: "The boys call me convic', because my trowsers is two kinds; and they take in school so early here I don't get no time to play shinny."

"Don't cry," said Lilly, putting her little white hand on his rough, bowed head, "you don't know how sorry I am for you."

That soft touch and tone made him Lilly's devoted slave from thenceforth.

"Sister Cecelia," said Lilly, as they walked home, "I would like to buy that little boy some clothes; his own hurt his feelings."

"I would not just now," said Saint Cecelia, "for he has been going to a heretic school, and needs punishing. Besides," she added, "we want our celebration of the Assumption to be very fine and suitable to the House of the Immaculate Heart, and it will take all the pupils' pocket-money from now until the fifteenth of August to get it up."

Lilly finished the walk to the convent in a deep muse. What was she thinking of? She had heard Ann Mora reproved, and had privately gone to her, asking, "Why did you leave this nice school?"

"Had to," said Ann.

"Did you learn anything in the other? Of course you did not. How foolish of you to go!" said Lilly, severely. "Come now, Ann, *did* you learn *one* thing in the month you were gone from here?"

"Yes," said Ann, suddenly, "I did, miss. I learnt it like as we was reading round one morning: 'The blood of Jesus Christ his Son cleanseth us from all sin.' I remembered it, 'cause it didn't say *her* Son."

"That was because you read in a heretic book," said Lilly.

"It's a mighty pretty verse anyhow, and I learned it to mother," said Ann.

Lilly walked back to the convent by Sister Cecelia, this verse ever in her mind, considering it in silence.

The nun at last said, "My child, what are you thinking of?"

"Saint Cecelia, is there any such verse as this?—'The blood of Jesus Christ his Son cleanseth us from all sin.'"

"I'm sure I don't know," said the nun.

"Perhaps it is in the Bible."

"Then I should not be expected to know, for, thank holy Mary! I never read a Bible. I should not think there could be such a verse in a good book, for I am sure the Church does not teach that we are cleansed from sin by *blood*, but by penance, absolution and the like."

"Saint Cecelia, is it very wicked to read the Bible?"

"Certainly, for the Church forbids it."

"But, Sister, my mother often bids me read a chapter to her."

"It is better to disobey your mother than the Church," said the nun, shortly. "However," she added, "since you are exposed to such temptations, you must avoid them when you can, and arm yourself against harm by frequent prayers."

"What particular prayers?" asked the docile child.

"The Hail Mary, the Angelus Domini and the Confiteor."

"The Lord's Prayer?" suggested Lilly.

"Yes, to be sure, that is a good prayer too. I have heard some bishops say it was the *best* prayer, but for my part, I put my trust in the Holy Virgin."

As they entered the convent gate the girls poured into the garden for recess.

"Go join your mates, my dear child," said Saint Cecelia.

Agnes Anthon, a girl of fifteen, who came to the convent for two hours each day to learn fancy-work, was introducing the game of "Characters" to the elder girls gathered in a beautiful arbor and eager in their amusement. They called Lilly to join them.

As she sat with them, watching the progress of

the game, the splashing waters of a fountain near by reminded her of the infant brothers who had lacked baptismal waters. Could she not, by an act of religion, then and there, do something for their salvation?

She turned her longing, intense look to some blue depth of distance far away. Her lips moved soundless. She almost held her breath.

"Lilly!" cried the girls.

"Quick, Lilly; it is your turn."

"Lilly, are you dreaming?"

"Bless me, the child's in a trance!" cried Grace.

"There, girls," said Lilly, turning delighted to her companions, "I've said the Hail Mary ten times!"

"Lilly, Lilly," said Agnes, "I see you have priestcraft on the brain, and I'm afraid you'll die of it."

"Lilly is much more religious than we are," said Grace, "though we have been confirmed and she has not."

"It is not confirmation that makes Christians, but a change of heart," said Agnes.

"What is a change of heart?" asked Grace.

"Why," said Agnes, who found it easier to assert than explain, "it is the heart being changed from the love of sin and the service of Satan to the love and service of God."

"Then, of course, as there is such a difference, when the heart is changed we know it," said Grace.

"I suppose so," replied Agnes.

"Then *my* heart has never been changed, for it's just the same as it always was," cried Adelaide.

"Unless it is changed you cannot enter heaven," said Agnes.

"Oh, Adelaide," said Lilly, "your heart was changed when you were baptized. Sister Cecelia says it is always so."

The large clock over the door of entrance to the convent from the garden struck the hour of noon.

Lilly turned from her companions. Agnes put her hand on Grace's shoulder. "What a hateful place that convent is," she said in a low tone. "I am fairly ashamed even of coming here to learn to do fancy-work. I would not, only my aunt insists so. Just as if there were no Protestants who could do elegant work as well as nuns!"

"Agnes," said Grace, slowly, "*I* think these convents are folly, at least for people of brains. Look at the Sisters. Some of them devoted to fine needle-work or water-color painting, and the others to acts of religion."

"The last is good enough, if they lived religion in the right way," said Agnes.

"Sometimes," said Grace, "I feel as if religion is the only thing to be thought of. I try with all my might to live up to what Father Murphy and the

Mother Superior tell me, but I don't get any satisfaction from it. Then I give my whole mind to study, and that satisfies me better. That is one thing that makes me dislike convents. I think the nuns are just machines. They only learn the surface of anything; they cannot reason. I have read a great deal of history—Richard has it—and I have read of such grand women who made fame for themselves, but not one of them was a nun."

"I'll tell you what my mother said about that once," replied Agnes. "She said the grandest things to reason on were what was right and what was wrong, that we might do the right. Now a Protestant on these questions goes to his Bible and his conscience, but a Romanist asks his priest, and cannot reason for himself. I heard the Catechism-class this morning reciting in answer to 'How shall we know what things we are to believe?' 'From the Catholic Church of God, which he has appointed to teach all nations all those things which he has revealed.' That was the answer."

Here Adelaide's laughing face was put between these two heads in close converse: "Girls, what *do* you think Lilly is doing? As soon as the clock struck she began the 'Angelus,' and went through the whole of it, and she does it three times a day!"

CHAPTER IV.

REVEREND MOTHERS OF THE CHILDREN.

THE family of one of the wealthiest merchants of the city was seated at dinner. With this family we have but little to do. The merchant had invited home with him a business acquaintance about to sail for Cuba. This latter gentleman was a person of wealth, as was well known to his host's family. The table was waited on by a maid-servant called Annette. She was evidently of French origin. Her hair was drawn back from her face, the ends curling, her cap was ornamented with pink ribbons, her teeth might be false, her cheeks were undeniably rouged; of her age it would be hard to judge. Her mistress pronounced her an admirable servant. She kept her eyes modestly cast down, and seemed intent only on performing her duties. While at table the merchant said to his guest, "Mr. Wynford, you have two children?"

"A boy and a girl," said Mr. Wynford. "My son goes to Cuba with me. My girl is now in the country, but my first business will be to look her out a school and place her in it before I sail."

"Have you any school in your mind?"

"None at all; I have only to look about. A good home is what I want for her, as the poor child has no mother."

Her duties at the table over, Annette left the house. She passed through many streets, looking behind her now and then, and at last stopped at a house which she might have reached by a much more direct route. It was a plain, three-story stone house, with heavy shutters, curtains that were nearly always down, double doors and a high iron fence. The house stood in but narrow grounds. Just at the rear was a high board fence, partly hiding the stables of Michael Shinn.

The place was unpretending enough, and had even on that summer evening a chilly, gloomy look.

Annette unlocked a side gate in the iron fence and went in. It is necessary to follow her closely, for in a few minutes even a detective would lose trace of her. She went in at the iron gate to all appearance a veritable serving-maid. Her whole manner changed as she unlocked a side door, and, entering the building, went up to one of many small rooms in the third story. It was a room with a narrow window, bare floor and walls, a poor, hard pallet in one corner, an

Annette.

Sister Clement.

One Person in two Characters.

Priest and Nun.

Page 81.

iron crucifix opposite it, a suit of nun's garments hanging against the wall.

Annette cast away her serving-maid finery, took off her high-heeled boots and grew shorter; removed her black wig and pink cap, and lo, thin, light hair; washed away the rouge and pearl powder, and there was a haggard, yellow face with whitish eyebrows. Next she clad herself in the dress of her order—a black alpaca gown, an apron of the same, reaching to the hem of the robe, a close black hood with a large cape, a white band across her brow, and white kerchief around her neck, a rosary and cross hung to her girdle. She was no longer Annette, she was Sister Clement.

Sister Clement went down to the sitting-room of this house. There were five women clad like herself busy on embroidery. They did not speak much as they worked. Sister Clement looked at them long enough to see that a person she wanted was not there; then pursued her way to the kitchen. Two Sisters were here—one getting supper for the household, the other baking coarse bread and making soup for a small charity-school they maintained. Again Sister Clement turned away, now to a dismal little corner-room—the oratory of the building. Kneeling before the altar was a gaunt woman, who seemed entirely absorbed in the prayers she was repeating. Sister Clement advanced in the twilight of the room and knelt down behind her Superior, occupying the time by saying the Litany and the Creed. After a few moments the Superior rose and looked about: "Daughter Clement!"

"Yes, Mother."

"A report?"

"Yes, Mother."

"Let it be important enough to have interrupted my prayers."

Sister Clement repeated the fragment of conversation from the dinner-table. As she was prosy and circumstantial in her recital, the Mother Superior's thoughts seemed turned away from her tale. She bent her head, groaned and beat her breast.

"Mother," said Sister Clement, impatiently.

"The father is rich and but two children?"

"Yes, Mother."

"He may die; he may be wrecked at sea; it is easy for men to die. Other men have died;" and again the Superior beat her breast with her long, bony hands.

"Yes, Mother, it is a girl and her money for the Church. Where shall she go and which Father shall I tell?"

The Superior flung off her own secret trouble and woke to energy: "Go to Father Murphy; he is the best man to meet strangers. The Convent of the

Immaculate Heart of Mary. Mother Robart is the best of the Superiors."

"Excepting yourself, Mother," said Sister Clement.

"Myself! I should scare the strangers. They would as soon give a ghoul a child to bring up. Your Mother Robart sits in the sunshine of favor, and *I* perish with remorse."

"You feel worse to-day, Mother Ignatia," said Sister Clement, moved to some tardy pity. "I dare say you have done more for the Church than Mother Robart. The Immaculate Heart is like the face of the clock, and this House Without a Name is the mainspring."

"Daughter Clement!" hissed Mother Ignatia, grasping the Sister's arm, "I have not eaten for two days; I have not slept for two nights. Last night I walked this house over nine times, and I tell you there was a ghost walked on either side of me, looking over my shoulder. I believe I am going mad!"

"I believe you are," said Sister Clement, and went away, while Mother Ignatia, kneeling, resumed her prayers and her groans.

Sister Clement let herself out the side door and the little iron gate. She came out a staid, thin, bent nun of about forty.

Sister Clement had reached the house of Rev. Father Murphy. He was in his private sitting-room—a handsomely furnished apartment. There was a bookcase containing two or three dozen books, and on the lower shelf, behind "Lives of the Saints," a box of chess men and a box of dominoes. The Father wore wrapper and slippers, presented on Christmas by the nuns of the Immaculate Heart. He reclined in a plush-covered easy-chair, and his feet rested on a hassock embroidered in the House Without a Name. On the table, at his side, was a plate of white Syrian grapes, the gift of one of the sheep. He was a Father, jolly and fat and fortunate. He was reading the *New York Ledger* and a *Protestant* magazine by turns. In the one was a story, showing what angels on earth are Sisters of Charity, and how holy are the Ursuline nuns—nourishers of orphans. In the other, a tale of a Protestant woman who became a lay sister to work peace to her soul. As Sister Clement was ringing at the front door, Father Murphy slapped down his paper and magazine upon the table, took two big grapes, and chuckled out: "There's your Protestant literature! The *Tablet* and the *Universe* would not be such fools. Ha, ha! that's the kind to give 'em!"

Here Sister Clement entered and told her tale of Mr. Wynford, who wanted a school for his daughter. She inquired if the Convent of the Immaculate Heart should be the place, and gave Mr. Wynford's name, age, business, present address, former residence and many particulars about him, which, to say the least, would have confounded her employers with her knowledge. But Sister Clement, laboring as maid-servant Annette, gathered every item of information afloat in the house. She tampered with letters, listened at doors, explored drawers, and in the present instance had relieved the pocket of Mr. Wynford's duster of one epistle, and read another carelessly left in his hat.

The conclusion of this business was, that Sister Clement should go to the Immaculate Heart, and make an appointment with Mother Robart to receive Father Murphy and a stranger at ten next day.

Sister Clement turned to go.

"I trust the Mother Ignatia is well," said the Father; "she is a very valuable daughter of the Church, and her life is particularly precious."

"Then you had better go and see her," said the nun; "she is fasting and keeping vigils, and seeing ghosts, and I think getting ready for her grave fast enough."

Sister Clement spoke indifferently. She cared little whether her superior lived or died. If she died, Sister Clement might reasonably look forward to being in charge of the House Without a Name.

Father Murphy, however, preferred that Ignatia

should live. He put on his hat and gloves, cast a last loving look on his grapes, and proceeded to the gray stone house, where he gained admission and a low obeisance. He strode to the chapel, where the nun, in coarse garb, yet kept her bootless vigils: "Rise up, daughter Ignatia!" he said, grandly.

The nun lifted her blood-shot eyes: "Oh, Father, my miseries have come back upon me like fiends from the pit. You are an exorcist, Father; deliver me from these spirits!"

"Some of your own kitchen's bread and soup will be the best exorcism, daughter," said Father Murphy, bluntly. "A weak body brings weak brains. You are laying yourself open to the attacks of the adversary. Follow me to the refectory."

Father Murphy, well-fed and portly, marched to the bare, dingy dining-room, where, at an uncovered pine table, the sisters took their coarse meals. Behind him went Ignatia, trembling with fasting and excitement, so that she could hardly walk.

The austere, morbid character of Ignatia swayed her household. There were with her only those sworn to the most rigid Jesuitical severities. Around them were none of the amenities of life. Hard fare, hard labor, hard religion—this the order of each dreary day. The light of heaven, social converse, bodily comfort, peace of mind—these all were denied to the few lonely fanatics gathered in that House Without a Name.

Father Murphy gave Ignatia one of the hard stools used as seats. A dim lamp was placed in the room where darkness came early, and the Father sent a shout to the kitchen, ordering soup and bread.

"I am sworn to fasting," faltered Ignatia.

"I release you," said Father Murphy, "and do not swear yourself to that again for a month. Our holy Church needs you, daughter Ignatia. There is no one to fill your place, if you fast yourself into your coffin." He passed into the parlor, where sat the Sisters, each with a copy of the Exercises of Ravignan.* It was their hour for study. "Daughter Maria, open the dispensary," said Father Murphy.

The nun addressed, the nurse of the house, unlocked a closet, and Father Murphy helped himself to an opiate, which he put into a wine-glass.

"Daughter Magdalena, open the store-closet," ordered the clerical censor.

As directed, this Sister unlocked another closet. Father Murphy coolly surveyed the contents, made the glass with the opiate half full from a bottle of

* "These exercises are not our institution; they are not even our rules; but I am convinced that they are its *soul* and its *source*. They have created the society, and they sustain it."—*Pere de Ravignan dans sa Defense des Jesuits.*

wine, and then reading the labels of the jelly tumblers, took down one marked to his taste and returned to the refectory. He put a spoonful of jelly on a saucer by the Superior, and calmly began eating the remainder from the glass himself, as he stood near her.

"Such a sinner as I am, Father, should have none of the good things of this life," said the Superior, eyeing the jelly as if it were an infernal machine. "I see terrible ghosts all the time."

"Such frequently arise from an empty stomach," said the matter-of-fact Father.

"I must atone for this refreshing of the body by vigils to-night," said the nun.

"You must drink that opiate and go to your pallet," said Father Murphy. "It is needless to atone for what *I* bid you do."

The nun had finished her supper. She took the wine-glass in her hand. "Drink it," ordered Father Murphy.

The Superior drank. "Unhappy that I am," she sighed. "I cannot sleep until I have confessed."

"It is not a week since you were confessed," said Father Murphy, impatiently.

"My sins lie heavy on my soul. If I die to-night unconfessed?"

"I'll confess you," said the Father shortly, and

opened the door of a very small room, used as a confessional. It was carpeted, and the sole furniture was a straight-backed wooden chair (which Father Murphy abhorred) and a stool.

Father Murphy took the chair. Ignatia knelt on the stool at his side, bent her head and folded her hands on her breast. She began in a low monotone: "I have to accuse myself of the nine ways of being accessory to others' sins: by counsel, by command, by consent, by provocation, by praise, by concealment, by partaking, by silence, by defence of ill done. I accuse myself of the seven deadly sins: of pride, covetousness, lust, wrath, gluttony, envy, sloth. I accuse myself of five sins against the Holy Ghost: presumption, despair, impugning truth, envy of others' good and obstinacy in sin. I accuse myself of the four sins crying to heaven for vengeance: willful murder —"

Here the indignation of Father Murphy broke out: "Daughter Ignatia, when were you guilty of these sins? This week?"

"No, Father."

"Since you took holy vows?"

"No, Father. In the evil days of my youth."

"Daughter Ignatia, this is utter folly. You have confessed these sins to me full nineteen times, and I have absolved you."

"But they lie heavy on my soul."

"They *cannot*, for I have dismissed them."

"Oh, reverend Father, they are crushing my heart. They are eating out my life. I groan over them every day. *They are not gone.*"

"The burden is of your morbid imagination. If there is any virtue in confession and absolution, your sins are utterly *gone.* Dare you defy the Church and say there is *no* virtue in her ordinances?"

"Far be it from me, Father," groaned Ignatia.

"If I have not benefited you by nineteen absolutions, what can you hope from the twentieth?" demanded Father Murphy, practically.

For reply, Ignatia sent out a low bitter wail: "My sins! my sins!"

The hard chair was getting unendurable: "Daughter Ignatia, *have* you finished your confession?" demanded the priest.

"Yes, Father," sighed Ignatia, despairingly.

"*Absolvo Te,*" said Father Murphy, rising, glad to be rid of the chair. Ignatia stood with bowed head. "Sleep," said Father Murphy, "is what you need to drive these phantoms from your brain. *Benedicite,* my daughter!"

He turned to go, but the nun sprang frantically after him and grasped his sleeve: "Father, if I should die—if I should die!"

"Send for me," said Father Murphy, pulling himself from her clasp. "I will administer extreme unction, and you will be *perfectly safe.* Regard these distresses as part of the purification of your soul."

He passed through the parlor, ordering Sister Magdalena, the housekeeper, to see her Superior at once to her pallet.

There, as the night-shadows lengthened over the city, and the sentinel stars looked down from the sky, the nun Ignatia lay locked in opium slumbers, while slowly before her sleeping vision dragged the fearful panorama of the past that haunted her by day. There was the city of Mexico, where she grew up a foreign trader's child. There, the fatal duel, provoked by herself, between brother and lover, where both were slain. There, the husband and child abandoned—her own reckless career—herself bending over a gambler's deathbed—her parents spurned—and then her broken maturity, chased by losses and fierce remorse and terror of death, hunted with the remnant of her fortune, a wretched suppliant for peace, to the feet of Rome. Despair, remorse, terror of retribution, vain longing to make restitution—these the fearful train that fed upon her vitals. To stop their gnawings she had given herself and her money to the Order of Jesuits. She had built this nameless House, gathered in these Sisters, and maintained all from her own means, while she visited upon herself the extremest rigors of her faith. Her house was Rome's spider-web spread in a secret place. But all in vain! in vain! Poor blind soul, with blind guides! One drop of blood from Calvary would have washed the mountains of her sins for ever away, let in on her crushed soul the sunlight of God's peace, and lapped her in eternal rest.

Behold you now in the morning the goodly Father Murphy sending in his card to Mr. Wynford at his hotel. Hear his courteous salutation, his delightful conversation, his profuse apologies for the liberty he has taken. *Will* Mr. Wynford carry to the Belen—the Jesuits' College at Havana—a child's portrait on ivory—a gift to an only brother—too precious to be entrusted to ordinary means of transmission? The young gentleman—one of two orphans—is studying at the Belen—an admirable institution, affording great facilities for studying Spanish. Mr. Wynford cannot fail to be interested in a walk through it. The reverend Brothers will escort him with pleasure. . . . . .

Yes, the original of the portrait is at the Convent of the Immaculate Heart—a delightful home school for girls. Mr. Wynford, of course, is a bachelor?

No, Mr. Wynford is the father of a girl whom he desires to place in school.

Indeed! The Reverend Father would not dictate, but Mr. Wynford might like to visit the House of the Immaculate Heart.

Mr. Wynford accedes, and precisely at ten is at the gate of a charming spider's web, quite unconscious that this appointment was made for him last night.

So the children of our Father at Rome work matters, and it is really surprising how we Protestants play into their hands.*

In the cheerful parlor of the Convent of the Immaculate Heart, Mother Robart received her guests. A tall, commanding woman was Mother Robart. She wore the usual dress of an Abbess, which became her well; but she was a Sybarite in holy orders. Her dress was of the richest and softest material; costly her rosary; costly her crucifix; costly and dainty every item from her headgear to her silken hose and kid shoes.

Vast the difference between Mother Ignatia and Mother Robart. To the gates of Rome had swept

* I cannot let pass this opportunity for expressing my deep sense of the favor our Father of R. has conferred upon us by calling on us, to *return*, welcomed and forgiven, to his paternal arms. For myself, I am quite happy to prefer a far country, feeding on Protestant husks, to the glories of such a prodigal's return.

Mother Robart, her fortune in her hands, a train of converts following her triumphant steps; coming with pride and pomp, like Naaman of old to Elisha's door; and Rome had not set within like a crabbed old prophet, refusing to come out, but had welcomed her with sounding honors, had shouted over the noble convent Mother Robart caused to rise; had made her an Abbess and sent her to Rome on special business; had explored other convents for the best chirographers, needle-women, music-teachers and so on; had given her the most gracious nuns, the most zealous lay sisters and privileges innumerable. Poor Ignatia, on the contrary, flying in terror, her all in her hands, the avenger of blood close behind, "sought peace and found none."

Mary of Magdala, mourning over sin, brought her box of precious ointment to a Guest at Simon's house. Happy woman! who bore her offering to the right feet. If she had poured the ointment upon the feet of Peter, probably the "seven devils" would have held her in possession until this day.

In Mother Robart's parlor were flowers and portfolios of drawings, and oil-paintings on the walls. It was a right pleasant room, and the Lady Superior assured her guest that here she gathered the pupils and Sisters about her for cheerful evening hours. So she did—the favored few.

When Mr. Wynford admired two small landscape oil-paintings, the Mother tranquilly remarked that they were done by Sister Anna, instructress in that art, though truth obliges us to confess that they were bought at auction.

Sister Cecelia was called to conduct the party over the building. She preceded them, voluble of tongue. Mother Robart majestically followed, Mr. Wynford and Father Murphy coming after, side by side. The door of a small parlor overlooking the garden was opened. "Oh," says Sister Cecelia, "I had forgotten this was the hour for fancy-work!"

In truth, Sister Josepha had been ordered to take the flower of the school to that attractive spot, where, in an open bow-window, were working and chatting Agnes Anthon, Grace, Adelaide and Lilly. They were busy on silk embroidery; their bright faces, tasteful dress and elegant work causing Mr. Wynford to wish his daughter among them. In the music-room the best pupil was very opportunely playing "Weber's Last Thought," a waltz of Reissiger's, though generally attributed to the greater Maestro. Then came the school-room, where the writing-books and Sister Cecelia's copies played an important part.

"I suppose," said Mr. Wynford to the Abbess, "you do not admit dancing?"

The Abbess was quick to read looks and tones: "Oh yes," she said, recognizing the gentleman's opinion, "we consider it very important—a delightful 'distraction,' the French call it. A mistress from the city instructs twice a week in my presence. We do not expect to bring our pupils up to be *Sisters*, but to take their proper places in the world and answer the demands of society."

"Beautiful institution!" murmured Father Murphy.

The chapel was next visited. What a grand altar-piece! Christ standing on the globe, a thorny crown in his hands, cherubs kneeling around. "I bought it the last time I was in Rome for eight hundred dollars in gold," says Mother Robart. A charming chapel, painted glass windows of choice designs, carvings and mouldings, soft carpets, antique seats, glowing plush cushions. A gem of a chapel. "Like some in Europe," says Mr. Wynford.

"I copied from one in Italy," replies the Abbess.

The dining-room was shown—a very different one from Mother Ignatia's. The dormitories—rows of snowy beds in the separate halls, the Sisters' place curtained off from the rest.

"A Sister always in each to secure order and prevent accident," says Saint Cecelia.

The children are pouring out for recess. Mr. Wynford naturally asks to see the one whose portrait he is to carry to Havana. Now there is no such child. But Father Murphy, with ready self-possession, asks the Abbess for a name not on the rolls, and the Mother, aptly catching the cue, replies that Sister Somebody has gone on an errand of mercy to a distant part of the city, and has taken the dear child with her to enjoy the fine day and cultivate benevolence.

A refection is provided in the parlor—lemonade, fruit, delicate, crisp little biscuit. Mr. Wynford thinks the Convent of the Immaculate Heart paradise, or its gate; the Abbess, magnificent (as indeed she is); and he engages to entrust his Estelle, aged thirteen, to her charge, and will deliver her at the convent the third day from that time.

"May I take this as a specimen of all convents?" asks Mr. Wynford, blandly, between lemonade and biscuit.

"They differ, of course, in minor points," replies the Abbess. "This is a wealthy House. There are some where the rule is stricter, the nuns being cloistered. There are others merely homes for Sisters, who are constantly among the poor, sick and dying. But one great aim animates them all and makes them similar—the desire of doing good." She made no mention of Houses Without Names.

"Beautiful institution!" said Mr. Wynford.

The guest departs with the priest. The Abbess, looking after him, is apparently engaged upon some arithmetical problem: "One hundred thousand—divided by two—fifty thousand; possible encumbrances. Take it at its lowest figure—thirty thousand."

The convent vacation came in October. This was because Mother Robart found that, if the school was opened during the summer, many girls, at other times day-scholars, became boarders while their parents or guardians were out of the city for summer journeys. Owing to these circumstances, Agnes Anthon, Grace and Adelaide were now boarding for a while at the Immaculate Heart.

The chief attention of the girls was taken up by the approaching celebration of the Assumption of the Blessed Virgin. We should except Agnes Anthon, who would not be persuaded to take any part in it. "I am a Protestant," she said, "and this is no work for Protestants. My mother would not like it."

"Do as you think best, my dear child," said Saint Cecelia, mildly, but privately warned her pupils against any intimacy with the young rebel: "She is a girl of insolent, obstinate, imperious spirit, quite unfit for a child of the Church to associate with. Adelaide, you have learned your Catechism—What are the seven virtues?"

"Humility— There I've forgotten it again!" laughed Adelaide.

"I am sorry for that. But you see that Agnes lacks the very first one."

"The last time I tried to learn Catechism was Consecration Day, and I left it to quarrel with Gracie over a satin sash," said Adelaide, with a burst of laughter.

"Grace, you can say the three eminent good works," said Saint Cecelia.

"I can't," said Grace, perversely. "I was busy quarreling over the sash too."

The girls did not look very quarrelsome as they stood with their arms about each other, but Grace was provoked at hearing Agnes condemned. Lilly, to comfort Sister Cecelia, said the good works: "Alms' deeds, prayer, fasting."

"You see that Agnes has none of those," said the nun, "therefore she is no fit friend for children of the Church. Lilly, say the three evangelical counsels."

"Voluntary poverty, perpetual chastity, entire obedience."

"I won't do 'em," said Adelaide, mischief in her eye. "I'm going to marry a rich man, live like a princess, and do just as I please."

"I want to be famous—to do great things," said Grace.

"If Princess Adelaide is a true Catholic, and if Sister Grace does great things for the Church, it will be very well," said Saint Cecelia. "My Lilly will take the three evangelical counsels into her heart?"

"Perhaps so," said Lilly, softly, a dreamy look coming into her violet eyes.

Sister Cecelia reached out her hand and drew her toward her. Was it by accident that Agnes came in humming—

"And the cruel spider caught her,
And quickly held her fast?"

Saint Cecelia did not look over-pleased at this interruption of her edifying converse with her pupils. She was cold to Agnes. Mother Robart was very gracious to Agnes, because she knew the girl was soon going to another school, and she wanted her to carry into the world pleasant impressions of the convent. "She is a stiff little Protestant now, but the seed sown here may one day spring," said the Abbess to Saint Cecelia. "I was not a Catholic myself when I left my convent school, but early impressions are strongest, and when I turned to religion at all, I turned to that in which I had been trained."

Agnes Anthon's father was with the American Legation at Rome. His wife had accompanied him to Italy for her health, but his means did not permit him to take Agnes; and besides, he wished her to attend to her studies at home. Agnes was a girl of unusual intellectual powers—had a retentive memory and a logical mind—had read much, and had been blessed with thorough teachers. After Saint Cecelia's warning, Lilly was little in Agnes' society, but Grace was completely bewitched by her new friend. Agnes had keen powers of sarcasm. She had studied Latin and read Virgil. She was Grace's beau ideal.

Richard Kemp frequently called at the parlor of his aunt the Abbess to see his half-sister Grace. Richard admired the Superior, though he did not admire her faith. Mother Robart, however, did not despair of converting him, as she had the rest of her family.

Richard was delighted at the accounts he received from Grace of Agnes, and decided within himself that it would be a grand thing to "prime" the girls for an attack on Father Murphy the first time he came among them. He warily got Grace into a determination to ask the priest concerning the Bible, and sent word to Agnes that invocation of the saints was borrowed from the Latins, tonsure from the Brahmins, and prayers for the dead were introduced by Æneas.

"I knew that, without Mr. Kemp telling me," said Agnes, proudly. She saw Richard's plan at once and was amused by it, but resolved to bring out her own weapons just when it suited best. "I would certainly ask the priest why I could not read the Holy Bible, if I were in your place," she said to Grace.

"I will some time," said Grace.

At the Convent of the Immaculate Heart of Mary were some fifty nuns, several lay sisters and a large number of pupils. These pupils were from five to eighteen years of age—some few of them Catholics, the majority Protestants, the reason for the scarcity of Romanists being that they were generally unable to pay the high rates demanded for tuition and extras. Mother Robart wanted her pupils to be from the upper classes of Protestants. Of these girls several had been privately received into full communion with the Church of Rome, their parents being in blissful ignorance of the fact, believing and often stating to their friends that "no efforts were made to proselyte, the Sisters discountenancing anything of the kind." In fact, there was a great apparent liberality and fairness. The pupils were let alone until it was evident what manner of spirits they were of, and then were tampered with so slyly as for some time to be unconscious of it themselves. Two-thirds of the pupils went to confession.* Of

* Quite recently a young Protestant lady, who is an inmate of one of these convents, told us that in three months nearly a score of Protestant young ladies had renounced their faith and been baptized into the Romish Church in the institution of which she is an inmate.—*Christian at Work.*

these was Lilly, who went entirely without the knowledge of her mother. All children of Papists are expected to confess after attaining the age of seven years.*

At one time the suspicions of Mrs. Schuyler were aroused, and she abruptly asked Lilly if she attended confession.

Terrified at the thought of betraying the nuns, the girl faltered, "No, ma'am."

This falsehood lay heavy on her tender spirit, and when next at confession she revealed it to Father Murphy.

"Ought I to tell mamma of it, and ask her to forgive me," inquired Lilly.

"You told the falsehood with good intention. It is the intention that makes the character of our acts. Being in behalf of the Church, the motive purified it. A good motive can purify perjury." †

On Saturday afternoon, therefore, Sisters Anna and Cecelia took each a band of pupils to confession. Thus all those who practiced this, which they supposed to be a duty, were confessed once each month.

The confessional adjoined the convent chapel, and

* See Catechism for use of Catholic Church in Archdiocese of Cincinnati, p. 33.

† One can swear that he has not done a thing, though he has really done it.—*Oper. Mor.*, p. 2, l. iii., c. 6, n. 13.

had a small parlor attached to it. In this parlor, the Sister in charge of the band of pupils maintained due gravity among them, while one of their number was engaged in the adjacent confessional in pouring out her sins—not to God, but to man. "Sister" would bid the girls spend the time of waiting in preparing themselves thoroughly for their duty, by "carefully examining their consciences upon the ten commandments, the seven deadly sins, etc," and, as each one passed her to go to Father Murphy, would say, solemnly, "He who willfully conceals a sin in confession commits a great sin by telling a lie to the Holy Ghost, and makes his confession nothing worth."

The confessional in the Convent of the Immaculate Heart of Mary was much more agreeable to Father Murphy than the dismal den at Ignatia's house. The ample, cushioned chair was an easy rest; the windows were daintily draperied; the carpet was soft; the temperature of the apartment just right the year round. There was none of the passionate remorse and self-upbraiding that fretted him in Ignatia—none of the ceaseless penances that were demanded at the House Without a Name, and which bored the comfortable Father most unmercifully. The childish penitents babbled out their little peccadilloes in musical monotony, interspersed now and then by ghostly questions which they did not half comprehend. Sometimes, if the day were warm or his dinner had been hearty, the holy Father dozed, all unsuspected by his neophytes.

Estelle Wynford had come to the convent. Her face combined, as did her blood, the Italian and English types. She was an impulsive, unsophisticated creature, ready to prattle all she knew. Yet, while her nature seemed all surface, there were clinging tenderness and uncompromising firmness in its depths. Estelle was, in truth, neither Catholic nor Protestant. Her father knew no worship but of himself. He looked upon religion as fanaticism, and held himself loftily above it. His children had about as much devotion as France during the Revolution. They regarded the Sabbath as a day for their ease and recreation; one creed was as good as another, and none essential. If Agnes Anthon fascinated Grace, Estelle charmed all the girls by her ardent, excitable temperament, her ready adaptation to any circumstances, and her acquaintance with foreign lands. It was now the summer term, when so many of the girls were boarding at the convent. Each morning they heard matins at six, and low mass at eight.

On Sunday morning there was a long service, then a Catechism recitation for all who chose to attend of the Protestants, the Romanists being obliged to be prepared with the lesson. "How liberal this was! no pressure upon the minds of Protestant pupils; perfect liberty allowed; coercion or proselyting not countenanced," I think I hear said by convent-admirers among every sect. The Protestants who did not desire to attend were, however, permitted to sit two seats off in full hearing. They might amuse themselves with books if they liked; but their seat was so discreetly chosen that there was not light enough to read conveniently. Between the Catechism in school and in church, and the prayers ordered and repeated aloud before and after meals, and on rising and retiring, the Protestant pupils could not avoid learning the whole of the precious compound during a very short attendance at the school. Besides, to attend and take part in this Sabbath recitation brought a heretic pupil much applause and commendation, and some desired privilege during the week, and would erase three discredit-marks from said pupil's roll. These things were thoroughly understood and acted upon, though the girls had never heard all these inducements formally set forth by the Sisters.

After dinner, and an hour or two for rambling in the garden and reading whatever literature the convent possessed—which was little indeed—the pupils were called to the school-room for two hours' study of lessons for the succeeding day, or writing their exercises or compositions.

"I will not do it," said Agnes Anthon; "it is a desecration of the Sabbath."

"No, daughter Agnes," said the stately Abbess, "we cannot desecrate the Sabbath by cultivation of the mind. I should not permit you to sew or take a dancing-lesson. But the mind is immortal, is spiritual. What we do for the mind we do for eternity. To learn the school-lessons for the ensuing day is perfectly proper employment."

"Such a proceeding is against my conscience," said Agnes; "and if you please, Mother Robart, my ideas of right and wrong are in my own keeping, and I must obey them."

"I shall not force you to do what you suppose to be wrong. You can spend the time, while the others are at study, by yourself in the organ loft," said the Abbess, coldly.

It was not long before there was another encounter with Agnes; indeed the girl took special delight in exciting a small passage-at-arms. She entered the music-room, where Estelle and Lilly were practicing a hymn for the coming celebration—"Star of the Sea and Queen of Heaven!"

"What heathenish music is that?" exclaimed Agnes.

Sister Cecelia was in charge of the room just then, and with smothered wrath in her voice she began with her usual formula, "My dear child," and proceeded: "Such shocking words are the outgrowings of a profane and evil heart. I shall report them to the Mother Superior."

Accordingly Agnes was presently summoned to the parlor, where the Abbess was occupied with several Sisters considering the arrangement of some tableaux.

"Daughter Agnes," said the Superior, sternly, "you have greatly distressed and offended us by the insult you have offered our Blessed Lady."

"I assure you, madam," said Agnes, "I have not said a word about the Virgin."

"But you have characterized a sacred hymn to her honor as heathenish."

"Why, Mother Robart, the hymn was 'Star of the Sea and Queen of Heaven.'"

"And by those titles we address the Holy Virgin."

"Then I beg ten thousand pardons. The ancients called *Juno* the Star of the Sea and Queen of Heaven, so of course it sounded to me as if they were singing to *her*, which would be utter folly in the nineteenth century," said Agnes, demurely, but with triumph in her downcast eyes.

Mother Robart bit her lip: "I trust, being now enlightened, you will not transgress again."

"Oh, certainly not," said Agnes, "unless I happen to hear some more *antiquity*, which to my ignorance shall seem out of place."

As this unrighteous leaven was working in the school, the Superior thought it best to give her pupils some especial instructions. They were, therefore, to spend the evening in the parlor with the Abbess. A basket of fine peaches was on hand to make the occasion more palatable. Sister Cecelia, Saint Sophia and one or two other nuns were met with them, and the darkness of their juvenile minds must needs presently vanish.

"Our next festival," said Mother Robart, "is that of the Assumption of the Blessed Virgin Mary. What does this mean?"

"It means," cried Lilly, with all the eagerness of full belief, "when the Virgin was taken soul and body into heaven."

"Are we to suppose that she never died?" asked Estelle.

"A venerable tradition tells us that she died; but before her body suffered corruption it was taken into heaven, to be there crowned as queen by her divine Son," replied Mother Robart.

"Since the world has demanded such clear historic proof of the Resurrection and Ascension of Jesus," said Agnes, "I should not think it would be satisfied with the authority of *mere tradition* on the point of the Assumption of the Virgin!"

"It can be clearly proved by logic as well as by tradition," said the Abbess. "How comes death into the world?"

"By sin," said Grace.

"The Virgin and her Son endured death out of their exceeding humility. But, as they were both entirely and equally without sin, it was impossible that they should see corruption," said the Superior. "They hallowed death and the grave by partaking of them, and then ascended into glory."

"But how can you prove," asked Agnes, "that the Virgin was undefiled, and how explain the doctrine of the Immaculate Conception?"

"I am speaking now," said the Abbess, severely, "to Catholics, or to those whose minds are open to receive *truth.* I trust there is no one but yourself who would dare so blasphemously to question this dogma of the Church. The Church is infallible, and I would not stoop to *prove* her assertions. We accept them as the voice of God."

Agnes dropped her head as if abashed, and the Superior, after this triumph, went on to say: "This doctrine of the Immaculate Conception is the most glorious prerogative of Mary—root of her being the Mother of Christ. When the foundation-stone of this convent was laid, I took a solemn vow that the 'Little Office of the Immaculate Conception' should every morning be said in full choir, knowing well that nothing could be more agreeable to the Holy Virgin."

"Sister Cecelia told me," said Lilly, "that I should not let a day pass without saying at least ten times, 'O Mary! conceived without sin, pray for us who have recourse to thee.'"

"Which of Holy Mary's two great privileges is the more important," asked Grace—"being the Mother of Jesus or being conceived without sin?"

"The last, undoubtedly," replied the Abbess, "for it was only *because* she was immaculate that Christ condescended to become her Son." *

"At the convent in Michigan, where I was two years," said Sister Sophia, "we spent the first ten days in December in adoration of the Holy Virgin, and she wrought three separate miracles for us. She extended the arms of her image in benediction, and she appeared clothed in light to one of the Sisters. She also appeared to a very obstinate heretic girl and converted her." Sister Sophia looked tranquil superiority at Agnes.

"I wish she would appear to me," said Agnes.

* From the "Ave Maria," a book for Catholic children.—See *Catholic Standard.*

"The Church has multiplied privileges, indulgences, prayers, orders and associations to those who have taken to their hearts this secret of the Immaculate Conception," said Mother Robart. "For myself, I had this name given to this House because I believe that doctrine to be the bulwark of our holy faith."

"It is singular," said the incorrigible Grace, "that this bulwark was not earlier understood. I have read that it was started in 1476 by the Gray Friars, and the Pope took it up and offered absolution to all who would add to the Ave Maria, 'And blessed be thy Mother Anna, from whom, without blot of original sin, proceeded thy Virgin flesh.'"

"You have read many heretical falsehoods," said the Superior, "but this one does not disprove the purity and truth of the doctrine we are sustaining."

"But when that doctrine was first held forth half the Catholic world called it an 'infernal heresy,'" said Agnes, boldly.

Agnes' torpedo had exploded with considerable effect. The nuns were horror-stricken, the pupils held their breath, the Abbess was red with fury.

"Sister Cecelia, conduct Agnes to her room, apart from the rest, and henceforth, while this holy House must be distressed by her presence, do you keep her in charge, that she may not contaminate our other pupils." Such was the Superior's mandate. When the room was relieved of the young heretic's presence, the Abbess said: "You see to what a pitch of wickedness a heretic can arrive. When I was in Rome, I saw many blessed relics of the Virgin, and knew of many miracles wrought by them and by the statue and person of our Lady. If you would gain heaven, there is no surer way than to worship the Blessed Virgin and hold fast to the doctrine of her Immaculate Conception." *

The day of the celebration of the "Assumption of the Virgin" was the gala day of the school year. The services in the chapel were of the most imposing order. The pupils who had been confirmed received the communion, and shocked might many Protestant parents have been to see their children kneeling in that act of idolatry. Among the exercises and entertainments of the school was a tableau of the grand altar-piece, in which, instead of Christ upon the globe, the Virgin was so represented, with an infant in her arms, and the loveliest of the pupils, white-robed and winged for the occasion, knelt about in adoration. It was a tableau arranged at great ex-

* The nearest approach as an object of worship to the Virgin Mary, as to-day set forth by the Church of Rome, was the Juno of the ancients. Juno was addressed by the same names, and an Immaculate Conception was also ascribed and celebrated to her honor.

pense and with fine effect, and was rapturously received by all the spectators. Most beautiful part of the picture was Lilly, who hardly looked as if she belonged to this rugged earth.

"My blessed child," said the Abbess, clasping the girl in her arms in the ante-room, "there is but one place in this world fit for you, and that is the sacred shelter of a convent. There may your purity and piety find its haven of rest!"

Ah, Lilly, Lilly! poor, ardent, misguided child! alas for this world if there is no purer place than a convent for spirits like thine! Is it the shadow of the coming ill, the agony of spirit, the loneliness and remorse of the coming day, that rises a cloud no bigger than a man's hand in thy morning sky?

Agnes was permitted under ban to view the ceremonies of the day. She was tired of the week of seclusion that had been forced upon her.

Richard Kemp saw her from afar, and slyly promised Adelaide a ring, for which she longed, if she would unexpectedly introduce him to Agnes, thus stealing a march upon Saint Cecelia and the Abbess. Adelaide, nothing loath, came up just as Richard had established himself near Agnes, and very charmingly introduced them.

"You do not seem to enjoy this occasion, Miss Anthon," said Richard.

"No, sir; the convent is a prison, and I can hear the clank of the chains under all the flowers and finery."

"There is a doleful-looking little nun who seems of your opinion," said Richard.

"That is a new Sister, a proselyte from Missouri."

"It seems," said Richard, "that half the nuns are proselytes, and half the proselytes are from Missouri."

"I have noticed that, and wondered at it," said Agnes.

"Poor Missouri," said Richard, "is an unfortunate State, almost without Protestant schools. The convents there make no more of swallowing the girls of a whole village than the whale did of Jonah."

"Nephew Richard," said the Abbess, sweeping down, "I do not allow promiscuous conversation; I am the guardian of my young ladies."

"My reverend aunt, I assure you I am the most harmless creature," began Richard. Saint Cecelia was on hand with laudable promptitude, and conveyed Agnes from the room.

"I was merely commenting on the unhappy look of yon nun," said Richard to his aunt.

"She is homesick," said the Abbess, her eagle eye scanning the nun in question. But in a few moments this nun also disappeared, and was seen no more.

CHAPTER V.

SECRET GUARDIANS OF THE CHILDREN.

ON the day after the celebration, Agnes was summoned to the parlor of the Superior.

"I have written to your aunt about you, daughter Agnes," said Mother Robart. "We have endeavored to treat you with all tenderness and consideration, but you have set yourself against us. We consider you a detriment to our school. Had you been entrusted to us as a regular pupil like others, we should have deemed it our duty with patience to bring you to a better mind. As you are only waiting here your father's selection of a school, we hope your departure to such a place as he shall choose will be hastened. We have written to your aunt that we can no longer entertain you to the damage of our House. She replies that it will be yet a fortnight before she shall return to take charge of you. We shall therefore send you for that fortnight to a House in the city, where there are no pupils to be injured by your insolence, your obstinacy and your misrepresentations."

"This convent," said Agnes, "is a palace, yet it is a prison still. I do not know where you are taking me, but I have heard that girls in convents are apt to make disappearances and never come to light again."

"Your insinuation is beneath contempt, daughter Agnes. Rest assured that, though this House where I send you may be lonely and severe, as soon as your aunt returns you shall be restored to her, and your departure from here is forced by your own rebellion against the proprieties of this institution."

Agnes did not reply. The Abbess had certainly gained the advantage of her, as, considering all circumstances, was only to be expected. All Agnes could say was childish impertinence. She was put in the very unpleasant position of being expelled from school—a fact of which her aunt would doubtless frequently remind her.

"Sister Cecelia will pack your trunk and then conduct you to your new home," said the Abbess.

"I should like to bid the girls good-bye," said Agnes.

"That I cannot permit," replied the Superior.

Agnes went up to the dormitory and stood by the window while Saint Cecelia concluded the preparations for her departure. The girls were playing in the garden. Agnes looked down upon them with tears in her eyes. Because she was not a Papist or a renegade she must be sent off somewhere by herself; and who knew if she should ever come back? She had read of little Mortara, of Eliza Burns, of Mary E. Smith and of many others who had been spirited off by priests and nuns. Poor child! she felt very miserable, yet was too proud to show it. The laughter of her companions came up to her like a wail; the sunlight was darkness; the heart in her bosom was like lead. This girl, you know, was not sixteen years old. She was far from father or mother, and her aunt did not care a penny for her. She thought it one of the misfortunes of her lot that she was not rich—that she was, indeed, in very moderate circumstances. But we, who know Rome so much better, can see that this was one of the best things that could have befallen her. She was not a prize worth making any trouble for. Had she been a larger fish, she might not have slipped so easily through the net of Rome.

Agnes' meditations were interrupted by the click of the lock as Saint Cecelia fastened her trunk.

"You will get on your sack and bonnet now," said the nun.

"Is it a long walk?" asked Agnes.

"We shall ride," said Saint Cecelia.

"Where is this House, and what is it called?" asked Agnes, trying to affect indifference.

"I have not been instructed to hold any conversation with you," replied that animate machine called Saint Cecelia.

They passed through deserted halls out the great door of the convent. No one met them. There was no kind look or farewell. Sister Cecelia was stern. Agnes ready—but too proud—to cry.

At the gate was a livery carriage from Michael Shinn's stables, driven by John Mora. He made a low reverence to Saint Cecelia, looked a little curiously at Agnes, and they were driven off. According to instructions, John took a roundabout way, and after nearly an hour's driving set Agnes and the nun down before the House Without a Name, and went off immediately. Saint Cecelia rang the bell, and the heavy front door opened for them after some delay. Even in August the halls of this nameless House were damp and chilly. Agnes was conducted to the bare parlor, where Mother Ignatia sat alone.

"This is the young woman the Mother Superior of the Immaculate Heart wishes to have remain here for two weeks," said Saint Cecelia.

"Our House is at the service of the Church," answered Ignatia.

Saint Cecelia bowed and went away. As she left the door a flaunting maid-servant entered the side gate. Saint Cecelia glanced at her curiously, only half a glimpse of the truth crossing her mind. It was Sister Clement.

Agnes stood yet in the parlor. Ignatia eyed her closely for a few minutes: then she spoke:

"This is a silent House. We are few of us here, wholly set apart from the vanities of this world and intent only on saving our souls. You will be required to obey our regulations while you are with us. Our fare is poor and coarse; our House is desolate; the flesh with us is mortified; only the soul is cared for. You can go to the room prepared for you. Your trunk is there. You will receive your orders as they are necessary."

She was taken to a small room in the third story. It had a curtainless window, which overlooked Michael Shinn's stables. As she entered it a nun came out of the next room. The nun was Sister Clement.

Sister Clement went down to the parlor, and presented herself before the Superior.

"There is a Protestant girl up stairs whom we are to take care of for two weeks," said Ignatia. "I put her in your care while you are here. She must conform to the rules of this House, occupy herself with work for our benefit, and fare as we do. She will be present at our exercises and keep the fast with us tomorrow."

"We have no orders to keep her or convert her?" asked Clement.

"No," said the Superior; "Father Murphy does not think she is worth making especial effort for."

Now this was not very flattering to Agnes. As the Superior thus stated Father Murphy's views, a hollow voice in the doorway said, "Any soul is worth taking especial pains for. Our Church has thought one soul worth fire and sword. If *one* heretic is in this House and leaves it unconverted, Rome is weakened by the loss of one servant, and blood will be found upon your garments."

The two nuns looked up. Ignatia rose quickly. Father Douay, a gaunt, eager, fiery-eyed priest stood in the doorway.

"Daughter Clement, you will attend to our charge," said the Superior.

"And what charge is this to whom you will be unfaithful, concerning whom you have received such base and cowardly orders?" demanded Father Douay.

Ignatia hastened to explain Agnes' position. "We shall make every effort to convert her," she said, "but our Director, Father Murphy, will not permit us to detain her or use force. It would be too open."

"Openly or in secret, it is your sworn duty to work for Rome," said Father Douay, smiting his skinny palms together as he spoke.

"In America our work is mostly done in secret," said Ignatia. "The land is not yet ripe for putting in the sickle openly. But it is ripening fast."

"In France, or, better still, in holy Spain,"* cried the Father, "our Church, with royal authority, commands and men obey. She is not forced to lurk in corners or to work in secret. She rules souls and minds and fortunes as she will."

"The day is coming, is coming!" said Ignatia, catching her breath. "There are great forces at work, wider and greater than men know."

"I will see this girl before I leave," said Father Douay.

Father Douay had been in this country but a year. We have translated his foreign idiom into plain English. He was a zealot of the first degree, a fiery fanatic, such as rushed at the head of troops of murderers on the fatal eve of Saint Bartholomew, or, brandishing a cross with frantic zeal, led on hosts of Crusaders to destruction.

We do not accord with hasty statements, to the effect that all priests recognize the mighty lie of Rome, that all nuns wish themselves free, that Rome's fasts and penances are a farce and a jest to

* These words were spoken before the recent revolution in Spain, which promises to give full liberty of conscience and protection to all religious creeds.

all but the mob of deluded foreigners and proselytes, the laity who crowd their churches. No, there are thousands of priests and nuns whom the serpent-bite has made mad—who are made drunken by draughts from the cup in her hand whom God has written "Mother of Harlots." With frightful passion they worship at the shrine of Rome. Her bonds eat into their flesh. Their brains reel under the pressure of their mental pain. They starve bodies and soul, and sink every better instinct of their natures, to do Rome service. They believe in her as the Hindu believes in Gunga—as the expiring wretch, under the wheels of Juggernaut, believes his god—as the infatuated widow, clamorous for the flaming pile, believes in the suttee.

Of such spirit were Mother Ignatia and Father Douay. The nun had heard of the zealous foreigner, and had asked permission for him to visit her, trusting that from his "holiness" and zeal she might obtain some medicine for her tortured soul. Glad to be freed for a while from his excited patient, Father Murphy, who, as we have seen, was intent rather on the temporalities than the spiritualities of the Church, had desired Father Douay to officiate for a while as confessor at the House Without a Name.

Ignatia had now the luxury of accusing herself of every sin ever heard of. She could bewail again the full record of her crimes, and chastise them anew with all the penances that tender Mother Church directs.

"Penance, penance and prayer must do away your iniquities, most wretched woman. Dare you for one day hold up your face as Head of this House, when you are doing nothing to cleanse yourself from these black enormities? Your sins are not done away; you have not driven them to the death; you have not confessed them fully and with self-abhorrence. You will be forsaken of God, of saints, of good angels, of the Holy Church, and, a miserable apostate, you will sink deeper than perdition." Thus Father Douay rated his wretched penitent.

"Take your shoes from your feet; put sackcloth on your flesh; rise to your prayers three hours before day; let the 'Confiteor' be for ever on your tongue; take but one meal a day, and that just after vespers. Be sure that, as long as these visions haunt your sleep and terrify your waking hours, they are evidences of the unappeased wrath of God. If drowsiness come upon you at your prayers, put your feet in ice-water or your finger in a flame. I can easily see why you are so lukewarm about that young heretic's conversion. It is because your own soul is in the hands of the devil."

Thus did this tender shepherd lead the strayed and wounded sheep.

And against this hardness, this refinement of cruelty, did Ignatia rebel? No; like the pagan, who thinks no physical suffering too great that he may save his soul, she accepted the horrible life thrust upon her, and recognized every cruel word, every indicated penance, as new proof of the holiness of her priest.

Oh, poor Ignatia, my heart aches for thee! What if to thy cowering soul, thus hunted by Rome's bitter Pharisees, had come that Tender One, saying, in his mercy, "Neither do I condemn thee; go and sin no more!" Very likely thy Rome-trained heart would have met such forgiveness with the old-time accusation, "He casteth out devils by Beelzebub, the prince of devils."

Sister Clement went to the little room whither Agnes had been conducted. She coldly surveyed the girl for a few seconds, and then said, "All these vanities of attire are here forbidden. Have you no black dress fit for a sinner to wear?"

Yes, Agnes had a black dress. At the Convent of the Immaculate Heart of Mary the pupils had been required to wear black two days in the week.

"Put on your black dress, comb your hair plainly behind your ears and come down to the parlor."

When Agnes was plainly attired in black, she went down to the parlor, where she was confronted by

Father Douay. The next half hour was spent in sharp cross-questioning and excited harangue. Agnes, having got into considerable trouble by the too free use of her tongue, maintained a complete silence.

The priest having left her, Sister Clement and five nuns entered. All took their places and their work. Agnes was given a stool in one corner, and a piece of canvas embroidery to fill up with a purple groundwork. Sister Clement then opened The Book of Hours and read in a rapid monotone until dinner-time. The Superior was not at dinner. The meal was of coarse bread and thin soup, exceedingly unpalatable to Agnes.

Back again to the parlor and to work. Sister Maria now was reader, and the "Exercises"—precious lore—she poured into the ears of the workers, as follows:—

"Next comes the exercise of the contemplation of hell. One should represent to himself hell, wide, great and profound, with vast flames, a horrible abyss. Secondly, the noise of groans, of wails, of cries of anguish, of struggling, of blasphemies, from those overwhelmed in the tempest of flames. Thirdly, the odor of smoke, of sulphur."* So Sister Maria read on, until Agnes almost felt as if

* "Les Exercises Spirituels des Jesuits."

she did really see, hear and smell these horrible things, and began saying to herself the twenty-third Psalm, the Beatitudes and any other Scriptures she knew, to keep her mind off the "Exercises."

Besides the reading and the work, were the stated hours of worship in the rude, dim chapel—at six o'clock, at midnight, at daylight and at ten o'clock. Friday was observed with much more severity in this House Without a Name than in the convent which Agnes had just left, or at Father Murphy's. At the Immaculate Heart of Mary, Friday's fast brought fish, eggs, buttered toast, fruit and cream and confections. Father Murphy fasted right royally on turtle soup, lobster salad, Delaware shad and whipt cream. In the House Without a Name they had a small allowance of bread and water after matins, and nothing more until after vespers, when they had water gruel and a crust of brown bread. In all these rigors Agnes must take part. She was roused at midnight to stumble down stairs by Sister Clement's side, and kneel dozing and shivering in the chapel.

"We want to show you," said Sister Clement, "that our religion is more than a name, and that we think the salvation of the soul worth a sacrifice."

"Christ was once offered a sacrifice to take away sin," said Agnes.

"To take away sin needs many sacrifices," replied Sister Clement.

Slipping away for a few moments from the silent embroiderers in the parlor, Agnes one afternoon wandered about the dismal house and into the still more dismal chapel. There was Ignatia, haggard, wild-eyed, barefooted, beating her breast and praying, bowed upon the floor. The evident misery, the fierce, ill-repressed excitement of the Superior had filled Agnes Anthon with a curious interest. She felt that Ignatia's heart was bleeding from a thousand wounds. She knew that she was tortured almost to insanity. When she found her there, praying huskily and groaning wearily, she felt as if the "Exercise of the Realization of Hell" were before her, and she stayed her steps and bent her head. When Ignatia's prayer was ended, as she was passing from the chapel to another of her penances—the dressing of loathsome sores for some paupers who came to her daily—she caught Agnes' eye regarding her with compassion, and addressed her in a broken voice: "Take warning, girl; it is thus that sins are expiated and man becomes just with God."

Agnes thought, as by an inspiration, of a sentence from an old, old book. She laid hold of the Superior's robe. "Clement of Rome has said," she cried, "we are not justified by our wisdom or piety, or the work we have done in holiness of heart, but by faith."

"Tempt me not, child," said the infatuated nun, "lest you and I sink together into endless fire."

Sister Clement had been ordered by Father Murphy to leave her place of service and report to him. She accordingly presented herself before him.

"You have left your place without exciting suspicion?" asked the very reverend Father.

"I quarreled with the cook and would not remain any longer in the house with her," said Clement, with a covert smile.

"You obtained a recommendation?"

"A most excellent one," replied Sister Clement, producing a document wherein the qualifications of the invaluable maid-servant Annette were set forth.

"We need more work of this kind," said Father Murphy; "and as we have found by many trials that Sister Maria is a staunch daughter of the Church and fit to be trusted, you can instruct her in various things necessary for her to understand, and transfer to her this recommendation. She will first obtain a situation as nurse-maid. In a few days the Superior of the Convent of the Immaculate Heart will indicate the proper place."

Sister Clement now returned to the House, and obtained permission for Sister Maria and herself to work at their embroidery in her own little room.

We do not mean to suggest a pleasant hour of work and gossip, such as two country girls might enjoy before milking-time; nor such gentle comparing of domestic notes as two good housewives engage in while sewing for Tom, Dick or Harry; neither school-girls' happy chit-chat, nor holy converse of two gospel-workers. Between these two lay the carping jealousies, the smothered rivalry, the petty spites that are inseparable from convent life.

Sister Clement was to instruct her inferior, and she made Sister Maria feel this fully. Sister Clement was well up the ladder of promotion. Before her lay the possibilities of a Superior's place and of a mission to Rome. In these things she craftily triumphed over Sister Maria. She took her up sharply, and in many ways manifested that she looked upon her with contempt. Of course, Sister Maria felt this, and while meekly learning, as in duty bound, she felt how delightful were sewing if her needle pricked in and out of dear Sister Clement instead of the canvas.

"I began by being a nurse-maid," said Sister Clement, "which is given to beginners as the easiest place. One must not be very devout, and one must be very respectful. I have done many things for my mistresses that no other servant would: it pays to flatter the pride of heretics. Among other things I have baptized their children," she added, with a sneer, "which was certainly a great favor. I have lived in three houses as nurse-maid, and have baptized, or had baptized, ten young children. Seven of these children I baptized myself—three I took to the cathedral. They are all on Father Murphy's rolls. Have you learned the formula of lay baptism?"

No; Sister Maria had not.

"I will instruct you at once," said Sister Clement. "This prayer-book is the infant; here is the water; attend." She rapidly made the sign of the cross over the water, dipped up a little in her hand and flung it over the book, muttering: "I baptize thee in the name of the Father, and of the Son, and of the Holy Ghost." Then, wiping the water from the book with her apron, she added: "I generally sign the cross on the child, and say an 'ave' at each point. Now, see if you can do it."

She handed over the book and the water, and Sister Maria performed the ceremony of baptism very creditably. Sister Clement continued her instructions:

"You must take special care that no one sees you. Of all things you must not be suspected to be other than a very humble, honest servant-girl. I have noticed that Sisters in disguise are the most highly prized of all servants. Once a child's grandmother saw me baptizing it. I do hate grandmothers; they are so sharp-eyed and for ever suspecting. She asked me what I was doing, and I told her that I was saying a charm I had learned in the old country, to keep the babe from being cross-eyed or a stammerer. One of the best qualifications of a Jesuit Sister is to lie well and quickly."

"I can do that," said Maria, meekly.

"I know you can," snapped Sister Clement; "I believe you have often lied to your confessor."

"What is to become of the baptized children after one leaves them and goes elsewhere?" asked Maria.

"Why, you fool," said the amiable Clement, "don't you know that they belong to the Church, and it is the priest's business to look after them? He sends a good, stiff Catholic girl after the place with a first-class recommendation, and there it is. Saint Cecelia at the 'Heart' has written five hundred recommendations, I dare say. In many places people let the nurse take the children to church, and always the nurse can take them walking and riding, and that goes a long way if one knows how to use opportunities."

"And what becomes of them in the end?" ventured Maria.

"You act as if you did not know our Church was looking forward to a day of power, when she can claim her own. I believe you're too great an idiot to work this way."

"I'll get ahead of *you*," hissed Maria.

"Well," said Sister Clement, smoothing her ruffled feelings, "stick to these three things—lying, humility and quickness to seize opportunity—and you *may* be able to do a *little* of what *I* have done."

It was the hour for the daily reading of "Exercises," and these gentle Sisters went down stairs. But just then arose a great commotion. Sister Magdalena had found Mother Ignatia lying on the chapel floor, apparently in a dying condition. She was carried to her room, or, more properly, cell, and laid on her pallet, while Father Murphy was sent for, to speed, with extreme unction and prayer, the parting soul.

While waiting for the Father's coming, the Sisters occupied themselves in various ways. Sister Clement with all propriety stood by her dying Superior, her face calm, peaceful in the assurance that the hour of her promotion was nigh at hand.

Agnes, who was not suffered to go out of sight, stood shivering before the presence of death in all his terrors. It was the Friday fast, but the two Sisters who served the kitchen availed themselves of the opportunity of making a full meal three hours earlier than the usual eating was allowed, while Sister Magdalena surreptitiously helped herself to some of her own wine and jelly.

At last Father Murphy arrived and stood by Ignatia's side. A quivering of throat and eyelids, and a short, spasmodic gasp at intervals, alone spoke of life.

"She is dying, Father; pray you administer the sacrament of extreme unction quickly," said Saint Clement.

Father Murphy had the holy oil in his pocket, but he bent over the patient, felt her pulse and touched her fleshless cheek.

"It's a clear case of starvation and exhaustion," he said. "What a dolt the woman is!" Then shouted in his stentorian voice, "Magdalena, bring me some wine; Joanna, get some beef-tea. She needs food more than anointing. Bring me a chair, and by Holy Mary, I'll perform a miracle and bring the dead to life," he added with a jolly wink; yet sitting down on the chair gingerly, as if fearing it would prove treacherous beneath his weight.

"Oh, Father, disturb her not; let her die in the odor of sanctity," suggested the disinterested Sister Clement.

"Not I, while the Church needs her," said Father Murphy. "Get me a spoon, daughter Clement: your turn will come some day; you will have her shoes after a while; but, bless me! I believe the creature's been going barefoot! That is Douay's work," he added under his breath, and as wine and spoon were ready, he forced the stimulant between the nun's blue lips. "Hurry that Joanna in the kitchen," he ordered, "and bring some brandy to rub this woman's feet and hands. Rub one of her hands, Agnes," he added to the girl near him; "you can have no better office than to wait on so good a Catholic."

Ignatia's mattress and pillow were of straw without sheets or pillow-case. The Father had been feeding his patient with modicums of wine and brandy, while the Sisters rubbed her feet, hands and head. Father Murphy bent over to notice the motion of Ignatia's throat, that he might judge better of the effect of his remedies. So doing, he lifted a little from his chair and moved the serge dress from her neck, which disclosed the fact that the poor, emaciated creature was dressed underneath her nun's robe in a horrible, rasping hair-cloth. The sight so shocked the worldly and jolly priest that he dropped himself heavily back, when his treacherous chair gave way beneath his ponderous person, and he went crashing to the floor, jarring the whole house. The Sisters crowded about their prostrate chief. The reverend Father speedily recovered himself, took a glass of brandy to settle his nerves, and ordered the inmates of the House to remove the sick woman's hair-cloth, put on proper garments, lay her on a soft and comfortable bed, and continue to administer wine and beef-tea until he came again. In a few days, Ignatia was able to sit up. Father Murphy then put the House in the temporary charge of Sister Clement, sent Sister Maria under the name and in the clothing of Annette to her place as nurse-maid, and informed Ignatia that she was for the present to be put in the hospital ward of the Convent of the Immaculate Heart of Mary, and given as an invalid into the charge of Mother Robart.

At this juncture, Saint Cecelia arrived, saying that Agnes Anthon's aunt had returned home and was ready to receive her niece. Agnes was therefore presented with a crucifix, a rosary, a Missal and a Book of Exercises, received the paternal benediction of Father Murphy, and with Saint Cecelia and Mother Ignatia was put into Michael Shinn's carriage, driven by John Mora, and by many devious and rapid turns taken back to the Convent of the Immaculate Heart.

Agnes knew that she had been somewhere in the city, but street, number or direction she could not tell.

Mother Robart received her banished pupil with dignified tenderness. She was rejoiced to hear so good an account of her, trusted that her whole life would reap the benefit of the last two weeks, should ever be glad to see her, and with a gracious kiss and blessing Agnes was consigned to Saint Cecelia to be taken to her aunt.

Behold now Mother Robart and her invalid charge Ignatia! Mother Robart living a lie and knowing it, yet staying her soul on the thought that her eternal chance was as good as that of millions who, through hundreds of years, have crowded the gates and ministered at the altars of Rome. Did she go down to perdition, she would go with a goodly train of popes and cardinals, and right reverend and very reverend and reverend clergy. Mother Robart knew one all-absorbing passion—ambition—the love of power; and this Rome gratified. She stood in the stately Convent of the Immaculate Heart of Mary, Sisters and servitors and pupils at her back, herself proud, flush with life and ease, admired and self-satisfied, ready to cry with Nebuchadnezzar, "Is not this great Babylon, which I have built for the house of the kingdom, by the might of my power and the honor of my majesty?"

And Ignatia, a bruised reed that Rome would utterly break, smoking flax which priestcraft would quench, starved and wounded body, starved and wounded spirit, believing entirely, yet wrecked by believing, a lie—still in bitterness of soul crying only, "Mea culpa! mea culpa!"

CHAPTER VI.

CONFIRMATION OF THE CHILDREN.

ALADDIN rubbed his lamp and summoned the genii. Father Murphy could with equal ease summon his helpers. He had thus called before him a sturdy pair—John Mora and Michael Shinn. Michael, as the richer man of the two, had ventured to balance himself on the corner of a chair, but his hesitation about so great a privilege as this so worked upon him that he was in instant danger of toppling over. John Mora held his felt hat uneasily before him, looking into it anxiously. With all these symptoms of a severe attack of reverence, Father Murphy was of course well pleased. He was established in his favorite chair, and he put first one foot on an ottoman and regarded it complacently, and then served the other in the same manner. He was not in too great haste to speak, thinking it better to allow the men to be fully impressed with the magnificence of his surroundings.

The children of our Father of Rome attending the

Cathedral of Saint Joseph the Just had just finished the devotion of the "Forty Hours." Father Murphy had entertained the Bishop in excellent style, and, having found it his duty to maintain the inner and outer man by various good dinners and suppers, was none the worse for the extra exertions he had been supposed to make. John Mora and Michael Shinn had found the "Forty Hours" a very different matter. They had fasted, had humbly approached the tribunal of penance, had heard, without understanding, the sermons, had listened to the fine music without appreciating it. They were very glad the "Forty Hours" were over, but were sure they must be a deal better for it.

"John Mora and Michael Shinn," said the sonorous voice of the reverend Father, "I have sent for you to show you how you may be yet more useful and worthy children of the Church. I trust you are ready to be all obedience and to take upon you whatever duties are set before you?"

"Yes, your honor's reverence," said the two men.

"The Church, as I have often told you," said Father Murphy, stretching himself back in his chair and assuming the tone and air of one about to give a lecture on political economy, "is a temporal as well as a spiritual kingdom. She claims to be mother and queen of nations. To uphold and extend her lawful temporal power, she needs strong muscles, keen wits and obedient hearts; and these she wants not in a helter-skelter mob, but in a regularly *organized* and *well-trained* body."

"And how many will it be, your reverence?" asked Michael Shinn.

"How many, my man? They will be counted by hundreds of thousands, here and over the sea."

"And is it just started, your honor?"

"No, Michael, the Church works slowly. This was ordered years ago. In silence and in patience our Church has laid her plans. She takes into this army of her faithful only the strongest and most zealous of her sons. One by one the reverend Fathers have picked out these men for years, and have sworn them into this organization. It is like a worm, from every severed part of which a new head will grow, and which destroying only increases. It is like a root which sends out a new plant every time it is divided, so that cutting it smaller only makes it larger. I defy this nation, I defy England, to search it out and crush it now!"

This was our reverend's priest's hobby; and speaking, his theme had grown upon him, until he rose from his seat and harangued his two men as if they had been a council. His enthusiasm was infectious.

"There's my hand on it!" cried John Mora, "as

will be proud to shed its last drop of blood in the holy cause, and carry a musket or a shillalah as the Church may bid me!"

"And what may the name of the 'band' be?" asked Michael Shinn.

"*The Fenians,*" said Father Murphy, deliberately.

"The Fenians is it?" cried John Mora, astounded: "sure it was only last week that Father Guire refused to confess a friend of mine for belonging to the Fenians, and troth I've been afraid to speak to the fellow since."

"*I* confessed him, so you need be afraid of him no longer. I'll give you a card with the time and place of meeting on it, and you'll find friends there and an officer ready to swear you in. As to Father Guire and the Fenians, let me tell you that there are some few priests who are kept in ignorance of these things, and there are many who must act as if they disapproved it. My men, the Church must seem to be on the fence about Fenianism. If, by any ill-luck, it falls into disgrace for a while, the Church must appear to have always condemned it. If it goes on prosperously, as Saint James permit, the Church can openly own it by and by. There's the Vicar-General at Chicago is a Fenian out and out,* while there's a

* This was before the Vicar-General died and was escorted to his grave by a body of *armed Fenians.*

priest in Buffalo who the other day refused to let a Fenian be buried in consecrated ground."

"Troth, what did the poor creature do?" asked John Mora.

"His body was privately conveyed to another Catholic burying-ground. Never fear, John—the Church will uphold the Fenians. The Pope will give each one an indulgence and absolution."

"And, your honor's reverence, suppose the law takes them up and handles them?"

"I should think you had seen, John, that the Church here is strong enough to clear any of her children before a jury if she once undertakes it. The Church works so that either the lawyers or the witnesses or the jury or the judge shall turn the verdict right for the faithful." *

"And, your reverence," said Michael Shinn, "might I be bold to say, men will be a poor mob unless they're armed; and where are the arms?"

"I see you take hold of it right, Michael," said Father Murphy: "let me tell you that there are magazines all over the country that are getting filled up; † and it is a good idea, my men, to make *Protest-*

* Witness the method of trial and its results in the case of Mary Ann Smith, abducted by Romanists from Newark, N. J.

† 20,000 rifles have been distributed among Fenians in the United States.—*Cincinnati Gazette.*

ants pay for these arms by bringing them out to *charity fairs* and *concerts*, eh?" and Father Murphy thrust his hands into his pockets and chuckled. He was a very dangerous fellow, this fat priest.

Now, as these two sons of Popery went homeward, or rather stableward, they passed a spacious building belonging to a Protestant religious society. Says John to Michael, "We may have that one day for a nunnery, eh?"

"We may that," says Michael, unctuously, "and yon's a grand house I may have for my own when the rise comes?"

"Troth, you may; and there's a brown stone house that Protestant dom*miny* lives in, it would make a very con*va*nient place for the old woman and me childher. Ha, ha!" replied John Mora.

Perhaps these two men were getting on faster than the reverend Father they had just left.

Of course, Father Murphy did not spend nearly all his time with Shinn & Co. or the Fenians. He looked after his flock with all vigilance. He was one day "going to and fro in the earth, and walking up and down in it," when he went into Mr. Kemp's, and, as the lady of the house was absent, he ordered Grace and Adelaide to be sent down to the parlor to receive his counsels.

He questioned them closely as to their observance

of fasts and prayers. For, although Father Murphy privately considered that himself had outgrown these things, he regarded them as admirable screws wherewith to keep the laity in working order. After these matters, he spoke of their friendships.

"I hope my daughters do not associate with Agnes Anthon. Mother Robart tells me she is a very naughty girl."

"She has gone away to boarding-school, so we could not see her if we wanted to," said Grace; "but, Father, she is a splendid girl—she is so smart. She only acted so at school for fun. She may come to the true Church yet."

"Perhaps she may," said the priest, dryly, "but until she does you had better not make a friend of her. Do you get letters from her?" he asked, quickly.

Grace seemed busy looking into the street, but Adelaide replied, "No, of course we do not."

"All your correspondence you should, like dutiful children, take to be inspected by Mother Robart."

"Why not to mother here at home?" asked Grace.

"Certainly show it to her too, but to Mother Robart especially, as she is your spiritual mother set over you by the holy Church."

(We see that, in a Jesuit's view, a mother the Church gives should be much nearer than one whom God gives.)

"Oh, well," said Adelaide, "there's no use talking; we never get any letters and are too lazy to write any."

"And what do you have to read? Do you borrow any books?"

"I borrowed a lot of fairy stories, and then I got Mrs. Southworth's novels," said Adelaide.

"They will not hurt you," said Father Murphy, smiling.

"I got Milton's 'Paradise Lost,'" said Grace. "I don't like novels."

"Milton!" cried Father Murphy; "go and bring it to me! It is an indecent, false and shameful book. To read it is quite enough to ruin you. Get me the book, and I will see it returned."

While Grace was getting the book, the keen eyes of the Father, searching the room, saw the corner of some volume which was thrust under the sofa pillow. He drew it forth to Adelaide's horror, and, dreadful to relate, it was a copy of Bunyan's Pilgrim's Progress—an elegant edition, with colored pictures. The first picture that caught the reverend Father's eye represented "Lord Hategood," strikingly gotten up as our Father of Rome in full pontifical array.*

Father Murphy shook the book, trembled, stamped, quivered and choked with rage. Adelaide fled to

* See Bunyan's Progress, London edition of Fred. Warne & Co.

the farthest part of the room, and Grace, returning with the copy of Milton, tarried on the door-sill, tears on her cheeks, anger in her eyes, ready either to fight or fly.

"Where did you get this vile, filthy, heretical book?" he demanded when able to articulate.

"From Annie Mott," faltered Grace.

"From a miserable little heretic!" cried the holy Father. "If ever you visit her, speak or bow to her again, you shall be shut up in a cell at the Immaculate Heart and kept on bread and water."

"I didn't know it was any harm," sobbed Grace. "I thought it was a pretty book, and there's one at the convent, only it isn't as pretty as this."

"Yes, there's a Catholic edition there, fit for reading; but this is a garbled heretical lie, and so I fling it in the fire; and in like manner may he that wrote it and he that sold it go to perdition!" He flung the book into the grate, and as it curled on the glowing coals, he seized the Paradise Lost from Grace, and seeing Annie Mott's name in it, he cast it also into the fire. Both the girls were crying bitterly. The priest's wrath cooled a little: "Will you promise to have no more to do with Annie Mott?"

"Yes," gasped Grace.

"And will you submit all your reading to Mother Robart's inspection?"

Priest Murphy burning "Bunyan" and "Milton."

Priest and Nun. Page 146

"Yes, sir," said Adelaide.

Father Murphy now prescribed for Grace a day's fasting, a certain number of prayers and the forfeiture of her month's allowance of pocket-money to the convent charity fund; and most likely would have gone on with his rebukes and penances, had he not seen the doctor's carriage at Judge Schuyler's door.

"What is the matter there?" he demanded.

"Uncle Schuyler had an apoplectic fit this noon," said Adelaide; "there is where mother is."

Here was a very valuable sheep in danger; so Father Murphy gave the girls his paternal benediction and went over the way.

Left alone, the girls cried until their excitement wore off. Then Grace said,

"Addie, what two big stories you told Father Murphy! You said we did not hear from Agnes, when we do; and that we get and write no letters, when we do."

"It is none of his business," said Adelaide, "and I sha'n't show my letters to Mother Robart."

"But it is shameful to tell lies," said Grace.

"No; Father Murphy has told me at confession that lies are right sometimes, and if they're right sometimes, they're right always. Anyhow, I like to tell them; they're convenient," said Adelaide. "As to those books, we'll tell Rick, and make him buy

Annie some new ones just like them, and take them to her."

Adelaide did this, and also got Rick to get two new copies, which she gave Grace, saying, "They are a birth-day present for you, *cherie;* keep them secret. It is so delicious to do things secretly, I think!" You see how Adelaide was bearing the legitimate fruits of Romish teachings.

Thinking he had been rather hasty with the girls, Father Murphy returned next day to talk with them more reasonably, and, of course, found them docile.

"May I read the Bible?" asked Grace in conversation.

"Certainly not. Do you not know that it is forbidden?"

"I thought it was," said Grace, "but I read in one of our Catholic papers that that is a heretic scandal, and that the Bible is allowed.* It said that 'the Church is anxious that the Bible should be circulated.'"

"That was written for the eyes of Protestants, and not for children of the Church," said Father Murphy, blandly.

"Say what you don't mean?" asked Grace, stretching open her eyes.

* Since this the Archbishop of Baltimore has written a tissue of contradictions on this subject, published in the *Catholic Standard.*

"Yes, if by that means we may win some to examine and receive the doctrines of the Holy Church, and be converted."

"And what does the Church really say about the Bible?" asked Grace.

"The Council of Trent says," replied Father Murphy, "that if the Bible is given to the people, there will result more trouble than advantage. No person can read the Bible without a written permit from the Bishop. No person who shall dare secretly read the Bible can receive absolution for his sins, and he who sells a Bible must be punished by fines and other penances, according as the Bishop shall judge of the quality of his *crime.* Lastly, priests themselves can neither read nor buy a Bible without the permission of their superiors." (Council of Trent, quoted by Monod.)

All this wisdom, of course, satisfied Grace; and the reverend Father was quite right in his deliverances, taking them from the "Regular Proceedings of the Council of Trent," which we hope he was scholar enough to read in the original Latin.

Meanwhile, Mother Ignatia was somewhat recruited at the Convent of the Immaculate Heart, though her vexed spirit found nothing congenial among those easy-going nuns. One melancholy face had moved her for a while to hope for a kindred soul. It was the face of the little pervert from Missouri. But Mother Ignatia was informed that the steadfastness of this nun was more than suspected; that she was never allowed to go into the street; that vigilant watch was kept over her night and day, and that she was not even trusted to go into the garden or to sleep alone.

Father Murphy now allowed Ignatia to resume the charge of the House Without a Name. Sister Clement must resign her briefly-held power. There was other work for her.

Judge Schuyler had been much shattered by his attack of apoplexy. Another might hurry him out of the world, and the Church must be ready for this event. Mother Robart told Lilly that it was very wrong for her to keep a Protestant maid when so many Catholic girls were needing good places. Lilly, acting under instructions, informed her mother that she could no longer be waited upon by Hannah.

"But, my daughter, Hannah is a faithful servant who does not merit dismissal. She is the maid I have chosen for you, and I must be mistress of my own house and keep such girls as I choose."

"It is my *duty* to have a maid of my own religion," faltered Lilly, still obeying orders received at the convent.

"It is your duty to obey your mother, and not

give her any trouble about the domestics," said Mrs. Schuyler.

"Dear mamma, do not hurt my conscience," cried Lilly; "do, please do, let me get another maid who shall be a Catholic!"

"Do not hurt my feelings, Lilly, by being thus ruled by strangers in every particular," said Mrs. Schuyler.

Further instructed, poor Lilly refused to be dressed by Hannah, wept continually, made her hair look very dreadfully in trying to arrange it herself, and constantly entreated "dear mamma" to let her do what was right; and yet the poor little soul was half heartbroken all the time by being *forced* thus to distress her mother.

Weak Mrs. Schuyler, yielding at last to husband and child, took Hannah as a seamstress for herself, though she did not need her, and Lilly was at liberty to get a maid recommended by Mother Robart. Mother Robart recommended "*Annette*," who resumed the "character" Sister Maria had been using, and was duly established at Judge Schuyler's. She was to act as a spy on the mistress of the house, to watch over the judge's symptoms, and to be a spiritual bellows to fan the fires of Lilly's devotion. She was also to drive off Hannah if possible. But this she could not do. Hannah loved her mistress with almost filial tenderness. Lilly became perfectly infatuated with her new maid. In her last place at service, Annette had found it necessary to simulate great vanity and lightness of demeanor: now her rôle was humility and devotion. As she dressed Lilly's hair she told her long legends of the saints, and would also relate what she called her own experiences, wherein devout Catholics had won over many of their friends and relatives. She had much to say of revelations, "made to her certain knowledge," where Our Lady, or Joseph the Just, or one of the long catalogue of saints, had supernaturally appeared to strengthen and console the faithful. The especial point Sister Clement had been instructed to make with Lilly was on her receiving the communion and being confirmed. This she did persistently and artfully, never dropping her character of the humble waiting-maid for one moment, but by every trifling circumstance bringing these points up in their "proper light."

And now the winter was passing away, and the first day of Lent this year fell on Lilly's birth-day. Mrs. Schuyler had intended to celebrate the day by some pleasant festival, but Lilly utterly refused this, her mind in fact being in a fearful excitement about being confirmed in the cathedral just after Easter, in direct opposition to her mother's commands—a step which she knew would make that dear patient mother entirely wretched, yet which Father Murphy and the nuns assured her she must at once take, after too long delay. Each month was dividing farther and farther asunder this mother and her only child, and putting Lilly still more and more under priestly domination. But a higher Power had ordered the events of that birth-day. Lilly came home from the service at the Cathedral of St. Joseph the Just to find her father at the point of death, stricken by another fit of his disease. Before night Judge Schuyler was dead. Fathers Murphy and Douay had stood over his insensible form as the spirit was departing, administering extreme unction and repeating the "offices" and prayers of the Church for the dying. When the scene was over, and only dead clay remained of the husband and parent, Annette conveyed the almost distracted Lilly to her apartment. Mrs. Schuyler being, as we have frequently stated, a weak woman, her distress overpowered her, and as fainting succeeded fainting, Hannah and the physician watched anxiously at her bedside until daybreak.

Meanwhile, priests and nuns, with Mrs. Kemp, presided in the chamber of death. The body of Judge Schuyler was suitably laid out, a crucifix upon his breast, holy water at his head, a prayer-book laid open at his feet, wax tapers burning about him with a sickly radiance in the growing light of dawn.

Poor Lilly, taken to her room, flung herself sobbing on the floor, refusing to be comforted. The invaluable Annette stood over her, wringing her hands and crying,

"Oh, miss; oh, my sweet miss; your father is dead; on your birth-day too! Oh, my dear miss, why did you not get confirmed, as they bid you? Here is a judgment on you, my dear miss. The saints and the Virgin are angry. Oh, I vow to them a fast on bread and water, and one hundred 'aves,' if their anger will cease."

"What shall I do? what shall I do?" shrieked Lilly.

"Oh, miss, make vows to them," cried Annette, dropping on her knees and rattling over "aves" in the pauses of her exhortations. "Vow to them to do your duty. Vow that you will keep this holy Lent with all your heart—that you will be confirmed and live a true daughter of the Church. Vow a gift to the convent. Vow a gift to the altar at Saint Joseph's. Oh, my dear miss, much I fear, if you do not, the angels will take away that blessed lady your mother," whom Sister Clement, alias Annette, cordially hated.

Need we doubt that Lilly made, in full faith and

earnestness, any number of vows? A little composed by these, she desired to go to her mother. All her grief and remorse were reawakened at seeing her mother's pale face, swollen eyelids and disheveled hair. She flung herself on the bed beside her, clasped her arms about her neck, and covering her mother's face with kisses, sobbed out, "Mother, oh, mother, it is my fault, I know it is; it is a judgment on your wicked Lilly that has brought so much trouble to you. Darling mother, forgive me!"

"Forgive *you*, Lilly!" cried Mrs. Schuyler; "my precious child, you are my only comfort."

Unhappy mother! unhappy child! born to be that mother's bitterest woe!

The judge was buried with all magnificence. He had not openly united with the True Church, but Father Murphy said he had done so privately; at all events, he had given to that Church's aid, upheld her institutions, placed his child in her hands, and plainly expressed his faith in her unity, purity and infallibility. His body was laid in consecrated ground; masses were said and sung for his soul; he was blessed and lauded and held up as an example, and Michael Shinn at that grand funeral reaped heavy profits from being a son of the True Church and obedient to the reverend Fathers.

And now we could have wished that, in the privacy of their grief, left to each other's love for solace, Lilly and her mother could have grown more closely together, and the child could have given her parent her entire confidence. But no; this the holy Mothers Rome and Robart could not permit. To the weeping widow could not be left the comfort of her child. Lilly was reminded of her vows—was told that she must go to the convent, and there remain for proper religious exercises and instructions until she had taken her communion and received confirmation at the hands of the Archbishop. Now, Mothers Rome and Robart could not have *forced* Lilly from her home and mother against the will of every one; but, cruelest sting of all, the child was brought to insist upon thus doing. It was set before her as a *religious duty* to leave her only parent alone in agony of spirit; and she was persuaded to demand it as her right and privilege thus to leave her mother in her grief—herself to go elsewhere for the good of her soul, and to prepare to disobey that mother's express commands. Oh cruel blow upon a heart already so sorely wounded!

To the convent went Lilly to remain six weeks, and to attend to such prayers, rites and reading as Mother Robart should ordain.

There was a week's school vacation during this Lent, and as Grace and Adelaide were now fully restored to Father Murphy's favor—Grace by absolute obedience, and Adelaide by cunning deceit, in which she very naturally delighted—Estelle Wynford was permitted to go to their house for a three days' visit, Mother Robart considering that, as the Kemps were of the faithful, a visit to them could do Estelle no harm, Richard being absent from home.

Mrs. Kemp, kind and friendly to everybody, and also intent on doing service to her Church, was naturally very attentive to her sister-in-law, Mrs. Schuyler, and spent much time with her. She was passing an evening with Mrs. Schuyler during Estelle's visit to Grace and Adelaide. The three girls, left to themselves in the parlor, began to amuse themselves with ghost stories, growing more and more extravagant in their narrations, until they had themselves fairly frightened—for all they were mature damsels of fifteen—and began to suspect supernatural influences in every wavering shadow or creaking door or window. "Oh," cried Adelaide, half earnest, half jesting, "I'm going to make Lucy come and sit in the hall near the register, for I'm dreadfully afraid." She ran off and ordered Lucy to her new post. Lucy came, but not alone. Annette had very justly decided that living as a spy at Mrs. Schuyler's did not prevent her exercising some surveillance at Mr. Kemp's. She had therefore gotten up an intimacy with Lucy, and was spending the evening with her. Adelaide bade Annette come and sit with Lucy in the hall, and the two maids having taken their places, Adelaide left the drawing-room door ajar, and putting her charming face at the crack, cried, "Now, girls, don't go away for your lives, for we are awfully afraid of ghosts."

The thread of ghostly narratives had been broken by Adelaide's short absence. "Let us talk of something else," said Estelle; "I'm tired of ghost stories."

"Let us tell our histories," said Grace.

"Oh yes," exclaimed Adelaide; "we will each be our own heroine."

"Sh-h-h," whispered Annette to Lucy in the hall; "let us hear the stories the young ladies are telling."

We all know about what Grace and Adelaide could tell; it is Estelle's story that will interest us most, as indeed it did Annette, sitting in the hall by the register.

"My mother," said Estelle, "was my father's second wife. When his first wife died he went to Italy to distract his mind from troubles. He left Martin, my half-brother, in Scotland with his nurse. Martin was just a little baby. In Italy father met mamma, who was a widow and quite young. In a year they were married, and they traveled about until I was born, which was in Paris, you know, and then they went to Scotland and got Martin, and we all lived together. Mamma loved Martin very much, and so did I. We had a governess sometimes; sometimes we went to school. Summers we journeyed about through England and Wales. We had no trouble; only Martin's grandfather died, and we did not mind that much, because we had never seen him, and he left Martin a good deal of money. We were happy until I was ten years old, and then mamma died, and we traveled about in Europe, and then came to this country; and father has not done traveling yet. He wants to distract his mind from trouble. Mamma left me some money, and her father is a very old man in Italy, and when he dies he will leave me some more money. You see I cannot be expected to care much for him, for I never saw him. I cared *so much* for my mamma, and I love my father and Martin to adoration."

Thus ended Estelle's tale—all marriage and money. Annette's eyes were fixed, her hands clasped.

"Wake up, Annette," whispered Lucy; "are you asleep?"

"Nearly," said Annette, aptly. But her mind was in a whirl of triumphant scheming.

The day for Lilly's confirmation had come. She

was allowed to dress at home for the occasion. Annette, the admirable, was a skillful dressing-maid. Saint Cecelia was in attendance to remind Lilly of her duties. The girl was dressed in white silk, and crowned with a wreath of lilies-of-the-valley of choicest workmanship — spotless white in all her attire, her golden hair falling like a halo about her face and shoulders. Poor Lilly! she was too fair for scenes like these.

"I must see, mamma," said Lilly, breaking away from nun and maid. She found her mother reclining in a large chair in her dressing-room, while Hannah, seated at her feet, read to her from the Psalms. "Oh, mamma, do speak to me," said Lilly.

Mrs. Schuyler took her in her arms: tears rained on the little devotee's upturned face.

"My poor, lost, misguided, deluded child!" sobbed Mrs. Schuyler.

* * * * * * *

Lilly, with many more, was kneeling in the grand Cathedral of Saint Joseph the Just. Trembling, she listened to the music, the Bishop's prayer, the monitions given, and then the Bishop made upon her forehead with chrism the sign of the cross, saying, "I sign thee with the sign of the cross, and I confirm thee with the chrism of salvation, in the name of the Father, and of the Son, and of the Holy Ghost."

He then gave her a little blow on the cheek, saying, "Peace be with you!"

This she had been taught was to put her in mind "that in confirmation she was strengthened to suffer with patience, and even to die with Christ."

Lilly had received "the Holy Eucharist." She had been taught, and fully believed, that under every fragment of bread and every sip of wine (which element, however, was strictly for priests) was "the flesh, blood, soul and divinity of the Lord Jesus, wholly there." * "Whole under each part." "In each morsel, wholly indivisible in each form and under each part of the form." She accepted it as true that he, "by the almighty power of God, did not leave heaven to come into the host, but was in heaven and in every one of the consecrated hosts in the world at the same time." She understood that Jesus became "really her nourishment." Poor, ignorant, earnest, illogical, deceived Lilly! she could not perceive the monstrous absurdity of five hundred Christs in the Church at once, ready for the mastication of the faithful. She could not see how wild the idea that Jesus, obedient to priestly benediction, should enter bodily into bread and wine. She could not see a hundred other follies, which Rome taught her as the very essence of wisdom. Re-

* See Roman Catholic Catechism for each of these quotations.

ceiving the Holy Eucharist at the same time were Estelle, Grace and Adelaide. Thus had the Holy Mother Rome nourished and brought up children.

PART SECOND.

SHOWING THE MANNER OF ROME'S CHILDREN.

"*The best of them is as a brier; the most upright is sharper than a thorn hedge.*"—MICAH vii. 4.

CHAPTER I.

NUN OR NOT.

THOUGH Father Murphy had placed full confidence in that pride of his flock, Judge Schuyler, he was, after the judge's death, in no little anxiety concerning the Schuyler property and Lilly. Father Murphy had often exhorted the judge to make his will, but was in ignorance whether his advice had been followed. Indeed the judge had experienced all his life a dread of death and whatever suggested it. If he had died intestate, Father Murphy greatly feared that the widow would be allowed more voice in settling the estate than would accord with the interests of Holy Mother Church. While he dared not exhibit the concern in this matter that oppressed him, Father Murphy hovered about, under pretence of sympathy and desire to afford religious consolation, seeking for every item of intelligence and every indication of the turn affairs were taking. Annette also was on the alert—noiseless and swift of step. Were gentlemen in the drawing-room, there were flowers, or glasses of water, or needed supplies of coal, or (lacking these) adroitly-contrived messages to bring Annette thither, tarrying long at the door, entering unexpectedly, meek and apparently pre-occupied. Often during these tedious days (for never did affairs seem to move so slowly) did Annette fly to Father Murphy with her budget of news. The good Father might have spared himself all distress. The will was found at last—short, clear, direct, cheering to the priest's heart. One-third of the property went to Mrs. Schuyler, the house belonging to this portion. The remaining two-thirds were for Lilly, and Father Murphy and Mr. Kemp were her guardians.

Lilly's doom was sealed.

Poor Mrs. Schuyler had been completely ignored. She had not been deemed a proper guardian for her child. Had her husband dreamed of the cruel pain he was inflicting, he might have paused as he drew up that will. Obtuse in all matters of the affections as he was, the judge supposed that, in leaving his wife a home and ample estate, he was doing all for her that heart could wish. Men, thought the judge, are the only persons fit for business. Men only should be the legal guardians of a child. Mrs. Schuyler was overwhelmed with anguish. She sent for her brother.

"Henry," she exclaimed, "my heart is broken! My poor Lilly, with that priest for her guardian, will be taken from her mother and be made miserable for life."

"Why, Maria," said Mr. Kemp, "I am as much Lilly's guardian as Father Murphy is, and I do not see how we are going to make her miserable. Who would think of taking her from you? Neither of *us*, I am sure. Lilly's prospects are certainly very cheering, with plenty of money, and guardians who desire only her comfort. You're excited, Maria; I know you do not like Father Murphy, but he is a very fine man, as you'd find him if you only put a little confidence in him. Harriet likes him greatly."

"But Harriet is a Catholic and I am not," said Mrs. Schuyler.

"You should not let religion interfere with your friendship or prejudice you," said Mr. Kemp. "I assure you Father Murphy is completely above underhand dealings. He has no bigotry about him. He is benevolent, and desires only everybody's happiness."

"I ought myself to have been made guardian of Lilly," said the weeping mother. "You and I, Henry, should have been the guardians."

"I know," said Mr. Kemp, complacently, "women always think so; but, my dear Maria, what do you know about business? Come, now—consider how much better off you are than if you had Lilly and her estate to attend to. I cannot let you find fault with the judge, Maria; I'm sure he has settled his affairs admirably." So amazed was Mr. Kemp at his sister's foolish fears that he must needs bring them up at his dinner-table, and request Harriet, his wife, to go over and talk with her a little.

Richard had been out of town since the funeral, and had just returned. He leaned back in his chair and emitted certain equivocal hums and half-whistles, which might signify his disapprobation of something.

"Well, Rick?" said his father, interrogatively.

"Father Murphy Lilly's guardian!" cried Richard.

"And why not?" said Mr. Kemp.

"To be sure," said Mrs. Kemp.

"I'd as soon think of asking a wolf to be guardian of a plump little lamb. Mind it, father, that wolf in a gown and cocked hat will swallow the little lamb and all her perquisites."

"That is laying the matter down pretty flatly, Rick. You appear to forget that *I'm* a guardian too;" and Mr. Kemp straightened himself majestically.

"I know you are," said Rick, the bold, "and when the time comes you'll be looking about and wondering what has become of the lamb, and if it was eaten with its own consent, as it was done so quietly, poor thing!"

Now, "poor thing" meant Lilly the lamb, and not her uncle-guardian, Mr. Kemp.

"Richard!" said Mr. Kemp between turkey and jelly, in a tone that indicated he was offended, within bounds of propriety, with the young man.

Mrs. Kemp resignedly folded her napkin and slipped it in its ring, as if to suggest that Richard's remarks had deprived her of any further appetite.

Richard's position at his father's may need explanation. He was a young man of ability, and possessed a fortune left him by his mother. He had been educated chiefly before Mr. Kemp became a pervert to Romanism, and while unfortunately lacking all religious feelings—as might only be expected when he had seen his father so coolly use religion as a stepping-stone in his political ladder—Richard was certainly not a Romanist. Strenuous had been Mother Robart's efforts to convert the young man, but she had found him the least impressible in all the circle of her relatives; for, though there was no relationship between them, the Abbess honored Richard with the title of nephew. Richard was free as air, dependent on nobody for support, liked for his generous, gentlemanly manners, and respected for his intelligence and morality. His living at his father's was accepted as a favor. Mr. Kemp had certainly a father's pride in his only son. He also found it convenient to have that son a business man and a man of property. He would not have offended him on any account, and, of course, would never be offended with him.

Madam Robart had not given up all hope of Richard's conversion. She was a persistent woman, and would never confess herself foiled; certainly not when she knew Richard admired her greatly as a handsome, daring, successful woman, and frequently allowed himself the pleasure of a call upon her. Still, Richard's calls were not sources of unmixed pleasure, for he often took the privilege of a dashing young nephew in teasing her, and was ready to attack all vulnerable points of her practice. On the occasion of one of these visits, Estelle entered the parlor to get a letter which had just arrived for her from Havana. Of course, the Abbess had read the letter—that was one of the rules of the institution; even the correspondence of father and child must be closely inspected, and the Abbess was particularly pleased with the contents of this letter, for it informed Estelle that her brother Martin had entered the Belen at Havana to remain some months and study the Spanish language. Here it may be well to mention the fictitious portrait which was made the occasion of Father Murphy's acquaintance with Mr.

Wynford and of Estelle's residence at the Convent of the Immaculate Heart of Mary, and now also of Martin's entering the Jesuit school at Havana. Let no one anticipate any trouble from the fact that the portrait on ivory was bought on a venture and directed to a person who never existed. That it was put in the care of a veritable Jesuit Father was sufficient to ensure the success of the little plan. And let no one think the subterfuge too small: the Jesuits *know the power of littles.* The wily Father of the Belen received the parcel with thanks, and a letter from Father Murphy soon enlightened him as to its meaning. He cultivated the acquaintance of Mr. Wynford and young Martin, and angled so skillfully for the lad that, after some months of travel about those fair equatorial islands, he entered the Belen as a pupil; and now, if the reverend Father at the Belen and the reverend Mother at the Immaculate Heart of Mary succeed, here will be two young proselytes and their fortunes—always that—for a prey in the teeth of Rome.

Richard, as we said, was sitting in his aunt's parlor when Estelle entered and departed.

"Well," said the tantalizing Richard, "is that another heretic in a fair way for conversion?"

"If she could claim to be anything before she came here," said the Abbess, "it was some style of pure pagan, as she had no creed at all, but only undefined notions of nature and fate."

"At present I suppose she is one of the true children of the Church; and that reminds me, aunt, that you are losing some of your zeal—you have not tried to proselyte me this long time."

"As for that, nephew," said the Abbess, with a calm smile, "you know that we never try to proselyte any one—it is against our principles. Those who do not come freely, urged only by conscience and reason, to the true Church, we do not wish within her bounds. If our system concerning proselyting is what you would make it appear, how do you account for not being a victim yourself?"

"Oh," said Richard, mischievously, "it is only weak-minded people that are proselyted." Then, as if impressed by some sudden thought, he threw himself into a tragic attitude and cried, "A thousand, ten thousand pardons, my dear aunt! Believe me, I am utterly incapable of personalities—unpleasant personalities."

"What a trifler you are, nephew!" said Mother Robart.

"Tell me, oh, tell me, do you pardon me?" cried Richard, preserving the air and attitude of an actor.

"Yes, yes; and in five minutes you will sin again," said Mother Robart, smiling.

She admired and liked her handsome, lively nephew, quite as well as if she had not been a reverend Abbess. After the schooled docility of the pupils, the respectful silliness of the Sisters, the restless fanaticism of Father Douay, and the worldly platitudes of Father Murphy, an hour with nephew Richard was to the Superior like a sip from De Leon's fountain, renewing the scenes of her youth.

[To Ignatia no such hours of relaxation ever came. Peace of conscience was a treasure for which she sought unresting, and sought where it might never be found.]

"Nephew Richard," said the Abbess, "you are a specimen of the effects of the false system of education prevalent in America. The schools and colleges in the United States ignore what is highest, and devote themselves to the inculcation of what is lower. From their curriculum they reject *religion.* In its narrow interpretation of the term *education,* the public-school system entirely ignores religion, and exhibits instead some shadowy outlines of revelation, which will suit everybody and benefit nobody." *

"Meaning," said Richard, with a bow, "that the religion they ignore is the precious logic of missal and tradition, and the Word of God is the revelation which 'suits every one and benefits none?'"

* Jas. M. McG., in *Catholic Standard.*

"Well, nephew, how much good has the study of the Bible done *you?*" said the keen Abbess. "Has it made you a religious man? No, nephew; our school system here is ruinous. It teaches only cultivation of the mind and conservation of the State."

"When it ought to teach the Church," said Richard.

"Yes," said his aunt, undaunted. "If it had taught *you* the *Church*, it might have saved you from being an infidel."

"I am not an infidel," cried Richard. "I reject the term as unworthy a thinking mind. I humbly confess I have seen some Christian Protestants whom I would be better for being like. But, with all deference to your opinion, aunt, I do not think I would be better for being Father Murphy, Father Hecker or Archbishop Hughes."

As Richard went home, it struck him as inconsistent that he neither owned nor read a book about which he was ready to quarrel with his aunt; therefore he stopped at a bookstore and purchased a very handsome Bible, bound in velvet and gilt, heavily cornered and clasped and fitted in a case. Taking it into the parlor, he mischievously dropped it into his step-mother's lap. She opened the parcel with some curiosity, but when she saw the Bible, drew back as if she had been stung.

"Richard, I'm surprised at you," she said, while Grace and Adelaide ran to examine it, exclaiming,

"Oh, what a pretty book! Is it for me, Richard—for me?"

"Why, ma'am, what have I done now?" asked Richard, as his step-mother took the book from her daughters.

"Why you have bought a *Bible* and brought it *here*, when you know we do not allow such books—to the girls at least."

"Girls," said Richard, pocketing his purchase and shaking his finger at his sisters, "remember that this Book is always to lie on my dressing-table, and if ever you go there and read it, it will be your own fault."

"It is a book quite unfit for them—entirely above their comprehension," said Mrs. Kemp.

At this Grace indignantly tossed her head.

Adelaide, from sheer perversity, ran several times into Richard's room and read in his Bible, but it did not suit her at all.

"I wouldn't believe such a book," she said one day to Grace; "it makes religion so *hard*. Any one wants to be *religious*, but who wants to take so much trouble about it? The idea of coming down so hard on sin and demanding so much repentance for it! How much easier our way is—just to rattle it off to Father Murphy once in a while, and have it all pardoned!"

"But the catechism says that to the priest's absolution we must join contrition, confession and satisfaction," said Grace.

"Nonsense!" said Adelaide. "The catechism don't mean what it says. I've tried both ways, and Father Murphy absolved me just the same. Now if he remits the sins, they *are* remitted, and what use is there in distressing one's self by being sorry, when one can get along without? I can prove to you in two minutes, Grace, that that answer in the catechism don't mean anything: What is the use of contrition when we get absolution? and why give satisfaction for sins which have been done away by absolution?"

"But, Adelaide, you make sin such a light thing!"

"It *is* a light thing," said Adelaide. "It *must* be a light thing if it can be done away by a priest's two words, by a few 'Aves,' or by a day's fasting, or by scratching one's skin, as nuns do, with a little hair-cloth. There's a book of poetry which I picked up at Agnes Anthon's when I went there to call, which makes a great deal more of sin than our Church does. It says:

'Though the mills of God grind slowly, yet they grind exceeding small;
Though with patience he stands waiting, with exactness grinds he all.'

But that, you know, is heretic nonsense; still, I do think it gives a greater idea to show God exacting for sin than to show him tossing it all over into the hands of a priest, as our Church says."

"Oh, but sin *is* a great thing—it is against *God*," said Grace.

"He doesn't count it great, or why should he let a few mean dollars pay for it?" said Adelaide, lazily dropping back in her chair and playing with her curls. "Come, now—God, owner of all the treasures of the universe, and having no need of money, allows *sin* to be paid for thus: Lies, so much—they're cheap, moreover; disobedience, so much; theft, so much; neglect of duty, so much. I'm beginning to learn the tariff, for it has left me short of pocket-money sometimes. When I'm twenty years older, I shall know it well."

Grace dropped her voice a little. She was approaching a forbidden theme: "Adelaide, in Rick's Bible, I saw, 'The blood of Jesus Christ, his son, cleanseth us from all sin.'"

"Well," said Adelaide, "*I* saw that 'Christ was once offered to bear the sins of many,' and that he is a '*free* gift.' That don't at all agree with penance and satisfaction and indulgences. That shows that the Bible is all wrong, and we ought not to read it any more. I sha'n't, for, as I told you, I don't like its doctrine about sin being such a serious matter."

"But, Adelaide, nothing will keep you from sin if you think it such a light thing," said Grace, anxiously.

"Nothing in life but expediency," said Adelaide, laughing. Dangerous doctrine this for a girl of sixteen!

It was now summer-time—glorious midsummer—yet the girls at the convent were still busy with school-duties. Their friends who were educated at other schools were at home for vacation, and among these was Agnes Anthon. Grace, obedient to her priest, had not dared to call upon Agnes; but Adelaide had done so from sheer perversity, as she had never been very fond of Agnes' society. Agnes herself called at the convent, said many pretty things to the Abbess and the Sisters, told them she often thought of the beautiful grounds and appointments of the Convent, and that her present school was a very plain-looking place in comparison.

"She has improved very much," said Saint Cecelia of Agnes.

"The seed here sown may be beginning to grow," said Mother Robart.

While Grace was repeating to Adelaide that precious verse she had found in Richard's Bible,

Lilly was hearing the same verse from other lips. Lilly was more and more with the nuns as each month passed by. She especially delighted in visiting the poor, the sick and the dying, and her liberal supplies of pocket-money were chiefly expended in relieving suffering. Perhaps if Mrs. Schuyler had roused herself to go abroad and seek out cases of necessity, and had taken her child to aid her in relieving their wants, she might not only have kept her with herself and more apart from her Sisters, but she might have given her mind healthier impulses, and, by showing her how to do works of charity herself, might have freed her from the notions that Romanists and members of "Holy Orders" are the only charitable people in the world—a notion that poor Lilly was not singular in holding. But unhappy, lonely and bewildered by the Romish toils she found winding about herself and child, suffering from feeble health and the apathy that grows upon inactive lives, she took no resolute and well-timed measures to recover her child from deceivers and self-deception.

Lilly's tender sympathies, extreme sensitiveness, enthusiasm and morbid imagination were carefully fostered by nun and priest. Before her mind were placed the lives of numerous saints, the religion of good works, the possibility of seeing miracles, prodigies and revelations; and, naturally given to meditation and devotion, Lilly gradually withdrew from youthful friends, and, when not busy in the school-room, was often, with a basket in her hand at Saint Cecelia's or Saint Sophia's side, visiting "good Catholics" who were ill, and who, if neglected, might fall a prey to Bible-Women or Colporteurs. It was thus that with Saint Cecelia—Annette, her waiting-maid, following with a basket well filled by Lilly's gifts—Lilly went to visit Ann Mora, who was laid up with a broken limb. Lilly had often seen Ann since the day when she found her at the foot of her class in the parochial school. She had given Ann and Pat many presents of clothes and money. When they made their first communion, their clothes and new prayer-books came from Lilly. She was regarded with tender love by them both. When she found that Ann had met with a serious accident, she insisted on going to see her at once, and was more liberal than usual in providing sick-room luxuries. Ann was tossing in a fevered sleep, her face flushed, her hair disordered, her hands moving restlessly, and ever and again talking in her dreams. Lilly and Saint Cecelia bent over the bed.

"The blood! the blood!" muttered Ann, "the blood of Jesus Christ—from sin, from all sin—cleanseth us from all sin!"

Lilly knew well where she had first heard those

words. Saint Cecelia did not recognize them, but looking up at Mrs. Mora, asked,

"What is she talking about?"

"It's meself that doesn't know; only it's some verse she's picked up, and she has it over all the time when she's dreaming."

Saint Cecelia was busy giving Mrs. Mora some orders and asking all manner of inquisitorial questions. Annette had been given the basket and permission to depart.

Ann Mora opened her heavy eyes, perhaps from some magnetic influence of the earnest gaze Lilly fixed upon her.

"Poor Ann!" said Lilly, "you are very sick, and you suffer much. Doesn't it help you to say your prayers?"

"I say 'em, miss," said Ann.

"And in your sleep you were saying something about blood cleansing from all sin."

Ann repeated the verse very promptly.

"Yes, I remember you told me you learned that in the heretic school you went to."

"I know I did," said Ann, "but I believe it holds the true religion for poor wicked folks like me. It's different from you, miss—it don't need blood, belike, to cleanse *your* sins."

Saint Cecelia had heard none of this, as it was

softly spoken. On the way home, Lilly, greatly disturbed, said,

"Ann talks very strangely, Saint Cecelia."

"Perhaps so—I did not notice—she is feverish and most likely out of her right mind."

Lilly was relieved by this supposition, but Ann's verse was not to be banished from her thoughts. So interested in Ann's illness and poverty was Lilly that she went to her Uncle Kemp's that evening to tell the girls about it. All the family but Grace had gone to the theatre. Grace had been kept at home by a slight headache, but was glad enough to see Lilly coming in to relieve the tedium of the moments she was spending on the sofa in the parlor.

"You do not seem to care for any pleasures, Lilly, but you devote yourself to acts of religion, just like a Sister," said Grace.

"It was always so with me," said Lilly; "death, heaven, angels—these were always in my mind when I was a little child. Nobody said much about religion to me until Mother Robart got me to convent school; then the Sisters and Father Murphy made it so plain to me and showed me how all one's life could be religion. I sometimes think I shall take the 'Three Evangelical Counsels' as the rule of my life and be a nun."

"Oh, Lilly! you would not, you could not,

leave your mother, your friends, your money, every pleasure in life and be a *nun!*"

"And why not, Grace? Ought I not even to leave my mother for God and the Church? Shall I love my money more than my soul, and the pleasures of this world more than heaven? Oh, Grace, only to think of dying and coming short of heaven!"

"But, Lilly, do those only get to heaven who follow the 'Evangelical Counsels' of 'perpetual charity, good works and voluntary poverty?'"

"Yes, to be sure, Grace; but no one dare expect forgiveness who despises a '*vocation.*' Father Murphy and Saint Cecelia, indeed all the Sisters, say that is surely my 'vocation.' Annette is a very pious girl, and she told me the other day, while she was dressing my hair, of a young lady who was persuaded to neglect her 'vocation,' and such dreadful troubles befell her, and such a doom followed all she loved, as drove her, after many years' resistance, to do her duty; and at thirty she took the veil and died a month after, very unhappy because she had neglected to do right so long."

"But, Lilly, I am sure your mother would die of grief if you were a nun."

"Why, Father Murphy says that I can be just as good a daughter—yes and better—to her than ever, and that it will surely be the means of her salvation.

Once I am a nun, she will give all up and be very happy, and a good Catholic, and then we shall not be divided for ever. Oh, Grace, just think how beautiful it is to live a pure, holy life, doing good continually—beginning heaven in this world! How much better, dear Grace, is the soul than the body!—how much nobler to live entirely for spiritual interests! How easy, then, it will be to lay by in the grave the body we have cared for so little, and enter heaven clothed with prayers and good deeds!"

"I wish I were like you, Lilly!" said Grace, with a sigh. "Very often all I care for seems to me so vain and trifling. I am so afraid of death, and feel as if I were not living for any usefulness. There will be weeks when I do not think of these things; then weeks when I am low-spirited and think of nothing else, and so long to be and do good. Sometimes I wish I were like Adelaide—not caring the least in the world for anything but pleasure and dress and admiration. She never worries about salvation—never feels so distressed about doing wrong—but oftener I wish I were like you. Oh dear!" and tears rolled over Grace's cheeks.

"Grace," said Lilly, kissing her cousin, "very likely if you should give up all your love of the world and deny yourself and be a nun, you would be much happier than you are now. May be it is your duty,

Grace; anyway, I am sure it would save your soul, and that is the most important."

"Well," said Grace, wiping her eyes, "I'll talk to Father Murphy about it." Then musing a moment, the innate ambition of her heart awoke. "It would be worth while to be like Aunt Margaret," she said. Mother Robart was still spoken of at times by her nieces as Aunt Margaret.

"Oh," said Lilly, "I never thought of being like her. *You* might, Grace, but I only look for some very quiet place as a working Sister. To nurse the sick and comfort the dying, that is all I want. It must have been grand to go to Rome as Aunt Margaret did, and see the Holy Pope and the grand churches, the relics, the miracles, the wood of the true cross, the handkerchief of Veronica, the very manger in which Holy Mary laid the infant Jesus. But I never expect to see these things. If I can do good among the worst and poorest, it is all I ask."

Poor Lilly! tender, loving, earnest heart, how deceived! Enter heaven "clothed with prayers and good works," instead of having on the righteousness of Jesus? Save her soul by being a nun? "By grace are ye saved through faith, and that not of yourselves; it is the gift of God."

Strictly forbidden, as Lilly had been by her priest, to mention this subject of her "vocation" to her mother, Mrs. Schuyler yet suspected what course of life was being urged upon her daughter, and asked Lilly if she intended to take this step.

"Oh, mother," said Lilly, nervously, "I am too young, too ignorant, to intend anything myself; I must take advice from my superiors."

"Why not then from me, your loving mother?"

"I know you would advise me not to do it, mother."

"And should not a child respect a mother's wishes, believe in a mother's judgment, trust a mother's love, Lilly?"

"Oh, mother, if it is my duty, ought I to let any love hinder me? Ought I to lose my soul? Father Murphy is my spiritual director, mother; he is to me the voice of God. I dare not disobey him; I must do as he says, for he is always right."

"Always right! My poor child! He is an artful and scheming man, deceiving you with falsehoods."

"If he had ever told me a falsehood," said Lilly, flushing, "I would never believe him again; but he has not; he is too good—he cannot. Mother, you do not like him because you are not of the true Church. Oh, mother, do turn from heresy and be a good Catholic, and save your soul, and make your Lilly happy!" cried the girl, flinging her arms about her mother and looking at her with tearful earnestness.

Mrs. Schuyler's next appeal was to her brother, Mr. Kemp.

"There has no step been taken in this matter; how can I begin to interfere on a mere notion?" said Mr. Kemp. "Besides, Maria, Lilly is old enough to choose for herself, and I do not think it right to meddle with what she considers her duty or makes her choice, when I can see no possible harm in it. Do you think she is forced in this matter?"

"She is given false notions of duty, and unjustly pressed and persuaded, until she does not know what she really wants or what is right," said Mrs. Schuyler.

"I will ask her if any threats or bribes or improper means are used to urge her," said Mr. Kemp, carelessly. But Lilly protested she was free to do as she pleased—that she was guided only by convictions of duty, and intended to do only what should seem right and for her highest happiness.

"I cannot take any steps to hinder her at all," said Mr. Kemp. "It would not be just; she must choose for herself, and I see no occasion for your anxiety, Maria—positively I don't."

While this point was being mooted, and Father Murphy was hot to have his ward and her property given to a holy Order, Mother Robart hesitated. Mother Robart owed a duty to her Church, but there was also a duty which she owed to her family. Did she join her strength to Father Murphy's and win Lilly to take a nun's vow, she would serve the Church and greatly enrich the convent. On the other hand, if she were the means of marrying Lilly to Richard, she would enrich her own family, and very likely bring Richard over to the Holy Catholic Church of our Father of Rome. Mother Robart hesitated. She was a woman with a mind and will of her own, and Father Murphy's orders were not reason sufficient for her, unless her own judgment agreed thereto.

She hesitated, we say, and her hesitation extended over the fall and winter. She wanted to be sure of her own ground. And while she hesitated she bade Lilly wait, not be precipitate—more good would be accomplished by caution than by haste. During these months, Richard, having been carefully sounded by his step-mother and by Madam Robart herself, the Abbess was persuaded that his marriage to Lilly was never to be.

"She's an angel," said Richard, "but I'm too human to want to marry an angel. I wish I'd been left her guardian. I'd run her off from convents, priests and nuns, and get some sensible folks to make a healthy, happy woman of her. Yes, she's an angel, pure and sweet as the flower they've named her after, but, with all deference to everybody, no Papist wife for me."

"I agree with you," said the Abbess, royally, to the priest—"Lilly must be a nun."

"I told you so from the first," said Father Murphy, tranquilly.

Thus was Lilly's fate decided in a secret conclave of two—a nun and a priest.

Lilly's example and her enthusiastic words had had very different effects on Grace and Adelaide. Adelaide, growing every day more bold and scoffing, mocked at the whole matter as the idlest piece of fanaticism—had her doubts altogether about souls and eternity, and said,

"If these things really are, let the Church take care of them; what else was such a great machine good for?"

Such words as these chilled the heart of Grace with sense of coming ill. Adelaide was letting go all religion, and where would she end? The girls loved each other, loved tenderly—the petty disputes of childish years had died away—but now there was some dark chasm widening between them hour by hour. Grace's craving, sympathetic, earnest nature had been much roused and touched by Lilly's devotion. Perhaps Lilly's was the only true and worthy course of life—the one herself must choose. She took these weighty questions to Father Murphy. The priest had come to visit these two lambs, Grace and Adelaide; and Grace tremblingly asked him what was her duty. Adelaide's lip curled, scornfully.

"A nun?" said Father Murphy. "A nun? and why would you enter a holy Order?"

"Perhaps it is my duty. If it is Lilly's, why not mine?" asked Grace.

"Because you are not Lilly," said the priest. "If the Church wanted you, she would tell you. No, no; you and Adelaide must serve us in the world; we do not want you in the convent."

"We are not *rich* enough to be nuns," said Adelaide, with covert sneer.

"No, not rich enough, nor poor enough. We want nuns with fortunes; nuns that can teach; nuns that can work; but for you, you shall uphold the Church in the world. You can look to marrying rich men and holding high position, and making your husbands good Catholics. Let me hear no more nonsense about being nuns."

"If we inherit fortunes, you'll take us, won't you?" said Adelaide the crafty.

Father Murphy looked keenly at her. "Yes; we would take you, too, to save you from turning heretic."

"Heretic!" said Adelaide, with spirit. "I'll never turn heretic!"

And now, as spring opened, Lilly was numbered among the Postulates.

CHAPTER II.

AGNES.—THE MISSOURI NUN.—ESTELLE.

THE passing seasons had brought our girls to their seventeenth year, Agnes being a few months older than the three cousins, and Estelle somewhat younger than these her chosen friends. A change had come to Agnes' outward life. Her father had died in Italy, her mother had returned home, with her coming a rich old Scotch uncle, who at once assumed the cares and privileges of guardian and provider to Agnes and her mother. This sturdy Scotchman boasted the blood of Covenanters, and Romanism was his favorite aversion. Having arrived with his niece, Mrs. Anthon, in the city, his first care was to secure a commodious house and make arrangements at once to have it suitably furnished. He had been shown many of the letters written by Agnes to her mother, and from that mother's fond lips had heard glowing accounts of her daughter. He was a liberal-minded and affectionate old man, and already disposed to receive his grand-niece with cordiality, and to give her every advantage that his ample means could procure. Judge, then, his indignation when he found that Agnes, having returned for the summer vacation of her school, had gone at her own request to be an inmate of the Convent of the Immaculate Heart of Mary. Mrs. Anthon was as much distressed and amazed as her uncle, and proposed going at once and bringing her daughter away. Mr. MacPherson, however, advised that she should send a messenger to the convent, stating her arrival and her address in the city, and desiring her daughter to come to her.

"Then we can talk to her without any of those nuns and priests to listen and interfere," said the wrathful Scot.

Mrs. Anthon took this advice, and her messenger returned with a line from Agnes, saying she would hasten to welcome her mother. But the day passed, and no Agnes appeared.

Agnes had indeed requested to be received at the Convent of the Immaculate Heart of Mary as a boarder, expressing a wish to receive instruction from Saints Anna and Sophia in music and embroidery. She was a changed girl, and the story of her having found a rich bachelor uncle having preceded her, Father Murphy and Mother Robart alike regretted that she had not been to them a more important object, and that they had not more zealously endeavored to secure her to the Holy Roman Church. Here was the hour of Father Douay's triumph over the short-sightedness of his compeers. Regrets seemed unnecessary, however; for without invitation or flattery, this unwary fly came near Mother Robart's glittering net and fluttered in. O rare occasion! Mother Robart was only too eager to meet the advances of her destined victim. Even without money, Agnes was now worth Rome's deepest wiles. Brilliant in appearance and in conversation, with a singular fascination of manner and a maturity far beyond her years, Agnes Anthon bade fair in the meridian of her life to rival the stately Abbess of the Immaculate Heart. And in this noble creature had the seeds of Romish instructions begun to stir with awakening life and to send forth blade and root? Agnes certainly desired as a favor admission to the convent, and she devoted herself to the society of the Sisters, read their books, went ever and anon to the Abbess for instruction, with a fair appearance of devotion took part in all the services of the chapel, spoke of the "dear convent," and in her self-chosen prison was happiest of the happy.

"I told you so," said Mother Robart to Saint Cecelia.

"The change is all owing to those two weeks with our daughter Ignatia," said Father Douay.

Lilly and Grace received the returned prodigal with acclamation. Grace was more entirely enraptured with her friend than ever; and Lilly, after long and earnest conversations with Agnes, would go to some of the nuns and tell with beaming eyes how docile, reverential and earnest Agnes had become.

Now arrived the line from Mrs. Anthon. Mother Robart sent for Agnes. "You will wish to see your mother at once," said the Superior.

"It is the evening of our festival," said Agnes, "and I do not want to go away. Mamma will be at the hotel to-morrow. Can't Saint Cecelia go there with me then? I don't exactly want to go alone, and I'd rather go when my stranger uncle is away. In fact," added Agnes, looking ingenuous and embarrassed, "I did not expect mamma so soon, and I want a little time to make up my mind what to say to her."

The Abbess smiled well pleased: "Your mother will wish you to leave us and remain with her."

"I'm resolved to stay until that embroidery is finished and I learn those organ chants," said Agnes, firmly.

"You know, dear daughter," said the Abbess, "that we should grieve to part with you—that you are dear indeed to us—all the dearer for the follies of your youth," she added, patting Agnes' cheek.

"I must do something to blot out the memory of those things from your mind, mother," said Agnes, "and I will."

"And what shall it be?" asked the Superior.

"Tell me yourself," said Agnes. "Shall I please you by taking the nun's veil? Sometimes I verily think I will."

"You would please me by being a true daughter of our Church, nun or not," said the Superior.

"Never fear, mother; the more I see and the longer I stay here, the more resolved I become. I will be to you more than your heart could wish," said Agnes.

That evening there was a festival at the convent—an affair of hymns and chants and prayers, altars dressed with flowers and offerings to the convent fund, in honor of Joseph and Mary. Mother Robart claimed that she knew the date of the betrothal of the pious pair, and thus celebrated it: In the convent chapel stood two statues on handsome pedestals, on the front of one pedestal being "S. J." in heavy gilded letters, on the other "S. M." These were covered and scattered over with choice flowers, while choirs of white-clad children sang their praise. This was the festival Agnes did not wish to leave.

In one corner of the chapel knelt apart the nun from Missouri. Poor thing! she was suspected of hating her convent and her vow, and desiring to fly from both. She had been kept locked up for a fortnight; but, giving some tokens of reviving piety, had been brought into the chapel and placed by herself to worship alone, the Pariah of the assembly. She was a forlorn, heavy-hearted creature—great contrast to Agnes, high in favor—the contrast being greater yet when Agnes, clothed in flowing white, with crown of flowers, in some of the evolutions of the evening swept near her for a moment—yes, and spoke to her. And yet the two were not greatly different in age, height or mien, only that one had been drawn down and wrecked in the Charybdis of conventual discipline, while the other yet hovered just without its gloomy edge.

After the festival was over, Saint Cecelia saw Agnes kneeling by the dormitory window, her head bent on her hands. Near her were a missal, a rosary and a crucifix. Saint Anna had left them there, but Saint Cecelia supposed them to belong to Agnes, and that the girl was at her prayers. She *was* either praying or thinking deeply.

The next morning Saint Cecelia accompanied Agnes to the hotel to see her mother. It was a tender meeting. Agnes was overjoyed to see her mother, who was in unusually good health, yet weeping over the loss of her husband. The mother was proud indeed of the daughter blooming into such gracious womanhood; yet her heart sickened with a deadly fear that upon that goodly blossom a fatal blight was creeping. To the mother the interview was unsatisfactory. Agnes did not wish to leave the convent at present—was busy with important duties, and described in glowing terms the splendid building and grounds and the stately Abbess of the Convent of the Immaculate Heart of Mary. There was a visiting-day next week, when her mother and uncle must come and see her, and they would then know how soon their house would be ready for them. Agnes kissed her mother and departed with the nun, who had been a mute third party at the meeting. Agnes departed, leaving the mother with a pain in her heart. The fact was, in these years of absence, Agnes had learned to be somewhat independent of her mother. But a mother never learns to do without her child. When Mr. MacPherson came in, Mrs. Anthon detailed to him her conversation with Agnes, and wept as she did so. Taking her handkerchief out to wipe her eyes, a bit of paper fluttered to the floor.

"That's Agnes' photograph," said Mrs. Anthon, picking it up. "Why, no, it isn't; it is a note for you. It is in Agnes' hand. How came it in my pocket?"

Her uncle read the note several times and put it in

his wallet. "Where's the picture, niece?" he asked.

"What is the note, uncle?" said Mrs. Anthon, anxiously. "She must have slipped it in my pocket when she put the picture there."

"What's in the note?" said Mr. MacPherson. "Ay, ay, what is in it? Didn't you tell me of some fuss the girl had once with those nuns and priests? Let us hear it again."

As Mrs. Anthon detailed the circumstances of Agnes' banishment from the convent, her uncle laughed long and loud. "Leave the girl to me a bit," he said.

"I shall certainly use all my authority to keep her from turning Papist," said Mrs. Anthon, with a spice of that firmness for which her daughter was noted. "Unfortunately, Agnes has been thrown into Romish hands, but I shall use all my endeavors now to nullify their influence."

When the mother and uncle visited Agnes at the convent, her uncle was rather cold to her. At leaving he said, firmly, "Mind you, niece, two weeks from yesterday, at two o'clock, I'll be here with a carriage to take you *home.*" [He had been instructed in this air and speech in Agnes' note.]

Agnes gave him one quick look and dropped her eyes.

"You will have trouble, dear daughter, but be firm," said the Mother Superior when the guests had departed.

"I must go with them for a while, mother, but I promise you I can come back when I want to, if you'll take me."

"My House and my heart are ever open to you, daughter Agnes," said the Abbess.

Agnes went up to a little room, which, being a boarder, she occupied alone, and threw herself on her bed. When she came down to tea she looked as if she had been crying. The nuns whispered that Agnes was going to be persecuted for the True Faith, and showed her much consideration. The nun from Missouri had been released from durance vile and taken into partial favor, as the day after the festival she informed her Superior that she had seen an angel in white, who bade her make her submission and be obedient. She now ventured an observation to Agnes:

"Dear Sister Agnes, it is better to suffer for doing right than because you have done wrong."

Agnes, who seemed in a melting mood, fell on her neck and said with a sob,

"Dear Sister, you and I must be true."

On this little scene the Abbess looked down benignantly.

As each day passed on, Agnes seemed to cling more

closely to her convent home. "One day less!" she would say to the Abbess, with a look of charming regret, and the Superior grew sure of her prize.

During these days a whisper that the convent was haunted, or angel-visited, got afloat. The penitent nun from Missouri admitted that she had seen a spirit, gracious in air and clad in spotless garments; and one or two others claimed equal perspicuity of vision. The Abbess laid the matter before the Rev. Father Murphy, stating that it was started by the nun from Missouri.

"The case is clear enough," said the Father, carelessly. "You had the girl in the dungeon a while, hadn't you?"

"In the dungeon a week, and in a cell in the east wing another week," replied the Abbess.

"Well, it is evident that her weak brain has been a little turned by solitary confinement. Likely she will never get her reason perfectly again, but as long as the aberration runs on angels and the like, it doesn't matter. She believes it so fully herself that these others are led away by it."

"After all," said the Abbess, smiling, "it will do no harm to have a 'miracle' for the pupils to talk about."

"None in the world," said the excellent priest.

This view of the case made the Abbess more lenient to a nun whom she must consider half crazed by her own hard usage; and as the nun seemed to like to stay in the cell where she had been shut up, she was permitted to do so. It was not far from Agnes' room, and the young girl often heard the Sister chanting to herself in her solitude. She always heard her with a smile.

The day set by Agnes' uncle came. Her trunk was packed and carried down, and she was ready to depart. She was dressed in deep mourning for her father. Agnes had bidden her young friends farewell, and sat waiting in the parlor with the Abbess and Saint Cecelia. It was school-time and the convent was quiet. The carriage was now at the gate. The dictatorial Scotch uncle had come, and he looked at his niece apparently ill pleased. The Abbess took her hopeful charge in her embrace.

"I cannot, I cannot," sobbed Agnes. "There, let me go. I must have one last look, one prayer, in my precious room alone, before I go."

She broke away from the Abbess and ran up stairs. In ten minutes she was back, her heavy black veil dropped, her handkerchief pressed to her eyes. She put her hand in her uncle's arm, trembling violently, and as he angrily conducted her down the steps she hid her face against him and waved a last farewell.

Flight of the Missouri Nun.

"Who would have thought she would feel it so?" said the Abbess. "We shall have her yet."

"She's got on her alpaca," said Saint Cecelia. "I thought it had been her merino."

Meanwhile, Mr. MacPherson put his niece in his carriage, rating her roundly.

"Out on that false, bewitching Church that has turned your brain! You, Agnes, with the blood of martyred Covenanters in your veins, traitor to the faith for which your fathers died! Have done with your shaking and crying, girl! I have no patience with you!"

His niece shrunk hiding into a corner of the carriage, and put a letter in his hand as they were driven rapidly away.

The nun from Missouri, kneeling in her cell, would not come out, but kept telling her beads and repeating her prayers all night—at least such was the report made to the Abbess the next morning. On hearing this, the Abbess bade Saint Cecelia order the nun to her presence, saying,

"I must find out what she means."

The order being given, the prostrate devotee arose, pulled her hood well over her bowed face and glided to the private parlor of the Superior. She stood there, her head drooping (thus concealing her features), and holding to a chair, as if for support.

Saint Cecelia left the room, and as she closed the door, the Abbess said,

"Look at me, daughter."

The nun slowly raised her head, pushed back her hood with both hands, and the handsome, dauntless face of Agnes Anthon met the Superior's eye.

"Agnes!" cried the Abbess, "what does this mean?"

"It means," said Agnes, boldly, "that I have turned Rome's weapons against herself. Here you teach us to deceive, and—I have deceived *you.*"

"What have you done?" exclaimed Mother Robart, sinking slowly back in her chair and folding her arms across her ample chest.

"I have set your poor little captive from Missouri free as air," said Agnes, throwing back her proud young head and eyeing the Superior unflinchingly. "She left with my uncle yesterday, and to-day he will be back for me; and," she added, meaningly, "if he does not find me, he has power and Scotch energy enough to turn your precious convent upside down."

"Wretched girl!" hissed the Abbess, clenching her hand, "I might have known this!"

"You *might*," said Agnes, haughtily, "but you trusted too much the power of Rome. Did you think you could make a pervert of *me?* Six months ago I read stories of the wretched captives whom Rome holds, until my blood was on fire. I remembered the unhappy girl you had brought here from the West. Her haggard face haunted me, and I laid my plans to come back here and watch what I could do for her. Each week the way has opened before me. I seized each chance as it came—and she has gone. I had *pride* in it, too," she added, with flashing eyes. "I was *proud* to pit my strength against yours!"

"How dare you, doomed and wicked girl, stand there before me, polluting the dress of our sacred Order?" cried Madam Robart, fiercely.

"I'll take off what I can," said Agnes coolly, throwing hood, cape and apron upon the floor. "What do you mean to do—blazon my exploit abroad, or send me away quietly with my uncle?"

"You have tampered with a poor nun whom we can prove crazy, and have taken her from the shelter which, when in her right mind, she loved."

"It was a prison she hated," said Agnes. "If you think her crazy about visions, why we arranged them between us. She has seconded me splendidly, making it a double pleasure to release her. You helped her run away from her relatives to *join* you, and, now, in order to escape from you, she has used some of the guile you taught her. I've fallen on her neck and slipped a note into her robe under your very eyes."

"Protestant!" hissed the superior. "Protestant worthy of the name! to live a life of falsehood and to lie to me so infamously day after day!"

"Oh, but you didn't understand me, Mother Robart,' replied Agnes, naïvely; "and if that were true, it is better to live a false life two months than all one's life, as— Well, I might have done this a better way, but this way suited me."

A furious ring of the great front-door bell just now sounded through the house.

"That's my uncle," said Agnes, cheerfully. There was a loud voice and a heavy stride in the hall, and Mr. MacPherson, pushing past the porteress and flinging the inner door wide open, made his way through the grand parlor to the withdrawing-room, where were those he sought.

"Where is my niece?" he demanded fiercely.

"Here, uncle!" cried Agnes bravely.

He caught her hands in both his and shook them vigorously. "Good girl! grand girl! I didn't know but they'd make way with you before I got here. Come, now, let me get you out of this den—maybe there's a trap-door under our feet."

"Sir, you insult me!" cried the Abbess. "Is this your Scotch politeness and manhood? By all means take that girl from this sacred roof—take her away from those whose courtesy she has returned with disrespect—whose candor she has answered with falsehood—whose religion and charity she has trampled under foot!"

Thus, you see, Mother Robart was not to be crushed. She could hold her own against great odds, and, defeated, appear to have conquered. As Mr. MacPherson, flushed and excited, carried off his niece, madam stood in the door of her parlor majestic as a queen dismissing a disgraced servitor.

Now was Agnes' hour of triumph. In her uncle's eyes she was a heroine. His friends were disposed to regard her in the same light. Hints of the matter crept into the papers. Grace and Adelaide told the story at home—Adelaide with unequivocal glee; Grace amazed, shocked, and yet with covert admiration of her whom she dared not call her friend. Richard took up the affair with enthusiasm, and presuming on the introduction given at the "Assumption" fête, hastened down to Mr. MacPherson's new abode to flatter and applaud.

In all this dangerous hum of adulation, one voice alone was silent—one anxious eye checked the undue exultation; and to shield her from the unwonted dangers of praise and popularity was the anxious thought of the young girl's best friend and guardian —her mother.

Uncle MacPherson, finding his fears put to flight, and his best hopes more than realized, was ready to exalt his niece to complete sovereignty over himself, and would have said to her, "What is thy petition? and it shall be granted thee; and what is thy request? even to the half of the kingdom, it shall be performed."

Mrs. Anthon wisely let a day or two of this exuberant rejoicing pass away. Then came the good maternal counsel and monition:—

"My daughter, no one rejoices more than I at that poor girl's escape. But tell me, was it philanthropy alone that put this difficult scheme in your head? Was it not also pride, and a desire to try your own ability at outwitting the Superior and priest, that urged you on?"

"Yes, mother," said Agnes, frankly; "it was all of these. I rejoiced in being able to defeat them, as well as to save that unhappy nun."

"And does it argue well, my child, for the crystal purity and frankness of your character, that you are able to outscheme old schemers and to deceive the teachers of deception?" and Mrs. Anthon looked down into the dark eyes of the girl sitting on a hassock at her feet, until Agnes blushed.

"Mother," said Agnes, "do you think I could ever deceive *you?*"

"I hope not, my child, and yet this ability to manœuvre and mislead is a fatal power. Perhaps you used it well this time, but you might indulge it to your ruin. I tremble when I think that for weeks you could live an unnatural life—a tissue of duplicity. Agnes, your work was well conceived—was boldly planned—was steadfastly carried out; and yet, my daughter, it shows that the child-like simplicity of your character is gone."

"Mother, in these years since we parted you expected me to change. I have been thrown on my own resources, forced to think and act for myself. You cannot expect me to be a *child* any longer."

"There are some characteristics of childhood, my Agnes, I would have you hold for ever. He who enters the kingdom of heaven must enter as a little child. Agnes, was your plan worthy of a *Christian?*"

"But, mother, I am not a Christian," said Agnes, in a subdued tone.

"Alas, you are not, my dear girl; and do you not know that, lacking the Christian's hope in Jesus, your soul will be lost despite all natural graces? Agnes, while you have set another free, are you a captive still? My highest wish for you is yet unsatisfied."

It is singular how averse we are by nature to a personal appeal concerning religion; how ready to turn the subject to our neighbor and away from ourselves. Proving this feeling, Agnes referred the matter of conversation to her uncle, who was slowly pacing up and down the room:

"Uncle, are you a Christian?"

"I am a professor of religion, niece," said Mr. MacPherson, slowly.

"And a *possessor?*" asked Agnes, with characteristic freedom.

The old gentleman walked up and down the room for some minutes in a deep muse.

"Well, Agnes," he said at last, stopping before her, "by the grace of God I believe I am; and yet, I fear, the most dead and crooked stick among all Christ's branches. Niece," he continued looking at Mrs. Anthon, "if I'm ever going to be worthy of the name of Christian, it is high time I woke up. Come now, 'As for me and my house we will serve the Lord' in right good earnest, by the Lord's help. No more dead-and-alive, sleepy service for me."

Agnes looked at the earnest face of her uncle, and saw also the joy sparkling in her mother's eyes. She felt this was a hope she did not cherish, an interest that had no place within her heart.

The remarks of Mrs. Anthon had opened Mr.

MacPherson's eyes to the fact that he might be in a fair way to spoil his niece. He considered her youth and inexperience, and saw plainly that it was better for her to return to her ordinary quiet life.

"No more boarding-school for you, Agnes," he said to her. "You must have another six months or so of hard study; but let it be in some school in the city, for we have here the very best, and you can live at home. There is no instruction can make up to you for lack of your mother's care and advice."

"I am sure I do not want to go away from mother again," said Agnes: and very soon after this she was busy with her studies in one of the best schools near her home.

Mr. MacPherson's name having been quite freely mentioned in the affair of the escaped nun, Mr. Kemp remembered that the MacPhersons of Edinburgh had been related to his mother's family, and finding that this MacPherson was a man of wealth, was sure he must be a cousin, distant one or two removes. Mr. Kemp had become a Romanist purely from political motives. It was not to be supposed that, when he might strengthen his social position and increase his acquaintance by searching out relationship with a man of fortune, he would hesitate because that person was inimical to Popery and utterly odious in the eyes of the priest. Accordingly he called on Mr.

MacPherson, and proved conclusively that they were relatives and should be the best possible friends. And now arose Mr. Kemp's first trouble from priestly interference in his family. He wished his wife and daughters to call on Mrs. Anthon and Agnes; but this Father Murphy positively forbade them to do. Again, Mr. Kemp insisted on inviting Mr. MacPherson to dinner, but when he came the lady of the house pleaded headache and could not appear at dinner. Adelaide and Grace were also absent, having unaccountably remained at the convent. So, while the table was covered with dainties and admirably served, the dinner-party consisted of a dull trio—Mr. Kemp, Mr. MacPherson and Richard—the first angry, the second surprised and the third wickedly delighted.

"One of the ways your priest has of proving true the Scripture, 'A man's foes shall be they of his own household,'" whispered Richard to his father.

After dinner the young gentleman went to his mother's dressing-room to pay his respects to her. She was lying comfortably on a lounge and reading a novel.

"I presume your illness is more mental than physical, as I see you are taking literature as a remedy?" said Rick.

Mrs. Kemp bit her lip and dropped her book.

"I hope you tried the truffles, as they were exceedingly nice, and fish, flesh and fowl were too good to miss," continued Richard, settling himself in a chair.

"Certainly; I intended to have everything in good style, even though I was too much indisposed to enjoy it myself," said Mrs. Kemp.

"You see now how impossible, and how exceedingly unpleasant, it would have been for me to look upon that matter about Lilly as you did," said Rick the unconquerable. "In case she were my wife, her priest would order her to have headaches half the time on account of my friends."

"Dear me, son Richard! you speak as if you had been quite sure of Lilly," said Mrs. Kemp, impatiently.

"It was Father Murphy I would need to be sure of—Lilly must have done just as she was bid," said Rick.

"Let us say no more about it," said Mrs. Kemp.

"You lost a great deal by not meeting MacPherson," rattled on Richard. "He's a prime article in the line of society. And there's Miss Agnes—she is a grand girl, I assure you. Your convents form none such. She can argue like a man, and does her own thinking. She hasn't been kept skimming the surface of a dozen paltry acquirements all her life, but what she has studied she has learned."

Wicked Richard! He knew this praise was "as vinegar to the teeth and smoke to the eyelids!"

About this time, under the calm seeming of the Convent of the Immaculate Heart of Mary a tempest was brewing. Although the Missouri nun had escaped as a bird from the snare of the fowler, yet she counted but one, and whatever money she brought to Mother Rome remained there. She was one nun gone, and the circumstances were aggravating. Now, however, a more serious loss threatened, and Mother Robart and Father Murphy gathered their forces to prevent it.

First, a Jesuit brother from the Belen of Havana arrived and brought news to Father Murphy that Martin Wynford had become very fond of the Brothers and their religion—dangerously so, his father thought—and on this account Mr. Wynford had removed him from the institution, saying he "did not intend to have his children made fanatics."

Next a letter arrived for Estelle from her father, bidding her mind her books, let the priests alone and not get her head turned on the subject of religion, as the pleasures of the world were before her. This letter found its grave in Mother Robart's pocket.

We must here revert to the fact that Mr. Wynford despised all religious feeling, and would have used these same measures had he supposed his children in danger of being converted to any faith whatever.

In the new schemes now developed by Father Murphy and Mother Robart, Lilly's trusty maid, the excellent Annette, was needed elsewhere. Her mission at Mrs. Schuyler's was accomplished. Lilly's fate was fixed. Hannah could not be ousted. In increasing distress, Mrs. Schuyler turned more and more to her Bible and her God, and *therefore* more and more from Rome. As Annette must go, Mother Robart suggested that Lilly should take Ann Mora, whom a slight lameness prevented from filling any but an easy situation, and have her trained to wait upon her.

"I am so sorry to lose you, Annette!" said Lilly.

"Thank you, miss, I am sorry enough to go, but I have a letter that my mother is dying, and go I must," said Annette, weeping.

An hour after Annette started "to see her dying mother," she was, to all outward appearance, hanging on the wall of an upper room in the House Without a Name, and Sister Clement was busy over embroidery and "exercises." Lilly would never have recognized Sister Clement as Annette; but she would doubtless have been amazed to see Annette's hair, bonnet, coat, dress and false teeth suspended on the otherwise bare wall of a nun's cell.

At night, Mother Ignatia, haggard, wretched, ghost-haunted and sin-burdened still, left the House Without a Name, accompanied by Sister Clement, and the two glided like black spectres toward the Convent of the Immaculate Heart. Did any deluded Protestant meet them, we suppose he concluded they were going on some blessed errand of mercy. After a while, Father Douay came up and walked silently before them—a third in this expedition of heavenly charity. Thus they reached the convent and entered Mother Robart's private room.

The matter in hand was this: Mr. Wynford would return in six months to the United States, and would then undoubtedly take Estelle from the convent. He might endeavor so to remove her before his return. To please the nuns, and personally with entire carelessness and indifference, Estelle had already received baptism, communion and confirmation. She therefore belonged to the Roman Catholic Church; they claimed her, mind, body and estate. And yet in blind, hardened America the law would inevitably insist upon her father's right to her. What was to be done? The first measures were to prevent her being taken at once from the convent. Mother Robart considered what she should do in the event of any third party being sent to place Estelle in some other school; and to allay the father's apprehensions,

Saint Cecelia was called upon to write a letter, in close imitation of Estelle's hand, and in reply to the one the Abbess had not seen fit to give to Estelle. In this forged letter Estelle would be supposed to tell her father of her increasing accomplishments, of her entire indifference to the religion of her school, of the admirable silence maintained by the Sisters on this subject, and of her own eager expectations of the time when he should introduce her to the gay world.

"The girl's parent," said the excellent Father Murphy, "is an atheist, and that is the same as being a Jew or a Protestant; it completely unfits him for being the guardian of this child."

"Estelle has been baptized," said Mother Robart, "and is therefore a member and a ward of the true Church, and we are bound to protect her spiritual interests. She is now by baptism entirely made over and born again into the holy kingdom, and can be compelled by force, if need be, to keep the unity of the faith and submit to the authority of the Church." *

"Courts of law acknowledge in parents in all cases a guardianship over the child," said Father Douay, "but ecclesiastical law—which is much higher authority—holds that the child is free, from its earliest reason, to submit to the Church, without

* *Brownson's Review*, July, 1864, p. 267.

regard to the wishes of the parent, and such submission once made must be maintained."*

"Yes," said Father Murphy, the autocrat of the occasion, "we must maintain the liberty of our daughter Estelle's conscience."

"Liberty of her conscience!" gasped Saint Cecelia, too greatly amazed to keep silence.

"Do you not know," said Mother Robart with severity, "that Father Hecker, in his excellent work on Liberty of Conscience, defines it as the 'right to embrace, profess and practice the Catholic religion?'"†

"I am so ignorant!" said Saint Cecelia, meekly.

"I should think you were," whispered Saint Clement with malice.

"The question of 'right' in this case," said the Abbess Robart, "is one no reasonable person would dispute."

"It would not be mentioned in any but these vile Protestant countries," said Father Douay, tartly.

"And," said Father Murphy, with a sardonic smile, "in this land there is *yet* civil law."

"Surely," said the sepulchral voice of Mother Ignatia, who had not before spoken, "there is not one of us who will not dare *any* consequences to obey the holy Church?"

* For similar views see *Catholic World* for July, 1868.

† "Plea for Liberty of Conscience," pp. 226–231.

"There are no consequences to be dared," said Father Murphy. "We can win a lawsuit if we have to sustain one. Have you never heard of supreme judges *promising* their interest to the Church as the price of their election? I have." * And he opened his mouth wide for a noiseless laugh that shook his sides.

"If," said Madam Robart, "we are all determined that this thing shall be, there remains only for us to discuss the 'how.'"

Now Mother Robart and Father Murphy were given to relieving the weariness of all difficult questions by discussing them over a dish piled high with tropic fruits, a solid silver basket of rich cake, and fragile little glasses of Italian wines, imported by the Superior herself "for sacramental purposes." But to-night the presence of Father Douay, Mother Ignatia and Clement hindered such refections. It was certainly trying.

Mother Robart remarked: "Estelle's chief inheritance will be from her maternal grandfather. He is very old and lives in a villa some eight or ten miles from Civita Vecchia, in Italy. I have his address from Estelle."

"It is fortunate," said Father Douay, "that I

* See page 123 of "Abduction of M. A. Smith." By Rev. H. Mattison, D. D.

know the priest in that neighborhood—a very zealous son of the Church."

"The grandfather is old and a good Catholic," said Mother Ignatia. "It is, then, only the father that stands in our way, and the seas are broad and storms and fevers are plenty, and it is easy for men to die—they die so many in a little time."

She groaned and struck her bosom, and looked fearfully over either shoulder, as if dreading that near her stood some terrible shapes.

As the result of this utterance and action, Mother Robart looked resigned to some severe infliction. Saint Clement and Father Murphy were evidently impatient and Saint Cecelia curious.

"We need not trust to *such* events," said Father Murphy. "Some men have nine lives, like a cat; and I have always noticed that if there is a man you want out of the way, he is the very one endowed in that fashion."

"This is an evil and ill-governed country," snarled Father Douay.

"Ah, well, we must wait for better times—they are coming," said Father Murphy, cheerfully.

"We must make our plan," said Mother Robart, decidedly. An excellent business woman was Mother Robart, whom nothing could divert from the main issues. "I do not see my way clearly."

"Daughter Clement some time since informed me she had gained some light on this subject of Estelle," said Father Murphy.

Mother Robart looked at her haughtily. How disgraceful that Sister Clement should have light denied to Superior Robart.

"I shall now get sent on a mission to Europe," thought Saint Clement.

"I shall most certainly put that nun down—she is too forward," said Mother Robart to herself.

"We are waiting for you, daughter Clement," said Father Douay.

Sister Saint Cecelia was nearly dying of jealousy.

"To lay my humble and worthless views before my spiritual superiors," said Clement, with a low reverence, "is a duty I perform with lowliness and confusion of face. Let me suggest then to this holy company, before which I stand unworthy, that Estelle is not Mr. Wynford's daughter." She looked around with covert triumph and proceeded in terse sentences: "Her mother was a widow. The first husband was Estelle's father. Estelle is a year older than represented to us. Mr. Wynford is not her rightful guardian. Her grandfather is her natural guardian, and can delegate his authority to these reverend Fathers and Mothers. We can obtain writings from the old grandfather. We can make out this case."

"And if we fail?" said Mother Robart, piqued.

"We *thought* we were right, and accept the stronger evidence," said Father Murphy, with a smile.

"It needs then some one to convince the old grandfather of this, and to obtain the testimony of the child's first nurse, the registers of the two marriages and of the girl's birth, all certified," said Mother Robart, rapidly.

"To obtain all this," said Father Douay, "we must send an agent over, to return with all speed, having accomplished what we need. In those blessed lands—France and Italy—the Church can obtain certified copies of whatever she needs."

"And a nun would be a less suspected agent than a priest," said Father Murphy.

"I offer my humble services to finish the work I have been able to begin," said Saint Clement, with ill-judged haste.

"Your services are far more valuable in this country," said Mother Robart, coldly. "I suggest as our envoy Saint Lorette—a French Sister, pious and wise, accustomed to travel, speaking foreign languages with facility and in every way suitable for this mission."

Thus Mother Robart circumvented poor Saint Clement. It was a small game, unworthy of her magnificent abilities; and the disappointment to

Clement was excruciating, like the very pangs of death—she had so set her heart on going and returning triumphant.

Soon after this convent-council, Lorette went on her mission fully armed, and in due time returned successful. Meanwhile, Estelle abode a pupil at the Immaculate Heart, ignorant of all these snares that were laid for her, and Mr. Wynford was still abroad, though on his homeward voyage.

Let us pause here in our story, and dropping (for once only) into statistics, show how easily in one city of the United States these Jesuit plotters might have been able to carry any case. Take warning, Americans all! The City of New York has, or recently had, these Roman Catholic officers: "Sheriff, Register, Controller, City Chamberlain, Corporation Counsel, Police Commissioner, President of the Croton Board, Acting Mayor, President of the Board of Aldermen, President of the Board of Councilmen, Clerk of the Common Council, Clerk of Supervisors, five Justices of the Courts of Record, all the Civil Justices, all the Police Justices but two, all the Police Court Clerks, three out of four Coroners, fourteen-nineteenths of the Common Council and eight-tenths of the Supervisors.*

Now we do not mean you to infer that our story is

* Extract from statistics published in the *New York Herald.*

laid in New York. This is only given as a sample of how Rome is winning the day.

When Mr. Wynford returned home, he was refused his daughter. He then sued out a writ of *habeas corpus*, and in obedience to said writ, Mother Robart appeared before the court and respectfully showed that the Estelle Wynford in said writ mentioned is in very deed Estelle *Latrelli*, committed to the care of Mother Robart by her natural guardian, her maternal grandfather, in proof whereof, etc., etc.

Madam Robart's counsel had plenty of certified copies of registers made in Italy. He had a priest's statement on oath, a nurse's statement, and lo! to complete the evidence, Saint Lorette testified that in the days of her youth she was the late Mrs. Wynford's maid and knew all about everything. The counsel also showed that Estelle does not resemble her pretended parent.

Astonished Mr. Wynford has no proofs of anything on hand. He swears most civilly and righteously that Estelle is his daughter. But two or three other people swear most civilly and *un*righteously against him. Estelle in anguish cries, "He is my father; he is—he is; I know he is; let me go to him!" has hysterics and gets sympathy from many. But Mother Robart wins her case, showing no triumph, only an apparent deep sense of duty, and Estelle is carried off to the convent. Her father is a wretched and amazed man, and all his friends—though, being a stranger in a strange land, he has but few—are indignant and ready with advice and encouragement, urging him to carry up the case and destroy all this false testimony and save his little daughter.

Richard was his strong partisan, and frequently his wrath boiled over. Mr. Kemp was laid up with gout just now and Richard attended to his business at the office. Mr. Kemp's friends came to console the invalid—as, for example, Rick, going to consult his father, found Father Murphy by his sofa, taking a hand at cards.

"Oh," said Richard, drawing back, "I beg your pardon. I was not aware that you were receiving *spiritual consolation.*" He went into the adjoining room, where Mrs. Kemp was seated by a window sewing, and flung himself into a chair. Presently, Father Murphy passed through the hall, and Mr. Kemp came slowly into the parlor occupied by his wife and son, evidently much vexed, and said, sharply,

"Richard, you are allowed many liberties and take many, but I consider your remark just now an insult to Father Murphy and myself."

"Perhaps it was. As far as you're concerned, pray excuse it," replied Richard. "But I longed for liberty to collar that priest and put him out of the house. I'm heated red hot on that subject just now. I have come from MacPherson's, where Mr. Wynford is staying, as unhappy a man as ever I saw. To think that those perjured fiends should take his child from him!" and the young man sprang up and began pacing the room in high excitement.

"Richard, Richard! what shocking language!" cried Mrs. Kemp, dropping her work.

"Those are rash accusations, sir; have a care!" said his father. "The case was fairly tried in open court before a learned judge, and the evidence all proved that the girl was not his, and that he had no legal right to her."

"Evidence!" cried Richard, fiercely. "And what kind of evidence? Collected by that pair of rascals, Douay and Murphy, after they knew what was wanted. I believe in my soul it was fabricated evidence, every word of it."

"Richard," said Mrs. Kemp, with unwonted firmness, "I cannot allow you to allege such crimes against holy priests and nuns—crimes at which the most hardened reprobates would tremble—perjury and—well, child-stealing in effect—State's prison offences! and you lay them to the charge of holy Orders!"

"And, ma'am, if you please, what was it they

played off on Father Chiniquy not long ago? Did not two witnesses swear point-blank against him what would put him in the penitentiary? and was not their evidence capable of being proven to be atrocious perjury, paid for by a priest? How ready they were to withdraw their suit, pay charges and make apologies. I tell you, ma'am, it is an outrageous system of fraud, and here's a case in point. A father is robbed of his child. You should see how it has furrowed his face and turned his hair gray. It makes my heart ache for him."

"Come, come, Rick," said Mr. Kemp, settling himself in the chair his son had abandoned, "this is all enthusiasm. You're young and excitable. Your feelings do you credit perhaps, yet you are old enough now to lay aside mere feeling. Don't you know it is the poorest kind of policy to vote with the losing side?" he asked with a grin.

"That your example has always taught me, but I decline the lesson," retorted Richard. "Here's a miserable wrong done that my heart bleeds to think over. To see, *in this country,* a man robbed of his child, groaning and weeping, utterly unmanned by the cruel blow! This is his reward for putting faith in Rome. Faith in Rome! When will people learn better?"

Richard was full to overflowing with indignation.

"I hope you do not think we shall let this Estelle case drop?" said he, angrily. "MacPherson and Wynford and I will carry it on to the death."

"I don't see what you have to do with it," said Mr. Kemp. "Don't play with edged tools."

"No, indeed," replied his son, "it will be no play, I can tell you. I'll pick them up and *use* them. And as to my having anything to do with it, it is with a righteous intention of seeing a bitter wrong righted."

"After all," said Mr. Kemp, coolly, "what is the difference? A father cannot expect to keep his daughters always. It is only giving her up a little sooner than he expected, and he must know she is well off and perfectly safe."

"You will talk less calmly about it if the question ever comes up concerning *your* girl," said Richard.

"My girl! impossible!" said Mr. Kemp.

"Of course it is," said Mrs. Kemp. "Everybody knows us."

"If it does not come up one way, it may in another," said Richard.

"There, there! you are perfectly rabid, Rick. Give me a cushion for my foot and let the matter drop," said Mr. Kemp.

"Well," said Mrs. Kemp, in her easy tone, "I am sure I am sorry for Mr. Wynford. Of course he and

Estelle are fond of each other, and it is hard for them to part. But I am sure Sister Margaret and Father Murphy are certain of their ground—feel that they are doing right, and regard it as a matter of positive duty. If it were proved that they were mistaken, they would not try to keep the girl one hour. If Mr. Wynford *can* establish his assertions, he had better do it; but I'm afraid the *perjury* will then come in play. There, there, son Rick! I did not mean to irritate you. Sit down and tell me what you are going to do. That will relieve your mind, so you can take us peaceably to the theatre to-night, as your father is laid up by his gout."

"As to telling you what we mean to do," said Richard, "would that be wise when you belong to the other side, and go to confession pretty often?" Having relieved himself by this last explosion, Richard added: "As to the theatre, I'll escort you there with all pleasure."

CHAPTER III.

THE WHITE VEIL.

A FEW weeks after the events just narrated, Mr. Wynford sailed for Europe, leaving his son Martin in charge of Mr. MacPherson.

"The lad is priest-bitten," said the Scot to Richard. "I see it in his eye and hear it in his tone; but I told him I'd have none of that nonsense. I've placed him in a good sound Protestant school, and I take him to church with me as a Protestant should; but, after all, I'm afraid he's like a deaf adder—his ears are stopped up with Romanism."

Richard, too, had his doubts about Martin, for once or twice he saw him coming from the house of Father Murphy or Father Douay. Martin, however, excused himself by saying he had been trying to get information of Estelle. Richard was anxious for news from Estelle. He had espoused Mr. Wynford's cause with ardor. He knew that the distracted father was now in Europe trying to collect evidence to vindicate the truth; and yet, should he succeed, he might return to this country to find that his child had been spirited away.

"There are a thousand ways," said Richard to Mr. MacPherson. "They can swear she has escaped, or get up a bogus death and interment. I doubt if he finds her again."

Richard had by this time been given over as a reprobate by his aunt, the Abbess, and was no longer allowed the privilege of calling at the convent. He endeavored to learn something about Estelle from Grace and Adelaide, who were yet pupils part of each day at the Immaculate Heart of Mary. He first questioned Grace:

"Have you seen Estelle lately, Grace?"

"No, she is sick," said Grace.

"What did she say about the trial?"

Grace looked away, without reply.

"What is the matter with Estelle? How long has she been ill?"

Still no answer.

"Grace, don't you think this is a horrible affair to take that poor girl from her father? Come, now, tell me something about her. Would you like to be kept a prisoner, as she is?"

"I can't tell you, Richard; don't ask me," said Grace, hastily. "I hate to think of this. We have been forbidden to speak of it, and Father Murphy will ask me."

She pulled away from her brother with tears in her eyes.

"They're spoiling a rare girl in you, Grace," said Richard.

His next attempt was with Adelaide.

"Adelaide, I want you to tell me something about Estelle."

"Why don't you ask Grace?" said Adelaide.

"I have, and she says she has been forbidden to reply."

"And don't you suppose I have been forbidden too?"

"It remains to be seen if you will obey. Come, Adelaide, tell me what you know, and I'll give you that set of pearls and turquoise you looked at yesterday."

"Bribing me, are you?" said Adelaide.

"Yes, if you'll take a bribe. I began years ago on bon-bons, and you know you have encouraged me."

"Mind, I hold you to your bargain, though my information will not be worth much. What do you want me to tell you?"

"What did Estelle say on the question at the trial?"

"Why, she said he *was* her father, and she said it so freely that the Sisters kept her away from the other girls."

"And how did she feel over the decision?"

"It's my belief," said Adelaide, "that her distress has thrown her into a brain fever. But the Sisters never say a word about her, and we are not allowed to see her."

"Do you think they have taken her away from the 'Heart?'"

"No, I think she's there."

"Well, finally, what do you suppose they are going to do with her?"

"Make a nun of her," said Adelaide, lightly. "She's got money. Father Murphy don't want Grace and me—we're not rich enough."

"Thank God for that!" said Richard. "Do you want that jewelry?"

"Yes, indeed. Mind you bring it to-night," cried the girl.

"Then I must get Grace the same to prevent questioning."

"H'm-m," said Adelaide; "she gets the pay and I do the work."

"Surely these few answers were but little work."

"Ah, but Father Murphy is so suspicious. I shall have to tell him a dozen lies next time I confess."

"I'm sorry for that," said Richard.

"I don't mind it," said Adelaide, flippantly. "I've been brought up to it."

"Yes," groaned Richard. "That's the way Rome trains up girls, and what sort of women will they turn out?"

Richard found himself very much entangled in the toils of Romanism just now, and raged inwardly. He had joined Mr. Wynford's cause with all the ardor of a generous, clear-sighted young man. He believed that Martin was deceiving his father and Mr. MacPherson, his guardian *pro tem.*, and yet he could not prove it. He was now seized by his aunt Schuyler in her agony of despair, and felt as trammeled and as exhausted as if he were swimming in a drowning man's death-grip.

The return of spring was bringing to Mrs. Schuyler a new installment of woe. Lilly was about to take the white veil.

By turns the heartbroken mother implored the two guardians of her child. Father Murphy urged her not to hinder her daughter of heaven—not to endeavor to thwart her dearest and holiest aspirations. Mr. Kemp said he could not interpose in a clear case of conscience. His niece must be happy in her own way; she was old enough to choose for herself.

Lilly, besought by every filial feeling and in every term of maternal endearment, would weep and wring her hands on account of her poor mother's grief. Yet she would claim that she must be the "Bride of Heaven" or lose her soul, and would implore her mother, even on her knees, to turn from heresy, yield to Rome—that one sacred, eternal and infallible Church; having done which, she would joyfully give Lilly to her "vocation."

The widow was in a sad strait. She had never loved the world, and had few friends or acquaintances outside of her own household. Her family had many of them become Romanists; her brother was taking sides against her; her child, weak, enthusiastic and obstinate, was being forced from her. Hannah, her faithful maid, alone stood by her. She reached for some other human helper, and grasped her nephew Richard.

Richard truly loved his aunt. He thought her a weak woman, whose weakness had all her life betrayed her own highest interests. But he knew her to be amiable, lovely and good. She was such as his boyish memories had pictured his own mother. She was the only one who would tell him long reminiscences of that mother. Yes, he was fond of his aunt Schuyler, and she was now wronged and cheated.

But what could Richard do? He could appeal to Lilly for one thing, and that he did, though as Lilly, ever obeying orders, habitually shunned him, it was difficult to find an opportunity. Richard persisted, however, and one day found her at the piano in the drawing-room. He went promptly to her, turned her gently about on the music-stool, and drawing a chair in front of her, sat down, saying,

"There now, Lilly! you must not run away this time. Your cousin Richard is not such a heathen as they make him out to be. See, I am a peaceable, well-meaning individual. Lilly, do you love your mother?"

"Why, Richard! what a question!" said Lilly, tearful at once.

"Do you owe her any duty—your first duty?"

"Of course I owe her duty, and I am glad to admit it, but not my first duty, Richard; that I owe to God."

"And do the demands of God and your mother conflict?"

"The wishes of my mother and the demands of the Church—which is the kingdom of God on earth—*do* conflict; but I believe, yes, I am sure, that if I am true to duty, my mother will be led to *her* duty, and agree to all the Church requires," said this child of Romanism.

"I do not come here to argue with you, Lilly," said Richard. "To argue with you would be to argue with your priest. But you have a heart, and I cannot believe that your priests have destroyed all its tenderness. If you persist in forsaking your mother by becoming a nun, you will kill her. I tell you, Lilly, she is now a heartbroken woman. The seeds of death have fallen upon her life, sown by *your* hand. Oh, Lilly, were she my mother, I would not so grieve her for the world. When you have lost her, little cousin, you will begin to know her worth."

Lilly's face and neck flushed crimson in the effort to refrain from a passionate burst of weeping. Tears trembled in her eyes as she struggled to reply: "It is not so, Cousin Rick; it cannot be so. I love my mother and I love her soul. Father Murphy says that if I despise my duty and neglect my 'vocation,' my mother and I will lead careless lives and die without hope of salvation; but if I am firm and do right, my dear mother will then be convinced of her error, she will be saved as the reward of my sacrifice, she will come into the convent for refuge, and together we shall spend our lives in that holy home."

"Lilly, *do* you believe this?" cried Richard.

"Yes, Richard, I *do* believe it as surely as I believe I am living and speaking to you. *Father Murphy says so.*"

Lilly spoke as earnestly and reverentially as if she were quoting the very voice of God.

Richard smote his hands together as an emphasis, saying, "Well does the Bible describe them: 'For this sort are they which creep into houses, and lead captive silly women.'"

This was not very polite of Richard, but Lilly was too absorbed in the main issues to take offence.

"The Bible, Rick?" she questioned.

"Yes, Lilly, the Bible. I read it, careless fellow as I am; and I tell you it describes what these priests are doing with you exactly, and Christ himself condemns it. Listen: 'For Moses said, Honor thy father and thy mother; . . . . but ye say, If a man shall say to his father or mother, it is Corban, that is to say, a gift, by whatsoever thou mightest be profited by me, ... ye suffer him no more to do aught for his father or his mother.' Now, Lilly, that is what your nuns and priests are doing. They do not say to you as God's law says, 'Honor thy mother,' but bid you make of yourself a gift, to profit her soul, and henceforth will let you do nothing more for her. Lilly, if she comes to die alone, brokenhearted, you will see you have been wrong."

"You need not quote the Bible to me, Rick," said

Lilly, what hardness she was capable of impressing itself upon her fair face, and the obstinacy she had heired from somewhere calming her voice and drying her eyes. "The Bible cannot be understood except by bishops and learned priests. You need not quote it to me, for, in the first place, yours is a heretic Bible, and in the next place, you cannot explain it properly."

Richard pushed back his chair and rose.

"Lilly," he said, gravely, "you have not gone to destruction unwarned."

He left the house, saying to himself,

"She has been filled with their lies, until she is no more capable of judging for herself than if she had been drugged."

He then went to his father's office, where he found that worthy alone, his chair tilted back, his feet on the window sill, enjoying a meerschaum and the daily paper.

"I'm like the good fairy in old tales, come to give you your second warning," said Richard. "Three, you know, are all you'll get, and then the ruin comes."

"Hul-lo!" cried Mr. Kemp, starting up so violently that his chair fell over and his pipe upset, "are stocks in that oil well of ours falling?"

"No, no," said Richard; "they were rising this morning. I am thinking of Lilly."

"Oh, Lilly? Bother on it, Rick; you've made me lose a pipe full of the best kind of tobacco, and crack this chair-back in the bargain. What's wrong with Lilly?"

"It is wrong enough. To see a girl like that deluded into a conventual life," said Richard, "and a mother deprived by men of her only child is a hard matter. It is akin to swearing a man's daughter away from him."

"Oh, you haven't got over *that*," said Mr. Kemp, coolly resuming his former position with refilled pipe. "I do not know but a convent is a very good place, and it is not my duty to prevent Lilly being happy in her own way, you see."

"I wonder, sir, that *you* do not see what a blight and desolation these nuns and priests make wherever they go. If they pass through a home, they leave the trail of the serpent over every good thing in it. What country have they ever ruled that has not withered and become effete under their influence? See what it is doing about *us*. There's Lilly, going to be lost to herself, her mother and society. There's Aunt Schuyler—all the sister you have, sir—going to die before her time of pure grief. There's Grace, she might be just as splendid a girl as Agnes Anthon if the nuns didn't dwarf her. There's Adelaide—we shall have trouble ahead with her—the girl is utterly reckless and untruthful. She knows no law but her own fancies, and yet she is as bright and pretty a girl as there is in the city."

"Why, you're putting it pretty strong, Richard," said Mr. Kemp, indolently.

"It is time it was put 'strong,'" said Richard. "Romanism is robbing parents of their children, husbands of their wives, is arming men from one end of the country to the other, is subverting the law and making the civil oath a nullity. Under its touch our progress, our happiness, our liberties, will crumble to ashes like Ginevra's hair."

"Eh!" said Mr. Kemp, looking up, "what was that story of Ginevra's hair? I've forgotten."

"Her hair, sir, crumbled to ashes as soon as a monk laid his hand on it."

"Oh yes. Very well put, Rick, very. Would tell in a political speech. But don't get over-excited, Richard, and run things into the ground. That was a start you gave me coming in; I'm not over it yet. And your warning was about Lilly?"

"Yes, sir. I told you Uncle Schuyler's will set a wolf to guard a lamb; that was *one* warning. She is going to take the White Veil; here is warning number *two*. The wolf has his mouth open and the lamb in his paws."

"Very good, very good," laughed Mr. Kemp. "When you run for Congress you'll need nobody to get up your speeches. You have quite a knack at the thing."

Richard retired disgusted.

Between Grace Kemp and Agnes Anthon there had been from their first acquaintance a sincere friendship. Now that Lilly had chosen a path so apart from her own, and that an unspoken separation and evil influence between herself and Adelaide was widening day by day, Grace felt more deeply the need of Agnes' companionship. This, however, was forbidden her by her priest. She was to have no intercourse with Agnes—no visiting, no books, no notes must pass between them, and on these points Father Murphy questioned her closely. Mr. Kemp deemed it expedient to cultivate Mr. MacPherson's friendship and attach him to his family. Mrs. Kemp unalterably refused to have anything to do with them; but Mr. Kemp considered Grace under his own control, and desired her to be intimate with Agnes.

"Mr. Kemp, I'm surprised at you!" said his wife. "Father Murphy decidedly forbids the girls associating with Agnes. She is in his opinion a very improper acquaintance."

"But I do not forbid them, and I expect to be

chief authority in such matters in my own house," said Mr. Kemp.

"*I* must obey Father Murphy, and refuse Adelaide such companions," said Mrs. Kemp, flushing.

"I shall not interfere with your rights over *Adelaide*," said Mr. Kemp, "though it is a pity that you regard your priest's whims more than your husband's interests; but I wish Agnes to be well received when she comes here."

"It must be by Grace then," interrupted Mrs. Kemp, with that persistency which a small mind can show about trifles.

"And I expect Grace to visit at Mr. MacPherson's and make herself agreeable there. I hope, Richard, that you find attractions there."

"I certainly do," said Richard, for this controversy had occurred at the dinner-table, "and I am glad that you expect Grace to exercise some freedom of choice as to her friends."

"Freedom of choice? why *I* choose for her," said Mr. Kemp.

"Oh, I see; you choose instead of Father Murphy. I dare say Grace will thank you for the selection, for she is really very fond of Miss Agnes."

"Hereafter, Grace," said Mr. Kemp, "I desire you to consult *me*, and not Father Murphy, about your friends. I consider myself quite as capable of directing you as any priest, and I shall be head of my own family. If I am a Roman Catholic, I do not expect to be a mere tool in a priest's hands. That will do for John Mora and Michael Shinn."

Grace's inclinations and her natural independence of character urged her to reject Father Murphy's interference about her intimacy with Agnes. Her father's orders and a long conversation with Richard decided her, and she resolved openly and frankly to act as her heart dictated about her favorite friend.

What Grace would do honestly, convinced by her reason, Adelaide delighted to follow secretly, from sheer perversity.

Adelaide did not find Agnes congenial, thought Mrs. Anthon was tiresome and Mr. MacPherson "sour." Yet one evening, when Richard and Grace left the house to visit Agnes, Adelaide said she was going with them as far as the residence of one of her Romish friends, and instead of stopping at her friend's accompanied them to Mr. MacPherson's.

"Why did you not tell plainly where you were going?" said Grace.

"Oh there would have been no fun in that, and it would have made such a fuss," returned Adelaide.

"I am glad to have you with us, but why not be frank?" said Richard. "If you play this game in one thing, you may in another."

"That is very true," replied Adelaide, unabashed.

"And I'm afraid, Adelaide, that you are on a wrong road."

"Pooh, pooh, Rick! how green and blue you are—a perfect old ogre! Here, Grace, come between us; I'm afraid the ogre will eat me up." Thus did Adelaide reject reproof.

Grace could not help contrasting Agnes' home and mother with her own. Mrs. Kemp was kind, attentive to the girls' dress and manners, ambitious for them, willing to spend an hour with them in idle gossip, or play a game of cards to pass away the evening. She was fond of the theatre, and took them there frequently, fostering Adelaide's growing passion for such entertainments. But to her children she was neither guide, instructor nor prudent friend. "For mercy's sake, ask Father Murphy or Saint this or that, and don't worry me," was her reply when appealed to for advice. She read nothing but the lightest possible literature; and as for conversation, there was little at Mr. Kemp's that could claim the name. Grace, fond of study, delighting in reading and with a naturally fine mind, missed in her own home those advantages which she found at Mr. MacPherson's. The best books of the day were there read and freely discussed. Literature, travels, science, the great discoveries of the age, were there the topics of conversation. Grace heard, and felt her mind expanding under favorable influences. Music, pictures, lectures, all these combined to elevate and refine. Grace saw that Mrs. Anthon was her daughter's closest friend and confidant, and the parental relationship assumed before her a hitherto unrecognized beauty. There was another theme freely mentioned at Mr. MacPherson's, to which Grace listened with growing interest; that was *religion*. The Church at large, the grand enterprises of Christianity, that particular body of God's people with which themselves were connected, the Bible and its doctrines, sermons which they heard, revivals, missionary work, these were common topics of conversation.

Grace had hitherto only heard forms extolled, prayers rattled off, the requirements of the priest referred to, and the necessity of observing the imposed fasts and saints' days.

Here there was an earnest religion of head and heart; here were children of God recognizing their Father's loving authority and cordially assenting thereto. This was a Christian household, and in Grace's heart the empire of Papism trembled. But prejudice is strong; the bonds of early instructions are clasped firmly, and the hour of her redemption was not nigh. If Grace heard with eagerness the serious remarks of her friends; if when, as sometimes happened, Mr. MacPherson had the family assembled for evening prayers before Grace and Richard had closed their visit, Grace looked upon these things as upon a new world full of sacred mysteries; if they stirred her heart with wonder and awoke the longing for a higher life; how were all impressions deepened when that new and higher life was begun in Agnes' heart; when the love of Christ and the hope of his eternal rest filled her soul; when Agnes from her own experience could tell Grace of God's goodness, and the fullness of his love! There was no backwardness nor shamefacedness about Agnes. She rejoiced in Jesus, and would that all should know it. She had found the pearl of price, and she wanted others with her to realize its worth.

Grace could not believe Agnes wrong, yet she dared not believe her right. She was tossed with serious doubts. Her friend said one thing, and her life exemplified her words. But the priest said something entirely different. His life did not recommend his doctrines; but then, you know, Grace had been taught to believe the priest God's oracle and the Romish Church infallible. She was too honest to accept a middle course. One of these two must be right, the other fatally wrong. Where should she rest? In her anxiety she sounded Adelaide a little on the subject, but received small consolation.

"I don't care one morsel about it," said Adelaide. "All I know is, that Father Murphy and the Church have promised to look out for me, and now they must do it. I was regenerated in baptism. I belong to the only true Church. I confess my sins and become as pure as a new-born babe every month. When I must die there will be masses and unction and all that, to make up for all deficiencies. Why should I bother myself about it? There is Agnes, she is too particular for me. She despises cards and frowns on the theatre. Now the theatre is *ma grande passion.* Grace, how *do* you think I would look on the stage? *Would* I be a star?"

Grace ventured to speak to Richard on this matter which so occupied her.

"What do I think of Agnes' religion?" said Richard. "Why it becomes her well."

"Oh, I did not mean *that,*" said Grace, drawing back.

Her brother caught the disappointment in her tone:

"Why, it is *real*—of course it is. I wish Aunt Schuyler had some of it. She needs it if any one does. She is miserable enough."

"Do you think Lilly is right?" questioned Grace.

"No, to be sure not. None of your Romish doctrine is right. It may have been purer once, but now it is like a cup of water which has had poison thrown into it—every drop is dangerous. You had better leave it, Grace, and stand where Agnes does."

Easy enough for Richard to say, but hard doctrine for Grace. Drop all she had ever believed—that wherein she had been educated? Drop all she really knew, and take up—what? She could not do it. *Then* she would be sure she was wrong, and *now* she was *not* sure she was right.

May came, fair month of flowers, and on its first Sabbath, Lilly was to take the White Veil in the chapel of the Convent of the Immaculate Heart of Mary.

Grace and Adelaide were eager about the occasion, Grace truly believing it a holy act and an acceptable sacrifice, Adelaide impatient ever for something new to see or hear.

"I can't go to the theatre to-day, and this will be next to it," she said lightly to Grace in the dressing-room.

"Oh, Adelaide, how can you? I'm frightened at you!" cried Grace.

Lucy, dressing the reckless girl's hair, sighed. The days had gone by when she might take the liberty of venturing a remonstrance to her young ladies.

Grace's mind was that morning as divided as ever.

She knew that, while Lilly would be receiving the White Veil in the convent chapel, Agnes in her own church would be taking upon herself the Christian's holy vow. Under any circumstances Grace would not have dared to look upon that simple ceremony, yet now her heart oscillated between the rite in which Lilly was to participate, obedient to Mother Robart and Father Murphy, while her wretched parent mourned at home, and the earnest act of Agnes, to be performed with the full sanction and under the eyes of her happy mother. Grace's face was troubled as she pondered these things. Adelaide watched her and shook her head.

"We must do something for you, Grace, my dear; you are growing blue!"

By what wiles Rome lures her victim! The allurements, promises and flatteries for the young proselyte, the flowery way spread before the postulant, the white crown and robe of confirmation, the spotless dress and veil before the black gown and veil. Ah, how like the snowy shroud and satin-lined coffin which precede the blackness of the grave!

If ever neophyte believed in the righteousness of her course, and the duty and sanctity of her vow, it was Lilly. The girl's whole soul was wrapt in her enthusiasm. She believed herself standing at the very gate of life. Almost in her hands she felt the golden harp of heaven. As she stood before the altar her violet eyes raised in an ecstasy, the chanting of the choir sounded like the welcoming of angels, her victory over earth complete.

Who can tell the mingled feelings of that cloud of nuns that filled the centre of the chapel? The Abbess, stately and benignant, looked on her favorite pupil with pride. She truly loved Lilly, and she meant to make her as happy as she could be—in a convent. She thought the girl rather unfitted for the serious activities of life, and henceforth what was lacking to her in reality her imagination might supply. She knew it was a sacrifice, in other meaning than Lilly put upon the term; yet perhaps Lilly would never find it out. As for Father Douay, he was not as earthly as Father Murphy—he had never lived in Italy,* and he really believed in his religion. In regard to Father Murphy—we will not venture an assertion—you know what Richard would have said: "The wolf was getting the first bite out of the plump lamb"—he found it very good and snapped his teeth in satisfaction.

* "It is hard to find an intelligent man . . . . who does not speak sneeringly, disparagingly or railingly against it [*the Romish Church*]. Judging from the state of public sentiment, ... you would declare the Church of Rome an ocular illusion, or at best a vast ecclesiastical mansion in ruins."—*Dr. Bellows' Letter from Rome.*

Adelaide looked on the kneeling figure, the beautiful face of her cousin, and the long soft folds of the White Veil, and thought it a charming "scene," and "what a pity there was not a larger audience!" Grace, wondering if Lilly's feet were indeed in the path of peace while her own soul was so tempest-tossed, and if Lilly were for ever safe, while *she* might linger on the brink of destruction, bowed her head and wept.

And where was Richard?

Richard's whole sympathies were with the robbed and unhappy mother. He felt that, sick, mind, heart and body, she was lying in her darkened room, attended only by the faithful Hannah. Perhaps his thoughts did rove to the solemn service of communion in the church where Agnes stood among the people of God, but he knew well where was the need of comfort, and his generous soul was ever ready to espouse the cause of the sorrowful and oppressed. As, alike in church and convent chapel such different services began, Hannah, bending over her mistress' bed, was saying,

"It is Mr. Richard, ma'am. He sends his love and duty to you, and hopes you will take comfort and not give way-like. He is sitting in the parlor, ma'am, and bids me say that he is comfortable with a book, and means to stay all day."

All we who have needed consolation know what a comfort it was to Mrs. Schuyler to think of her nephew's sympathy and nearness—coming to her house in its gloom, waiting not far from her with a son's dutiful affection. She felt that she was not quite alone. The spasmodic sobs that had shaken her frame melted in a gentle rain of tears.

"Might I read to you, ma'am?" said Hannah. Bearing her mistress' burden, the faithful servant had often searched the Holy Book for words of cheer. She knew well where to read, and soon through the stillness of that upper chamber broke the tender echoes: "For the Lord hath called thee as a woman forsaken and grieved in spirit," and so on, culling out precious promises, until from the pitiful weakness of the present and the failure of all creature help, the mourner's heart had been turned to Him from whom all goodness flows.

That evening, Grace, depressed by the conflicting emotions of the day, was sitting in her own apartment, while Mrs. Kemp and Adelaide were yawning out the time in the drawing-room.

"How beautiful Lilly looked!" cried Adelaide for the twentieth time.

"Beautiful indeed," said Mrs. Kemp.

"But to be a nun—to be buried in a convent!" added Adelaide.

"Yes, horrible!" replied the devout mother; "but I dare say it suits Lilly."

"Mother," said Adelaide, "something is wrong with Grace. She is getting almost as religious as Lilly. You have no idea how grave she is and what queer things she says. How *awful* it would be to have her get 'pious' now, and we to be introduced into society next winter! Now, mother, you really *must* do something about it."

"Is it so, Adelaide? Dear, dear! it is quite time you were out of school and having a part in the world and seeing something of *life.* Yes indeed, we must do something to distract her mind and stir her up a little. Grace serious and devout! Horrors! I should be bored to death!"

CHAPTER IV.

VEIL AND WREATH.

AMONG the particularly interested spectators on the occasion of Lilly's taking the white veil were Pat and Ann Mora.

"It's a born shame," whispered Pat to his sister, as they stood humbly near the door of the chapel. "I don't believe in this kind of thing. I never could bear the Sisters nor Father Murphy either."

"Oh, Pat!" said Ann, turning pale at her brother's presumption, and weeping faster than ever between the excitement of the scene and misery at losing her place as Lilly's maid; for Lilly was now to find a home at the convent and learn to wait upon herself. "But it *is* dreadful-like to see her giving herself away so. Oh dear! it looks just as if she was dead and buried and an angel," added Ann, incoherently.

"I tell you, Ann," continued Pat, in his stealthy whisper, "this isn't the religion for poor folks. What a mint of money has been spent on this place in stone and glass and finery! And look how St. Joseph's was squeezed out of us poor sinners, when there ain't a winter but them as they call good Catholics is starving with want, and depending on Protestants to give them bread to eat."

"Hus-s-h!" said Ann, fearful; "it ain't a week since father said as there were dungeons under the Cathedral to shut folks up in as dared turn against the Church!"

"Father's been no better man since he turned Fenian," said Pat. "If it wasn't for mother I'd leave him. He's taken food out of my mouth and clothes off my body to give money to the priest, and that's what I call unnatural;" and he gave a bitter memory to the parti-colored trowsers which had wounded his earlier years. Pat confided entirely in his sister Ann, and presently whispered in her ear,

"I've got a *trac* as I picked up t'other day, and if half as it says about Holy Mother Church is true, we'd better slip away from her."

* * * * * * *

Grace soon got a better pair of spectacles than a tract through which to look at Rome. The anxiety and distress of mind kindled by witnessing the ceremony in the chapel, filled her with fears that her intimacy with Agnes was wrong and an injury to her—that she was endangering herself by this disobedience to her Church and priest, and she resolved to refrain from visiting at Mr. MacPherson's for the present. Providence guiding her, however, she met Agnes in the street, who gave her a warm greeting and demanded the reason of her absence.

"I love you as much as ever, Agnes," said Grace, flushing, "but—"

"Ah, I see. Come into this bookstore a moment, so that I can speak to you. I have a little business here." They entered; Agnes gave a rapid order at the counter and stepped aside with Grace. "Are you happy, Grace?"

"Yes, or at least I ought to be; but I wish I *knew* what was right, and was *sure* I was doing it."

"Grace, I am praying for you that your way may be made plain," said Agnes, tenderly. Grace looked up with a grateful smile. A parcel was just then laid near Agnes' hand; she took it. "Grace, you wish to know the truth, and here it is so plain that a fool might understand. Grace, if you love me do not refuse me my request, that you will take home this Bible and read it. I ask you to do it, Grace, because I *know* it is the power of God unto salvation. Grace, will you take it?"

Grace hesitated, considered, yielded. By a strong effort one of the old shackles was broken, and she dared to believe that she might read the word of God. She gave the promise. Later she repented, and wished she had not promised. But her word was gone beyond recall. At intervals she read, then again laid the volume out of sight, distrusting it. Father Murphy did not ask her about Bibles now. He saw with satisfaction that she no longer visited her heretic friend, and he thought his stray one had returned to the Romish fold again. Little did he dream that a power stronger against Rome than Agnes was in Grace's keeping.

Had Adelaide warned her mother that Grace showed symptoms of smallpox or insanity, Mrs. Kemp could not have been more disturbed than at the information that her step-daughter was "getting pious," in Adelaide's phraseology, or, in other words, was concerned for the salvation of her soul. That a member of the "True Church" should be distressed on account of sin and desire peace with God, was to Mrs. Kemp perfectly inexplicable. Being a Catholic, surely Grace was safe, and what more could she desire than safety? Mrs. Kemp had looked forward with much satisfaction to the time when she could introduce to the gay world two such beautiful girls as Grace and Adelaide—girls accomplished, fresh, charming in manner and accustomed to the best society, with money enough for all the demands of fashion in dress and entertainments—girls who must inevitably make fashionable marriages, and whose weddings Mrs. Kemp could celebrate with great *eclat* to her own intense gratification. Should these, Mrs. Kemp's highest hopes, be frustrated by having Grace suddenly weaned from the follies of this world and looking for a better life at God's right hand? Never.

The next question was, what was to be done at once to enliven Grace and "*distract*" her mind. Summer was approaching, the autumn would see school-days ended, and the beginning of the gay season would bring the time suitable for the introduction of Grace and Adelaide to the world of fashion.

"If it had not been for Richard, and the way he persuaded his father," said Mrs. Kemp, "the girls would have been introduced last winter." After further reflection, she added: "What a blessing that it is time to procure the summer fashions! The grand openings will be in two or three days, and the girls shall go with me to procure what is stylish and becoming, and then we must take them to Niagara."

The shopping occasions proved very successful. The girls were enraptured with hats, silks and laces, as girls will be. They thought their mother very liberal and the "styles" very charming. All went on gayly. Grace was as eager over patterns as Adelaide, and her Bible lay untouched in the bottom of a drawer. The girls no longer desired to repeat each other in dress, but each consulted her own taste, giving themselves thus the benefit of endless diversity.

The subject of going to Niagara being broached, Mrs. Kemp found her husband less tractable. Time enough for that next year. The way she managed matters it would be an enormous expense. She could go where she pleased, and let the girls board at the convent and attend to their music. As for himself, Mr. Kemp was unusually busy, and had no time for pleasure-trips. He was gathering up all his surplus means for a new speculation—a silver mine that would make his fortune, and be much better than an oil well. Thus Mr. Kemp. But now Richard, sometimes such a hindrance to his step-mother, came to the rescue. He would accompany her. He would be responsible for the girls' expenses, and his mother might arrange the trip to suit herself. It may be ungenerous to hint that Richard was in any way influenced to this gracious offer by the fact that Mr. MacPherson's family were going to Niagara at the very time Mrs. Kemp wished to go, and that by a little judicious management on Richard's part they might be fellow-travelers. Mrs. Kemp was in the height of her glory, the girls elated, the weather propitious. The carriage reached the depôt in ample time, and they secured plenty of seats on the shady side of the car. Nothing had been forgotten.

"Ma," said Adelaide, pulling her mother's sleeve, "there are the Anthons and Mr. MacPherson!"

"Bless me, so they are! and Richard is talking to them!" replied Mrs. Kemp.

"Ma," said Adelaide again, "Rick says they're going to Niagara!"

Mrs. Kemp pulled out her eye-glasses and slowly scanned the parties in question.

"Agnes is certainly a magnificent girl, and Mrs. Anthon has 'tone,' and has traveled in Europe. Really they look well, decidedly well. Girls, now as we are away from home and from Father Murphy, and as they are surely desirable acquaintances, I think we had better cultivate them."

Thus, having delivered her opinion, the next time the cars stopped, Mrs. Kemp was escorted by Richard to Mrs. Anthon and introduced—was charmed to see "dear Agnes," glad they were going to Niagara, and on that especial day and train of all things, proposed that they should take seats nearer together at the first opportunity, and so forth.

Mrs. Anthon, agreeable to every one, and mindful of Agnes and Grace, received these advances graciously, and the party were soon in the same part of the car, Agnes and Grace sharing a seat, Adelaide rattling her pretty nothings to Mr. MacPherson, and the two mothers exchanging opinions and experiences with a cordiality that set Father Murphy at defiance.

While enjoying everything about them with youthful zest, amused or pleased by their fellow-travelers, catching every mirthful incident and admiring the diversity of country over which they passed, exchanging opinions and relating past adventures, Agnes and Grace did not neglect the great theme on which they often before had conversed. Grace confessed her anxieties, her present carelessness, the Bible by fits consulted and rejected; but as she talked, the interest, which in her heart might slumber, but never die, revived.

As the days of the excursion passed away, Mrs. Kemp frequently congratulated herself on having found such agreeable acquaintances. At Niagara, being intent only on the follies and fashions of the day, she failed to notice that Adelaide seemed much delighted with the society of two or three people who were entire strangers to her mother, or that Grace and Agnes were as often seated in the shade of some broad tree on Goat Island, reading, as engaged in lively discourse with their friends.

"Ma," said Adelaide, as they strolled down one morning for a new view of the mighty cataract, "do see Grace and Agnes; quite rural, aren't they? Hats off, under a tree reading. What book is it they have?"

Scene on Goat Island, Niagara.

Priest and Nun. Page 262.

Mrs. Kemp turned her lorgnette that way.

"An album, I suppose," she said, catching a glimpse of the crimson velvet cover, against which Grace's white hand lay in clear relief.

"They must be fond of their friends, to bring their pictures out here to look at!" laughed Adelaide.

But instead of a treasury of friends' faces, the girls were studying the Bible—God's mirror, where the hearts of men are laid bare.

On one of those days Agnes gave Grace a volume containing the lives of some of the martyrs, and called upon Richard to guarantee the veracity of the book.

"Grace says she will read it if it is *true*," said Agnes.

"Certainly it is true—a plain matter of history," said Richard. "It will be more interesting than a novel, Grace, and at the same time a narration of facts."

Grace read the book after she had returned home. She could not enjoy as much theatre-going as Adelaide and her mother, and on some evenings, when she had declined to accompany them to the play, she would sit in her room, comfortably arranged in a soft wrapper, her brown hair veiling her face and shoulders, her head supported upon her hand, reading intently the lives of those who had witnessed a good confession for the testimony of Jesus Christ. So stirred was her heart by these tales that she cautiously referred the subject to Father Murphy, saying,

"Will you tell me what I am to believe about persecutions, martyrdoms and inquisitions? I see these things mentioned everywhere, and hear them cast up against our Church. Some Romanists utterly deny them, and say that they are libels—that the Church has never countenanced these things. But those who deny are refuted by other Romanists and by the voice of history."

Father Murphy smilingly replied,

"In this country girls are too much educated. It fills their heads with questions. *Belief*, daughter Grace, is better than *questioning*. Your sister Adelaide is much safer than you are, inasmuch as she does not meddle in things too high for her. Yet, as you ask me, I do not deny persecutions and so-called martyrdoms of heretics, or the glorious Inquisition. I rather *justify* them, and thus: The Holy Roman Catholic Church, my daughter, is queen of kingdoms and of churches. He who rejects and abandons her is guilty of *high treason* and *rebellion.** These, you

* "Mother and Mistress of all churches."—*Creed of Pius IX.* Hence inferred the RHEIMS annotators, "All heretics are at once rebellious subjects and disobedient children, and their punishment is to be like that of *thieves* and *traitors*." Quoted by R. J. Breckinridge.

know, are crimes, by the common consent of mankind punishable with *death*, and the higher the authority against which a man rebels, the more severe the manner of his capital punishment should be. Every heretic is a *rebel* and a *traitor;* therefore you need not marvel at the righteous severity of the holy Church to *some*, but at her leniency to others."

And so the summer and the autumn sped. The step-sisters were school-girls no longer. Mother Robart said they had finished their course at the convent with credit to themselves. We must not suppose from this, however, that the girls were good scholars, or thorough in any branch of education. They had merely skimmed the surface of their lessons in the most trivial manner, for it is not the policy of Rome to educate her pupils in anything but Papism. Grace had learned something at the convent in spite of all the disadvantages. She was in some things wiser than her teachers. But Adelaide was delightfully shallow—a good sample and trophy of the training of nuns and priests.

With lavish expenditure, Mrs. Kemp was preparing for her daughters wardrobes which should eclipse all their acquaintances, and, added to their beauty and charming manners, make them the belles of the season. The grand party which was to usher them into a round of pleasures was ever in her mind. Adelaide, wild with excitement, dreamed only of brilliant successes and boundless popularity. Grace, more moderately vain than her step-sister, and yet dazzled and bewildered, was slipping within the rapid circles of the vortex of worldliness.

By some strange fatality, the day selected by Mrs. Kemp for the splendid party on which she had fixed her heart was the very one chosen by the Abbess for Lilly's taking the Black Veil and the irrevocable vow. This was discovered too late for either party to change their plans.

"After all," said Mrs. Kemp, complacently, "I do not know as it signifies. The ceremony at the convent will be in the morning, and of course we shall all be there. I cannot see that the two affairs will interfere in the least."

"Yet," said Adelaide, "it *does* seem like going to a funeral in the morning and a wedding in the evening."

"And even that has to be done sometimes," said Mrs. Kemp. "I have only to beg, my dear Grace, that *you* will not be so impressed with the scenes of the morning that you will be dull and moping all the evening. What Lilly does is right and pleasant for her; but you have a different life before you, and you must set yourself to succeed in it."

"And what shall it profit a man if he gain the

whole world and lose his own soul?" The fearful question started out before Grace as plainly as if a spirit-hand were writing it on the wall in words of fire. A sudden anguish seized her. Lose her soul! Thin was the crust of life on which she trod. If it broke beneath her feet, what then? She envied Lilly. On that day to which they were now looking forward, how much better Lilly, sworn the bride of heaven, than herself, offered at the shrine of the world! Better? Then came the suspicion that Lilly might be deluded, that her sacrifice was false and unacceptable to God, and Scripture clinched the thought by the remembered assertion: "Not by works of righteousness that we have done; but by the precious blood of Christ, as of a lamb without blemish and without spot."

And did such thoughts cross Lilly's mind? In these earliest days of separation her heart was sick with a yearning for her mother. Her thoughts rested on that mother alone and unhappy, and over her fair young face the shadows thickened. Lilly had been *promised* that if she did her own duty her mother would unquestionably be brought to see the error of her ways and to come into the same convent with her child, where they would be united in a bond that even death could not sunder. This belief gave Lilly courage to act well her part. She never for one moment doubted the assurances of Father Murphy and Mother Robart. To be sure, when she talked of her hopes to Father Douay, he met them very differently:

"Whether her mother were lost or saved, it was her duty to obey the Church. She must renounce these earthly affections; they were quite unworthy a child of the Church. That longing to be united to her mother was old leaven that must be done away. This separation was the best thing that could happen to her. If her mother continued obstinate, Lilly must utterly renounce her. She must be to Lilly as a heathen and a publican." Thus Father Douay.

But this was hard doctrine, and Lilly could not bear it. It was a blow that paralyzed her heart. She had ever been ruled and guided by her affections and her imagination, and the cold, sharp dealings of Father Douay were as death itself. Nature rose and cried out that she could not, would not give up her mother. She clung to the repeated promises of the Abbess and her spiritual director; and yet a chill fear crept over her, because as yet there was no sign of those promises being fulfilled. I do not think Father Murphy ever expected that Mrs. Schuyler would adopt the religion of her child. He greatly desired it, but there was less and less prospect of such a consummation of all these plottings. One thing

Lilly insisted on. On the afternoon before she took her final vow she must spend two hours alone with her mother at her own home. In vain the priest and Superior argued that such an act was inexpedient, perhaps unprecedented—that Lilly's duty was to spend her time in solemn preparation for the great event of her life—that visiting her mother would excite her and disperse all her solemn thoughts.

"If I cannot do this," wept Lilly, "I shall die! I must make one more effort to convert my mother."

"But surely, child," said the Abbess, "Father Murphy can argue much better than you, and a visit from him would be more effectual."

"It is not argument that can prevail, but love," said Lilly, clinging to the Superior's neck in a passion of sobbing. "My mother loves me, and she may listen to me."

At last Lilly won her cause and was allowed to go, under charge of Saint Cecelia, to her mother's house and see her mother alone. She obtained this permission—first, on account of the Abbess' partiality; next, because she was so frail that they feared refusal would make her too ill for the next day's ceremonies; and lastly, because she *might* win her mother at this eleventh hour, and what a consummation devoutly to be wished for was that!

When Hannah opened the door to Lilly and Saint Cecelia, the faithful maiden involuntarily burst into tears. If that had been a house of death, there could not have been more weeping or oppressive gloom.

"Don't, Hannah!" said Lilly, in a choked, petulant voice. "Take Saint Cecelia into the parlor, and do not come to mamma's room while I am there."

She ran up stairs, shaking off Saint Cecelia's detaining grasp. The quick ear of love recognized the coming footsteps. Mrs. Schuyler rose from her couch, and as Lilly opened the door extended to her her arms. The mother and child were clasped in a long embrace. Then they looked into each other's faces, and what bitter revelations! Mrs. Schuyler had grown haggard and old; gray hairs were plentiful above her wan brow; her eyes were sunken and their light was wept away; for this delusion of her child had been worse than death. From Lilly's cheek the soft rose-tint had faded; her eyes were sorrowful from hope long deferred; of her delicate frame the rounded outlines were wanting; her little hand was thin, almost transparent.

"Lilly," groaned her mother, "that convent is killing you!"

"No, mother, not the convent; that is a blessed home, but my heart is sick waiting and longing for you. Then I have been very diligent at my duties, and much more engaged in acts of religion than our Mother"—how the word cut Mrs. Schuyler's heart!—"thinks is good for me. But, mamma, it is all for your sake, to save your soul. Oh, mamma, dearest mamma, I can never, never come back to you; but you can come to me. Do not destroy yourself and break your Lilly's heart. Come to the true Church; come to the convent, and we can perform all our duties together. We can give ourselves to heaven, watch over each other's feebleness and be buried in one grave, my mother, oh, my mother!"

Mrs. Schuyler had dropped into an easy-chair, and Lilly, kneeling on a foot-cushion beside her, resting on her bosom and encircled by her arms, aided the pleading of her lips by the earnest entreaty of her tear-filled eyes.

"Oh, Lilly, my precious one!" said Mrs. Schuyler, with a strong effort, conquering the spasmodic catching of her breath, while her heart beat fearfully under Lilly's arm, "this can never be. My bitter griefs are driving me nearer my Saviour, and therefore farther from Rome. Lilly, hear what your mother has learned in the heaviest afflictions that ever woman had to bear: *Only the blood of Jesus can save our souls.* You are deceived, and miserably deluded, if you think your nun's vow and your convent life can take you into heaven. Oh, Lilly, leave them even now. My child, I entreat you, I command you, come back to your duty! come back to your unfaithful and bitterly repentant mother, and we will serve the Lord together."

"Mother, mother! do not tempt me. I *cannot* come back. I should be for ever accursed. There is but one hope for us, mother. Come to me; come to the convent. Be converted to the true faith. Oh, mother, my mother, come!"

"Lilly," said Mrs. Schuyler, in agony, "I have a sure hope in Jesus my Saviour, and I cannot give it up. God helping me, through all these dreadful woes, I will live and die a Protestant. And yet for you, my darling, my own beloved, poor, innocent, unhappy victim of your mother's weakness and of priestly wiles, I believe that God will save you yet. Yet, Lilly, if the Lord bears long before he avenges me at my crying, I shall not live to see the joyful day. I see myself dying, slowly but certainly, my poor child."

Lilly's arms tightened convulsively about her mother: "I must go back to my convent," she moaned, "and if you do not come to me, we may never meet again. My mother, be persuaded. I think this grief will kill me. Mother, *will* you refuse me?"

"Lilly," said Mrs. Schuyler, endeavoring to speak

calmly, "I shall send for you when I am dying. Will you come?"

"Oh, mother, must I see you die a heretic?"

"You shall see me die a Christian. You shall hear what witness I bear in death to the efficacy of Jesus' blood. Daughter, will you come?"

"Mother," returned Lilly, "I hope I may send for you to see me die. But if I must live, and you send for me, can you think I would not fly to you and nurse you and get your last look and blessing? Do you doubt my love—do you doubt my humanity?"

"No," said Mrs. Schuyler, slowly; "I do not doubt you; yet you are a toy in stronger hands. Something tells me we shall never meet again in this world. But the Lord will be better to you than I have been. He will not reject my tardy penitence and prayer. He will let me see you enter heaven. Daughter, we have never knelt in prayer together. Kneel with me now, and let me commend you, poor, helpless lamb among the destroyers, to *his* keeping."

Awed and wondering, Lilly knelt, encircled by her mother's arms, and Mrs. Schuyler, in a passion of love and grief, poured out a prayer that amazed, hushed and overwhelmed her unhappy child; a prayer that left Lilly no doubt of her mother's nearness to God; a prayer which outweighed all the set prayers of Rome; a prayer which dwelt in her trembling spirit day by day, her sweetest, saddest memory, and which it seemed must bring its answer.

That had been a tender but terrible interview. All night Hannah watched over her mistress, while the anxious Richard waited below and the physician exerted his best skill to save his patient. The morning found disease baffled for the present; but as the doctor drew on coat and gloves in the hall, he said to Richard,

"These attacks are of the heart, and will one day prove fatal."

As for Lilly, she could scarcely reach the convent, supported by Saint Cecelia's arm; and the Abbess, partly pitying and tender, partly anxious for next day's rites, upbraiding herself for having let Lilly make this wretched visit, by hours of soothing, by skillful arguments, by deceitful promises, by monotonous repetitions of prayers, and especially by administering nervines and cordials, at last had calmed her neophyte to rest.

How different, with the next morning's dawning, were the circumstances and occupations of those two families with which we begun our story! Mrs. Schuyler, lying a helpless, exhausted invalid in her darkened room; Lilly being carefully made ready for the solemn mockery before her; Mrs. Kemp in a bustle of preparation for the festivities of the evening, sending forth her couriers first to the wine-merchant, then to the confectioner's, and anon to upholsterer and mantuamaker; Grace and Adelaide obsequiously waited on by madame, the dressmaker, and her forewoman, for the last trial and retouching of their elaborate costumes—jewels, flowers, dances, fashions and all manner of frivolities on their minds and tongues.

And now, from Adelaide: "We must not be late at the convent. Be quick, madame, we have an engagement. Our cousin takes the veil at eleven. Lucy, my gray silk suit, my lace set—Lucy, the best one, and those turquoises. Yes, my bonnet with blue ribbons and plume; one cannot be very *prononcée* at the chapel, you know, Grace."

And Grace, not behindhand with the vanities of this life: "Lucy, lay out that black velvet suit and the hat to match. Yes, you may give me the jet and pearl jewelry; I think that most suitable to the occasion. Don't you, Adelaide?"

"Yes, for *you*, certainly; it suits your style. Madame, you are sure this method of trimming is becoming to my figure?"

"*Charmante*," says madame. "*C'est* bewitching. Mademoiselle is so—ah, what you call it?—so *beaute piquante*, ah!"

They start for the chapel, and all the way Adelaide's head is filled with visions that would have frightened Grace; and Grace's mind, slowly turning from her own anticipated triumphs and pleasures, gives a gentle sigh to her aunt Schuyler—is glad she is better, and wearily goes over the old wonder, Who is right and who is wrong?

What shall we say to the scene in the convent chapel? Lilly, the fair, the young, the innocent, is dead to the world for ever, buried beyond recall, lost in a sad oblivion; her tomb, her record, only in her mother's bleeding heart. Instead of Lilly dead, we are henceforth to have "Sister Mary Anna," a pale, frightened young nun, in whose heart is gnawing the worm of an imperishable grief, eating her life away. Sister Mary Anna, erst Lilly, has received the gloomy, black veil and the symbolical ring that make her the Bride of Christ for ever. A horrid lie and mockery. Not these gloomy rites for the eternal nuptials—far other bridal that whereof John writes the exultant Epithalamium, "I will show thee the Bride, the Lamb's wife, that great city, the holy Jerusalem, descending out of heaven from God, having the glory of God; and her light like unto a stone most precious. And to her was granted that she should be arrayed in fine linen, clean and white. Let us be glad and rejoice and give honor to him; for the marriage of the Lamb is come! Write, Blessed and happy are they which are called unto the marriage supper of the Lamb." Thus we gather up the echoes of the song of the latest seer.

It must not be for one moment supposed that the little sigh which Grace gave her aunt was the only notice Mrs. Schuyler received from her brother's family at this juncture. By no means. Mrs. Kemp, early in the morning, sent Lucy over the way with regards and inquiries. Mr. Kemp called himself, entered his sister's bed-room on tip-toe, took for a second her limp hand—"Hoped she was better. She must not give way so; everything was going right. She must be cheerful and conquer this nervousness. Exercise, society, these were the tonics she needed. Mrs. Kemp and the girls were very busy to-day, but would be over to-morrow," etc.

At his dinner-table Mr. Kemp freely expressed the opinion that "Maria was nervous and low-spirited; she gave way to trifles; she was hysterical. It was a great pity that she had always been so weak. It was absurd in her to make such an ado over Lilly: the girl was not dead. If Maria had buried her daughter, one might look on Maria's distress with a few grains of allowance, but as she had only taken the veil, why it was too ridiculous."

Richard shared his aunt's unhappiness, and longed to do something for her. He strolled to the florist's and ordered two of the most beautiful bouquets that could be made for the two girls; then he procured a third just as beautiful and sent it up by Hannah to his aunt. After that he found it only reasonable to go to Mr. MacPherson's and ask Mrs. Anthon to go and visit Mrs. Schuyler; and this was, after all, the very best thing he could do.

Mr. Kemp had given an especial order to have Mr. MacPherson and Mrs. Anthon and Agnes invited to the grand reception which so filled his wife's thoughts. Father Murphy had expected this, and expressly ordered Mrs. Kemp to send no such invitations. Mrs. Kemp was in a dilemma. She endeavored to persuade Father Murphy that the compliment would do no harm, but Father Murphy was endowed with a pig-headed obstinacy, and would not abandon his point. He was resolved that the MacPherson household should be outcasts and publicans, as far as he could compass it. Mrs. Kemp then sought to convince her husband that an invitation would not be accepted, and therefore had better not be sent; but the husband was as obstinate as the priest. And now, as Mrs. Kemp wishes agreed with the spiritual Fathers, and yet as Mr. Kemp was to foot the bills for this occasion, and could not be too violently opposed, Mrs. Kemp undertook to write a note which should not be delivered, and thus upon the lad Matt could fall the blame. But Mr. Kemp had been a Romanist long enough to know that his wife would contravene and deceive him, and that her priest was "full of all subtlety and mischief." He unexpectedly secured the dainty, scented, rose-hued missive, and said he preferred Richard should be their Mercury to Mrs. Anthon, and thus make sure of there being no mistake. Mrs. Kemp being thus foiled, accepted the situation gracefully. She had done what she could to obey Mother Church. She did not want Agnes Anthon set beside her girls on that eventful evening, but as it could not be helped, she was not the woman to distress herself about it.

Thus it happened that Mr. MacPherson and Agnes were present for an hour, admired the young ladies and the rooms to Mrs. Kemp's satisfaction, and then withdrew, also to her satisfaction.

We have mentioned Father Murphy's intention of making the MacPherson household outcasts as far as he could. Mrs. Anthon never thought of attributing to *him* the difficulty she experienced with servants. One after another, they framed some excuse and left her, and Mrs. Anthon, not keen enough to consider that all these maidens, who changed as kaleidoscopic visions, were Papists, wondered and lamented over her housewifely afflictions. Did Father Murphy relent, that he sent her a servant, humble, capable and well recommended? Send one he did—a servant in a brown gown and black silk apron, a check silk bonnet and a check woolen shawl—a red-haired, white-faced girl, not very young, and a most excellent chamber-maid. This servant came out of the side gate of the House Without a Name. As she did so she met a furbelowed nurse-maid coming in with a child in her arm.

"Going to have him baptized, Sister Maria?" asked the proposed chamber-maid.

"Yes; is Father Murphy in there?"

Clement made a sign for yes, and added:

"He's just been marking out my line, but I think I've practiced enough to know myself. You're going to leave where you are, and be sent ladies' maid to a young bride who used to go to the Convent of the Immaculate Heart. You can have the recommendation I got from Schuyler's. It is under the pillow in my room. I'm chamber-maid now."

"Eh, you're coming down?" sneered Maria, changing the elegantly-dressed infant to her other arm.

"Only for a little while. There's a boy for me to look after, too. Mother Ignatia is carrying on the working and fasting worse than ever. I've been in a week, and it will be your turn soon."

The two parted, and Annette was soon busy in Mrs. Anthon's house, sweeping, dusting and polishing in an exemplary manner. Drawers, writing-desks, portfolios, etc., were of course systematically gone through with; but the especial object of Annette's curiosity was Mr. MacPherson's escritoire, and that the wary old Scotchman kept fast locked. It was not very difficult to get an impression of the lock and have a key made; but when this was done, to her great mortification there was little to be found, as all the inner compartments were under the ward of another lock. Sister Clement, alias Annette, had two especial missions at Mr. MacPherson's. One was to secure intelligence concerning Mr. Wynford and his movements. The escritoire she must therefore penetrate, and by having three keys made, she succeeded in having that piece of furniture entirely at her mercy. At this juncture, Mr. MacPherson, pursuing his wrathful investigations of Papism, became highly excited on the subject of Popish spies in families, and casting about for some one to suspect, he fixed upon Annette.

"I don't like that girl," he said to his niece; "she looks like a Jesuit."

"She is an admirable servant," said Mrs. Anthon.

"So they all are," said Mr. MacPherson, grimly.

"I'll send her away if you like," replied Mrs. Anthon.

"No, you needn't go so far as *that*," answered the

old gentleman, "but I'll take all my private papers down to my office. I *know* there are no spies in petticoats there."

So just as Annette was all ready for a nocturnal investigation of Mr. MacPherson's correspondence and private papers, the objects of her solicitude were carried out of the house, and half her mission came to an untimely end.

Alas, for the other object! It was too surely obtained. Annette baffled the vigilance of Mr. MacPherson. Through her did Martin Wynford receive letters, books and papers from the Rev. Fathers Murphy and Douay, and from the Jesuits at the Belen. By her the lad's ears were filled with the tales and superstitions of Romanism, which, mounting to his brain like poisonous vapors, overpowered his reason and his sense of duty, and while no one suspected his danger, he had gone nearer and nearer, and now was in the serpent's coils and carried away. Aided by Annette, Martin Wynford escaped from his friends. By night Annette helped him carry away all his valuables. The next morning he went off early, as to school, and did not return.

Mr. MacPherson waited up for him at night. When it was quite late, Annette came down stairs in shawl and wrapper and "Begged ten thousands of pardons; but she had let Mr. Martin in two hours ago and had forgotten to mention it. He had said his head ached and had gone to bed." She then ran up stairs, softly entered Martin's vacant chamber, and locking the door, simulated deep, steady breathing. Mr. MacPherson, coming to the room, concluded that his ward was asleep and passed on.

The next morning Annette was found composedly setting the apartment in order, and innocently supposing Mr. Martin had gone out for an early walk. By this connivance of the pretended Annette, Martin made good his flight, and all Mr. MacPherson's efforts failed to track him.

This was a heavy blow to the old guardian. He felt keenly for the father robbed of both his idolized children.

"I cannot tell Wynford of it," said Mr. MacPherson to his niece; "indeed I cannot. He'll go crazy, or get brain fever and die among strangers. No, no; we'll let him get all the evidence he can to sustain his suit and get the girl back, or they are all lost. I can hunt for the lad myself."

He did continue his search, expending time and money, but unsuccessfully.

As Mrs. Schuyler had lost one child, so had Mr. Wynford lost two. Doubtless the first blame lay at their own door. If the lambs are not well tended, we must expect the wolf will carry them away. Had

Mr. Wynford been an earnest and intelligent Protestant, instead of a cold-hearted unbeliever, his children would not thus have been deliberately thrown among snares. Had he done his duty, the Convent of the Immaculate Heart of Mary and the Belen would not have obtained possession of his son and daughter. But how many are thus unfaithful!

CHAPTER V.

REAPING THE WHIRLWIND.

THE months flew by. One while Grace would be swept along in the rapid current of fashionable dissipation. Again she would tremble at thoughts of a wasted life, a conscience ill at ease, a heart burdened with unforgiven sin. She would read the Bible until stung by remorse and knowing not what to do; then would hide it away and hasten to drown her bitter reflections by new gayeties. Adelaide appeared light-hearted as a butterfly borne on the wings of every truant wind, ever in a brilliant land of sunshine and of flowers. Grace felt that Adelaide had concealments from them all, that she was living a double life, that there was something hidden—a life behind the scenes, where other than her own family could come. Mrs. Kemp was perfectly satisfied with everybody—a little better satisfied with Adelaide than with Grace perhaps, but getting on admirably with both. The silver mine was doing wonderfully, money was plenty; she felt as if she had come out into a wealthy place, and she was bound to enjoy it. *She* would see that her girls married well; Father Murphy *of course* would see that they behaved well. What had she to do with their characters when they went regularly to the confessional?

Not so Richard. He did not think Grace in the wisest and most skillful hands. He had learned to measure mothers by Mrs. Anthon, and he thought Mrs. Kemp painfully deficient. He watched Grace and her friends with tender interest, and doing so, his eyes were opened to the fact that there was a vast difference between Grace and Adelaide. Grace was all frankness—Adelaide delighted in subtilty. Self-constituted guardian of these two young ladies, Richard was not long in discovering that Adelaide had some acquaintances unknown to the rest of the family, that she was extravagantly enamored of the stage, and that some mornings, when she civilly declined Grace's companionship, she found her way to the green-room of the theatre.

Concerning these deviations Richard spoke with Adelaide privately.

She first denied, then grew angry and spoke violently of his interference.

"Why do you not play the spy to Grace?" she cried.

"I play the spy on nobody," replied Richard, calmly. "As for Grace, you know well, Adelaide, that she is frank and open in her dealings. There is your danger, Adelaide. You are not honest about your actions. It amuses you to deceive people. Do not be angry with me that I speak plainly. I see you open to a thousand dangers. Truth, Adelaide, is the young heart's best palladium. Truth may be your safety, deceitfulness will be your ruin."

Adelaide laughed boldly.

"You and I have been very differently taught," she answered. "I have been instructed that I may deceive when it is expedient. In fact, that when it is useful to health, honor or wealth, a lie is *very right.** Now, if it is very right one time, it is very right always. The only question is of convenience, and it is always convenient."

"Adelaide!" exclaimed Richard, much shocked, "it cannot be that your religion is responsible for these false and shameful opinions. Grace is also a Papist, and she would blush to entertain them."

"You are pleased to be very complimentary," said Adelaide, mockingly, "but you cannot abash *me* by your disapproval, even so boldly expressed. Grace is no proper sample of Romanism. Accept me as the legitimate fruit of the tree of Papism. I am in my opinions very like Father Murphy, the Abbess, the

* Sanchez. Quoted by Sauvestre, page 44 of "Monita Secreta," 16th edition.

Sisters and my own mother. *They* think it expedient to keep these opinions in the background. I bring them forward plainly—first, because I like to shock people, and lastly, because they are my sole excuse."

"The girl is going to destruction," said Richard to himself; "but it must be that her mother is able to control her, and I shall open her eyes." As he wished to take no underhand measures, he chose an occasion when Mrs. Kemp, Adelaide and himself were alone together. Grace had just left the room, and Adelaide was rising to follow her, when Richard laid a detaining clasp on her arm, and said to his stepmother: "By your leave, madam, I have a somewhat serious charge to prefer against this young lady. Not being blessed with our mature years and judgment, she has made some acquaintances which I am sure will be an injury to her."

Horrible visions of seamstresses, clerks and other employés, rose before Mrs. Kemp's mind.

"Adelaide," she demanded, "what does this mean?"

"Since Rick knows so well, let him speak," said Adelaide, sulkily.

"Then I will speak," said Richard, firmly. "Adelaide has formed friendships with some of the actors and actresses at the ——— Theatre. She visits them, walks with them, and is to be found at times in their green-room. To be thus behind the scenes may be bewitching to a young girl's imagination, but you will see, madam, that such acquaintances are dangerous and inadmissible."

Mrs. Kemp's face grew dark, but Adelaide resolved to win her mother over.

"Neither dangerous nor inadmissible," she cried. "I have but one friend among those Richard mentions, and that is Madame Leplatte, who on the bills is called Camilla Donatelli. I met her at the Falls last summer, and I'm sure she had the most splendid toilette of any lady there. As to her being '*dangerous*,' she is a perfect lady and very fashionable. Some of the wealthiest people in town call on her. I cannot see how my visiting her is '*inadmissible*.' She boards at the best hotel, and when I went to the green-room with her, I went in her carriage."

Richard saw that Mrs. Kemp was going over to the enemy.

"I assure you, ma'am," he said, "I take the liberty of speaking because I have the same interest in Adelaide that I have in Grace, and—"

"You have no business to have the same interest in me that you have in Grace!" exclaimed Adelaide, furiously.

"My dear child, don't quarrel," interposed Mrs. Kemp.

"And," continued Richard, "I think if an elder brother does his duty, he can be a great blessing and protector to his sisters."

"Thank you, Rick. I am sure—" began Mrs. Kemp.

"And I must be allowed to say," hurried on Richard, "that I think the kind of fashion and visitors that Madame Leplatte, as she calls herself, may be suited with, very unsuitable for a young lady in Adelaide's position. Madame and her guests may not be unimpeachable—they are not generally considered so—and if Adelaide attaches herself to them, she is likely to fall out of our set entirely."

"Let me alone!" cried Adelaide, striking Richard's detaining hand with all her small might. "I shall choose my own friends. Madame has the finest laces and jewels in the city; and if you want to prove her respectability, just look into her card-basket and see whose names you find there! She speaks Italian like an angel! Let me go, Rick."

Richard laughed, and caught in his broad palm the small clenched hand descending for another blow.

"Come, mother," he cried, "express your high displeasure, which I am sure will bring this girl to her senses. Banish the Leplatte & Co.'s friendship by an edict like that of the Medes and Persians, and then I will speedily make my peace with miss by whatever offering she may demand."

"Mother, don't you listen to him. Madame Leplatte is splendid, and you don't know how useful she might be to us—some private theatricals—"

Mrs. Kemp, unhappy mother, caught the bait—

"Let the child alone, Richard," she said, easily. "I'm sure there is no harm done. You're over-particular. If Adelaide were going wrong, I'm sure Father Murphy would stop it. And, as you say, Adelaide, some private theatricals *would* be just the thing to set against Mrs. Storms' concerts. I have been worried to death with the stir her concerts have been making, which is all that keeps those red-haired girls of hers in fashion."

During these remarks of Mrs. Kemp, Richard had stalked out of the room.

"Rick is utterly unendurable," said Adelaide, angrily.

"He's a regular blue Puritan, thanks to those Anthons, and is getting worse and worse," said Mrs. Kemp. "But he is a kind-hearted fellow and generous in gifts."

"Yes, he does make nice presents," conceded Adelaide. "And, mother, couldn't we get a few to help us, issue about a hundred and fifty invitations, get a stage up and have a little drama and some tableaux with madame to assist. It would take admirably. We would have a *recherche* supper after the play. Do, mother; it will be better than a grand reception, and Grace and I will choose our own parts. Say yes, mother!"

"I do not know but we could manage it," said Mrs. Kemp, meditatively, "if you could secure madame; and I suppose she has a handsome theatrical wardrobe?"

"Oh, elegant, mother! you've no idea; and we could hire some costumes through her, and nobody know a word about it. Our dress would then be complete, and not so very expensive. You could get Carter to manage the stage and curtains, and cover the stage with those carpets you took off the parlor last spring, and hire some scenery—what is needed for parlor-acting—and most likely madame could find us a prompter who understands the business, to ensure against failure. Come, mother, promise!"

By this time Mrs. Kemp was as eager as her light-headed daughter.

"I will make all the arrangements with Madame Leplatte," said Adelaide, "as I know just where and when to find her. She is going to the cathedral with me on Sunday, and wants me to take dinner with her in her private parlor afterward; then I can talk it over with her."

"You will surely not dine at the public table?" said Mrs. Kemp, uneasily.

"Oh no, indeed! Madame always dines in her parlor with a few friends on Sunday. It is very private, I assure you, and madame is a married lady and, of course, a suitable chaperon; and then, mother, it is only a very small and private dinner, as you may know, for I shall go right from the cathedral, and in the same dress I wear there. You had just as lief, mother?"

"Well—yes, perhaps so," said Mrs. Kemp, slowly.

On the next Sunday, Adelaide wore a purple silk, trimmed with white lace, to the cathedral, and her mother saw her nodding and smiling at her from a distant seat, beside a splendidly-dressed and handsome woman.

When Adelaide was inquired for after service, Mrs. Kemp said, "She is dining with a friend." Richard at once suspected who this friend was, and inviting Grace to go with him to spend an hour with their Aunt Schuyler, he talked the whole matter over with her, and warned her against Adelaide's new companions. Grace was as averse to such intimacies as Richard. "It is of no use for me to speak to Adelaide," she said, sadly. "She would only be vexed at me, and she never tells me anything now, as she used to."

Despite this dislike of Adelaide's theatrical friends, Grace was wavering about the private exhibition that Mrs. Kemp was now arranging. Conscience, Agnes and Richard urged her to have nothing to do with it; Mrs. Kemp, Adelaide and the lively fancies of youth persuaded her to enjoy it. Her mind trembled in the balance; one hour she thought it a waste of time, likely to throw her among ineligible associates—for Grace was not sufficiently enlightened to apply to them any other title—and that the exhibition would be opposed to that maidenly reserve which she preferred. Again, the enticements of dress, vanity, display, and the persuasions of Adelaide and Mrs. Kemp would be in the ascendant.

Really anxious to be right, at confession Grace referred the subject to Father Murphy:

"Were not Adelaide's friends of the theatre objectionable?"

Father Murphy settled himself comfortably in his easy-chair, stretched out his slippered feet, puffed his thick lips, and did not so consider it. Madame Leplatte was a good Catholic, attended cathedral ever and anon, came sometimes to confession, was not niggardly in giving, accepted humbly all imposed penances, was a much better friend than that heretic, doomed to perdition, Agnes Anthon.

"But these theatricals, Father?" persisted this anxious inquirer; "ought I to take part in them—are they right?"

"The Church of Rome has ever countenanced these diversions," said the excellent priest. "People must have some entertainments, and the Church is a loving mother, not too strict with obedient children. The theatre cultivates the taste, the memory, the mind generally. There are many things more dangerous than theatre-going and acting; as, for instance, the friendship of heretics, reading forbidden books, questioning the dicta of the Church and the authority of your priest."

Grace was evidently out of favor, and she began to weep: "I try and do my duty, Father."

"Your duty, your *sole* duty, is obedience. Pay no attention to the evil speech of your heretic brother. Have nothing to do with Agnes Anthon or her heaven-abandoned mother; read none of their books; follow none of their counsels. Do not set yourself up as better than Adelaide. She is a better Catholic and much nearer the kingdom of heaven than are you. As to these theatricals, take part in them, for they will distract your mind and do you good."

Richard had remonstrated with his father as to the present dramatic infatuation, and as to the style of guest about to be admitted to his house.

"True, Rick," said the worthy head of the family, "it does cost a mint of money to keep the family in the advance in good society. The fashions of the day would ruin——you know that fellow who made everything he touched gold."

"Midas?" suggested Richard.

"Yes, thank you, that's it. But the well and the mines pay admirably; we can stand it, and when the girls are married the crisis will be past."

"Oh, I wasn't meaning the money, but the wisdom, the propriety of the thing."

"I don't expect women to exercise wisdom," said Mr. Kemp; "but your mother is well posted in all the proprieties."

"It is a fact, sir, that Adelaide is not keeping the company she ought."

"I cannot interfere with Adelaide. She belongs to her mother," said Mr. Kemp, loftily. "Don't borrow trouble, Rick. Your whole duty to the girls will be to give them each a handsome silver service when they get married, eh?"

"I would gladly give Adelaide half a dozen such if I might see her suitably married to-morrow," retorted Richard. "The next thing we shall suffer the disgrace of having her adopt the profession, and herself become a third-rate actress in some theatre."

"What utter folly!" said Mr. Kemp, laughing.

* * * * * * *

"Adelaide," asked Richard, "what note was that tied in the bouquet you threw on the stage last night?"

"Just one to madame about our play. I thought it would be funny to send it so. But, Richard, I can't bear you. You are so interfering!" said Adelaide, pettishly.

Again Richard asked, "Adelaide, who was that stranger I saw you walking with on —— street last evening?"

"Only madame's husband. I was just going to see her. What harm in that? I hate to be watched so; I hate you for doing it!" exclaimed Adelaide, her eyes glowing and her foot stamped in anger.

"I do not watch you. I assure you I saw you by the merest accident. But oh, Adelaide, be warned in time!"

"Be warned of what?—that I am growing old and must one day die?" retorted Adelaide with a mocking whine.

"Quit all this, Adelaide, and come, I will take you and Grace for a trip to Cuba and be gone a couple of months. Perhaps Aunt Schuyler or Mrs. Anthon would go with us," said the distressed Richard.

"I won't do it," said Adelaide, turning away.

About taking part in the private drama, Grace hesitated and could reach no conclusion. She learned her part, but said she would not play it; so another young lady learned it also, as a *corps de reserve.* Mrs. Kemp would not have endured this vacillation, but she was now wholly committed to the play, and wished to conquer Richard, whom she believed at the bottom of Grace's hesitation.

On the very evening of the exhibition, Richard knocked at the door of the young ladies' room. Lucy came out.

"I want to see Miss Grace," explained Richard.

"She is dressing," said Lucy. But presently Grace came out, a cashmere wrapper enveloping her, and her hair all braids and ornaments, shining from Lucy's manipulations.

"Grace," said Richard, "I've seen that famous 'prompter' mother has discovered, who passes for Monsieur Leplatte, I think. As to madame, I abhor the sight of her. Mother and Adelaide are completely infatuated. Come over to Aunt Schuyler's with me, and spend the evening while all this farce and folly are going on. Don't let the evil angel get the better of you any further. Finish up some plain dressing and come on. See"—holding up his watch—"I give you ten minutes to array yourself; meanwhile I wait in the hall."

Grace drew a long breath, resolutely compressed her lips, went into her dressing-room, and seeking no aid from Lucy, put on a dark-green silk, fastened it with a cluster of carbuncles at the throat, and throwing her opera-cloak about her, returned to her brother.

"Thank you, Grace," said Richard, drawing her hand through his arm and leading her quickly down stairs, and giving a message to the footman, they were soon at Mrs. Schuyler's. By this act Grace incurred the anger of her mother and priest, and the scorn of Adelaide, who would not cease to ridicule her.

This entertainment was the great event of the winter at Mrs. Kemp's. Otherwise life passed in the usual round of parties, balls, opera and theatre-going, the services at the cathedral and the convent chapel being sandwiched between. Like other Romanists, our friends attempted to cut the Gordian knot of Scripture, and to serve God and Mammon. We cannot say that in this double service Grace found peace. Her heart was like the troubled sea that had never rest, and still against the awakening voice of the Spirit strove in her that mighty trio—the world, the flesh and the devil, the latter in the crafty guise of the creed of Rome.

* * * * * * *

Since that bitter visit to her mother and her home on the eve of her taking the veil, Lilly had not seen her only parent. Mrs. Schuyler now left her house only at times for a short ride, or on Sabbaths, when she felt unusually well, to attend the service in her own church.

She was surely dying. The return of her daughter could not have saved her now, though it might have healed the wounds in her aching heart. As for Lilly, she was not the strong, zealous Romanist her Abbess and priest had expected she would be. The elasticity of her nature had gone. She was meek, obedient, devout, thinking no penances or exercises too heavy, and yet there was a crushed, grieved, anxious look about her, that told she was far from finding the rest and satisfaction she sought.

Instead of continuing her life of active ministrations to the sick and destitute, Lilly now seldom left the convent. She hovered about the hospital ward in the Convent of the Immaculate Heart of Mary, or lingered alone in the chapel, gazing on pictures and statuary with a feeling between religious adoration and her innate love of the beautiful. If she wandered in the garden, it was when the pupils were in the school-room, and she might stray in shaded walks and by dripping fountains alone; and then too often the painful memories of those days when she, a happy girl, could go nightly to her home and mother —that home now by her own act desolated, and that mother by her only child crushed and made miserable—that mother, whom her spiritual instructors assured her must, bearing fearful penalties, drift farther and farther from her through the cycles of eternity—these memories, we say, would make the poor, pale nun, Sister Mary Anna, sadly weep.

One nun among the black-garbed throng who filled the convent was more often with Lilly (for so we must call her despite her new name of Sister Mary Anna) than the others, not from any congeniality between them, but that neither was care-free enough to envy, jar and bicker like the rest. This was the French nun from Paris—Sister Lorette. She was of more than middle age, of a hard, unhappy face, and a moaning, weary tone, that touched Lilly as the revealing of a sorrow deeper than her own. Lorette's trouble was indeed worse than Lilly's; for Lilly, grieved, was not yet the prey of either remorse or despair. She believed she had done right, and that her thorny way was the path of duty.

As Lilly was not like some of the gentle Sisters—a tale-bearer and a spy—Lorette's surcharged heart would sometimes in her presence break forth in sharp, terrible speech.

"Don't tell me of heretics!" she said, fiercely, one

day. "*I* am more surely lost than ever heretic that lived. They tell me there are some people who do not believe in a hell; but *I* do not believe in a heaven. For me every year has been a sharper pain—every day I grow harder. How can this hardness and bitterness pass by death into endless glory? I believe that after death will follow the increasing agony that shall slowly wear the spirit out, destroying its ethereal essence atom by atom until all be gone, and we be nothing as before we began to be. I have heard such things in France. This baby-land has only milk-and-sugar doctrines of immortal safety and happiness."

Lilly shrunk from her terrified.

"What is there dreadful in that?" demanded Lorette, sarcastically. "Is it dreadful that drops of water are invisibly taken up by the sun—that they are carried away in scorching heats and known no more—that air and water wear the particles of a rock until there *is not* what once there *was*, and that is all?"

"Ah, but nothing is lost," said Lilly, gently. "It does not cease to be. In the black cloud, in solution in the water, on the wings of the wind, though you may not find the lost particles of water and rock, yet they are there."

"And what difference," demanded Lorette, "is it

whether our aching, wretched souls are entirely annihilated, or are slowly gathered up into some mighty existence in which we lose our separate consciousness, our individuality? Ah, in France we reason more than here of these things, and we do not believe all the twaddle of purgatory and heaven. Don't think I am afraid to die. I wish I *could* die. Life is a curse, and death is the beginning of the end. Once out of this dull body, that wants so much and gets so little, the fiercer fires, whose kind we cannot tell, will begin the destruction that must some time have an end. Ah, yes," she drew a long, slow breath between her teeth like a serpent's hiss, "I wish I *could* die, and I sometimes say to myself, 'I *will* die.'"

Lorette turned away, and Lilly, trembling and shivering, reached her own little cell. She could not weep. A blind, cold horror came over her. Here was Lorette, a child of the convent and the nursling of the Church; Lorette, who had neither heretical breath nor bread; Lorette, the confidential messenger, the "beloved Sister," the good Catholic; Lorette, of whose salvation nuns and priests would proclaim absolute certainty, who might (who knows?) one day get into the calendar; and yet she had flung open to poor Lilly the door of her heart, and lo! all within was ravening and wickedness, and cursing, doubts and misbeliefs and dead men's bones. It was a new burden, and Lilly must bear it in secret, for she could not betray Lorette's confidence. We must pity this poor child, who until now had believed the convent infallibly the gate of heaven, and the vow of the order the passport to the skies. After some wretched days a solution of these difficulties occurred to her. She sought Lorette and inquired if she regretted her vows?

No, Lorette regretted nothing.

Was she weary of the convent and anxious to leave it?

No, Lorette would do as illy in the world as the caged bird would do in the woods. The convent was her home.

Did she reject the Romish faith?

Oh, no, she was a good Catholic.

Was she at all a heretic?

By no means. Lorette despised heretics. She was simply a wretched woman, with no hope in this world and none in the next.

How shall we think Lilly contrasted this statement of belief with her mother's fervent prayer?

Meanwhile, Sister Clement, as Annette, was at Mr. MacPherson's, and one day, while dusting the hall, she heard a carriage stop before the door. She looked out and saw Mr. Wynford leaping from a city hack, portmanteau in hand. Annette fled up stairs,

Priest Murphy—Cards—Whiskey Punch, etc.

Page 305.

and while Mrs. Anthon and Agnes were greeting their guest in the parlor, and sending for Mr. MacPherson to come and welcome him, and alas! break to him the news of Martin's flight, Annette, in hat and shawl, passed out the area door, asking the cook to tell the mistress that she was wild with the toothache and was going to the dentist. Annette did not wait this time to hang her present seeming on the attic wall in the House Without a Name, in order to visit Father Murphy as nun Clement; but she sped to the priest's house without delay. Mr. Wynford had returned with a brightened face, a step and mien that told success! This was news of importance.

In fact, in her excitement and headlong haste, winged by the words she had heard Mr. Wynford shout to his friends as he met them—"All right, all right!"—Sister Clement committed an indiscretion unprecedented in her exemplary life. She pulled the bell at Father Murphy's door, and then, too eager to wait to have it answered, which in that dwelling was always a work of time, probably hasty preparations for visitors having to be made, Sister Clement pushed open the door, crossed the hall and admitted herself. Ah! Father Murphy, the housekeeper (his aunt, you know), the housekeeper's nephew and the nephew's cousin were engaged in playing cards. Near at hand stood a steaming and mighty pitcher of hot whisky punch,* which perfumed the room with the odor of liquor, lemon and spice. This was flanked on one side by a high dish of ruddy apples, and on the other by a frosted silver basket of fruit-cake.

Oh goodly spectacle! Oh goodly Father! who knew how to take his portion in this life. Was this Father Murphy's notion of *otium cum dig.*, as the seniors have it?

Annette, abashed, let the door swing together between herself and the jolly group of card-players, and stood without, her head dropped, and groaning (between envy and fear) worse then ever Peri at the Paradisaic gate.

Father Murphy, seeing a furbelowed and gorgeous damsel of the maid-servant description thus appear and disappear at his door, graciously went out to her. Annette fell on her knees, exclaiming, "Forgive me, holy Father! the cause was urgent; my haste overcame my decorum!"

"Daughter Clement!" cried the priest.

"With weighty news to plead my excuse. See, I have not even been to the House to lay aside my

* "In Pittsburg, after the consecration of a Bishop, they had a great consecration dinner, with a long list of wines and ales, whiskies and brandies on the bill, and several of the Bishops got gloriously drunk—all this on the Sabbath."—*Pittsburg Christian Advocate*, quoted by Dr. Mattison.

dress. I trusted to being supposed by passers-by a penitent for confession."

"Rise up, daughter," said Father Murphy in his deepest tone, judging from the stir in his parlor that his co-revelers had made good their escape. "Rise up and report your business. We—hem-m—the Scripture bids us be all things to all men—and—a still higher authority—hem-m—the *Monita*—h-m-m—the Rules of our Order—*Visitentur crelso, et jucundis colloquiis ac facetiis*, etc.; which means, daughter Clement, Let one visit often and entertain one's guests in an agreeable manner, and with pleasantries, according to the humor and inclination of each one.* Rise and enter my parlor."

Clement's discoveries were soon unfolded, and as Father Murphy must have a clear record in this matter, the crafty sister was bidden to report to her Superior, put on her proper garb and go to the Convent of the Immaculate Heart to bear to Mother Robart the united wisdom of Father Murphy and Mother Ignatia. John Mora was sent with a message from "Annette" to Mrs. Anthon, stating that the trusty servant had met with an injury in crossing a street, and was taken to her aunt's in the country, John to be the bearer of her clothing and wages. As for John, he did not know but

* Secreta Monita, chap. vii., sec. 4.

there was a real Annette for whom Sister Clement was agent.

On the following morning, Mr. Wynford, on the plea of having new and important evidence for his case, obtained a new writ of *habeas corpus*, wherein Mother Robart, Superior of the Convent of the Immaculate Heart, was ordered to have the body of Estelle Wynford, or, as previously pleaded, Estelle Latrelli, at the City Hall on the following day at ten o'clock, there to do and receive what should then and there be considered concerning her.

And now Mr. Wynford was torn by conflicting emotions—joy at the prospect of recovering his daughter, and misery over the ingratitude and loss of his son—one moment weeping and groaning, the next taking courage. Richard was exultant at the thought of next day's triumph, and in his earnest, manly way was doing his best to comfort this father, who had grown suddenly old in his prime, and crying, like aged Jacob, "If I am bereaved of my children, I am bereaved." Mr. MacPherson feared some new priestly artifice. A new blow was, in fact, impending. Before the court next day appeared the gracious and stately Abbess of the Immaculate Heart in person, her very presence inspiring respect, and on her oath declared that the girl Estelle Latrelli having been legally committed to her keeping, she had in all good faith endeavored to fulfill her duties as guardian; that her ward had been wayward and rebellious, choosing evil and eschewing good, and despite all entreaties, gentle coercion and due vigilance, had made good her escape from the convent on the fifth day of March, and had gone none knew whither.

The Abbess explained that, though she watched with maternal solicitude over her pupils and nuns, yet they might get away from her if escape was their desire. Thank heaven, no such desire had ever been shown, save by one poor crazed nun and this unhappy Estelle! The Abbess with mild indignation asserted that her convent was a "home," and not a "jail;" its inmates were a "family," not "prisoners." Estelle was gone, and as her guardian she had sought her far and near. A detective swore that on the 6th of March he had been notified of this flight and requested to look for the girl. Two policemen swore that they had been on the watch. Father Murphy and four Sisters made a deposition, declaring that they knew of Estelle's departure, of the Abbess' efforts to recover her, and of the failure of said efforts. The Mother Superior further took oath that Estelle had left her, and she had no knowledge of her whereabouts. John Mora and Michael Shinn testified that, feed by Father Murphy to look for Mother Robart's ward, they had searched, and but yesterday had heard of a girl answering to her description, who, after a reckless life of several weeks in an alley (the name of which was given), had, with some like-minded companions, started for New Orleans. The matter was hotly prosecuted on both sides with witnesses, depositions, oaths, arguments, but in the midst of it the agonized father was carried insensible from the court-room. The holy Abbess of the Immaculate Heart of Mary sat calm and mild behind her veil during the whole scene. Time and money were freely but unavailingly spent by Richard and Mr. MacPherson in this case, while poor Mr. Wynford lay burnt with fever and with distracted brain, unable to defend his cause or carry it on, and wildly shrieking the names of his lost children.

CHAPTER VI.

THE GATES OF DEATH.

SINCE the private theatricals, when Madame Leplatte and one or two of her friends had been admitted to Mrs. Kemp's house, Adelaide had grown constantly more intimate with these actors. Even her mother began to be awake to her danger, on account of the frequent hints received that Adelaide's society was unworthy of her position. Now and then a friend suggested to Mr. Kemp that perchance his step-daughter might sacrifice the family respectability by making her début on the boards of the ——— Theatre. But remonstrance and entreaty came too late, and availed but little with the wayward girl.

"You liked them well enough when they were convenient to you. Now, why should I drop them when they are convenient to me?" demanded Adelaide, disrespectfully. "If the theatre is not proper, why have I always been taken to it? If actors and actresses are not proper people, why does the public encourage them by crowding to the play? If to be an actress is disgraceful, why are whole columns of newspapers given to praising them, and why are bouquets thrown on the stage by the dozen? If being an actress is not disgraceful, what are you talking so to me for?"

Thus Adelaide would retort on her friends.

If the family storm rose too high, she would say,

"Well, there! what is all this coil about? I'm sure I have nothing to do with them now. I got tired of that company a month ago."

But this household knew each other well enough not to believe bold assertions.

It is useless to linger over this portion of the family history. Adelaide was a good Catholic. She was an average specimen of the training of nuns and priests. What more was wanted? Her relatives felt a good deal more was wanted when the dénoûment came. Adelaide left home to spend a day and a night with a friend of her convent days in a distant part of the city. On the afternoon of the second day, while the family were seated at dinner, came a note from the wayward girl, containing a certificate of her marriage to Mons. Paul Luolli, and boldly demanding that her personal property should be sent to the hotel, where her family knew too well that she had often visited Madame Leplatte. A letter to Grace arrived at the same time, detailing the recent proceedings, stating that her friend where she was visiting, Madame Leplatte and two others had composed the wedding-party, and that they had gone to a town twenty miles away, and been duly married in the Romish church by a priest. She was now at the ——— Hotel, in a handsome suite of rooms, and would be pleased to receive her family at any time. This bold, dashing, careless letter was worthy of Adelaide Grant, and that is all we can say for it.

"I know the rascal!" cried Richard. "I traced him out long ago, but none of you would listen to my warnings. He is Madame Leplatte's own brother, but was introduced here as her husband on the occasion of that unhappy theatrical. What do you suppose he has married the girl for but her little fortune and the name of the family?"

"Oh, oh! here's a pretty thing!" groaned Mr. Kemp. "My step-daughter, Adelaide Grant, married to an actor! It will be in all the papers and on everybody's tongue, and how can I ever hold up my head again?"

"Well, ma'am," cried the angry Richard, "you see how much Father Murphy has done toward keeping your daughter right. Not that I blame him or think him responsible. Every mother should guard and guide her own children. But I complain of a religion that publicly offers to lift the responsibility off parental shoulders, and rest it—goodness knows where!"

"Stop, Rick, stop!" exclaimed Grace, who had run around the table to her step-mother, and was supporting her in her arms; for Mrs. Kemp, after gazing wildly for some seconds at her husband and Richard, and making inarticulate efforts to speak, had fallen back in her chair in hysterics that threatened to end in spasms.

Richard muttered something between his teeth, and called for the footman to assist him in carrying Mrs. Kemp up stairs, while Mr. Kemp, in his anger utterly regardless of his wife, whom he considered the primary cause of this misfortune, strode wrathfully up stairs, and bade Lucy collect every article that had ever belonged to Adelaide and send it to the address she had given.

"Don't leave a trace of her in the house!" he cried.

It was easy to say, "Do not leave a trace of her;" but were not her traces everywhere? The lively, pretty, saucy, agreeable girl could not so quickly be cast out. The house was filled with mourning, as if the destroying angel, who went sword in hand through Egypt, had been there. Lucy wept until she could hardly see to dress Grace's hair. Mrs. Kemp kept her bed and refused to be comforted. Mr.

Kemp was angry and Rick gloomy. The servants spoke in low tones and looked melancholy enough. Grace, forbidden by her father to visit Adelaide, went nowhere, and at her books, work, meals or music would inopportunely burst into tears and rush off to her room. Adelaide's departure had left a miserable void. The family happiness had been made shipwreck, because the parents had not been true to the trust reposed in them by God—because Adelaide had been instructed to deceive, and had never been trained to a sense of her own responsibility. She had had no "calling and election to make sure," for she was in the good ship of Romanism, which she was told celestial breezes would inevitably waft into the port of peace.

But, says one, these things happen in Protestant families. Very true; but it is because parents are unfaithful. "The Lord is not slack concerning his promises," and he has pledged himself to second the good efforts of parents for their children. If Protestant parents were but *faithful*, their children would not be traitors to themselves, like Adelaide, or proselytes to Rome, like Lilly.

Hearing of the trouble in her brother's house, Mrs. Schuyler, carefully supported on Hannah's arm, went to visit her mourning sister-in-law. Consumption had set its fatal seal on Mrs. Schuyler's hectic cheek and in her bright and sunken eyes. Richard met her at the door and aided her to reach Mrs. Kemp's chamber. The feeble woman, looking as if her days on earth were numbered and very few, bent over the bed, where, refusing all consolation, the unfaithful and heavily-punished mother lay. "I have come to weep with you, sister, for I too have lost a child; I have a child who living is dead to me."

"Ah," replied Mrs. Kemp, "but your trouble is not like mine. Your child, devoted to a holy life, abides in all happiness and honor, and her praise is on every one's lips, while not a tongue in the city but will tell of my child's wicked folly. What can I look forward to for my Adelaide but a roving, disappointed, unhappy life? How will she repent this step when repentance is too late!"

"Repentance unto God is never too late," said Mrs. Schuyler, dropping her head on her hands, "and unless a merciful God interpose, I do not see but my child is as surely lost as yours."

There was a silence for a few moments; both mothers were weeping. Mrs. Schuyler was the first to speak:

"Let us not brood over our trials in a hopeless spirit. How strongly comes to me the question, 'Wherefore should a living man complain, a man for the punishment of his sins?' For myself, I see that I am reaping what in my negligence I sowed. Let us rather turn ourselves unto the Lord, 'who has smitten and who can heal, who has wounded and alone shall bind us up.' I can tell you from my own experience that the Lord is good, and a stronghold in the day of trouble; he helpeth all who come to him; 'He will heal all our backslidings and love us freely.' Let us give the remnant of our lives to him, instead of to the world. You have longer to live than I—I may never come here again—I think I shall not—but you in the years before you can serve the Lord if you will. Seek him in his written Word."

She spoke in a low tone, and with many pauses from shortness of breath. Mrs. Kemp knew she was in hearty earnest, and also saw that she was a dying woman. She replied:

"I am glad, sister Schuyler, if you have found anything to make you happy. I'm sure you need it. I don't want anything of that kind, though. I've been a member of the True Church nearly twenty years, and I feel that my spiritual interests are in good hands. I only want one thing—I want to retrieve this disgrace of Adelaide's. I want to be sure she will never disgrace us by going on the stage. Oh, if I could only get her home again! Richard, *do* you think we could get her divorced from that man and bring her back?"

Richard was standing at the window with his back to the room, apparently looking out into the street from the small aperture between the curtain and casing. Mrs. Kemp kept her room darkened as an indication of the state of her feelings. Richard had listened to his aunt with strong emotion. His step-mother's words jarred harshly on his ear. He replied, shortly:

"I can't see, ma'am, as that would make the matter any better; and, besides, she is of age, and there is no pretext for such proceedings. Grace sent a note to-day to Father Murphy. I suppose she asked him to go and see Adelaide; and most likely you will have the light of his wisdom on the question, as soon as his reverence finds time to give it."

"Sister Kemp," said Mrs. Schuyler, "we ought both to have trained up our children for the Lord, and then we should not have been brought to suffer in them."

"I'm sure," said Mrs. Kemp, "that if I'd known my daughter was to act in this way, I would much rather have had her go in a convent; but she was so fond of life that I do not think I could have forced her to take the veil, and I hoped she would gain a brilliant position in society. Now all is lost, and nothing can do us any good."

"'Who shall show us any good? Lord, lift thou up the light of thy countenance upon us,'" said Mrs.

Schuyler, softly: but her words were "as water on the flinty rock."

After a short stay, Richard aided her home. She dropped back in her chair exhausted, and he stood fanning her. When she became able to speak, she said,

"Richard, you are like a son to me."

Then taking up a small Bible from a table near, she pointed out a verse. Richard read:

"Be watchful and strengthen the things which remain, that are ready to die."

"That," said Mrs. Schuyler, "is all that is left for me to do, Richard. I have thought you had some interest in religion. Is that ready to die?"

"I am almost afraid so," said Richard, soberly.

Mrs. Schuyler took his strong hand in her thin white fingers.

"Richard, won't you seek the Lord until you find him?"

Richard looked down in earnest silence. It was a solemn question, and he was weighing well his answer. A promise to himself and this dying woman might never be taken back.

"Yes, aunt, I will;" he said it with all his heart.

Father Murphy visited Adelaide and made his report. Her husband and his sister were good Catholics, and willing to be better ones. They all had promised obedience to the Church and attention to their religious duties. The match for Adelaide was a very bad one, and the Father was greatly disappointed. He had rather have had Adelaide and her little fortune in the nunnery than thus thrown away. He had hoped Grace and Adelaide would marry rich Protestants, who would pledge themselves to the true faith.

Grace was now much more of an object to Father Murphy than she had been. Mr. Kemp, instead of exhausting his whole income each year by extravagant living, as had once been the case, was now, though living with equal display, laying up a fortune from successful speculations. Grace, as one of his two children, might look to inheriting half the estate.

Mrs. Kemp visited Adelaide, was partially reconciled, and extorted from her a promise that she would never appear as an actress in the city where they resided; and if she took such character in other places, it should be under an assumed name. The mother gained this pledge by declaring that, if Adelaide crossed her in this matter, she should not receive a penny of her mother's private estate.

Lucy, with many tears and protestations, left Grace's service "to go wait on poor Miss Adelaide." Grace took Ann Mora, who was now quite skillful, as her maid.

Mr. Kemp would not permit Grace to visit Adelaide, nor admit Adelaide to his house; and Grace mourned sincerely for the step-sister she had so truly loved and so entirely lost. After some months of this total separation, chance threw these two together. Grace, going one day to confession, waited in Father Murphy's parlor until some penitent, who was already occupying the priest, should retire. Grace was bending over a vase of tuberoses placed upon a table, when the rustle of a dress and the gentle closing of a door told that some one had come from the confessional. She felt that "some one" stop close beside her—looked up—it was Adelaide.

She clasped her in her arms, forgetting and forgiving all the neglect and treachery of the past, remembering only the joy of meeting. In a moment, Father Murphy, waiting within, was forgotten, and the two girls in low, eager tones were exchanging questions, answers, protestations and regrets. Father Murphy, guessing how affairs stood, came into the room and flung himself into his great chair, benevolently prepared to allow the long-separated friends to converse, if they chose, in his presence. "Come and see me," said Adelaide.

"I cannot. Father won't allow it. Go to his office and make friends with him, and then perhaps I can come," said Grace.

"Nonsense!" said Adelaide; "you are of age; come when he don't know it."

"No," said Grace, firmly. "There is where you went wrong, Adelaide."

"Daughter Grace, you are right," said Father Murphy.

Adelaide pouted.

"Oh, Adelaide, how could you do so wrong?" asked Grace.

"Don't talk about that," said Adelaide, daringly. "I have confessed all and done penance, and now I am all right. I have had absolution, and it is just the same as if I had never done wrong. *Absolvo Te*, you know;" and she looked gayly toward the listening priest.

"Daughter Adelaide," cried Father Murphy, sternly, "you have little of the true spirit of our religion. Where is the hearty penitence you professed? I am seriously angry at these light words."

"Then I will confess them the next time I come Good-bye, Father!" and Adelaide tripped away, leaving Grace weeping and the confessor astounded. In fact, Adelaide's husband and Madame Leplatte were in heart infidels, and were teaching her their pernicious views.

And now the autumn had come once more, and over the two opposite mansions where our story has lingered hung the shadow of death. Battling bodily for life with unexpected tenacity, and in spirit longing unutterably to be gone to her Father's house, Mrs. Schuyler had worn out the lengthening weeks, and now the end was nigh. Again and again had she sent for her child. Hannah, Richard, even Mr. Kemp, had gone to the convent and pleaded for the daughter's presence at the dying bed. They were heard in silence or obtained promises which were never fulfilled. Father Murphy was appealed to, and referred petitioners to the Abbess. The Abbess, besieged, referred them to the priest. It was an endless round game of diplomacy. Meanwhile, in fevered sleep, the dying mother moaned her Lilly's name. Mrs. Anthon and Agnes wept over her. Tears of pity and wrath shone in Richard's eyes. Hannah lamented the "hardness of the nuns and priests" unceasingly. It was a sorrowful deathbed, yet this long-afflicted woman was prepared to die, ready to depart and be with Christ.

Over the way the death-angel also hovered, and over an unwilling victim. Fever had seized upon Grace, was scorching in her veins, burning in her eyes and filling her head with fearful visions. She cried out that she could not die. In vain they tried to comfort her. She read in despairing faces that they felt her doom was sealed. In vain Father

Murphy and the Sisters told her all was right—the Church would secure her eternal happiness. She had read enough of that hidden Bible to know that more than the Church is needed to make a man just with God. "I am not safe, I am not safe!" she would cry. "Save me, save me! let me get well, and I will attend to nothing but the salvation of my soul!" Sister Clement had come as nurse. She suggested prayers unnumbered, vows, visits to convents and churches, gifts—all that Rome offers to buy the salvation of the soul; but still her patient cried, "Save me! I cannot die! These things are not helping me. I feel that all is wrong!"

"There has been some mischief at work stirring her up so," said the priest to the nun. "Daughter Grace, cease to doubt the holy Church; cast aside your fears; resign your heresies and drop yourself into the arms of the Church as a child to its mother's breast. The Church will carry you to safety."

"I cannot, I cannot!" cried Grace. "Tell me something higher and better. I have tried the Church and the Virgin and the Saints, and they are not helping me. Tell me something quickly, or I am lost!"

In one of the lulls, when Ann Mora could speak to her young mistress unheard, she whispered, "Dear miss, let all go and catch hold of this: 'The blood of Jesus Christ cleanseth from all sin.' Oh, if you only knew the good it's done *me*, miss."

"Say it again," said Grace; and Ann said it again and again.

"Call for Richard," said Grace. Richard was sometimes by his dying sister and sometimes by his dying aunt.

"Rick," gasped Grace, "tell me something that will help me."

"Believe on the Lord Jesus Christ and thou shalt be saved," said Richard. "Let go all else and cleave to that. 'Look unto me and be saved,' says your Saviour. Look unto him alone."

"Bring me Agnes, bring me Agnes! She knows the way!" cried Grace; and Richard brought Agnes from Mrs. Schuyler to his sister. But now arose a tumult in the sick room. The Sister and the Father declared that, if the heretic remained, themselves would depart and doom the dying girl to perdition. This distracted Grace so that she could hardly heed anything. Her disease increased each moment. "I will go," said Agnes, bending over to kiss her friend, and whispering, "Grace, look only to Jesus; he taketh away all your sin."

Fearing that the patient might seem to die a Protestant, Father Murphy sustained and urged the physician's giving a powerful opiate. It was the last resort; it might help her; or, too feeble to bear it, Grace might in her stupor pass out of life—better to die thus unconscious than a Protestant.

Agnes Anthon, overcome by the heartrending scenes she had witnessed, was conveyed home by her mother.

All night the watchers' tapers burned in the opposite windows. Richard and Hannah waited by Mrs. Schuyler, the hired nurse sleeping quite exhausted, and Clement, Ann Mora and Mrs. Kemp tarried at Grace's bedside.

When the stars were setting, the warfare of Mrs. Schuyler was over, and earth, life and trouble dropped together like heavy shackles from her ascending spirit. She had entered into glory, and had attained at last to the full realization of that blessed truth, that "the sufferings of this present time are not worthy to be compared with the glory that shall be revealed in us."

Meanwhile, on slow pulsations, Grace was drifting nearer and nearer "the iron gates of Time" that stood ajar before her. Cast through them by some heavy swell, into what night and shadows should Grace Kemp be gone?

PART THIRD.

SHOWING HOW ROME'S CHILDREN REBELLED AGAINST HER.

CHAPTER I.

GRACE'S RECOVERY, AND THE RESULTS OF HER SICKNESS.

GRACE came slowly back to life. After the first days of utter weakness, when, the fever having burnt itself away, she lay barely conscious of existence and not realizing her recent danger and escape, came solemn thoughts of her hours of terror and remorse, and of the vows she had paid in the day of her distress. She had been fully shown her unfitness for the death that must surely overtake her; and not like some, who with the release from immediate danger throw aside all their anxieties, Grace saw in the prolonging of her days space for repentance.

While these thoughts were occupying her mind, the mind of Father Murphy was also busy devising how he should secure the girl for Romanism. He feared that the empire of Romish superstition was in her heart doomed to its fall. He thought it possible that Grace might have entirely forgotten those hours and fears; but if she recalled them, she must be convinced that they were the offspring of a brain wandering from disease.

Grace did recall them. Her religious feelings, if less wild, were yet as earnest as in the moments of immediate peril. Agnes was kept from her; her mother could only say, "Talk to the priest," and in Richard she had not learned to expect a religious guide. To Father Murphy, her spiritual director from her childhood, she naturally turned.

"I am going to lead a different life, Father. I want to be prepared for death, and what to do exactly I do not know."

"That the Church—the only guide in such cases—will show you, daughter."

"But, Father, the directions and consolations of the Church did not do me any good just when I wanted them most," replied Grace.

"They *did* do you good, but your diseased mind prevented your recognizing it. Had you died, now—thanks to the offices of the Church—you would be in Paradise."

"In that case," said Grace, "if I am perfectly safe, there can be no more for me to do."

"You are safe," replied the priest, "yet there is always something more for us to do. We can rise higher and higher in the religious life. Do you feel ready to accept the fact of your safety, and there rest?"

"No, I do not," said Grace, "for I cannot believe what you call that fact. I was indeed very ill and greatly terrified; but I was fully conscious, and I saw plainly that I was in the utmost danger. Eternal loss was before me."

"Then," said the priest, "you must have some heavy burden of heresy or crime unconfessed upon your soul."

"No, I have not," said Grace. "I have always been faithful at confession. I felt that I was apart from God, unholy and without any fitness to come into his presence."

"You had the fitness of a member of the only True Church."

"That was not enough for me," said Grace. "I needed something more. Indeed, Father, the only thing that gave me any comfort—and that I could not properly seize—was that some one whispered in my ear: 'The blood of Jesus Christ, his Son, cleanseth us from all sin.'"

"Very true; it does cleanse us from all sin; but it must be properly applied. It must come to us through the proper channels—the regular succession of the priesthood; and must be made effectual by penitence, prayer, satisfaction, penance and priestly absolution."

"Ah, but suppose the wretched sinner at the point

of death could not have all these things—he must be cleansed by the blood of Jesus at once or die unforgiven—what then?"

"You suppose a case which could only happen to a heretic," replied the priest, "and such an one has no right to expect anything but destruction."

"Well, Father," said Grace, "I feel in my own soul that I am not prepared to meet my God. Did I think I must die to-morrow in just the state I am in to-day, I should be in convulsions of terror."

"You would have extreme unction and the prayers for the dying."

"You remember I did have them, and they did not do me any good," replied Grace. "My Catechism tells me, 'Extreme unction is a sacrament that gives grace to die well,' but it did not give me that grace."

"That was because you were to get well," said the artful priest. "We only get dying grace when we are absolutely in a dying state."

"I am going to be *sure* now," said Grace. "If there is such a thing as surety and knowledge of God's love, I mean to seek until I find it. I shall not live with the sword of destruction hanging over my head any more. I do not want to know that death by some sudden onslaught can kill me soul and body. I want to make sure of my soul, as I have never been sure of it."

"You must be a dreadful sinner," said Father Murphy.

"I am," said Grace, simply. "You have no idea how wicked I seem to myself."

"Worse than Adelaide?" asked the wily confessor.

"Oh, incomparably worse; because Adelaide never had, and quenched, such serious reflections and spiritual longings as I have. Now, Father, what must I do? Or is there nothing I can do?"

"Oh yes; you must do a great deal, and the Church will do the rest. You had better withdraw yourself entirely from the world, and devote yourself to Acts of Religion for the present, until you are so fully nurtured and instructed in the true faith that doubts and fears shall never come to you again. Of course you know that if you are to find peace and safety, you are to find it in the Holy Catholic Church, and in none other. As you are now too weak to *do* much, you can listen to the prayers and readings of your nurse, who is a pious Sister, and can meditate on the 'Seven Works of Charity' and on the 'Four Cardinal Virtues.'"

"And what shall Sister Clement read to me?" asked Grace, for the nun was for once without any disguise or alias.

"'Flowers of Mary' will be soothing to your

mind; so will the 'Life of Blessed Mary Ann of Jesus,' 'Life of the Blessed Virgin,' and 'The Month of Mary.' Something calming and elevating is what you want now."

"I want something to *teach* me," groaned Grace, hiding her face on her pillow.

If the "Purgatorian Consoler" had then been published, very likely the reverend Father might have recommended that.

While Sister Clement tediously read the books which the priest had indicated, or at times the prayer-book and the "Spiritual Exercises," the earnest craving after truth grew in Grace's soul day by day. The memory of her terrors was abiding. Hers was no excited, frantic truth-seeking. It was an earnest, steady reaching to the light. The Spirit of God was at work in her, and all the false soothing of her religion would not lull her into indifference. As her health returned, and she regained her usual strength, so that Sister Clement need no longer hold her position as nurse, and as Father Murphy saw that his disciple had no mind to return to the follies of the life she had been living, and to leave the great question of her salvation yet unsettled, he proposed that she should go to the Convent of the Immaculate Heart of Mary, and there remain until her mind regained its accustomed tone. We suppose the excellent Father judged that, if it were possible for conviction of sin and desire after holiness to be quenched, convent life was the most effectual means of doing it.

To this plan Grace readily assented, for she was in earnest after salvation, and would take any means to obtain it. If her priest recommended the solitude and gravity of a cloister life for a time, that she would accept.

Mr. Kemp thought his daughter feeble in health, and that retirement would be beneficial to her, and Mrs. Kemp, since losing Adelaide, had lost her zest for the gayeties she had loved, and experienced some mortification in meeting her fashionable friends. She was glad that Grace would not at once demand a renewal of last winter's amusements; and besides, she had deemed it proper to put on mourning for Mrs. Schuyler, and that would also be a hindrance.

Richard remonstrated, but no one heeded him. Richard was not living at home now. He was in the late residence of Mrs. Schuyler. Mrs. Schuyler had left Richard her sole heir, providing that, if Lilly left the convent and returned to Protestantism, the house, its furnishing and one-half the remainder of the property should be hers. One clause in the will earnestly prayed Richard to keep the home in its present state, and to comply with this request the young man took up his abode there, served by the old family servants who had for years lived with his aunt, Hannah only not remaining. Her occupation was now gone, and she departed, having received a sum left her by her mistress sufficient to enable her to set up housekeeping in two rooms with an aged aunt, and also having received Mrs. Schuyler's sewing machine, by which she knew well how to earn her daily bread.

From Lilly, the fact of her mother's increasing illness, and at last of her death, had been carefully concealed. She was assured that her mother had recovered from her excitement and distress of mind, and was living very comfortably in her home, in improving health.

The young nun was permitted to see none of her relatives and none of her former acquaintances. She was told she must be fully weaned from the world wherein she had lived, that she must be *dead* to it, and that to bring about this happy result she must see and hear nothing from outside life until such sights and sounds could find her utterly unmoved. In this policy Grace was carefully instructed when she was recommended to find in the convent a refuge from the beseechings of the Spirit of God. But Grace was of very different stuff from Lilly, and with her different arguments were needed.

"You must by no means give Lilly information

of her mother's death," said the Abbess. "The dear child has an aggravated form of heart disease, and the news, however carefully told, would kill her."

"But how shall I answer if she asks me?" said Grace.

"She has been forbidden to ask you any questions."

"But, Mother, I should think the torture of anxiety and suspense would be worse to her than any certainty."

"Daughter 'Mary Anna' has learned that obedience is a pleasure and not a torture," replied the Abbess.

Grace doubted if obedience were the pleasure it was suggested to be, when she saw Lilly's large, mournful eyes following her at times with such a look of anguished questioning and entreaty. She would return the look only by a glance of love, melting into tears. The two cousins were kept much apart. Grace was not a "religious." She was not a suitable companion for the younger nuns. She must find her society in the Abbess and older Sisters, who could instruct her. Lilly was not a teaching Sister, nor a lay Sister, and was therefore kept apart from the pupils and from the work of the outer world. Grace was neither a pupil nor a Sister, but had come to find spiritual instruction, and she also was kept apart from the school. The two led very secluded and also unhappy lives.

Lorette, the French nun, frequently sought Grace when she might converse with her alone.

"What brought you to a convent?" she asked.

"I wish to be better."

"And you came to a convent to grow better!" cried Lorette, with a scornful laugh.

"Yes. That is, to give my undisturbed attention to religious things."

"What," replied Lorette, "should interest a handsome young girl like yourself in religion?"

"Because," answered Grace, "life must inevitably end in death, and I wish to learn to die well."

"Extreme unction will give you that grace," said Lorette, sneeringly.

"A changed heart more likely," said Grace.

"Eh!" cried Lorette, "that is what the Huguenots and the Paris Protestants are always prating about. *We* don't deal in such things. I'm afraid you are not a good Catholic."

"Oh yes, I am," returned Grace, earnestly. "I am sure I am."

"Good Catholics do not worry themselves about dying. Come, I will tell you how to do it. Shut your eyes and make the leap in the dark, just as if you were jumping from yon roof of the convent. It is sure destruction any how."

Grace shuddered and drew back:

"You would not talk so if you had ever been as near dying as I have."

"And you would not talk so if you had grown as sick of living as I have. To go back to the roof, I'm sure it would be easier to make up one's mind, set one's teeth and jump off, than to wait in horror for some one to push you over."

"Ah, but the *pushing* one could not help. To voluntarily take such a leap to certain death would be a great sin."

"And when one's sins are piled as high as a mountain, what harm to add a little more, a *coup de grace*, eh? But if you are getting on that discussion of right and wrong, excuse me, for I am weary of it. We cannot measure that, even in France, where we discuss everything."

"Familiarity breeds contempt," is an adage almost too common to quote. It proved true in Grace's case with the convent. The gloss of that life wore off, and she saw the children of the convent as trivial, as fickle, as irreligious in absolute fact, as the children of the world; and more aggravating, as they were more narrow-minded and capable of more petty meannesses.

Grace wondered if Lilly saw things as she did, and if being bound for life to these people and this home were wearing her to a shadow. But Lilly was neither keen-sighted nor censorious. If a little condemnatory thought crept into her mind, she banished it as unjust and inconsistent with her vow.

When Grace unfolded her thoughts about the Sisters to the Abbess her aunt, Mother Robart smiled.

"My daughters are not what they should be, I admit," she replied, "but *that* you must attribute to their own infirmity, and not to the rule under which they live. You see in Sister Mary Anna a true Sister. I trust my daughters can find nothing amiss in *me*. If you read the Lives of the Saints, the Lives of Saint Bridget, Saint Agnes of Rome, Saint Zita, Saint Margaret of Cortona, Saints Elizabeth, Theresa and Angela, you will find those whose example you should emulate, and whose holiness there is every hope that as a Sister you would approach."

Indeed continually before Grace was now set a convent life as her highest aim. Her priest, the Abbess, Lilly, when allowed to speak to her, the elder nuns, all by sly suggestions urged this consecration upon her.

"You may do better than the rest; you may reform the convent. You are stronger-minded than

Mary Anna, and you could have more positive influence," said Father Douay.

Ann Mora had been permitted to go home until Grace should need her services again. She came up to the convent in great trouble. Her mother was very ill, and she wanted Miss Grace to come and see her, and one of the Sisters. Grace had frequently been sent out with one of the nuns to visit the sick. It was one of the means they were using to beguile her. She now went with Saint Cecelia to the bedside of Mrs. Mora. The woman was evidently very ill. The sight of a person so near death revived in Grace's mind all the terrors she had herself experienced.

"Are you afraid to die, Mrs. Mora?" she asked.

"I *was*," said the woman, "but I ain't now."

"Have you confessed yourself?" asked Saint Cecelia.

"I have that, and got absolution."

"Of course, then, she need have no fears, and she has always lived a good Catholic," said Saint Cecelia.

There was one very good thing about Saint Cecelia. She had an absolute passion for nursing the sick. She was not less eminent as a nurse than as a scribe. She delighted in "sick-room cookery," and in compounding pills and teas, as thoroughly as any wise old New England grandmother. She was given far more in her visitations to healing the outer than the inner being, which was fortunate; for she was a good nurse for the body, but when it came to the mind, there poor Cecelia was the most miserable of spiritual quacks. She now felt sure that Mrs. Mora needed a drink and a poultice of true convent make, and going to the stove in the small place used as a kitchen, she was soon in her element, cooking and stirring, and, if the truth must be told, filling the room with vile odors. But this drink and this poultice must be administered hot, therefore must be made then and there.

While Saint Cecelia was thus busied at the stove, Grace sat by Mrs. Mora. "It is not so much confession and the priest that comforts me and makes me content to die," she said in a faint voice; "but Pat and Ann have a deal to tell me that cheers me amazing. There's Ann's old verse about the cleansing blood; *that* is food and medicine. Then there's another about 'Look unto me and be saved,' and there's 'Lord, remember me for good,' a prayer which it does me more good to say than all the 'Aves' in the book. You see, miss, I'm a poor, ignorant woman, and belike not wise enough to feel the priest's talk. And Pat, he bids me never tell the priest of his sayings, or I'd get him into the cathedral dungeons, he says, which, you know, miss, I could never do for my boy. Ann says, You can trust Miss Grace, says

Ann. Says I to me boy, Pat, tell me no more that I may not tell the priest; but Pat tells on, and I've no heart to stop him; it does me such a power of good."

"Well, if it comforts you, believe it," said Grace. "When I was sick I could not find anything to do that would help me." She spoke sadly.

"And it is not *doing* that is our part, Pat says. He's been to a Mission of some sort, evenings, miss. Don't tell of him, dear. His father thinks he's roystering round town, but he's at his learning meanwhiles, and he knows how to talk better than a priest of them all. 'Mother,' says he, 'it isn't that you can do anything. Quit your hold, mother, and just drop right into them strong arms as is held out to you.'"

"The priest told me that—to fall into the arms of the Church; but I must have been very wicked, for it did not help me," said Grace.

"We're all wicked, dear; but it was not falling into the arms of the Church Pat meant. His riverence told me that, and never a thought of comfort did it do me. Says Pat, 'It is not the Church, mother; just drop into the strong arms of the Son of Mary himself.' It's my believing, miss, that we don't hear half enough about him. How could we? there's such a host of saints for us to learn of." She sighed as if oppressed by her knowledge of the holy saints, and here Sister Cecelia came in with her tea and poultice.

Grace had gone there to do good, but it seemed to her as if she carried away more good than she brought. That, however, is a common experience.

Grace, in the position of a spiritual patient at the Convent of the Immaculate Heart of Mary, was not improving in a manner to suit her physicians, Fathers Murphy and Douay. They considered that a change of treatment might be efficacious. If the Convent of the Immaculate Heart of Mary was the theological apothecary shop, the House Without a Name was the theological water-cure, and thither it was considered expedient to send her.

The conversation with Mrs. Mora, giving her a little light, only increased her agitation. Where were those strong, ready arms? Of *what* should she loose her hold, to cast herself into them? Would she assuredly be held in a rescuing clasp?

Harassed by these doubts, the proposal to send her to another convent was welcome. She was sick of the shallowness and falseness of her present abode. She firmly believed that somewhere in the Catholic Church she should find the truth she sought; and this new convent, "small and of strict rule," might show it to her.

She requested permission to go once more with Saint Cecelia to visit Mrs. Mora; and the Abbess, seeing nothing singular in this, as Ann had been Grace's maid and very faithful during her young mistress' illness, gave the required permission.

Saint Cecelia had no poultices to attend to, and kept close to the young lady and the patient.

"And you feel happy and ready to die?" queried Grace.

"All good Catholics do," said Saint Cecelia, rebukingly.

"I'm trusting in the Lord Jesus," said Mrs. Mora.

"I hope you are not forgetting your patron saint," said the nun.

"I try to forget nothing," said Mrs. Mora; "but my mind is weak like, and I'm only able to hold fast a little that's good."

"You must have Ann read to you in the prayer-book," said Grace.

"She does," replied Mrs. Mora, "and some of it I take to wonderful."

"You ought to 'take to' all of it," said Saint Cecelia.

"There's some of it I don't understand," submitted the invalid.

"Oh well, there's the misfortune of being ignorant," said the Saint.

"Ann reads me the Act of Contrition from her Catechism, and I understand that," said Mrs. Mora.

"I think you are doing very well," said the nun, presently.

Mrs. Mora was weak and dropped into little dozes even as she was talking. She came out of one just then, and muttered,

"It's the blood—the blood, miss, as does it all."

"She's wandering," whispered the nun, and signified that the visit had better end. They left the room, and then the nun returned for a moment, leaving Grace in the hall. The door of a room opposite to where Grace stood was open. A girl, evidently in a consumption, lay on a bed, and near her, reading from a Bible, was a well-dressed young woman whose back was turned toward the door. As Saint Cecelia came out of Mrs. Mora's, the reader had probably come to the end of her chapter, for her voice was still.

"That is one of those foolish Bible-women," said Saint Cecelia, going down stairs. "Just as if common people could understand the Bible!"

Yet Grace thought it a sweet scene, and she had observed that the face of the consumptive was as earnest and peaceful as an angel's might be.

* * * * * * *

Sister Clement conducted Grace to the House

Without a Name. They went, as usual, by a crooked and indirect route. Said the nun to her young charge,

"You will find this House very different from yonder convent. We are not the Sisters of ease and luxury. But with us life is short and eternity long. Religion is our business, and we seek not to please ourselves, but to save our souls in the Church's way. We are the workers of the Church, and we are few in number, quiet and stern in our lives. It has been *my* lot to live—in my business as nurse—in many wealthy homes. I have not reaped the full benefit of our Institution; but I have done my duty, and look to my reward."

Thus Saint Clement magnified herself.

The nun unlocked the side gate and with Grace entered the rear of the building. The kitchen was darkened by the high fences of Michael Shinn's stables; but it was clean, and in the open oven loaves of bread were slowly baking, while a kettle of vegetables simmered on the top of the stove. No cook was visible. They passed into the refectory, which was silent as a grave. There was the long table with its delf ware and no cloth, and with stools placed far apart on either side. The blinds were closed, and the little light in the room came through the upper part of the windows. The place was chilly and gloomy.

"They are in the chapel," said Sister Clement, and led Grace through the bare hall to the oratory.

Here were plain seats, two shrines, an altar covered with an embroidered cloth, bouquets of wax flowers under a picture of "Our Lady of Sorrows," and on the bare floor five or six nuns kneeling, praying in rapid undertones.

The gloom, the severe plainness of the whitewashed walls, the bare floors and benches, the altar with its unlighted tapers, the ghastly crucifix of ebony with a figure in carved ivory and gilded rays glaring behind the figure, the agonized face of the pictured Virgin gleaming down from its black frame, the shrine at the left, where Ignatia's patron saint, Mary Magdalene, was painted as kneeling with disheveled hair and box of ointment broken in her hand,—all these things, together with the bowed, swaying, black-robed figures of the nuns, and the wailing sound of their subdued voices in prayer, touched Grace's heart. Like Clement, she dipped her hand in the basin of holy water at the chapel door, crossed herself, and kneeling in the narrow aisle, joined her voice to the others in prayer.

The devotions of the hour over, Ignatia rose, and without a glance at any one, left the chapel, the Sisters following in their order, the cooks going toward the kitchen, the other nuns (only four of them now) entering what we may call, despite its poverty, their parlor. Clement and Grace closed this little procession, and once in the parlor, handed Mother Ignatia a sealed note from the Abbess Robart. When Mother Ignatia had read it,

"This is the young Sister," said Clement.

"Beloved daughter, you are welcome," said the Superior, with something of a wistful look at her new charge.

She then exchanged a few words apart with Clement. As they were speaking the clock struck twelve. The nuns all rose and with much seriousness repeated, "Blessed be the hours in which our Lord was born and crucified for us." They then went silently into the refectory, Clement taking the place of honor next the Mother, and Grace, as the last comer, being placed at the foot of the table. All remained standing while Ignatia prayed: "Bless us, O Lord, and these thy gifts which we are about to receive from thy bounty, through Christ our Lord;" and then all joined in low tones, "Hail, Mary, full of grace, the Lord is with thee. Blessed art thou among women, and blessed is the fruit of thy womb, Jesus. Holy Mary! Mother of God! pray for us sinners, now and at the hour of our death."

They now seated themselves to eat. Grace found the bare table and coarse plate repulsive, the high stool most uncomfortable; and for one who had fared sumptuously every day the plain vegetables boiled with salt meat, and the brown bread with its modicum of butter, were exceedingly distasteful. For the annoyance she experienced at these things she took herself seriously to task.

"How can I repine at such trifles when my soul is in jeopardy every hour? How can I consider these things too mean for me, when I know I am undeserving of a moment's existence?"

No one spoke during the meal. When it was ended they bent their heads, and Ignatia said,

"We give thee thanks, O Almighty God, for all thy benefits, who livest and reignest, world without end;" and all the nuns added, in a low chorus, "O most Holy Virgin, who hast had the happiness of being the Mother of God, be a mother to me. Pray for me, now and at the hour of my death!" They then returned to the parlor, and took their work—endless embroidery—from a box, and bending over it, they whispered, "O my God! I offer to thee this work! Vouchsafe to give it thy blessing! O my good angel! protect me! enlighten me! guard all my actions!"

"Now, my daughter, follow me," said Ignatia to Grace, and led her from the parlor to the upper part of the house, to a narrow room—her own apartment.

The furniture was of pine painted white, and consisted of a low, narrow bed, a chair, a table with a missal and a crucifix, and a small shelf against the wall, by the side of which hung a metal basin foi toilette purposes, fastened by a chain. Ignatia sat down on the foot of the bed, gave Grace the chair, and gazed long and sadly at her. The fire within had burnt away Ignatia's flesh and the healthful color from her cheeks. Her hair lay prematurely whitened on her furrowed brow. Her eyes were sunken, and told the piteous, simple, old-time tale—"They lifted up their voice and wept until they had no more power to weep." Ah, that was no good gray head whitened with the almond blossoming of age, but a head bleached like dry bones by the burning heats and tempests of life. Before her was Grace, cast after the fairest model of girlhood, a favorite child of luxury, with small white hands and dainty skin, her silken chestnut hair bound closely about her well-shaped head, her figure elastic and healthful, her dress bespeaking wealth and refined taste, all marking her as coming from a far softer sphere than this. Amid the bareness and the meanness of these surroundings, she was like some fair, tropic blossom set within a Greenlander's poor dwelling.

"Child, what brought you here?" asked Ignatia, half impatiently.

"Because I think my soul of greater worth than anything else, and I want it to be safe."

"*You* can never have done anything to jeopardize your soul," said Ignatia, wonderingly.

"I cannot trust to any such idea as that," said Grace. "I have been near dying, and found myself unready for the change."

"But after your home—after the convent where you have been, can you endure this hard life with us?"

"It is hard," said Grace, "but it is earnest, and I am in earnest. It seemed to me at dinner that everything was poor and dreary, and I thought how worldly I was to care for such things. I wish, Mother, you could tell me what to do. I hear that you have left the world and devoted your property to establishing this House, and that for many years you have asked nothing for yourself, but serve yourself with the poorest, devote your life to the greatest rigors and take upon you every hard burden. You must have found peace in this life or you would not pursue it so long. They tell me you are a very holy woman. Teach me, Mother, for I want to be holy."

"A holy woman! a woman that has found peace!" cried Ignatia, striking her breast. "Oh, child, how little they know me! I am only a woman who cannot deceive you. I am not holy, for still the old corruption cleaves to me, and has eaten so deep into my soul that I have found nothing to take it away. The past — the fearful, bitter past—clings to me. There is blood on my soul. I have trampled all the law under my feet. So vile am I that all these years of penance and good works have lifted me nothing nearer heaven. Girl, do you, with your fair face and innocent soul, come to *me* to learn the way of *peace?* The way of peace I seek with bitter groans and tears, and find it not, because—" and she lifted up the wail of the "Confiteor"—"'I have sinned exceedingly, through my fault—through my fault—through my most grevious fault.'"

And Grace, taking up the words, added, "Wherefore, I do beseech the blessed Mary, ever Virgin, blessed Michael the Archangel, blessed John the Baptist, the holy apostles Peter and Paul, and all the saints, to pray to the Lord, our God, for me!"

"Oh, child!" cried Ignatia, "a million of times, surely, must I have entreated all those holy ones to aid me. Either they have not heard or my sins are far beyond their helping; and still I must pray on, for our Church affords us no other way."

"And there can be no other," said Grace, with a thought of Mrs. Mora.

"Other? No: thank God, amid all my crimes, I have not added the last and worst—I have never been a heretic."

"And, Mother, as I am a seeker after peace with God, do you commend to me this way of practicing austerities and good works to obtain it?"

"Yes, my daughter, seek thus and you will find. Your sins are of a dye less deep than mine. Pursue this way you find us in, and you will arrive at a blessed destiny."

Together they returned to the parlor. Grace took some work. Ignatia opened "Raccolta," a collection of indulgenced prayers, and read until tea-time. After tea, which was much the same as dinner, and was preceded by attending vespers in the oratory, Magdalena read the "Glories of Joseph" until eight, when all recited six prayers in the chapel and retired to their cells. There were to be other prayers at midnight and at daybreak.

"Child," said Ignatia to Grace, "if you would serve your God in all humility, leave off to-morrow these trappings that only minister to your vanity;" pointing to the girl's collar and cuffs and a set of jet and pearl jewelry. Grace, anxious to do her duty, obeyed, but felt awkward and half-dressed and untidy, involuntarily wasting more thoughts on her appearance than if she had been suitably dressed.

Thus the days passed in fulfilling the ritual of the convent and in reading of books of devotion "to Mary," "to Joseph," "to the Sacred Heart," etc.

It is natural to the human heart to desire to save itself, and to cherish the idea of getting into heaven by good works. Grace fell readily into this delusive hope. The earnest belief of those about her and their fanatical austerities attracted her imagination. She thought the nuns at the Immaculate Heart were playing at religion, but in this House Without a Name they were truly living it. She became blindly infatuated. Ignatia looked upon her as a saint. The Sisters, feeling less jealousy of one so far different than they did of each other, petted her. Father Douay assured her she was exactly right, and Father Murphy, secretly considering that if Grace and her prospective inheritance came into this "House," its bounds might be enlarged, and it might become an admirable retreat for those whose faith was wavering, added his voice to the general acclamation. Grace informed her confessor that her chief desire was to take the veil and become fully an inmate of her present abode.

Sometimes what she had heard from Mrs. Mora and Agnes came back to her and filled her with vague uneasiness. But these thoughts were uncomfortable, and she banished them. Thus the powers of darkness were striving for the possession of our Grace against the Spirit of God.

CHAPTER II.

RICHARD'S TEST.

FATHER MURPHY undertook to be Grace's ambassador to her father, to propose her taking the veil. The reverend Father was very glad Richard was not present, and with a prolixity of speech that would have done credit to the Circumlocution Office, broached the subject.

"*My* daughter take the veil!" cried Mr. Kemp.

"She has such virtuous intention, imitating the example of your niece."

"But, sir, I had no right to expect anything of my niece. She must do as she chose, and she was a very different girl from Grace. My daughter owes something to herself, to her family, to society."

"And that debt she may best discharge by representing her family in the Church," insinuated the good Father.

"My daughter is beside herself—she is moody and moping—she is infatuated. I have been considering her making a suitable marriage, and here, like a baby, she is crying after a white and a black veil.

Upon my word, sir, I'd as soon send her to a lunatic asylum."

"And how dare a son of the Church speak in this way of her most cherished institutions?" cried the priest, angrily.

"The institutions are admirable, but not for my daughter," replied Mr. Kemp. "As to the family, it is well represented by my niece and my sister-in-law the Abbess." Here Richard entered. "I say, Rick, here's Grace wants to be a nun. What shall we reply to that? Order her to come home, get married and forget such notions?"

Richard marked squares and triangles on the office-table with a small ruler. Presently he answered:

"No, sir. But I should first bring her home and see if that is her fixed and unbiased desire."

"It *is* her settled and unbiased desire," replied the priest.

"And she is stubborn enough when she gets a notion," said Mr. Kemp, gloomily.

"I do not think you can change her mind by any *fair* means," said the polite priest.

"*We* shall use no *unfair* means," retorted Richard.

So Grace was brought home, and was found resolute enough. A nun she would be, and nothing else. Her soul was above all price, and here was the only way to save it. She was disgusted with the world and all its follies. She wanted something real, and could find it in the convent.

Father Murphy came often to Mr. Kemp's house.

"I am glad your sister feels and expresses herself so earnestly," said he to Richard. "It may convince you that our Sisters are not, as you claim, a body of deceivers."

"I never claimed that," said Richard. "They are themselves, for the most part, thoroughly deceived. Weak-minded and half educated, fed on superstition from their cradles, they are puppets in your hands—your stool-pigeons to catch other unwary youth."

To Grace, Richard said:

"I'm astonished at you, Grace! Why will you throw yourself away?"

"I am not throwing myself away," replied Grace. "I have found the best way of living. I shall give myself to good works. I do no longer belong to myself—I belong to God—to the Church. You remember, Rick,

'Heaven doth with us, as we with torches—
Not light them for themselves.'

I am now to live for the light of others."

Richard looked fondly in her eager, resolute young face.

"I will reply to you from that same author:

> 'Oh, cunning enemy, that to catch a saint,
> With saints doth bait thy hook! Most dangerous
> Is that temptation that doth goad us on
> To sin in loving virtue.'

Poor Grace! you want to do right, but you are taking a lamentably wrong way."

Said Mr. Kemp to his son:

"Rick, what is to be done? that girl is bent on destruction."

"It is a pity you didn't see that in Lilly's case," said Rick.

"That was very different. Lilly was fit for nothing else, but Grace would be completely thrown away. *What* can we do?"

"Listen to my wisdom," quoth Rick. "Grace is obstinate and you cannot alter her. But you can make the priest refuse her. Just tell him that if she *will* be a nun she may, but you shall consider her thus provided for, and shall at once cut her off from any share in your property. Do that. Offer to draw up the will cutting off the 'nun' at once, and let the priest see it; and I tell you he won't have her. They want her money."

"Eh! think so?" cried Mr. Kemp.

"Take my word for it. Try it—come now."

Mr. Kemp slapped his son jovially on the shoulders.

"Rick, you're my comfort. Counselor Kemp, your good health. I'll try that priest this very day—but—suppose, Rick, he wants the girl any way?"

"He won't," said Rick; "but, if he does, I'll take her off on a trip to Europe, to give her a better mind. Just say to him, 'If you get my girl, you get her portionless.' Try it."

Mr. Kemp did try it. The priest argued, he raged; but Mr. Kemp got more firm.

"If Grace enters any convent, she forfeits all share in my property, and the whole estate will go to Richard. If she enters after my death, she must give up all she has inherited. She shall inherit property only on condition that she is never a nun."

"The Church will anathematize you," cried the priest.

"In America we don't mind *that*," said Mr. Kemp. "I can go back where I came from, and I vow if I do, I'll build a mission chapel for a peace-offering."

Both priest and Mr. Kemp lost their tempers, and were sufficiently hot and ridiculous. However, next week, after seeing the Abbess, and finding from her that there was no hope of changing Mr. Kemp's mind, Father Murphy told Grace to give up all thought of her "vocation," and serve the Church in society—"Children ought to obey their parents."

"Not when parents resist the Church," flamed Grace.

"The Church resigns her claims," said the priest, meekly.

Grace persisted. The Father persisted. He would not have her now on any account.

Grace cried and sulked and stormed in a very unedifying and unchristian manner; but everybody was obdurate, and finally yielding, as the weak must, to the parties in power, she said that she would spend a month in the Convent of the Immaculate Heart of Mary to get reconciled to her disappointment, and would then return to such life as her parents dictated. The world, the flesh and the devil had, you see, very nearly got the upper hand of Grace.

At the convent Grace met Lilly alone for a few minutes.

"Grace, you wanted to be a nun, and they would not let you?"

"Yes," sighed Grace.

"And you are unhappy about it, Grace?" she asked, wistfully.

"Yes, Lilly."

"Oh, Grace, it is the kindest thing—" She checked herself, twisted her thin hands together and looked piteously at her cousin. "Grace, Grace," she burst forth, "where is my mother? my own, own mother?" and then, as if terrified at her disobedience to orders, fled away without waiting for a reply.

The deep religious impressions were already wearing away from Grace's heart. She did not know that she had almost grieved away Him who will not always strive with men. But God had mercy on her ignorance.

She met Lorette. "Ah," said the Frenchwoman with a sneer, "the good little daughter cannot be a nun!"

Tears came into Grace's eyes: "I do not want to, Saint Lorette."

"Ah, trying to get sweet water from a bitter spring—trying to breathe in life from a corpse! Take my advice: rush through life until it gets so cruel that you can endure no longer, and then make the leap in the dark."

"Make it one's self, Saint Lorette!" cried Grace. "How could one?"

"Shall I show you how? Soon!" said the Parisienne.

"But all reason—all natural feeling—all conscience cry out against that!" exclaimed Grace.

"For the first, mine is astray; for the second, it is dead; for the third, I never had it," said Lorette, turning away.

Grace thought of Antonio:

"Ay, sir, where lies that?
For I feel not
This deity in my bosom."

Next day a panic spread in the convent, leaped from lip to lip and from heart to heart, before Mother Robart could cover up all horror with fair seeming. Lorette had been found in her cell, stretched on her pallet, dead by her own hand. The air of the little apartment was loaded with the smell of the poison she had taken. On the whitewashed wall over her head was written with charcoal, "I find the beginning of the end. I have made the leap in the dark."

The nuns had crowded into the room. Lilly fell fainting across the feet of the corpse. The Abbess, ever first to gain tranquillity, said, "To your prayers, my daughters. Leave this body with the nurses. Go, pray for your Sister's soul. I have long known that she was not in her right mind, but I little thought her insanity would take this turn. Go, my children, pray the saints to have pity and intercede for the forgiveness of an unconscious act."

Grace stood as one amazed. "Insane?" reasoned she. "Yes, of course, Lorette must have been insane." Yet still a voice seemed shouting in her ear a sentence from that Bible which was locked among her possessions at home: "Except ye repent, ye shall all likewise perish!"

In a moment she recognized her growing indifference, her self-confidence and her spiritual pride. The last state of her heart, indeed, seemed worse than the first She was bowed with remorse and penitence. She sought a retired corner of the chapel and knelt just behind the statue of Saint Joseph the Just. Before her was the shrine and image of Mary; near by, the crucifix, the altar-piece, the figures of angels; all about upon the painted windows were pictures of the saints. At the door stood a marble angel with a sword and scroll. Here were indeed "all the idols of the house of Rome, portrayed upon the walls round about." Here was one of the chambers of imagery.

In all the convent there was at this time no more earnest, troubled spirit than Grace. She strove in an agony to pray, but the prayers of Rome died on her pallid lips. This was the hour of the Spirit's victory. Before her mind rose up forgotten words of the "Book" she had by turns read and despised: "They have no knowledge that set up the wood of their graven image, and pray unto a god that cannot save. Look unto *Me* and be saved, all ye ends of the earth, for I am God, and there is none else." "There is no other name given under heaven whereby men can be saved." "And I fell down to worship before the feet of the angel; then said he unto me, See thou do it not, for I am thy fellow-servant; worship God."

What, indeed, were these images, or, rising above the images, who were they to whom nearly all her prayers were addressed, but fellow-servants of the saints and creatures of God's bounty? "Worship God." It was a sacred spell that set her spirit free. As to Huss in the college of Prague, to Luther on Pilate's staircase, to Charlotte de Bourbon in the convent of Jouarre, came the hour of deliverance to Grace. She saw the way of truth shining clearly before her, and in that way eternal mercy set her feet. She saw Jesus her all-sufficient Saviour, and between her soul and his goodness was now no host of saints and angels to block the way. To his ear of love could she address her own plea. It needed not "blessed John the Baptist, blessed Michael the archangel and all the saints" to beseech her Lord for her. His own compassion pleaded her cause. She left the chapel, wrapped herself in her cloak and went out into the garden, her heart full of a new hope which she could hardly define. The next few days she passed as one in a dream, only longing to get home to read her Bible. Saint Lorette was buried with all due solemnities. Lilly was in the sick ward, very ill, and Grace went, under guard of Saint Cecelia, to see her.

"Grace," said Lilly, "are you going to be a nun?" How faint and far away her voice sounded!

' No, Lilly, I am going home." Grace thought Lilly's thin hand held hers with a warmer pressure as she made this answer, and that a look of gladness stole into her sad eyes. Then there was such a beseeching, longing, intense gaze as almost made Grace say, "Dear Lilly, your mother is in heaven." But Lilly was very weak and ill, and Grace dared not make the communication. Then, too, Saint Cecelia was standing by, who would be furiously angry, and besides would promptly deny Mrs. Schuyler's salvation. So Grace only bent down and kissed Lilly several times, and said, "Good-bye." It was a last good-bye, and she went away.

As she went down stairs, she was informed that her father wanted to see her in the Abbess' parlor.

"Come, Grace," was his salutation; "are you resolved to be a nun against the decrees of the Church and State, represented by the Abbess and myself?"

"No, father, I am ready to go home."

"Very good then. When will you go?"

"To-day—now—with you," replied Grace, cheerfully.

"Grace is frightened," said the Mother. "One of our Sisters, one who was mildly insane, is dead, and poor Lilly is quite ill. Grace is gloomy, and wants to get into the world again."

"It is quite astonishing how many of your nuns

go insane!" said Mr. Kemp. "That one that ran off by favor of Agnes Anthon was crazy I believe, and in 1835 I remember there were a number of nuns escaped in different parts of the country, and they were all crazy."

"Other people besides nuns are crazy," said the Abbess, shortly.

"Yes, yes, I suppose so; but, after all, isn't it quite enough to craze a young woman to be mewed up in narrow bounds, saying prayers and living on meagre diet?"

"We don't say prayers all the time, nor do *we* have poor fare," said the Abbess, laughing.

"Well, I suppose *you* do manage things better than they do in some places; but here is my 'fair penitent' in her bonnet. Come, Grace, home with you, and in less than a year you shall send your Abbess-aunt your wedding-cards and a box of cake."

"No, I won't," said Grace.

"Bless me! has the girl got a new crotchet?" cried Mr. Kemp.

Grace went home. Spring was dressing the earth in beauty. As the new summer was dawning in flower and leaf and verdant sod, a summer of joy and fruitage was growing upon Grace's spirit. She returned to the study of her Bible. She weighed Protestantism well, and conversed often on this subject with Richard and Agnes. As her mother was too self-absorbed and her father too busy to notice her, and as she dropped the works of Romanism only one by one, as she was convinced of their futility, she was for the present not interfered with.

At the convent, Lilly had risen from her sick-bed more frail and shadowy than ever, looking like some mild, fair, young ghost. Her state moved the Abbess to sincere pity. She saw that the girl's life was utterly wasted and blighted, that she had been sorely deceived, and was doomed to an early death. She was a submissive, faithful, gentle daughter of the Church, and against her not one word could be spoken. She had claim upon some tenderness and amelioration of a life that was evidently too hard for her. Consulting with the priests and the Bishop, Mother Robart concluded that the best help for Lilly would be to allow her to go out at times with some of the elder Sisters on errands of mercy. She could become interested in the sick and for young children, making for them delicacies suited to their condition and articles of clothing. The change and the new interest might be better for her than medicine, and would minister to both mind and body.

Thus Lilly was permitted to go out with safe guides to designated localities—all far removed from her early home—and gradually she grew a little better. A new, unacknowledged hope had grown up in Lilly's heart, that in these hours outside of the convent she might see her mother—might beg her to come once in a while to speak with her at the convent-door, or failing in that, she might have one look at the dear face, and, herself unseen, be assured of her mother's health and comfort. Unhappy Lilly!

So the summer passed away. Grace was at Saratoga, Niagara, the Thousand Islands, the seaside, far away from Father Murphy, enjoying the society of Mrs. Anthon, Agnes and Richard, and others of her friends. A gloom fell over them sometimes when they thought of Mr. Wynford, who from city to city was seeking his lost children, a prematurely old man. Here he would think he had a trace of Estelle, there of Martin; but as he sought them, ever, like mocking will-o'-the-wisps, they fled his coming. Richard still believed Martin at the Belen, and Estelle hidden in that city graced by the Convent of the Immaculate Heart of Mary; but Mr. Wynford had hunted there in vain.

Lilly had now grown accustomed to leaving the convent at times to labor among the sick. The Abbess felt less anxiety than formerly about these walks, and indeed congratulated herself upon their good effect, the more as Father Douay had objected to the present course of action, and had advocated sending

Lilly to Mother Ignatia. Mother Robart did not wish Mother Ignatia to be deemed a more experienced trainer of young nuns than herself. She secretly felt that Father Douay thought Ignatia a greater saint than herself, and was piqued thereby. She loved Lilly, and did not want her to die, and pointed triumphantly to her improvement, saying,

"If she had gone to our dear Sister Ignatia, she would have been in her coffin months ago."

The Lord disposes all things as he will. After all the days when Lilly had gone out with Saint Maria, Cecelia or Sophia, came the first, the only day that she was out alone. It was a warm day early in October. Lilly went out with Saint Cecelia on a visit to an invalid. Farther from the convent a Catholic widow had just died, and Saint Cecelia was anxious to hasten to her house, to secure her children for the Catholic orphan asylum. Lilly felt too faint to take the additional walk.

"I will go back to the convent," she said. "I am very weak to-day."

Cecelia left her, and she walked slowly toward the not distant convent. Her figure was bowed by ill-health, her veil was dropped over her face, already nearly hidden in her large black bonnet. Little was this Sister Mary Anna like to Lilly of years ago. But the eye of love is keen, and good Hannah, passing that way, recognized her young mistress. She rushed to her and caught her hand:

"Oh, Miss Lilly, Miss Lilly, I must speak to you. How sick and worn you look! It softens my heart that was grown hard to you, miss. But how could it ever be that them as was to you neither kith nor kin could set you against that blessed angel, your mother!"

That name unlocked Lilly's long-sealed lips. "Hannah," she exclaimed, "how is my mother?"

"And how is she, Miss Lilly? How should she be but well? dear saint that she was, and kind to me as if I was of her own blood. Do you ask me how she is? Hasn't she been in glory these twelve months?"

"Hannah," gasped Lilly, clutching the woman with both hands, "tell me, *is my mother dead!*"

"Is she dead? To be sure, Miss Lilly. What else should she be but dead after dying for six long weeks, lying just at the gate, you may say, and could neither get out nor in for the longing to see you? Times and times did we send, praying you just to come to say one good word to her parting soul, that she might go in peace, and still you wouldn't come, and still she lingered. Ah, it was a sad sight to see. How could you? how could you?"

Hannah had no other thought than that Lilly had

despised her mother's dying wish; and, as she recalled the painful incidents of Mrs. Schuyler's last days, her heart burned with indignation. In her excitement and ignorance she hurried on, unconscious what effect her communication was having on the unfortunate nun beside her.

Lilly's heart had given a mighty bound at the first word which revealed her mother's death. Then it had labored slowly and heavily, a chill creeping over her; but still her one thought was to hear the whole of Hannah's tale, that some one word of comfort might be gathered from it. The noisy, jostling street was no place for such a conference. The stir made her sick and dizzy. She forgot the convent and its rules. For her the world held now but one person—that was Hannah, who had watched her mother's last hours. "Hannah, I cannot hear you in the street; it makes me sick. Where can I go that you may tell me?"

"My room," said Hannah, "is in a little court not far off. It is a quiet place; come there. Take my arm if you are weak."

"Go on; I will come after you," said Lilly, with a vague thought of Hannah's secular dress and of exciting attention. They proceeded in silence for two squares, then came to the narrow street or alley that led to Hannah's home, and turned into it.

"Hannah, your arm!" said Lilly, gasping. "I shall fall."

Hannah supported the thin, trembling frame. A memory of the round, rosy, dimpled girl upon whom she had waited filled her with tender pity. This blanched, withered, sobbing nun was so different from the soft-eyed, light-footed girl!

"Here's my room," said Hannah, unlocking the door. "Thanks to your mother, it is decent; and the old lady is out to-day, so it is empty for us. Here's the big rocking-chair, Miss Lilly. Here, let me put a stool to your feet and fan you. There, you're faint, my dear. The convent has ruined you, miss."

"Water!" groaned Lilly.

Hannah brought a glass of fresh water, and stood with anxious looks until Lilly seemed a little revived.

"Sit down, Hannah; tell me all; when was it? what was the matter? what did my mother say? how did she feel? Don't forget anything."

"I can't forget—not I," said Hannah. "The dear lady never gave a smile after she lost you. Mrs. Anthon was a good friend to her, and Mr. Richard was like a son; but who could make up for you as she doted on, miss? She went into a consumption, and left the house less and less, and she was that meek and gentle, praying and hearing the Bible and talking of religion. Don't tell me of Saints and Sisters. I know your mother was holier than any of them. A true child of heaven was she, miss, and if ever a soul found rest, it was hers, that I know."

Lilly's arm resting on the chair, her face being hidden in her handkerchief, and she making no answer and giving no sign of life except by the slow throbbing of her heart, evident through the folds of her black garb, Hannah went on:

"She longed for you, miss. She could not die until she saw you. It's my belief that that longing held her here and kept her out of heaven a good month. We sent, over and over again, to the convent, praying and begging for the love of mercy that you'd come just for one hour, but never an answer did we get. Nuns, they tell us, are to visit the sick and the dying; but my dear mistress, as might have had some claim on a convent, might have died alone for all them. Ah, Miss Lilly, she'd watch the door with such large eyes by the hour, saying, 'Hannah, she'll come—my only child—my poor Lilly.' And then at night she'd turn from the food I offered her that heartsick, and put her face to the wall and pray, miss, and all I'd hear would be a sob and your name. Ah, my heart aches yet for them days. Why didn't you come, Miss Lilly?"

"Go on—go on," said Lilly.

"'Hannah,' says your mother to me, miss, 'if ever you see my poor child, tell her I loved her to the end, as she may never know. Tell her I prayed the Lord to bring her to heaven, but she must trust in Jesus and nothing else. Tell her not to mourn over the past, but to see to it that she meets me in heaven.' That's what the kindest mother and mistress as ever breathed says to me, Miss Lilly, for you."

A pause. Then Lilly impatiently motioned with her hand.

"Well, the end came on, miss, and your cousin, Miss Grace, was not like to live, and the nurse she was wore out, and Mrs. Anthon took Miss Agnes home. We had sent for you again that day, to the convent and to the priest, but you never came; and as it grew night, miss, and she saw you were not coming, the tears rolled down her cheeks, and she being too weak, I wiped them away. Bless the Lord, who is more pitiful than men, that was the last weeping ever she did. Mr. Richard came in to watch. She dozed a bit, and that minute she lost herself sleeping a little she would say your name. Ah me! I cried like a baby, and Mr. Rick, he leaned over the foot of the bed watching her, and, big man as he is, when he saw how worn out and sharp her face was, and how her eyes were sunk in her head, and her breath coming shorter every minute, and she sobbing in her sleep like a grieved child, he stood wiping away his tears fast enough. Well, miss, it's nearly all told now. It was the turn of the night: says I to Mr. Richard, 'If she lives an hour, she'll live a day.' Just then she opened her eyes, and pointed up, looking to Mr. Rick. Says he—I learned the verse afterward—'And God shall wipe away all tears from their eyes: and there shall be no more death, neither sorrow, nor crying; neither shall there be any more pain; for the former things are passed away.' She smiled at that, but her smile had got to be as sad as other people's crying. Then she holds out her hands, as if groping for somebody in the dark. Says I to myself, 'It's a hard lot to be the mother of a child and ask for it in vain at the last.' Then she says half your name, and belike she never finished it, for she was out of this life the next minute, and perhaps she found something better to say."

Hannah's tale was ended. She could not know Lilly's unhappy position, and her heart was hard to the poor nun. Her hearer sat for some time in the same attitude in which she had listened to the sad account. When at last she lifted her face, Hannah was terrified at her pallor and at the intense agony written on every drawn, pinched feature. "Oh, Miss

Lilly, Miss Lilly! I've broke your poor heart. Oh, miss, don't take on so; your mother left only her love and blessing. Miss, that convent is clear poison to you; don't you go back. Bide here while I call Mr. Richard, as will put you in your own home and guard you from all the priests and nuns in the country."

"Help me down stairs and through the alley, Hannah. It is time I got back," said Lilly.

"Oh, miss," persuaded Hannah, helping her as she was bidden, "ain't your heart set again them, and isn't your life just eat up with them? Do you go home and bide there, and it is wicked Hannah that will work all her life to make up to you for breaking to you such news."

Lilly made no reply. When they got to the street she dropped her veil, said, "Good-bye, Hannah," and went slowly on her way. Hannah, shading her eyes from the rays of the setting sun, looked after her, wiping now and then a tear with the corner of her apron, and murmuring to herself, "Poor, feeble young thing! She's not long for this here evil world. Why, why *didn't* she let me go with her to that jail gate? She looks as if she'd drop down." When Lilly was fairly out of sight, the faithful servant-woman returned to her own room.

As for Lilly, she felt herself in the hands of her foes. She had been cruelly, bitterly deceived. Utter falsehoods had been told her. The Abbess and Director had been false to her in this matter—why not in others? Yet she was a nun, and the wide world offered her no home but one—she had taken upon her a solemn vow—orphan and desolate, the Church her only parent—so to the convent she turned her trembling feet. A heavy blow had fallen upon her. Every word of Hannah's story was burning in her brain like fire—her dying mother! her deserted mother!—and then, either her mother was lost or herself was on the road to ruin. On, on, on, she tottered—the convent was in sight—there was the gate—but, once within, what should she do? What should she say to those who had lied to her, and who had kept her from her mother's dying bed? The last step—her hand reached out to the latch—a mist swam before her eyes—the convent seemed to reel and bow as in an earthquake—its windows, flashing in the sunlight, were whirling fires—the echoes of the city were as the surging of the stormy sea or the rush of winds through the forests.

A little later there was a loud ring at the convent door. Some passers-by had found a nun lying insensible at the half-open convent gate, and were bringing her into her "home"—the house of the "Immaculate Heart of Mary."

Saint Cecelia shortly returned, and told Mother

Robart how she had parted with Sister Mary Anna.

"She has been very long coming. She must have rested somewhere, and fainted at last from fatigue," said the Abbess, and then sharply upbraided Saint Cecelia for neglect and ordered her to her cell.

It was long before, under the utmost care, Lilly revived. As she returned to consciousness, the Abbess sent the other nuns from her, lest their presence should fatigue her, and herself remained with her favorite charge.

"My dear daughter, you are very ill," she said, bending over the pallet of the poor little Sister.

Lilly lifted her emaciated hand and pushed the Abbess from her with what strength she had.

"You have deceived me," she cried, gazing wildly at her. "My mother is dead! and you told me she was alive and well!"

"My child, you are dreaming," said the Abbess, clasping her repelling hand.

"No, no—you despised her dying prayer—you deprived me of her blessing—she died alone, in sorrow;" and she strove to withdraw her hand.

"My daughter, this is a feverish fancy," said Mother Robart.

"It is bitter truth. Let me go, Mother; you have deceived me; yes, when I *trusted* you. I have seen one who stood where *I* should have been—at my mother's deathbed," she said, turning away with pitiful sobs.

The Superior was neither more nor less than woman —a hard woman, but so is many a one not an Abbess: in her heart she anathematized Saint Cecelia, and then she looked on Lilly with pity, greatly mixed with self-upbraiding. Here was happiness wrecked, a life untimely blighted, a perfect trust, alas! most foully betrayed. The Abbess had loved this girl with what love she had—she loved her still. Anger she often felt, but now her eyes were wet with unaccustomed tears.

"My daughter, my dear daughter, I have labored for your good," she said. "In all the world you have no truer friend than I. Yes, your mother *is* dead, but I loved you too well to break your heart by the news. It was the will of God. We must all die some time, my daughter. Complain not of Heaven. Address your prayers to those tender interceding saints who have tasted human sorrows, and have freely offered you their aid."

Lilly turned her wild gaze to the Superior's face.

"You, *you* and Father Murphy I have trusted as I have the saints. I saw you as God's holy servants. You have deceived me—why will not the saints also? Whom can I trust, to whom can I go?"

"Hush, daughter. We have labored for your good as we have had authority from Heaven. You are a child in knowledge and cannot understand these things. All we have done is right and best: be humble, yield your rebellious passions, your earthly love, and submit to the will of God and the decrees of your spiritual guides."

What could Lilly do but submit? She was a poor bruised reed whom Rome had utterly broken. What power of resistance was there in her? As the weeks went by, she gathered enough strength feebly to mingle with the other Sisters; but her trust and confidence were gone, she was quite bereft of hope, an apathy crept over her, dull and listless she joined in her duties, and listened to the voices of others as one whose heart was dead within her. She grew to be such a tacit reproach to the Abbess that that admirable woman was ready for anything that should work a change.

Father Douay urged again that Sister Mary Anna should be sent to Mother Ignatia. The entire change might be beneficial. The severe routine might wake her from private sorrows all unworthy of a nun.

Mother Robart consented to her temporary removal. Father Murphy was quite discouraged about her case. He did not see what was for the best, and as she was no longer a temporal interest, as the Church had her fortune secure, we may say truthfully that the Father did not particularly care what course was taken for the short remainder of Lilly's life, provided only she remained a Papist and a nun. Mother Robart and Father Douay might make her happy or miserable in their own way.

Sending Lilly to the House Without a Name was giving the spiritual invalid too violent a remedy. What was a tonic—so supposed—to Grace, was a poison to Lilly.

Here was a new experience, a hardness, a severity, an excitement, which was positively horrible to the sensitive, delicate young nun. Mother Ignatia upbraided her new charge with grieving over private sorrows and cherishing natural affection, when she ought to be bemoaning sin and expiating the follies of her life. Lilly withered away under this influence, like some frail flower under the fierce blasts of winter. She became too feeble to leave her bed. Her mind appeared utterly torpid. Mother Ignatia despaired of aiding her, and Mother Robart, hearing of her low state, had her brought home to the Convent of the Immaculate Heart to die.

Pat Mora, working for Michael Shinn, drove the carriage that removed Lilly from the House Without a Name, and the honest fellow shed some tears over her miserable condition.

CHAPTER III.

A DYING ACTOR.

WHILE Lilly was coming back to the Convent of the Immaculate Heart to die, her cousin Grace, over whom more beneficent stars seemed to shine, was returning full of life and health to her home.

It had not once entered Grace's mind that any one would dare to interfere positively with her change of faith. Grace, though brought up a Papist, was a thorough American. She was old enough and wise enough to judge for herself. All this summer she had attended Protestant churches, eschewed Romish books, studied her Bible and offered her heart's desires in her own words to God; and she meant to do so still. The church of which Mrs. Anthon and Agnes were members seemed most like a "home" to Grace, and thither, as Sabbath bells called the hosts of God's Church militant to worship, went Grace and Richard.

Arousing to a sense of this innovation, Mrs. Kemp

discoursed awhile on the "proprieties of life" and the ignorance and vulgarity of heretics. Finding these words fell like unfeathered arrows, short of their aim, she shed a few futile tears, and then, like other Romish matrons, betook herself to her priest. You see, she never thought of appealing to her husband, the father of this girl, for any aid or counsel. The stout and ruddy spiritual Father and Director, who, acting out his natural self, might have made a capital Falstaff, was Mrs. Kemp's "guide, philosopher and friend."

Father Murphy listened, his wrath gathering like a winter storm.

"I'll see this wretched and reckless girl," he cried, "and shall order her to the convent until she recovers her senses and takes an oath of future obedience. It all comes of your own folly and obstinacy, woman. Did I not tell you years ago to use your influence to turn your husband against that villain of a son, who has poisoned your house with his heretical blasphemies? He has told me to my face that our religion is idolatry, and is carnal and not spiritual, and that the Pope is *not* God's vicegerent; and yet, woman, you tolerate him, you flatter him, you permit him in your house and at your table."

"But," ventured Mrs. Kemp, "the house and table are my husband's."

"Your husband," shouted the priest, "is a miserable, lukewarm, shuffling changeling! He has no more devotion than a brute beast, and worships himself and works for himself. The less he has to do with you and your affairs, the better for you, mark that."

Mrs. Kemp wept; not because she was distressed to hear her husband thus roundly censured, but because she was frightened and nervous and perfectly amazed and confounded to find this Falstaff in canonicals so angry with her. Her tears encouraged the wearer of cincture, alb and stole to yet stronger denunciations: "As for you, traitorous woman, your allegiance is to the Church first, the Church always, the Church only. This man was united to you by grace of the only true Church, and just for so much and for so long as that Church deems fit and wise. Henceforth you will take your orders from *me;* and the first is, that you forbid that scandalous step-son your presence; that you neither speak to him nor recognize him; and yet further, that you strictly obey whatever orders I give you for reclaiming this deluded girl, Grace Kemp. If you want authority for that, you can take it from our blessed Lady: 'Whatsoever he saith unto you, do it.'"

For this blasphemy the Lord did not strike Father Murphy dead. God works slowly in mighty circles, in which our earthly visions see but infinitesimal parts.

Mrs. Kemp was that worst of all caitiffs, a moral coward. She succumbed entirely before this outburst of priestly wrath, and went home quite ready to obey, no matter what was the command.

The next day Grace was ordered to the parlor, and was catechized, lectured, argued with and berated for three long hours by Father Murphy.

She was grieved and then angry. She answered as might be expected, sometimes aptly and sometimes weakly; sometimes well and sometimes ill; was now white with excitement, then flushed with indignation, and again tearful from passion, but held her own to the last. As the contest drew to a close, she kept her peace, gathering her forces for a final assertion of her faith, while Father Murphy fairly exhausted himself in a mingled exhortation and denunciation.

"Sir," cried Grace, clearly, "one thing I can say, 'Whereas I was blind, now I see.' God has converted my soul and enlightened my eyes, and henceforth neither saint nor sinner shall come between my soul and its Maker. *You* claim apostolic succession and divine inspiration. *I* have learned that God dwelleth by his Holy Spirit in every holy and contrite heart. Henceforth I accept God as my Father and do renounce the Pope; I accept Christ as my

Mediator, and renounce the mediation of the saints; I accept the Holy Spirit as my counselor, and do for ever renounce the Church of Rome and all her delusions."

She then rose, and with her head held rather too high for a follower of Jesus the Nazarene, left the room. Our Grace was not then perfect, nor do we think she ever will be while in this body of death.

Grace was ordered to the convent, that "the Superior might converse with her on religion;" but the girl knew very well what that meant, and went not. Father Douay came to see her, and was even a worse enemy than Father Murphy, inasmuch as he was a more crafty reasoner and more thoroughly in earnest. Still, Grace was aided to detect fallacies, even when she was not wise enough or skillful enough to frame an answer, and these attacks only left her firmer in the faith she had espoused. The Lord had done great things for her, and no one could argue their realization out of her rejoicing soul. In these new hopes she consecrated herself to Him who had washed her from her sins in his own blood, and, standing by Richard's side before the congregation of God's people, took upon herself the solemn vows of the Protestant Church. Brother and sister were now united in their highest hopes.

Mrs. Kemp did not once fail in following out the

daily programme dictated to her by her confessor, and the result was such a series of persecutions that Grace asked permission of her father to take up her abode across the way with her brother. During all this contest, Mr. Kemp had maintained strict neutrality. He would not quarrel with Richard and Grace; he would not quarrel with his wife and the priest. He had oil-wells and silver-mines on the brain, but by no means religion either on the brain or heart. When Grace appealed to him for permission to go to Richard's home, he signified his royal pleasure that everybody should do just as they pleased, and so Mrs. Kemp soon found herself in solitary state, deprived of both the girls from whose successes in society she had hoped so much. She was disappointed, and grew sour and low-spirited.

With that broad benevolence that springs from Christian hope and joy, Grace's heart turned toward Adelaide, the sharer of her childish happiness, longing to lead her to Jesus. Mr. Kemp's prohibition about intercourse between the girls was not recalled, but Grace determined that she would for once see her step-sister and unfold to her her new desires. Adelaide had been absent from the city all summer and was now no longer to be found in the extravagant apartments at the hotel, but in much plainer quarters in a less fashionable street, in a quiet and respectable boarding-house, in whose four stories were quartered different grades of lodgers. Adelaide and her husband occupied commodious second-story rooms, while madame, her sister-in-law, was established in a similar room on the other side of the hall. Lucy was yet retained, but she informed Grace privately that she acted as maid to both the ladies, neither being able to afford a separate attendant. There was no carriage kept now, and the toilettes of these children of pleasure were less expensive; indeed, Madame Leplatte and her brother, Mons. Luolli, had been theatrical comets rather than fixed stars, and their reign was passing away. Adelaide looked worn and peevish, and seemed rather irritated than pleased to see Grace, but presently assumed a debonair manner, which was painfully foiled by her anxious, weary eyes and the look of bitterness that was growing habitual to her once lovely mouth.

Grace inferred that Adelaide had heard of her change of religion from Father Murphy; but Adelaide asserted that she "had not been near Father Murphy for an age." She listened with a supercilious smile as Grace told of her new hope.

"I do not wish to dispute what you say," she exclaimed, "but though these things are true to you they cannot be true to me. I could not bear the yoke of Rome, worldly as it is, and how do you think your Puritanism would suit *me?* My husband believes in nothing, and I begin to think that is the most sensible creed of all." And Adelaide laughed, her laugh a shrill sad echo of the joyous past.

Grace's eyes filled with tears and she turned away to hide them. Doing so, she looked out of the door, which was set open to the hall, as the room was over warm, and saw a young woman clad in blue and gray passing up to another floor, a thick, black book in one hand, and her blue-lined, squirrel muff in the other. Grace recognized the figure and style of dress in a moment. It was the Bible-woman she had seen beside the consumptive girl the day she was visiting Mrs. Mora.

"Adelaide, who is that?" she asked, quickly.

"I'm sure I don't know," said Adelaide; "some very common person I suppose. She boards here, and has a room in the attic where those wretched little dormer windows stick out. She is a Bible-woman I think."

It was useless to try and impress Adelaide. Grace fairly wept over her, and not wishing to meet Mons. Luolli when he came back from playing billiards, took her leave. She had closed Adelaide's door and reached the stairs, when, taking a sudden resolve, she turned and went up staircase after staircase, until she arrived at the attic. Tapping at the door, she was bidden to come in, and entering saw the young Bible-woman sitting at the window, her head resting on her hand and her eyes fixed on a volume in her lap.

She rose at once, saying, "Pardon me, I should have opened the door, but I was not expecting visitors. I seldom have any."

"And pardon *me*," said Grace, taking the proffered chair, "for intruding on you in this manner. I can only give a child's reason for doing so, 'I wanted to;' but I think I have seen you before in No. 15 Anne street. I came from the room of a sick woman, and you were reading to an invalid in a room opposite."

"Very likely," said the Bible-woman. "I had a young girl to visit in that neighborhood, but she is dead."

"I was with a Sister of Charity—Saint Cecelia," said Grace.

The young women started violently, flushed and looked away in either fear or aversion, so that Grace blushed and explained: "I was a Romanist then, but now I am a Protestant—a member of the Fourth Church. My name is Grace Kemp."

"I am glad you are a Protestant," said the young woman; "so am I one." But she shook as with some strong emotion, and looked about her neat little room as if for a place of refuge.

"You spend your life in doing good and telling of Jesus," said Grace, "and I have a step-sister here, Mrs. Luolli, who never thinks of these things; and as my father does not like me to visit her, I cannot often speak to her of those great themes—the sinner and his Saviour. Won't you speak to her of them sometimes?"

"I never see her," said the Bible-reader. "She is on the first floor and I live up here. See, I cook my coffee and eggs here by the gas, and this is my closet and pantry," pulling back, as she spoke, a sliding-door under some book-shelves, and displaying a tiny cupboard, where were some tin cans carefully covered, a baker's loaf, and some dishes.

Grace looked with interest. Here was such a new way of living; and the room, with its books, its few little pictures, its white bed and gay carpet, was so neat and cheery. Still she held to the point she had made, and said, even with tearful entreaty, "But if she should be sick, or alone, or unhappy, can you not say a few words for the Saviour?"

"I think you are in earnest," was the singular reply.

"In earnest! Indeed I am!" cried Grace.

"And *you* are Grace Kemp?"

"I am. Have you heard of me before?"

"Is Miss Agnes Anthon in the city?" was the next inquiry of this incomprehensible young woman.

Grace readily gave Agnes' address. She could

make no progress in conversation, and withdrew disappointed, yet attracted in spite of herself. She told the incident to Agnes. A few weeks after she called at this house again. Adelaide was out shopping and the Bible-reader had moved. This she reported to Agnes. "I know all about it," said Agnes, smiling; "you frightened her away."

"I did!" cried Grace, "how could I?"

"Some day I may have permission to tell you," said Agnes.

Not an hour before, this same Bible-woman had been in Agnes' little boudoir; and Agnes had said to her, "Yes, go by all means. You should be neither cowardly nor foolhardy, and this will be neither. Go and see her."

The person thus referred to was Adelaide; and the Bible-reader, having gone directly to her from Agnes, was even now in her room. Adelaide was lying on a sofa, where she had passed most of the day, as she was suffering from a cold. Her cheeks were flushed with a slight fever, her hair was disordered, and ever and anon she passed her hand over her temples to soothe their throbbing pain. Her theatrical friends had been all day at the green-room, very busy with a new play. Adelaide was lonesome. The Bible-reader's was a mild, winning face; you could see she had endured sharp trials and conflicts, and her heart had grown old and wise; she was one of those people who unconsciously win every one's confidence, and are the receptacles of the woes of all their acquaintances. She sat down by Adelaide, chased away her pain by the magnetic touch of her cool, soft hand, and talked to her in a low, sweet tone that calmed the restless invalid like tender chords of minor music. Adelaide was pouring forth her troubles before she was aware. She was so differently situated from what she had been at home; she missed the society she once could claim; she had been so rash and hasty, and now felt so lost and out of place; once she had everything she wanted, but now she felt cramped and narrowed; her family were ashamed of her, and was not that too bad? Sometimes she wished she were dead.

Here the soft-voiced visitor spoke of the hereafter, of troubles that should lift us up, should purify our souls—"Whom the Lord loveth he chasteneth;" and grievous chastisement works goodly fruit; and then, as Adelaide looked impatient, the Bible-reader, striving to recommend the truth, and to bring that home by degrees, which would not be received abruptly, quoted from another source,

"Sweet are the uses of adversity;
Which, like the toad ugly and venomous,
Wears yet a precious jewel in its head."

"Oh, but you know the toad hasn't any jewel in its head!" said Adelaide; "and, dear me! I have not told you half my troubles yet; I am getting to look just as old; and then my husband has such a cough; and when he plays in the theatre two or three nights in succession, he raises blood, and I know he'll die of hæmorrhage; and isn't it dreadful to think so? Now in this new play he has to speak so much and so loudly, I'm frightened to death about it. Oh, you've no idea what a world of trouble I have!"

The visitor tried to tell her of Jesus and of God's love; and begged her to speak to her husband of these things.

"He don't believe in any of them," said Adelaide. "He would only laugh, and begin to sing French songs like

'Au banquet de vie,' etc.,

and then, religion and theatre actors! who ever heard of such a thing!"

The visitor saw she could make no impression just then, and, as she had no time for gossip, took her leave.

In the same house, in the room she had herself lately occupied, was a young girl, a clerk in a store, sick, and she was going to see her. She visited this girl several times after, and offered her services as watcher with her when she was ill enough to need one. Thus it came about, that she was in the house a week later, at night; and, about eleven o'clock, one of the servants stayed with the patient while the Bible-woman went to the kitchen to prepare some things that would be needed before morning. As this young nurse was returning to her charge, a server with glasses and bottles in her hand, an excited group thronged in at the front door. Mons. Paul Luolli was carried in by two of the subordinates of the theatre, and was closely followed by his sister and Adelaide. The three were in brilliant attire, Mons. Luolli in the dress of an Italian count, which character he had been acting. His lace frills, gorgeous chains, and velvet surtout were covered with ominous stains, and the handkerchief pressed to his lips was red with blood. Madame Leplatte had hastily gathered up her white satin skirt and velvet train, flung about her bare neck and arms a heavy cloak, and tied a thick veil over her flowing wig and the gilded diadem on her brow. Adelaide, in her choicest dress, had occupied one of the private boxes, and now her silks and laces and down-trimmed opera cloak were spotted, like her husband's, with the blood she had attempted to stanch. A physician followed closely after the patient, and Mons. Paul was laid back in a reclining-chair in his own room.

The Bible-woman set down her server and went to offer her aid, which was greatly needed, indeed, as Adelaide and Madame Leplatte could only weep and wring their hands in dismay.

Mons. Paul motioned to indicate the distress this occasioned him.

"Compose yourselves, ladies," said the doctor; "we hope to conquer this trouble presently." But, even as he spoke, another rush of crimson put to flight his hopes.

"Doctor, this is fatal," whispered the Bible-woman, as she aided his endeavors for his patient. This was now evident to all.

"Let us send for a priest!" cried Adelaide. "Oh, Paul, let me send for a priest!"

But the actor would not give any sign of consent. It was a terrible scene—the excitement—the terror—the pallor of approaching death—the fantastic and gaudy dresses of the central group. That there was no hope was plain to all; and still, at intervals, rejecting the Bible-woman's tender words of truth, did Adelaide clamor for her priest. At last she was permitted to send for Father Murphy.

"He will not get here for an hour," said madame.

After the message was sent to him, the Bible-woman seemed listening, amid the silence or the sobbing, for some sound from beyond.

The dews of death stood on the dying actor's white face.

"Only a few seconds more," whispered the physician.

"The priest will never get here!" cried Adelaide, wildly.

"Monsieur Luolli, turn your thoughts to Jesus," said the Bible-woman in his ear.

The actor's lip curled, and summoning all his strength, he said, "Let me die as becomes a Frenchman and a philosopher. Bring me a glass of wine; your prosing priest will never get here. Wine, I say."

His sister handed him a glass of wine, helping his trembling hand to hold it. He pushed the Bible-woman and surgeon from him, feebly,—

"Your health, belle Adelaide; we all must die!"

The glass dropped—a rush of life-blood met the wine at his lips. He fell slowly back with one convulsive quiver.

"He has gone," said the doctor. Just at this juncture, the portly form of Father Murphy appeared in the door. The Bible-woman glided out in an opposite direction.

"Had you no one but yourselves here?" asked the priest, signing the cross over the dead body.

"A Bible-woman was here—but she must have gone," said madame, looking about.

Death of Paul Luolli.

Priest and Nun. Page 398.

"The Bible-women are impostors, and fly from the face of the Fathers of the True Church," said the pompous priest.

Meanwhile the Bible-woman had gone to her patient in the attic, and had locked the door, and, as she moved about the little room, she was praying.

When the word came to Mrs. Kemp of the death of Paul Luolli, she went to Adelaide.

"I will order your mourning for you," she said, "and as soon as the funeral is over you had better go to the convent for two or three months, until the whole matter has been quieted, and you can afterward come home."

She remained with her daughter all that day; but did not return to the funeral. Richard and Grace went, however. The body was to be met at St. Joseph's by Father Murphy.

Richard went in the carriage with Adelaide, and was to take her to the convent when the burial was over.

"It is a poor place for you to go, Adelaide," said Richard. "You should look to God rather than to man for comfort; you are welcome to come to my house, if you will."

"I'd rather go to the convent," said Adelaide, wearily. "I feel dreadfully, and would only be a burden to you and Grace, and it is so quiet at the Immaculate Heart. Take me there."

Grace remained behind at the boarding-place to gather up Adelaide's possessions, and to send them to the convent with Lucy. All was done at last,—it was four o'clock—Lucy had gone—Grace put on her cloak and stood by the fireplace drawing up her gloves — somebody touched her arm—it was the Bible-woman—Grace thought that her pale, calm face, contrasted with the cluster of small blue flowers and the broad blue strings of her bonnet, looked like a sweet wood violet.

"Don't you know me?" said the Bible-woman.

"Yes; but not your name."

"I saw you, years ago, and I was afraid of you lately; but Miss Anthon said I could trust you."

"I am sure I don't remember you," said Grace.

"I saw you with your schoolmates in the chapel at the 'Heart.' I was with the other nuns behind the grating generally. I was the 'Missouri Sister,' and Miss Agnes helped me to escape."

"Is it possible!" cried Grace, seizing both her hands; "and you a Bible-woman!"

They sat down before the fire. The Bible-woman loosed her cloak and untied her hat, and, as Grace listened with intense interest, she told her where she had found refuge, and then found Jesus; how her parents were dead, and she had recovered some small part of their property, enough for her simple wants;

and how, as health and active labor had changed her much, she had ventured back to work as a Bible-woman in the very city where she had passed months of what seemed a hopeless captivity.

"I have done some good I think," she said, "and, as you see, I dress so entirely different, and look so changed that I am not afraid of being discovered. I shun all nuns and priests," she added.

It was time for Grace to hasten home. She parted from the Bible-woman at the door, promising to see her often.

Mrs. Kemp felt sincerely grateful to Richard for the kindness he showed Adelaide at this time. She would have liked to thank him for it, but dared not, on account of Father Murphy. She was not forbidden intercourse with Grace, and sometimes she was cross and sometimes kind, and sometimes she stormed and sometimes entreated.

One day she persuaded Grace to go with her to the convent chapel to vespers, that they might see Adelaide. Grace went because she had heard nothing from Lilly for some time and wanted to see her if possible. She had heard that Lilly's life was despaired of, and again that she was better. She wanted to catch a glimpse of her, and give her one sympathizing look, if nothing more.

"You know, mother," said Grace, "that I go to

vespers as a simple spectator, or, rather, to see Adelaide and Lilly, not to worship."

"What ruinous infatuation!" sighed Mrs. Kemp.

They were in the street, and Richard met them. Grace told him where they were going. "I will go with you," said Rick, "everybody is admitted as a visitor at vespers."

Mrs. Kemp held up her head and walked on alone, leaving Grace to follow with her brother. They entered by the door of the chapel, that opened from the street. At the lower part of the chapel was the grating, behind which the cloistered nuns were gathered. Near this grating was a door opening into the main hall of entrance to the building. Adelaide, some boarders, pupils and visitors, Mother Robart, a few of the "Saints" and Father Murphy were in the chapel, from which most of the ornaments had been removed as it was Lent. Grace took her position as near the grating as she dared. She thought she saw a feeble figure seated in a chair, as one unable to kneel and stand, and that a pallid face was turned toward her own.

Grace sat down, with Richard in the seat behind her, cast her eyes to the floor and remained perfectly quiet until the services, which were that day of unusual length, were ended. She wished neither to honor nor to insult. She felt sorry that she had gone there, when the first notes of the choir fell on her ear. She hoped that it would not be construed into a concession on her part. How natural to her seemed all the words and acts, filling ear and eye. How long she had taken part in them; and now what rank idolatry they seemed. She wondered that all these things had ever been religion to her. She knew just where the different persons were standing. There were the postulants in white caps and black dresses; there, the novices in their snowy veils; there, some of the black-veiled Sisters; and here, the cloistered nuns. The choir sang the Litany of the Sacred Heart. Again the clear, well-trained voices rose in

> "Root of Jesse, Gate of morn,
> Whence the world's true light is born;"

which must not at all be understood as applying to Jesus, but to the Virgin Mary. Then at last came the Litany of the Blessed Virgin. Father Murphy intoned the Antiphon—*Sub tuum præsidium confugimus*, etc., or, in plain English, "We fly to thy patronage, O Holy Mother of God," etc.

It went on after three invocations, through forty-five different titles of honor to the Virgin—then again the antiphon and then the oremus. Grace was very tired when it was all over, and wondered that it had never been so wearisome to her in other days. But in those days she had believed in it all most heartily, and that had relieved it of its monotony.

The services ended, the visitors began to depart at the chapel door. Grace, however, familiar with the building, quickly opened the door beside the grating, and pulled the bell for the porteress. The nuns, from their secluded place of attendance on service, were dispersing to their cells, crossing to do so a hall at right angles with the one where Grace stood. Lilly lingered behind the others. The porteress came running along the corridor, dropping hastily on one knee as she passed Lilly—for this reverence is rendered by postulants to the veiled Sisters—and, obeying the motion of Grace's hand, proceeded to unlock the great door. Grace for one moment clasped Lilly's wasted hand, gave her one loving look, whispered "Look to Jesus," and hastened from the convent. She met Richard outside the gate. "I did not know but the monster had swallowed you alive," he said.

"Oh, they cannot secure me, I know them too well," said Grace, laughing.

"Did you see Lilly?" asked Richard.

"Yes, poor little creature; she does not look as if she would be in this world very long. I thought when I looked at her what a farce that set phrase is, 'Vowed to the perpetual adoration;' she seems rather vowed to a pitiful endurance. The hall where they have their cells is so dark and chilly, and those little narrow cells with their bareness and their thick walls are enough to kill her. Lilly's life is now much more severe and hard than it used to be; almost as if they were trying to put her out of the way."

Richard sighed: "Yes, and we are going back to the house that might have been such a happy home to her. I wish she had it now I am sure."

"Adelaide told me *she* had almost a mind to be a Sister, because she hates to go home so. She thinks father will be angry at her, and that all her set will be whispering and wondering, and perhaps will not recognize her."

"An admirable reason truly for a 'religious life,'" said Richard, scornfully. "I suppose also her feeble mind is beguiled with this glamour thrown around 'holy orders' and vows, veils and Sisters. It was only yesterday that I read a poem on Sisters of Charity, that is quite enough in itself tc turn some of those weak heads that so greatly abound. The last verse is such a climax of extravagance, and indeed of profanity that I cannot but remember it; it runs thus—

'Still mindful as now of the sufferer's story,
Arresting the thunders of wrath as they roll,
Intervene as a cloud between us and his glory
And shield from his lightnings the shuddering soul.'

That is the first half, and you see it invokes a Sister

of Charity, as only Christ himself should be invoked. The remainder is:

> 'As mild as the moonbeam in autumn descending,
> That lightning extinguished by mercy shall fall,
> While He hears, with the wail of a penitent blending,
> Thy prayer, Holy Daughter of Vincent de Paul.'"

Grace was silent awhile, then looking up in her brother's face, she said,

"God has been better to me than I have been to myself or I should have been one of these same Sisters. But, Richard, many of them are more sinned against than sinning. They are deceived, and are the decoys used by the priests to deceive others. And some of the priests are deceived too. There is Father Douay, thoroughly, frantically in earnest; but, if to be a Christian is to be like Christ, you could hardly imagine any one farther from that holy likeness than he is."

"Always excepting Father Murphy," said Richard; "and what a shocking thing it is that such a trio, as our proud, self-serving, self-willed aunt Robart, a fanatic like Douay, and a plethoric old glutton and wine-bibber, like Father Murphy, have full control of the destinies of a houseful of Sisters, novices and pupils, like the Immaculate Heart of Mary."

"I like Father Murphy better than Father Douay," said Grace. "He is more *human.*"

CHAPTER IV.

LILLY'S FLIGHT.

MRS. MORA had not long been buried, when John, to the exceeding grief of his children, brought home a new wife as unlike their mother as possible. The second Mrs. Mora was a loud-voiced Romanist, fond of quarreling and gossip, not over tidy, and loving well her whisky punch. She particularly disliked Pat, and imposed upon Ann many and unthanked tasks. Against these things Pat rebelled.

"What's the use of biding here, Ann?" he said to his sister. "Father's never been the same since he joined the Fenians, and this woman he has brought home is the plague of my life. I'm of age and making my wages, and you're of age and can sew a rare good hand. We'll hire two rooms and live by ourselves, and you can keep the house and sew what you like, and for the rest I'll take care of you as a brother should."

This plan suited Ann exactly. The rooms were hired, well away from their father's abode; second-hand furniture was bought and furbished up; blue and white crockery made glad Ann's eyes; and, having taken what belonged to them from their early home, they were ready to set out in life by themselves.

John Mora was very angry, and so was his new wife, who wanted the work and wages of the young people. They brought their grievances before Father Murphy, and he laid his commands on Pat and his sister to live at home, attend confession, and pay their tithes, or be in danger of eternal ruin.

"That's not for man to say, your Reverence," said Pat. "The Bible tells us that all God requires is to 'do justly, to love mercy and to walk humbly with God.' There's never a word of church or priest in it."

The next day, being safely established in their new rooms, and very delightfully sitting down to a little supper prepared by Ann, and invitingly set forth on a brown table-cloth and blue china, Pat said to Ann, "Ann, me girl, let us two turn over a new leaf entirely. We will quit the Catholic Church, for you don't believe in it nor do I. There's a tidy little chapel near by, and there we'll go to meetings, and we'll study our Bible and the tracs, as becomes good Christians."

"Yes indeed, Pat," said Ann. "That's just what I'd like. I don't care for our Church, because it never teaches the only thing that comes home to my heart, and that is, 'The blood of Jesus Christ his Son, cleanseth us from all sin.'"

The next morning Pat went off to his work early, but soon returned with a lowering brow. "Father and the priest have made Michael Shinn discharge me," he said; "and now what am I to do, with no work and a house on me hands?"

"Never fear," said Ann, cheerfully. "Scour the knives, and bring water and coal in for me, while I tidy myself, and go talk to Miss Grace, and get me some sewing. Belike I'll find a place for you anent I get home again."

Her courage was infectious. Pat performed the household tasks she had assigned him, and betook himself to reading "tracs," while Ann, hopeful and vigorous, if she was a little lame, went to see Miss Grace.

"And so," said Grace, "they have made Michael Shinn discharge your brother, because you could not live with your stepmother."

"Oh, if you please, miss," replied Ann, "that ain't all the reason! We've turned, miss—we ain't Catholics any more—Pat and me has been slipping away these many years. We don't feel like that's the Church for poor folks, and it puts us far off from God, and the Lord Jesus, miss, and it sets in between a host of saints and priests and the Pope, and well we know *they* don't care for us, so what are poor folks to do?"

"But, Ann, dropping the Church of Rome, I hope you do not mean to drop all religion."

"Oh, no, if you please, Miss Grace, we are far from doing *that!* Why, miss, if poor folks, as haven't got no very great of a portion in this world, have also no hope for the next, again what are they to do? Oh, we're to study the Bible! and being ignorant, we are likewise going to Sunday-school and church, and if you've got any advisement for us, Miss Grace, we'd be very thankful."

"I will only advise one thing," replied Grace; "that you do not wander from place to place, but if the gospel of Jesus is preached in that chapel near you, as I am sure it is, that you go there regularly and constantly, and find there your religious home. And now you want some sewing?"

"I'd be so thankful for it, and do my best endeavor on it," said Ann.

"I can give you a parcel, and a note to Miss Anthon, who will furnish you with some more. As for Pat—"

"Yes, miss," said Ann, eagerly.

"Tell him to go to Mr. MacPherson's office at three o'clock. I will go there before that, and see what Mr. MacPherson thinks he can do for him."

Thus Ann went away comforted, and that afternoon Pat was hired in a provision broker's at good wages.

"And it's a blessed thing to have friends," said Ann Mora.

Going one morning to do her small marketing, Ann encountered Hannah on a similar errand; and, with the ready friendship of their class, they had soon exchanged sketches of their experiences. They walked a square or two together with their baskets, and Hannah detailed her interview with "her blessed Miss Lilly." "Ah," she said, "nights and nights I've laid awake mourning over my hardness to her, poor lamb, and I'd go from here to Californy on my knees if I might only make up to her for it."

"And you are living now with the old lady, your aunt?" said Ann.

"I'm living alone," said Hannah, "the Lord's took the old lady, a thing she was waiting for long. I'm no ways lonesome or afraid. I've my work to do, and I go about much among the sick. It saves 'em from falling in with 'Sisters' sometimes, and 'Sisters' is people I own to a grudge to, for haven't they just spoiled and broken up Miss Lilly, that might have been now in her own house, the sweetest woman in all the city?"

And now that the spring-time had come, and the

flowers were pushing up through the garden mould, through the chill darkness of Lilly's heart had pressed up a new desire. Perhaps something of the new life and freedom of spring had stolen to her through the crevices of her cell. She walked in the convent-garden now and then, and breathed in a little added vigor, and this fed her one ardent hope. We have mentioned the tenacity, or obstinacy, that was in Lilly's disposition. An idea could gain complete mastery over her, and all things would minister to it. Now she had brooded over the great deception that had been practiced upon her, until she had distrusted everybody about her and had watched them for faults. Suspecting evil, she had found it. She saw herself the victim of a mighty lie, the prisoner of deceivers; she felt the chains that falsehood and selfishness had bound about her cutting into her heart, and she meditated only how she might break them off and die free. She knew she must die; but oh, she longed to die where true faces looked upon her, where the blue sky could meet her eyes, where the last ministries of earth were the offspring of affection, and not of service vowed in ignorance. Kneeling in the cell or in the chapel—for Lilly was not ready to cast off Rome—it seemed as if the stone walls were stooping in and crushing her, and as if the air was thick and poisoned. There she could not stay. She would not be a toy, a puppet in stronger hands. She would get away from these her masters, and be nursed by Hannah as in her childhood. The fitful fever of life should cool from her veins, and free, she should sink under the cold, welcome waters of death. It would be very good to be buried in the potters' field, with nothing to mark her grave, where grass and wild flowers should grow above her at their will, and barefoot children and homely robins come to her resting-place to play.

Of these dreamings no one suspected Lilly. She had long been silent and morbid; she was the favorite of Mother Robart, and yet the Abbess could not bear to see her often, she was such a miserable wreck. The other nuns thought her some saint, like those that had graced the mediæval Church, and filled the Calendar; they had not the least idea of being like her, and did not particularly enjoy her society, yet it was quite delightful to witness her holiness, for evidently the earth would soon rattle upon her coffin-lid.

Father Murphy was convinced that Lilly's mind was shattered. So long in the confessional her voice had died into inarticulate murmurs, and when he had plied her with questions, she had started, and replied absently, "I don't know, Father," that he had grown tired of it, and he had prepared for her a set form, which he supposed comprehended everything, and had bade her learn it and repeat it; and, as from this form he never changed, the question of her weariness of convent-life did not come up between them. It was not that Lilly had resolved to break her solemn vow. She had only a fierce desire to get away from the convent, tc some hiding-place, to have Hannah near her to tell over and over the reminiscences of her mother, and by these, as a tender song, to be lulled into a mornless sleep. Hers was indeed an innocent plot, to steal away and die like a wounded doe.

Fixed in this wish, she was alert for opportunity; and, not being suspected, she was not watched, and being so very feeble and a favorite, she was more indulged and had more chances for carrying out her intention; and so, one morning when the earth was sweet with May, she slipped away into the outer world. She had hidden her rope girdle, rosary and crucifix under a seat in the chapel, and had taken a white sunbonnet and a little check shawl from a peg near the school-room. Her mind was in such a ferment, that she was then a harmless maniac, never reasoning, only bent on one thing—escape,—and instinctively taking the best means to that end. Poor Lilly! it was as if her black veil had grown large, and floated cut, and darkened over all the horizon of her life.

She had stolen away.

I pause—she had not gone from the grasp of Rome

alone—Grace also had gone, and the Missouri Sister, and Mrs. Mora, and Ann, and her brother; and Lorette and Adelaide had turned to Infidelity. It was thus that the children, whom Rome had fed on dry crusts, had rebelled against her scanty providings, and some had bethought themselves of going direct to the good table of their Father, to claim the children's abundant bread. They would not feed any longer on miserable husks, for the Elder Brother had cried to them of wine and milk and honey, and bread indeed; and, though their tyrant foster-mother blocked the way and raised loud hubbub, and put hosts of angels and saints and priests and nuns, and Father Pope and all his Cardinals to hinder their progress, they were struggling into their true Father's house and the table of the kingdom.

"Blessed is he that shall eat bread in the kingdom of God."

Now much I fear me, faint-hearted and double-faced Protestants, for whose especial benefit I am writing, that you will say to yourselves right comfortably, "If this is the way Rome's children rebel, why Rome is sure to die out, and we need not hasten her doom; let us take our ease and go our ways, for Rome is crumbling to her fall."

I will tell you, no. Awake before it is too late. While some of Rome's stronger and wiser children are rebelling against her, are coming out of Babylon and shaking off her sins, *we are feeding her by ten thousand streams.* Turn your eyes to England, once strong in God, and see how there, in one little year, two peers, nine clergymen and 2000 laymen and women have gone over to Rome. See how, in one fleet-footed century, from fourteen Romish noblemen, they have come to claim sixty-four, while in the House of Commons sit thirty-eight Papists to toil for Rome. And in our own country, Father Hecker tells us that *seven-tenths of all the Protestant children sent to Romish schools become perverts;* and can you estimate how many such children there are? Then, too, how many silly women with money go over to Rome, and take their fortunes to build convents. I could tell you of two such not twenty miles from each other; and one of these openly avows her purpose of using her House entirely as a school for Protestant girls, to bring them to Rome, and she already counts her trophies by many tens. And unless Protestants "be watchful and take warning" what shall be the end? Bloodshed, war, disaster, the wheels of progress and civilization reversed, and the fearful drama of the last eight years re-enacted with tenfold horrors. Verily,

"The times are very evil
And the days are waxing late."

* * * * * * *

Lilly, with excited brain, entered the city's streets, now long untrodden by her, and with sudden strength pressed on, anxious only to put wide distance between herself and the Convent of the Immaculate Heart of Mary. She knew not which way to turn. She had nothing in common with the fashionable avenues; she was fearful of the foul courts and narrow alleys; but she instinctively turned into quiet streets, apart from business thoroughfares where everything frightened her, and chose the resorts of humble independence, the more, as she had some dim recollection of having met Hannah in such a place. This Lilly, who should have been a strong and happy woman filling well a noble sphere, was a poor scared creature, not fit to take care of herself, who would soon drop down of fatigue. But the tender Shepherd of the sheep was watching over this strayed, torn, bleeding lamb, which had been watched by wolves and folded in their den. She was going on as fast as she could, beginning to stagger a little in eagerness and exhaustion, when a healthful young woman in a gingham dress and cape passed her, with a wicker basket on her arm. The young woman limped a little, but her step was strong for all that. She was clean and wholesome-looking, altogether a cheerful and attractive young person. She had been to market, and the wicker basket contained a marrow bone, a bunch of yellow carrots, a bunch of dark green, curly parsely, and some brown-coated potatoes, suggestive of good soup. As she passed the bent form of the fugitive nun, there was such a contrast as forced itself even on bewildered Lilly, causing her to utter a feeble outcry, and then, sensible of her own utter weakness, to grasp the picket fence for support. The cry reached the young woman's ear, and she was one to whose heart the way was short and easy. She turned, and coming back, said,

"Oh, ma'am, I'm afraid you're ill—take my arm—what can I do for you?" and looking under the white sun-bonnet—"Oh, Miss Lilly, Miss Lilly."

Lilly threw up her hands appealingly. Ann Mora understood her, took in at one glance her mixed attire. "Bless you, dear miss, my house isn't more than a stone's throw from here. This is a by corner where no one will see us. I'll tie on my apron so as to make you more changed like. There now, come on, take my arm and walk as stiff as you can. I'll see you safe in five minutes. Don't fear; there ain't a Catholic on our street, miss, dear."

So Lilly took new heart, and pressed on, and was presently in Ann's second-story room, she knew not how;—but the basket of marketing stood on the white pine table, and the door was locked—and then Ann had to catch her as she fell and carry her insensible into her own little room.

"Bless her, she'll come to after a bit," said Ann to herself. "I'll take off these hateful clothes." And, quick at her office of ladies' maid, Ann soon had the shrunken figure draped in one of her own night-dresses—you may be sure she chose the very best—which was as white and smooth as the best washing and ironing could make it. Then she put a clean case on the pillow, and laid the feeble form to rest, spreading over her her very nicest pink and green quilt, which was far too fine for ordinary use, and so kept folded away in a towel. Then she bathed her forehead, and rubbed her hands, and when Lilly had come back to life again, said, "Now I'll make you a cup of tea and a bite of toast, miss dear." This she did, and at the same time made the soup for herself and Pat. When she brought in the tea and toast very neatly and daintily served, Lilly ate and was refreshed.

"Miss Lilly," said Ann, kneeling by the bed "whom shall I send for to come to you?"

"Don't send for anybody," cried Lilly, trembling at once, "don't, don't, dont,"—then wailed out, "I want Hannah."

"I can get Hannah," said Ann. "I'll go speak with her this afternoon, and bid her come just on the edge of evening."

"No, no," said Lilly, grasping her tightly; "don't leave me, I'm afraid."

"You needn't be afraid at all; I'll lock the door," said Ann.

"Don't go," cried Lilly. "If they find me, if they get me. Oh, you can't tell how terrible!"

"They sha'n't get you, miss. There now! I'll lock this door—see, it's strong—and Pat shall bide from his work and read his book in the next room. The broad-shouldered boy that he is, half a dozen couldn't fright him."

So with much soothing, and after the "broad-shouldered boy" had presented himself at the door, and with his humble respects had prayed her not to be afraid, Lilly let Ann go for Hannah, and while she was gone slumbered quietly, forgetting all her fears.

At evening Hannah was ready to come, but not empty-handed. She considered that Ann was a poor girl, just at housekeeping, and so she took from a trunk of choice stores, left her by Mrs. Schuyler, linen sheets, ruffled pillow-cases, and damask towels. At a druggist's she spent such a sum as she would never have laid out for herself on brushes, perfumery, and toilette soaps. And with these things to show her penitence for past hardness, Hannah appeared at Ann Mora's, and was soon bending over her "dear miss," weeping and caressing her.

Pat was sent back to Hannah's house under cover

of darkness, to bring a bundle she had left where he could find it.

"It is the mistress' clothes as she left me, and far too good for me to put on," explained Hannah to Ann, "and there I've had them laid up in lavender, and there they are all ready for miss."

She then inquired with particularity into the supper that had been provided for the invalid. Ann meekly submitted the bill of fare; and the two young women amicably divided their loving cares for their idol.

That night Lilly slept sweetly. Hannah napped in a rocking-chair near her. Pat resigned his bed in the outer room to Ann, and himself lay on the floor, which he declared he was quite ready to do for a hundred years, if it would in any way benefit Miss Lilly.

Lilly manifested the most extreme dread of having her whereabouts made known to anybody, lest thereby she might be again delivered to the convent. She was unable to lift her head from her pillow, but lay in calm content, waited upon with the utmost tenderness by Hannah. She would not have a physician, but was willing to take any remedy Hannah suggested. The faithful maid was sure no power on earth could save the young patient; yet she felt guilty about this neglect of medical aid. Lilly was very determined, however, and her word was Hannah's law. Her fits of terror were pitiful, and returned at every mention of bringing any one to see her.

Hannah had cherished her stricken charge thus for a week, contributing her own share to the family expenses, and aiding Ann with her sewing, when one morning she went to the market to get a fowl for making broth.

"A fresh young spring chicken fit for a sick body," she said. A black-eyed, slender, sallow-handed woman, with linen apron and straw bonnet, a serving-woman-looking person, stood near her, and turning about said, "An invalid, eh?"

Now Hannah was garrulous, alas like many another woman, and she replied with a sigh, "Yes, consumption, dying with it too, the sweetest young lady—"

"I'm a gentleman's cook," explained the stranger, to inspire confidence. "I do my own marketing. I give my master my best work, and I want the best to do with. Ah, consumption you say?"

"Yes, consumption, like her mother before her," said foolish Hannah.

"If you please," cried some one, pulling Hannah's sleeve, "*would* you come tell me which of these fish to buy?" And, as obliging Hannah turned away with her to examine the scaly victims of hook and net, she said, "Oh, go home—keep silent, do—that is a Jesuit spy—Annette—she lived at Mrs. Judge Schuyler's once."

The ground seemed to reel under Hannah's feet. Had she betrayed Miss Lilly! "Don't look so," said the Bible-woman. "These fish, sir, please—go back and don't tell her where you live—don't go straight home—she'll follow you, and I'll follow her."

And so it was. But Hannah went to her own home, and, when her spy was gone, hastened by crooked ways to Ann Mora's. Not far from there she met the Bible-woman.

"I looked from my window a week ago," she said, "and saw a person tying an apron on a very feeble young woman, and helping her along to some place in this neighborhood."

"Oh, it's all done!" groaned Hannah, wringing her hands.

"It need not be. I'm sure the feeble young woman was some unhappy nun, and now, if she has any true, strong friends, you had better let them take care of her."

"As sure as I'm alive," said Hannah to herself, "Mr. Richard shall know of all this before night."

She entered Ann's rooms. Ann stood by Lilly's bed. Hannah heard the invalid's sweet, childlike voice, as she said, "I came here to die, Ann, and it won't be long now. You are very good to me, Ann. Ann, tell me that verse."

"What verse, miss?" asked Ann.

"A verse you told me long ago."

"A verse?" said Ann, doubtfully, "what could it be? Oh yes, now I know, to be sure! There is but one chief verse in all the world to me: 'The blood of Jesus Christ his Son, cleanseth us from all sin.' Oh, Miss Lilly, what a power of good it does to take that verse into one's heart! It's all you need. The Bible says those 'who sometime were afar off are made nigh by the blood of Christ.' It is only to let Jesus wash out all he finds amiss in us in his own blood, and set us before the Father clean once for all."

Lilly looked very calm and peaceful. Hannah knelt down and took her hands. "Miss, dear, don't deny me; I'm going for your cousin, Mr. Richard. He's strong to take care of you, miss, and he knows the law and can do more for you than we know to."

"Well, go, Hannah," said Lilly, absently. "Ann, do you think I can get near to Jesus, and be washed in his blood?"

"Yes, sure, miss, only put out of your mind the notion of those interfering saints, and say to him, 'Lord here am I.'"

Fear gave speed to Hannah. She thought that she had betrayed her young lady into the hands of her enemies, and imagined that already they were carrying her off by force to the convent. She stopped at the warehouse where Pat was busy, and bade him "hurry home to protect that dear young lamb, while she went to call them as had a right to do it."

Pat dashed off, hardly waiting to snatch his cap.

With many sighs and much self-condemnation did Hannah tell her tale to Mr. Richard. "To think," she said, "of that sweet young lady, born to all luxury, now hiding like a thief, in a servant-woman's house, and all along of them dreadful nuns, sir! Not but what the house is clean and the air good, and I've done my endeavor to get her what was right for her station; but oh, Mr. Richard, what sort of treatment is a bare floor and a pine bedstead for a young lady like Miss Lilly, sir?"

To call a skillful physician, a friend of his own, to take a carriage and hurry said physician into it, with Hannah, and to dash off in the direction of Pat Mora's, was short work for Richard Kemp.

Ann and her brother, with anxious faces, were keeping guard in the outer room. They brightened considerably when they saw Richard and his coadjutors.

"Is Miss Lilly awake?" asked Hannah.

"That she is, and lying as peaceful as a dove, like as she'd never want anything more in this world."

Hannah acted as *avant courier*, and then ushered in Richard.

Lilly raised her eyes with a smile, and too feeble to speak much, or even extend her hand, said, softly, "Rick."

How the old name touched him! His eyes filled.

"My mother," said Lilly, softly.

"She left you her love and blessing," said Richard. "Do not fear anything, Lilly; I can take care of you. You shall go to your own home, to your mother's room, Lilly, and Grace shall watch over you. I have brought a doctor here for you, Lilly. You must get well, now you are safe."

Perhaps his strong, fearless presence encouraged Lilly; she did not appear frightened, and the doctor came in. After a short visit he retired to the outer room.

"Doctor," said Richard, "my cousin must not stay here another hour. The house I live in is her property, and she must be taken there at once."

"She would not reach there alive," said the doctor. "She has but a few hours to live, and any exertion would rob her of those. Just make her comfortable here. She is very nicely cared for I see already. I might leave her some stimulant, but I doubt if she could swallow it; you have no idea how low she is."

Richard was shocked. "If you have anything

that will lend her a little strength let her have it," he said. "There is one subject on which I must speak tc her. The poor child has been beguiled in the convent so long, that she very likely knows nothing of the way of salvation."

The doctor sat down to write a prescription. "Let her be quiet," he said, "don't bring any new faces about her, nor have more than two in the room at once. A little excitement would be fatal."

After the doctor was gone Richard said, "Hannah, I shall stay here most of the time while Miss Lilly lives. I wish you to take the carriage we came in and go bring from my house whatever will add to your young lady's comfort, and bring her some flowers from the green-house,—she always loved flowers."

He then asked Ann and Pat to move their stove and kitchen furniture into a vacant room across the hall for which he would pay, that no noise or heat might disturb the invalid. "As for you, Pat," he said, "you stay here and watch that street-door. I'll see that you lose neither place nor wages."

Hannah having helped herself liberally at "Mr. Richard's," Lilly had now in her room many of the luxuries of her home. She smiled at the dainty bouquets in their Parian vases; but ice-pitcher, toilette sets, silver server and fine china, did not appear to be noticed.

"There is your mother's Bible, Miss Lilly," said Hannah.

Tears came into Lilly's eyes.

"I'll read you some of the passages she marked," said Richard.

Shortly after noon Pat called Richard in haste. "There's the convent-carriage at the door," he said, "and Father Douay and two of the Saints in it."

"Go into the hall," said Richard. "I'll lock the door. Never mention me; but firmly and quietly refuse them entrance, and suggest that nothing but the law, and a writ of habeas corpus shall make you surrender."

"That I will, sir," said the sturdy youth, relishing his task.

"In the name of the Holy Church," said Father Douay, to the "broad-shouldered boy" he found leaning against the outer room door, "open this door, and give into our hands our escaped Sister, Mary Anna."

"Your Reverence," said Pat, "it's the name of the law of the land, and not of the Holy Church, that opens this same door."

"The everlasting curses of the true Church shall destroy your soul," said Father Douay, in a voice that caused Saints Clement and Cecelia to tremble, "if you refuse obedience."

"Curses like chickens get home to roost," said Pat.

"If you refuse, your door shall be broken open," said his Reverence.

"Then ye'll have to try your strength agin me at a wr*a*stle," said Pat; "and I'll have the law of ye atop of that. My house is as good to me as another man's is to him."

"I shall soon raise force enough to bring you down," cried Father Douay.

"Not in this neighborhood," said Pat, "wasn't I out of conceit with the Holy Church when I came here? This is a *Protestant* neighborhood, your Reverence, and I'm not the ijit [idiot] that would live where me roof would be burnt over me heretic head, or me tea would be seasoned with arsenic."

"At least," said Father Douay, trying another plan, "let these holy Sisters go in to converse with that unfortunate young woman."

"It was a poor time for the doves when they took the hawk into the cote to instruct 'em," replied Pat, smiling. "Your honor has an honest man's chance. Get a *haby corpy* [habeas corpus] and I'll surrender."

After some further parley, the intruders returned to the convent carriage, an affair which, with its black curtains shut close down, looked like an odd-fashioned hearse, and were driven away. Before dark a writ ordering Patrick Mora to produce the body of Sister

Mary Anna at court, at eleven o'clock next day, was served upon the sturdy Celt.

"I take my orders from you, Mr. Richard," said Pat, exhibiting to him the writ.

"I'll give them to you in the morning," said Richard. While these waves of tumult and trouble were beating around her, Lilly lay unconscious of all, a deep calm settling over her, her soul lifted above all cares of earth.

"Lilly," said Richard, "the way of salvation is plain and simple, but it has been hidden from you by a hundred forms and human traditions."

"Those have all been cleared away, Rick, like clouds from before the sun. They are gone; and now I see only the cross of Christ,—Jesus dying for me,—and willing for me to come to him."

This was said in whispers with many a pause.

"And, Lilly, do you trust in none other?"

"In none other, Rick."

"Nor in your blameless life, nor in good works."

"I have none—a sinner, I need a Saviour."

"And who is he?"

"Jesus, the Son of God."

Hannah came to administer a cordial, and then felt her hand and her pulse.

"Only a little longer, Hannah," whispered Lilly, and Hannah wept.

The next morning Richard gave Pat his instructions. "Go to court and respond to the judge that you are not a principal in the affair; that the young lady is actually dying, as Doctor ——— will certify; that she is at your house by accident; that I am paying her board, and am responsible for her; and to me must the writ be addressed. That will give us one day more."

Pat obeyed orders; the doctor and Mr. MacPherson bore out his testimony, and a writ was served on Richard Kemp, ordering him to produce Sister Mary Anna at court at eleven o'clock next day, or show good and sufficient reason for the contrary.

Pat guarded his doors like a young lion; and slowly ebbed the last hours of Lilly Schuyler's life.

CHAPTER V.

LILLY'S DEATH.—THE TWO PRISONERS.

"MR. RICHARD, if Miss Lilly lives past twelve o'clock, she'll live till the turn of the night, when folks is most like to die. She'll slip off at twelve or four, sir." So said Hannah to Mr. Richard. It was a remark she had made at many deathbeds. They were keeping watch alone together, as they had done over Mrs. Schuyler.

"Mr. Richard, do you believe in guardian angels, sir?" asked Hannah, presently.

Richard did not reply. He was watching his cousin intently. Her breath was so feeble it scarce seemed as if she breathed at all.

"Because, sir," pursued the maid, "*I do;* and I feel as if her mother was Miss Lilly's guardian angel, all ready, sir, to carry her soul up to the right gate, sir. I can just be *sure* she is hovering over her child, as gracious an angel as ever was, sir. Ah, Mr. Richard, won't that be a happy meeting! Haven't I heard prayers on prayers from my lady for that blessed girl, and don't I see them answered? Never tell me the Lord ain't an Answerer of prayer. I know he *is*."

Lilly's lips parted in her sleep to a softly-uttered word, "Mother."

"I told you so," said Hannah.

Later she opened her eyes with an effort to breathe. Richard lifted up her head and pillow on his strong arm. Hannah brought a cordial.

"Don't trouble her with it," said Richard.

"Rick!" said Lilly, clearly, "the blood of Jesus Christ his Son—"

"Is that your trust, Lilly?"

"All my trust, Rick." Her head drooped.

"Your young lady has gone, Hannah," said Richard, restoring the pillow to its place. Then, all the sweet child-life and the poisoned girlhood of his cousin rose up before him, and Richard Kemp went out and wept.

While Ann went in to assist Hannah, Richard called Pat, and the two departed together. They proceeded to Father Murphy's. Unseasonable as was the hour (now about five o'clock in the morning), they requested admittance on business, were taken to the parlor, and presently the holy Father came down in dressing-gown and slippers.

"You know who I am," said Richard, savagely, "and you know I have been ordered to produce in court my cousin, Lilly Schuyler. She is lying dead, God having freed her an hour ago from a life she found too hard. I have witnesses ready, and shall, if it is your pleasure, show the court how *you* deceived your ward, and shortened her days in the miseries of that prison, the Convent of the Immaculate Heart of Mary. Sir, I lay her death at your door!" And Richard struck his fist on the table till it shook and rattled under the blow.

"Of course if the erring and unhappy young woman is really dead, it is not necessary for us to say anything more about it," replied Father Murphy.

Richard went home to leave some directions with Grace. At the proper time he went to court and sat two hours, but none of the convent party were on hand. The case was pretty generally known by this time, and many glances of sympathy were directed to him as he sat with his hat crowded down over his eyes, in sad meditation. Pat was at home guarding his house. When Richard returned there at one o'clock, all was in order, according to the directions he had given. Hannah had gone to the undertaker's, and all matters had been quietly hastened. Pat and Ann were in the kitchen. Hannah, in the mourning she had worn for Mrs. Schuyler, sat reading her Bible in the outer room. The most perfect stillness reigned, and the inner door was shut.

"Will you please see Miss Lilly, sir?" said Hannah. Richard entered the room. It was spotlessly neat, with fresh curtains, bedspread, and stand-covers of snowy whiteness. The coffin-lid with its silver plate was laid on the bed. Two carpenters' tressels had been set in the centre of the room, and covered with a linen sheet, which fell in ample folds to the floor. On these stood the coffin. Richard stepped forward noiselessly, and stood, with folded arms, gazing into that narrow resting-place.

Lilly was worthy of her name—indeed a lily, broken in the midst of its fragrance and beauty. Her hair had been cut in the convent, but Hannah, loving the old-time task, had curled it childishly about the still face. No more the red cross glared upon her bosom, but over the white merino of her shroud her fair hands were clasped prayerfully, and filled with flowers. About her head, in her hands, over her breast and still form, even to the feet, had Hannah scattered the treasures of the florist—white violets, lilies, camellias, cape jasmine, wax-like rose-buds and hyacinths, snowdrops, and all kindred white and perfumed blossoms—flowers with fragrant souls were they, which souls they were breathing out over the early dead.

"Asleep in Jesus," said Richard; for there was smiling peace on the flower-encircled face.

"If you please, Mr. Richard," said Hannah, "here's the undertaker and his men and the hearse, sir"—with a sob—"obeying your orders, and the carriages too."

Richard motioned without speaking, and stood aside. The undertaker's men lifted the coffin-lid from the bed.

"If you please, Mr. Richard, at your house won't you have it off again for Miss Grace as loved her, and Miss Agnes, and for the old servants?"

"If they wish it," said Richard.

Hannah and Ann bent over the foot of the coffin, their tears falling on the flowers, an unaccustomed dew. There was no one nearer of kin than cousin, to press a kiss on that cold face. She was the last of a house in which Rome had made ruthless havoc.

They fastened down the coffin-lid, and Lilly was hidden out of sight. There was a hearse at the door, a carriage behind it for Richard, another for Hannah and Ann. This small procession crept slowly through the streets, and at last stopped before the Schuyler mansion. The door was open wide, the shutters already bowed and wearing the badge of death. Mr. Kemp, Mr. MacPherson, the doctor, and three other gentlemen stood on the walk with crape on hats and arms. They lifted the coffin from the hearse and carried it in. It was thus that the heiress of the house came home. She had entered into her heritage —eternal rest.

Then came the simple funeral service, and then the small train of carriages, filled with friends who had been hastily gathered, bore Lilly Schuyler to the family vault, and a place by her mother's side. Richard's friends had advised quiet and short delay under the singular and painful circumstances of this case.

That this escape, this death, this burial made no small stir at the convent, who will doubt it? Saint Clement, her situation as cook resigned, was at the House Without a Name brooding over her defeat. She had taken to herself great credit for the manner in which she had discovered Lilly's hiding-place. Baffled at finding Hannah's house closed, and that Hannah had been absent from it a week, she had fixed her suspicions on Mr. Richard's residence. At fault again, with an unerring instinct like a blood-hound on the scent, she had tracked her quarry straight to Ann Mora's humble room. But after all she was foiled! She had not carried her prisoner in triumph to her cell. Sister Saint Clement thought there were a great many disappointments in life. A good while ago she had wanted to go on a mission to Europe, but Lorette had been sent in her place, on the poor plea that she spoke better French! And here was Mother Ignatia, into whose sandals she was all ready to step, who was a living skeleton, consumed daily by all manner of mental horrors, and yet likely to live to the age of Methusaleh, and see Saint Clement herself safely laid in her coffin. It was a cruel thing to be remanded every now and then to the House Without a Name, and put at all sorts of rigors, and set on a level with Saint Sophia, and Saint Magdalena, or even with the cooking Sisters in the kitchen. How very humiliating to be considered no better than Sister Maria, who had not a soul or capacity above nursing children, and bringing heretic babies to her priest to be baptized! There was no telling how cutting it was to hear how useful was Mother Ignatia, and how valuable to the Church, and how much worshipful obedience was due to her.

Saint Clement had one safety-valve for all the furies roused within her by these trials;—and that was a prisoner shut up in the fourth story. "I like to take care of prisoners," said she, between her set teeth. Truly she did; and she ruled this prisoner most unmercifully. She took her small and poor allowances of food; hung up in her room horrid pictures of fictitious saints and martyrs; and, if she heard through the thin wall or ill-hung door, the clear, strong voice of her prisoner, she rushed in, shook her fiercely, or even treated her to a mild specimen of garrote with her handkerchief. "I'll have the heresy out of her yet," said she to herself.

It was quite wonderful how this prisoner, a young girl, sustained this treatment. She kept her elastic health and spirits, like some strong plant that thrives on being crushed and twisted, and rudely handled. She was of mixed blood, sprung of two races, one of which has never learned to yield a point, and the other knows how to endure through ages of oppression, strong in the hope of good to come. She was Scotch and Italian. She was *Estelle.* We know how long she had been a prisoner; and here she was in the very heart of the city, caged in an attic of that nameless House, while her father sought her from place to place with a love that would not grow weary or faint-hearted.

It is useless to tell how Estelle was treated to vigils, fastings, prayers and exhortations, how all that Rome could do to break her spirit had been ineffectually done. She kept her lips closed in chapel and confessional. The few books in the case in the sacristy were untouched by her. Her crafty Italian vein found outlet in deceiving sometimes even these vigilant jailers, and getting a surreptitious meal or rest or jibe, merely to amuse herself by the getting of it. She fed her life on hopes set purposely a long way off, that she might not grow heartsick too soon.

When Estelle found herself denied to her own

father, when the bond that united her to her brother Martin was by the Abbess Robart rejected, her whole soul burned with hatred to a creed to which she had in outward act subscribed, while her heart was not with it. Above all things, Estelle now hated Rome, the Church which had robbed her of liberty and relatives. Mother Robart and the reverend Fathers had endeavored to make their proceedings plausible to Estelle, and to win her interest and affection for a convent life. They told her that, if she took and cherished holy vows, she would be one day a Superior—the glittering bait held out before many ambitious young spirits—should visit Europe on special missions, and go in high favor to Italy, the land she loved. Nothing could persuade Estelle. She had seen nothing of religion but what she had seen in Rome, and that she hated with a perfect hatred. If we could only say that it was faith in God, love for religion pure and undefiled, that sustained this girl under her persecutions; if we could set her before you as a fair young martyr for the truth, gladly would it be done. But Estelle was strong in a prejudice rather than a principle. She was upheld by pride instead of faith. She was not a lover of God. Yet, God was good to her, and, even in this House Without a Name, he gave her a friend. This one light in Estelle's darkness illustrates the truth that people are rarely, if ever, as miserable as they might be. There is ever below the "deepest depth" of misery, a "deeper depth" that might be tried. On this side eternity the most wretched has ever some one consolation.

And who was Estelle's friend in this prison? The Italian nun, Magdalena. She was not enough her friend to free her; she dared not do that; but she was enough her friend to secretly supply her with food, with materials for fancy-work, with pencil and paper; for these things Ignatia denied Estelle, that by utter loneliness and tedium, she might sooner break her spirit. There were hours when Magdalena could steal into that narrow upper chamber to talk to Estelle; and her talk was never directed to efforts for her conversion; it was all of the fair native land for which this nun was homesick.

"I love you," Magdalena would say to Estelle, "for you came from Italy. You have blood in your veins like mine. You have touched the hands of my country-people. You can remember our vineyards, our little homes, our dress, our songs. You have seen the flowers and loved the skies that I have seen and loved. You have seen Florence, and Venice and the Bay of Naples. There are those in Italy that loved me once, but now they have forgotten the poor girl who was made a Sister and sent far away from her lovely land. Yes, I love you. You can speak to me in my own tongue, and can tell me the songs you heard them sing in Italy; and you think the land shall be free some day; ah, so my father said."

Besides such prattle as this, Magdalena would tell Estelle the small news of the house—when Maria came and went, how much work was done, what patients came for Mother Ignatia's doctoring, and what new privations Mother Ignatia imposed upon herself. Thus Estelle had something to think about, and did not feel utterly detached from the outer world. She was sure she would get free one day.

Mother Ignatia disliked Estelle.

By this time Adelaide had grown tired of the convent, and wanted to go home. Mrs. Kemp represented this matter to her husband. "Adelaide had married very poorly to be sure, but she was a widow now, young enough to retrieve the past; she had better come home and let all things be as they had once been."

"Yes," Mr. Kemp said; but added, that if he could put up with his wife's daughter, his wife could certainly return the favor in kind. People were talking because Grace could not live at home. They had better gather up the scattered fragments of the household, and put them together as well as they could. If Adelaide came home and Mr. Kemp made no reflections on the past, so Grace must come home and Mrs. Kemp must cease to hector her about religion.

Therefore Adelaide came from the convent, and Grace crossed the street from Richard's, and Lucy was restored to her former place. But the tie that had bound the step-sisters was broken. They did not longer share one room, and had very little in common.

Mr. Kemp was doing his best to make his family comfortable. He had consented to go to Saratoga for the summer, and had not denied new carpets and rosewood furniture for the newly-occupied bed-rooms. He had even agreed to a proposition for exchanging the family carriage for a handsomer one. How astonishing, then, that a priest could lead the wife and step-daughter to plot together to deceive and wound him in the cruelest manner. Yet so it was.

Father Murphy told Mrs. Kemp, that he had waited long enough for Grace to return peaceably to the Romish fold, and now she must be *forced* to come. Adelaide was not a good Catholic, but she was not a Protestant, and while she gloried in infidelity during sunshine, as soon as the storms of life broke over her she would run cowardly back to the Holy Church. But Grace was a positive trophy to Protestantism, and such she must not remain. Father Murphy had no doubt that a few weeks of judicious management, away from Richard, Agnes and other Protestant friends, would restore Grace to her former opinions. She might be induced to make solemn oath to be faithful to the Church for ever; or she might be made to take the veil, and so be saved from heresy. To aid him in this precious plan he won Mrs. Kemp and Adelaide—Mrs. Kemp because she was afraid to disobey her priest—Adelaide because she was envious of Grace, piqued at her step-father, and fond of malice and mischief anyway.

They managed it very nicely. Mrs. Kemp and her husband went off one day with the carriage. Mrs. Kemp had planned the excursion, but so adroitly that Mr. Kemp supposed it had all proceeded from himself. Adelaide urged Grace to go out shopping, and volunteered to hire a hack for the occasion. She insisted so strongly that she had her own way, and, according to previous agreement with them, Michael Shinn furnished the carriage and John Mora drove.

They went about here and there. Adelaide bought both pictures and bonbons which demanded close attention. At last they stopped before a chill, shut-up, iron-fenced, dreary house, so like a good many others that Grace did not know she had ever been there before.

"Come in here with me, Gracie," rattled Adelaide. "Mrs. Barry says here is the best mantuamaker. She works for absolutely nothing, and such a fit! Put your veil down, do, this wind would tan one to an Indian. Hold up your dress, Gracie, the walk is so dirty!" The door was opened by a young woman in a gay pink calico, and in the hall a red carpet had been put down for the nonce. Grace therefore suspected nothing, and they went into a side room. Adelaide mumbled something about "seeing madame," and ran through an opposite door.

Grace was alone—she looked about—how stupid she had been! This was verily the parlor of Mother Ignatia's house. There was a footstool, a tidy, a worked table-cover, a bouquet and an ice-pitcher,—things set there to beguile her memory at the first glance; but they could be carried away in a minute with the red carpet in the hall and the maid's pink dress; and surely it was Mother Ignatia's House. She tried the doors, tried the windows, thought she heard the sound of wheels without, and felt she was a victim to Adelaide's treachery.

A chill of terror passed over her, then she grew hot with rage. It could not be possible that they should dare imprison her. Then she thought of the many queer things they had done, and she remembered Estelle, and her heart sank.

Half an hour passed. The door opened very gently—it is astonishing how quiet everything in a convent is—and there stood Mother Ignatia. Grace looked at her angrily, and did not speak. She tried to think the reverend Mother the most detestable-looking person she had ever seen; but, for all that, pity stirred in her heart at the sight of her wan, pinched features and anguished eyes. "How in the world had this Superior existed until the present time?" This question thrust itself so boldly upon Grace that it almost drove off those other questions, how and why she herself got here, and when should she get away?

"My dear daughter, how rejoiced I am to see *you!*" said Ignatia.

"And how surprised *I* am to see *you!*" replied Grace.

"I have been very unhappy about you, daughter."

"If you had wanted to see me, you knew where I lived, or, if you could not come, you could have sent me a note, asking in an honorable way that I should visit you. I came here with my sister on some pretext of hers, and now I find her gone, and myself locked in. I am in no mood to talk with you, Mother. Open your front door, and let me go home."

"Home, my daughter? There is a heavenly

home, on which in youthful folly you have turned your back. Dear child, you are in deadly peril, lest those gates of mercy are closed on you for ever. False teachers have beguiled your youth; you are here to set your feet firmly in the true way. My daughter, I have grieved for you, and wept over you."

"If I am wrong, you are not responsible for it," said Grace. "I am satisfied that I am right. I am of age to choose for myself, and if I choose wrong on my head be the wrong. You have no right to use force, and violence, and underhand means to bring me to *your* notions." And Grace, frightened and excited, sat down and sobbed wildly. From this Mother Ignatia argued that Grace was of a weak nature, and could be easily moved; but she did not comprehend that in that weak nature dwelt eternal strength, sent from above.

As Grace sat, her face hidden in her hands, weeping bitterly, Mother Ignatia stood near her, and in a low voice repeated several forms of prayer. At last Grace looked up. "Mother Ignatia, are you not going to let me go home to my friends?"

"Your home, dear child, is the true Church. *We* are your friends."

"But you have no right to keep me here—a person of my age—in a free land. Have you no respect for the law?"

"We recognize no law but obedience to the Church," said the Superior. "To the Church we are for ever children, and never too old to obey or be coerced to obedience. I do not act for myself; I act as the Church bids me."

"And what has the Church done for you that you should be so submissive to her?" demanded Grace.

"I have been a wayward, stubborn, rebellious child," said the Superior, sadly. "The Church has been better to me than I deserve. I have merited nothing at her hands."

"And because the Church has made you miserable, *you* want to make me miserable. You are a cruel, wicked woman. You *can* let me go home, you know you can. What have I ever done to you, Mother Ignatia, that you should hate me?"

The Superior had sat down by Grace, and was resting her head on her hand, with her arm supported on the back of Grace's chair. She looked sadly at the young girl, and tried to clasp her hand. Grace jerked it away. "My child, I love you."

"It is a poor kind of love that persecutes, and is unjust and breaks one's heart," asseverated Grace.

"Mine *is* a poor love; alas, it is poor to mortals and to Heaven! My love has been the curse of those I spent it on. I thought that it was dead until you came to me, so fair, so young, so obedient, so gentle to me who for years had known no gentleness, so ready to believe well of my poor life. My child, I *do* love you."

"Let me go home then," cried Grace. "Show your love in one good way. You are keeping me here to be scolded and persecuted by Father Murphy and Father Douay, and I hate them and am afraid of them."

"They are true servants of the Church," said Ignatia. "There is nothing to fear from them, and it is wrong to hate them."

"If you say you love me, and yet keep me here," cried Grace, "I shall never believe you again."

"Perhaps it is better that you did not," said the Superior, mournfully. "None ever trusted me, but I made them wretched. My daughter, they tell me you have left the faith of your youth and become a heretic."

"I have left the Church of Rome, and returned to that pure faith from which many years ago Rome departed," retorted Grace.

"Poor deluded child! they tell me you have accepted one of the many wicked forms of that perverted belief, Calvinism—the creed of a wicked, cruel, bigoted man, a true child of the Evil One."

"You are greatly mistaken, Mother," said Grace. "I have gone back to the pure faith of St. Augustine, or rather, to the holy doctrines of Jesus of Nazareth."

"And where, my child, can you find *them*, but in the one true holy Church? Let not evil men delude your tender mind. You were here with me once, a gentle, faithful, obedient child of the Church. I hoped that you would take holy orders, and come here to abide with me. On you I built great hopes for this House I have planted. Dear child, am I to be disappointed?"

"I have seen my errors, and accepted a faith from which I shall never turn. You may tear me to pieces, Mother Ignatia, and you shall not get the Protestantism out of me. You might as well let me go."

"Be satisfied, my daughter: *that* I cannot do."

"Then I shall run away," said Grace, angrily.

Mother Ignatia gave a sad, incredulous smile. She knew her House was strong. "Promise me one thing, my daughter, that you will here honestly and humbly examine the doctrines of our Church, and see how broad, how firm, how glorious they are. Rome invites your study. The True Church is not afraid to have her faith examined. In the sacristy you will find volumes in which the questions at issue are ably and clearly discussed. Examine them with an unprejudiced mind. It is all the True Church asks of you. Do that, and convinced of your delusions, you will joyfully return to your proper faith. For this are you here."

"Then I shall not do it," said Grace, pettishly. "You will make nothing by this cruel, shameful imprisonment; and my friends shall punish you for it, too."

"I am used to harshness and unkindness," said Ignatia, dropping her eyes. "I have borne it long, and none can be harder upon me than myself."

Grace looked upon her gray hairs and her pallid face, and felt a little remorse. Ignatia quickly discerned it. "May I not ask this one little attention to my wishes," she said, softly—"I who have sinned so much, and suffered so much?"

"And why do you ask it? How can it benefit *you?*"

"If I might be the humble means of leading so precious a child back to the True Church, it might be accepted as some little atonement for sins black and many."

"There is but one atonement for sin," said Grace, "the blood of Christ."

"We must do something to win the interference of that blood; so says the infallible Church," replied Ignatia.

"Christ shed his blood *freely* for all men," said Grace.

"His blood is not such a trifle that we can gain it for nothing," answered Ignatia. "If it is worth having it is worth working for. If it were not so, would I have spent years striving for the cleansing?"

"And how long have you striven?" asked Grace.

"Twelve years," groaned the Superior.

"And if you were ever to obtain it in that way, do you not think you might before this?"

"Child, you can never realize the number and blackness of my sins," said Ignatia.

"You remind me of the case of a woman who lived many years ago, when Jesus was on earth."

"A case like mine? Never, never," said the nun, dreamily.

"Yes; she had striven for help for twelve years. At last she thought she would go to Jesus. The apostles stood about him, but she did not pay any attention to them. Jesus was all she wanted, and she pressed up to him. She fell on her knees, reached out her hand, touched but the hem of his garment, and all her trouble was gone. Her help you see came *directly* from Jesus."

Ignatia looked up with a heavy sigh. "It is a pleasant story," she said. "I wish her lot was mine. Come, child, you are not a prisoner, only a wanderer come home. Your cell is a small one within mine, and I shall have you with me always. Only set your mind to learn the truth." She took her hand and led her from the room. The red carpet was gone from the hall already.

Grace struggled to draw her toward the front door. "Oh, Mother Ignatia, let me go—let me go."

"It is useless, child, it is useless. Do you ask me to add to my other crimes this, worst of all?" She led Grace to the sacristy, and taking from the shelves several books, laid them down before her, reading their titles as she did so:—"Protestantism Weighed and Found Wanting," "Protestantism and Infidelity," "Plain Talk to Protestants," "Evidences of Catholicity," "Principles of Church Authority," "Burnett's Path." We think it a great pity that she did not have "Protestantism a Failure," to add to the precious list. It is such a clincher in the way of argument.

And now see Grace deprived by the nuns of her worldly attire, going about with Mother Ignatia from morning until night.

CHAPTER VI.

PLOTTINGS.—THE CHOLERA.—THE BROKEN SNARE.

OF course, among the other bits of information that poor Magdalena took to Estelle in her stolen hours of gossip, she told her that Grace was in the house, and how and why she came there. The voluble Italienne had never learned a primary principle of Jesuitism, namely, to hold her tongue. She gave the information along with other indifferent matters, having not the slightest idea that Estelle had ever before heard of Grace; and Estelle, wise girl, gave no sign of special interest. It seemed to Estelle that it would be so easy to escape from the convent if one was not shut up in one room! All her fear was that Grace would get away before she found out about herself. She began to set before Magdalena how she would like to see this strange young woman—such a change, such an event—she was so tired, so lonesome—only to see her—only to speak five minutes, only one minute, dear Magdalena. And she argued her case in Italian to win more surely the heart of the nun.

A meeting between Estelle and Grace was of all things not to be desired, from a Murphy point of view. It might lead to the very worst results. And such a meeting would never have taken place, had not Saint Clement been called away to act as nurse to a rich man dying at a boarding-place, whom it was desirable to convert in his last hours. Annette was ready to go; here was a case that suited her peculiar talents. She signalized her departure by putting her prisoner on short rations for the day, and Estelle was in a state of semi-starvation when Magdalena in the evening privately conveyed to her two biscuits and some loaf sugar. Magdalena, being the housekeeping Sister, she could do this conveniently. When she had brought it, she leaned against the door and discoursed in her native tongue on the delights of sardines and maccaroni.

"What were you saying to the prisoner?" said sharp-eared Saint Sophia, who had drifted to that part of the House, a self-constituted vigilance committee. "My prayers and the Blessed Hours," replied the veracious Saint Magdalena.

Grace had not dropped out of her ordinary home-life unnoticed. Richard was absent from the city—a fact which had caused Father Murphy to look on this as a favorable time for the execution of his plans; but on the first night of her absence, about bed-time,

Mr. Kemp suddenly noticed that his daughter was away. Mrs. Kemp lazily opined that she had gone to stay all night with some of her friends—with Agnes very likely. Of course, she was not then expected at breakfast, and no more was said until the six-o'clock dinner. Then Mrs. Kemp "didn't know—feared something was wrong. Grace had asked Adelaide to go out shopping, and had suddenly left her before a dressmaker's, and had not returned."

Adelaide began to whimper: "She could not bear to walk and so had hired a hack. *Merci!* no, she did not know *what* hack it was; how should she? would not know if she saw it again. Grace left her, and she was pretty sure she saw a Scotch-looking man getting into the hack. Grace had hinted this; but then Grace was such a dear girl, she had never suspected."

Now Mamma Kemp came to the rescue. She "had seen several things she thought strange. There had been letters speaking of a trip to Scotland, and all such things. She had merely glanced at them; but feeling it her duty to look at them again, they were gone. Mr. Kemp would hear soon enough; letters always came in such cases." And Mamma Kemp looked at Adelaide, and Adelaide grew red, and they both retired behind their handkerchiefs. This was good acting, and Mr. Kemp did not suspect them. They were quite perfect in the parts Father Murphy had assigned them. Presently, Mrs. Kemp "did not wish to be harsh, but most likely this was the reason Grace became a Protestant."

Mr. Kemp was at his wits' end, and as was eminently proper his wife became his counselor. "Such matters were so much better hushed up. They had better keep all quiet; perhaps there would be some good explanation; anyway, she and Adelaide were willing to say that Grace was off on a visit, until they knew something for certain. He might quietly look at the list of passengers on departed ships, and might make some inquiries at the ticket-offices."

Mr. Kemp "did not know what better to do than to take this advice. He was ignorant of the ways of young women; and, if Adelaide had acted in this manner, why might not Grace? It was very hard and he wished Rick was home."

Adelaide took an early opportunity to call on the Anthons, and tell them Grace had gone from the city on a visit. She and Mrs. Kemp took all pains to keep up the illusion they had begun for Mr. Kemp. By the time Richard got home, Mr. Kemp thoroughly believed his wife's view of Grace's disappearance. Richard did not believe it. He took counsel with the Anthons, and concluded that Grace had been kidnapped. But that seemed a ridiculous idea, and they had no shadow of foundation for it, save that they believed her a pious and sensible girl who would not run away from her family. Richard searched for her as best he could, but his father was nervously anxious "to have the affair kept quiet," and the young man was bewildered by the tissue of falsehood that Mrs. Kemp and her daughter spread before him.

Now Richard might have searched constantly, boldly and wisely, without once coming near Grace's true prison. Who knew anything of that Nameless House? A few poor Romanists went there for medicine and for doles of soup and bread, without knowing what sort of place it was. Few, even, were the nuns who knew of this House. Its exterior was blank as an idiot's face. John Mora knew it was "some sort of a holy place like." Michael Shinn believed it a "little 'ospital." Saint Cecelia had been there now and then. It was a hidden snare—hidden all too well. Get any one in there, and Mother Church might defy everybody to get them out again.

But there was one sleepless Eye that watched that House Without a Name by night and by day. To that watching care did Grace appeal. Believing herself shut out from all human aid, she cried to God to bring her out of prison. While daily her faith was assailed, she cried that she might never deny the truth, but that God would bring her trial quickly to an end.

After a while Magdalena was prevailed on to take Grace secretly to Estelle's room.

"You wicked girl," said Magdalena, "you never told me that you knew her!"

"How could I tell you that I knew her before I saw her," said Estelle, releasing herself from Grace's embrace.

"You deceive me," said Magdalena, sulkily. Then Estelle overwhelmed her with Italian, and caresses, until she agreed to leave them alone together for a while.

"Grace," said Estelle, "you must contrive to get away, you have such a good chance."

"I have no chance at all," said Grace. "You have no idea how it is."

"You will find a way," said Estelle; "and then—oh, Grace, think how I have been treated—my brother—my father"—and Estelle wept.

"I'll not go away without you," said Grace. "But you can get this Magdalena to let us both go—to go with us. It is evident she will do anything for you."

"Almost anything but that," said Estelle, crossly. "She is a doll-baby and a coward. She is afraid to do that—afraid of her priest. She could not get up courage enough to do anything important."

"But we could plan it all, and you could persuade her to do certain things which we had marked out."

"I have planned it, fifty times over, but she takes fright at the least little hint of it—says this is a good-enough place—she wishes she had never come into it—but what would she do in the world? If Magdalena is our only hope we might as well die in despair."

"God is our hope," said Grace, earnestly. "He will hear our cries."

"It might be," said Estelle, turning the subject, "that if we got all ready for a start, even to the door open, and gave poor Magdalena a pull, and said 'Come out, and we shall take you to the land of grapes and maccaroni,' she might get her liberty before she realized what a dreadful thing she was doing. I think I'd like to help the good simpleton that much."

"As they have in a manner stolen me from myself," said Grace, "I feel as if I should like to return the compliment by taking off one of their dupes."

"By that rule we ought to take off two at least," said Estelle; and these two prisoners laughed, for they were young and hopeful, and not suffering any present pain. Thank God for the care-free hearts of youth!

The main object of this House Without a Name was to have it a perfectly secret place, unknown to almost every one, where difficult cases might be quietly handled. *Rome is not able yet to get the olden Inquisition restored in America, but she makes small and gradual approaches to it in prisons like this.* The force of Sisters kept in this House was very small, because only thus could entire seclusion be secured. Mother Ignatia, Saint Magdalena the housekeeper, Saint Sophia the nurse and doctress, Saints Clement and Maria, who were so often abroad, and two Sisters in the kitchen, made up the present number. Of these, Saint Sophia visited the sick and a small school which was under their supervision, and all the time that could be spared from other duties was given to embroidering articles for sale; for this institution was not wealthy.

Grace was required to spend her time in embroidering. She would not read the books in the sacristy; and so she embroidered, and Mother Ignatia read them to her.

"Oh, my dear daughter," said the Superior, "if you would only read these invaluable books yourself!"

"I shall not read them here where I am a prisoner," said Grace. "If I can go home, I promise you that I will read them there, every one."

"But with what benefit, my daughter, when you would have your heretic books and friends to bewilder your young mind with false arguments and sophistries that might cheat the wisest?"

"Don't you think yourself," said Grace, "that it is very cruel and wicked to keep me here in this way?"

"How much better," said Ignatia, "is the soul than the body! Dear child, consider how *I* endure and toil, to destroy these fleshly sins and inclinings, and to save my soul."

"You will find, Mother," replied Grace, "that you have 'spent your money for that which is not bread, and your labor for that which satisfieth not.' Tell me, Mother, do you *love* Jesus?"

Ignatia drew back as in horror. "Love!" she cried; "dare such a wretch as I offer my love to the Holy One? It is not love but penitence that I must feel. When at last my works are remembered, and all my groans and tears have washed away my iniquities, then, when I am clean, may I offer my heart's devotion to the Son of God."

"There is just where you are wrong, Mother, believe me," said Grace. "We must love Jesus 'because he first loved us'—love first, and *that* shall teach us to repent."

"You cannot be right, my poor innocent child," said Ignatia, stroking Grace's soft hair; "for, if that were true, my priests would have told me of it. Father Douay says I am not penitent enough. My child, the rack would be heaven to what mental agonies I suffer. Father Murphy says all is right; I am only nervous; I must be content, be at rest, be at peace. Ah, child, how *can* I have rest or peace when ten thousand furies possess my soul?"

"Since your two spiritual doctors differ, Mother," said Grace, "take the prescription of a third; if you try which, your own heart shall soon divine its efficacy."

"My own heart!" cried the Superior, "I would not trust that; it is full of all wickedness."

Mother Ignatia was very kind to Grace. She read to her, exhorted her, tried to reason with her, and kept her ever at her side. With Mother Ignatia Grace went many times in the twenty-four hours to the chapel, and while there, unlike Naaman in the house of Rimmon, she would not bow. "O stubborn knees that will not bend before the holy Lady and her blessed Son!" Ignatia would lament, holding Grace's hand, and trying to draw her down to the brick floor beside her. Then she would pour out many prayers for herself and for this poor, unhappy, deluded girl.

As may be supposed, this House, where sunshine never came, where vigils were multiplied, and fasts were a customary exercise, where the food was coarse and poor, and where disease was ever and anon coming with its odors, was a tempting harvest-field ready for the mowing of the reaper, Death. The only wonder is that he delayed so long. But now, as the July heats scorched the city, on poisoned miasmatic breezes, and in ships from over the sea, the cholera came; and here and there, like grasses under the mower's scythe, its victims fell. First it visited the crowded homes of poverty, and it was while it delayed there, and the terror of the pestilence had scarcely begun, that Saint Sophia went to some sufferers in a foul, reeking den, and gave them first medicine and then baptism, and held the crucifix before their dying eyes, and murmured Pater Nosters and Ave Marias in their deafened ears, and folded up their clammy, dead hands over little crosses, and so came home with the disease creeping through all her veins. Poor Saint Sophia told of the ravages of the pestilence, and fear spread through all the House. The two Sisters who especially presided over the cooking and kitchen were terribly alarmed. They were Germans and had lost friends by this sickness in "Faderland," and it was their chief dread. One was quite sure she felt the symptoms of the malady already.

That was a night of trouble. The disease fastened relentlessly on Saint Sophia, and in the darkness of her little cell, lighted by one poor taper, the Sisters and the Superior gathered to see her die. They administered what remedies they could, and sorely wanted a physician and a priest; but Clement and Maria were away, Magdalena had never been outside the front door of the House, the German Sisters were ignorant of the city, were dull, little acquainted with English, and terrified almost out of their senses. One of the Germans knelt sobbing and praying in a corner of Sophia's cell. The other wailed without the door. Death had never come to this House before, and now he surprised them armed with his wildest terrors. Magdalena and Mother Ignatia saw the struggle for life ended, and Saint Sophia lying helpless on her pallet; then spread a sheet over her, and locked the door of the cell.

"You, Magdalena, must go for the reverend Father," said Mother Ignatia—"and for a doctor," she added—for she felt already the grasp of the pestilence upon herself.

Grace had held aloof from Saint Sophia's cell. She felt that she was not there needed, and the scene was too fearful to look upon. But now that Mother Ignatia was seized, she applied herself to do what she could for her relief. Her mind was also divided between sympathy for the sufferer and a hope of her own escape. She thought of Estelle, and appealing to Magdalena that she would not want the young girl to die of this plague alone, she besought her to bring her to the lower part of the house.

Saint Ignatia signed assent, and, her features pinched and her hands already chilling, begged for a doctor and a priest. The terrors of death had indeed taken hold upon her. She was in an agony of pain and fright. Grace indeed desired the presence of a physician; but felt that if Father Douay or Murphy came her hopes of release were gone. She urged Magdalena to allow her to go for help; but the nun had just enough of reason and stupidity left, amid her terror, to keep the House locked and her prisoners safe.

The German Sisters were now nearly frantic. They believed the city was full of the plague and did not doubt that corpses were piled in every street. They had come to this House from a convent situated three miles out of the city on a breezy hill, and their one idea was to get there once more. They believed that to do so they must crowd their way through dead bodies; but the love of life was strong in them, and their sole hope lay in getting to this remote and healthy convent. Magdalena told them they must go for a doctor and a priest, and tried to gather some directions for their guidance from the Superior's quivering lips. The German Sisters consented to go together, and Magdalena let them depart.

"If they get people here we are lost," whispered Grace to Estelle.

"Don't be afraid of *them*," replied Estelle, who from her foreign rambles could speak a little of many languages. "They said to each other that the convent of Santa Clara lay due east of the city; they could guide themselves by the sun and get there; it would be time enough to send help then. And Santa Clara is full four miles from here."

"We are as strong now as Magdalena," said Grace; for she and Estelle talked apart as the Sister with poultices, hot water, camphor, and brandy, toiled weeping over her Superior. "Let us force the keys away from her, and run for it. You are less likely to get along than I. Go up stairs and get the clothes I wore here, and put them on. They hang on the wall of Annette's room—Sister Clement, you know. Be quick, Estelle! and bring some of the holy Sister's trumpery for me."

It was a time of day when no one ever came near this Nameless House, the reverend Fathers making their appearance, if at all, in the latter part of the afternoon. Things looked hopeful for the young prisoners. Estelle sped up stairs, though she was weak from long imprisonment. Grace could not leave the Superior without some kind words. She aided Magdalena for a moment or two, and, wiping the damps from the contracted forehead of the dying Superior, said, "Mother, do you know me?"

Ignatia grasped her hand.

"You are so ill, Mother." Another pressure replied.

"And are you ready to die, Mother?"

A fearful groan burst from the writhing figure.

"Mother," cried Grace, "now, at this last hour, cast yourself on Jesus. Offer one earnest prayer to him alone. Let all else go, and seize him. He is *ready* to save, *able* to save."

Magdalena ran up with holy water and a crucifix; then brought an image of our Lady, and held it high before the blearing eyes. Ignatia turned her gaze to Grace. "Mother, trust *him*. Trust the Saviour!"

Ignatia's eyes closed. Grace thought her in a stupor.

Estelle at this moment ran in, wearing Grace's clothes, with Annette's habiliments in her arms. "Now or never!" she cried. Magdalena stared. Estelle dropped the garments and went up behind the nun, grasping her closely in her lithe arms. Grace jerked the keys from her side, and began to pull on the clothes that lay on the floor.

"Magdalena," said Estelle, "we are going to let ourselves out, and be free. Keep still, Magdalena, you cannot prevent us." But Magdalena gave a shriek of dismay.

"Going!" she cried, holding to the girls, "and leave me alone, with a dead woman and with *her* dying? The House is full of ghosts—I won't stay—if you will go I go—I cannot stay alone with dead people and spectres!"

"Come on, then, with us," said Estelle. "But she will betray us, Grace, by her looks, if she goes in this dress, and we chance to meet nuns or priests. Let her have part of those clothes, and I will give her this blue veil for her head."

Estelle began hurriedly dressing the nun, quite relishing the idea of eloping with her, while the poor Sister had no thought of anything but to get away from dead bodies, and not be left to brave the cholera alone in a haunted house.

"Magdalena—Sister Magdalena, stay here," cried Grace. "We do not want you with us, and you will not leave your Superior to die alone. Shame on you, stay here!"

"Let her come," said Estelle. "Magdalena, in three months you shall eat sardines in Italy."

"Magdalena, stay here and take care of your dying Mother!" cried Grace.

"If I stay here I shall die of cholera, and be murdered by ghosts," shrieked Magdalena.

"Let her come. What is the Superior to her? She is quite unconscious; maybe she is dead; let us leave her alone," said Estelle; "we have not one minute to lose."

The three turned, Grace reluctantly, when Mother Ignatia opened her eyes, and gave a piercing scream.

"I cannot leave her to die alone," said Grace. "Estelle, escape yourself. Take the little money that is in that tin box; get off to the noisy parts of the city, and hire a hack to take you to Vane street, No. 16, which is Mr. MacPherson's. Get a hack with a colored driver, or you may be in the hands of some Catholic who knows you. Tell Rick where I am, and that he must come to help me. If I get out alone I will be home before night."

She wrapped the thin shawl, which she had put on, about Magdalena, and with the caution, "Oh, Estelle, this is your last chance, be careful," unlocked for them the front door, and saw them hasten away. Magdalena had made signs of staying with Grace; but Grace said, firmly, "If you stay, I go." So the nun ran away from ghosts and the cholera, and Grace remained in that gloomy prison, where one figure was already lying stark and still under the folds of the white sheet, and where Ignatia was groaning in the agonies of death uncheered by the hope of heaven.

Grace knelt by Mother Ignatia administering what remedies she knew, praying with her, exhorting her to rest in this extreme hour on the Merciful One, to know no name but his. Ignatia grasped her with a clasp of terror and despair. Grace shivered and trembled on that sultry morning, as if in the chill of a winter's day. She was in terror of infuriated priests coming there, and wondered if she could not bar them out at one door and escape by another; but ah, the fences were high and their gates were locked. Every wheel on the street, every foot on the pavement, was as a death-knell to her. She feared that presently Estelle and Magdalena would be brought in captured. I hold her a heroine for staying as she did, and for nearly two hours her heroism sustained her. Then the death-rattle sounded in Ignatia's throat, her limbs relaxed, her eyes wide open stared stonily. Grace spread a handkerchief over the terrible face, drew up the counterpane smoothly, put on the tawdry hat of servant-maid Annette, and fled as for her life. She saw a nun three squares off, and thought she saw also a priest. She was ready to drop on the pavement, but passed blindly along—growing warm enough now, but oh, so weak—east, two squares, south, three squares, looking for a street she knew. Here was James street. She brightened; she had heard of that street. And now she came to a stone church, with three flights of retreating stone steps leading to doors that gave deep shelters. As she was passing this church, she heard her name called. To her amazement, there were Estelle and Magdalena! They said they had got bewildered and frightened, and had hidden there, waiting for they knew not what.

"Keep to this side of the street, keep pace with me as I go on the other pavement, and do as I do; come," said Grace.

In fifteen minutes she found a hack whose driver she believed she could trust, and putting her silly companions into it, stepped in herself, dropped the curtains, and said, "Drive fast," having first given Mr. MacPherson's address; and then waited almost wild with anxiety, to reach the familiar house. She knew the old gentleman hated summer traveling, and would not shut his house up for the hot season.

Now, on reaching 16 Vane street, the hack-driver saw a curious performance. One of his three passengers flung some loose money on the sidewalk, and then they all rushed up the steps, and one tore wildly at the bell, another attacked the door-handle, while the third hung upon both; and presently the door swung back and they all seemed precipitated into the cool depth of the hall.

"Them is three *luny*tics," said the hackman, "lucky I got rid of 'em."

It seemed a house full of lunatics five minutes after, when Mrs. Anthon ran down stairs from her sewing-machine, Agnes from letter-writing in the

"Them is three *Luny*tics—lucky I got rid of 'em!"

Priest and Nun. Page 472.

library, Mr. MacPherson from the darkened parlor, where he had been endeavoring to keep cool; and when poor Mr. Wynford, who had been sick in his bed two days, heard a voice whose tones were echoing in his sad heart for ever, and came staggering down stairs in his wrapper, to add to the general confusion by fainting in the hall.

How Richard happened to come in just at that hour was a mystery that Agnes might have explained. He seized Grace in a grasp very uncomfortable considering the heat. Mr. MacPherson was first about to turn Magdalena into the street for a "wicked nun," and then was ready to hide her in the china-closet for safe-keeping.

"Magdalena," said Estelle that evening, "you are a nun no longer."

"Not a nun?" said Magdalena, who was in a state of bewilderment. "What am I then?"

"A free woman," cried Estelle, "and you shall gather grapes in Italy."

"If this woman desires to return to her convent, we must not detain her," said Mr. MacPherson.

"What was that about Italy?" demanded Magdalena.

"My father says if you want to go there, some friends of his will take you with them, they start next week, and you can go with them as maid."

"I shall go to Italy, mia Italia!" cried Magdalena, in a rapture.

Magdalena went to Italy. She was a useless body, but her friends were patient. She ate maccaroni and sardines, and gathered familiar fruits; but she was lonely and bewildered by the noisy world, and, in less than a year knocked at the gate of a House of Franciscan Sisters in Naples, was admitted and came out no more.

Estelle was with her father. He scarcely suffered her to go out of his sight, proposed many places where they might be *safe*, but ended by living at Mr. MacPherson's. He had proofs now such as would have overthrown the case made out by Madame Robart, but it came up in court no more. He was a broken man, and his friends desired only to lengthen out his life by quiet and tender care. In the shelter of a Christian home, the father and daughter learned the peace of God.

Martin most likely is a Jesuit priest. When he grows old and wise in Rome, like others he will mock at the "Fifteen Mysteries," and jest over the "Seven Sacraments," * and find amusement in the credulity of the unlearned.

Probably Sister Saint Clement has attained the end of her ambition, the rule of the House Without

* See Le Pape et L'Evangile, par J. J. Maurette, cure de Serres.

a Name, but into that House may we enter no more!

The return of Grace revealed the deception practiced by her step-mother and Adelaide. Mr. Kemp was both a grieved and an angry man. He rushed the delinquent feminines home from Saratoga, and bade his wife prepare for a separation, as he would by no means endure a woman who had robbed him of his child, and at the order of a priest so basely deceived him. Mrs. Kemp declared that Father Murphy had nothing to do with the affair; and, indeed, they could prove nothing except against Adelaide. In a separation from her husband Mrs. Kemp saw a disgrace for which her Church could offer no compensation; and Adelaide was sure they could no longer have a carriage or a saloon parlor. So deep was their humility and professed penitence, that the threat of separation was never carried into execution, although the healing of the wounds caused by Romish priestcraft was never so thorough as to efface the bitter memory or to hide the unsightly scars.

Of that household Grace never made one. Her brother's home was hers.

See, dear Americans, what Rome can do for you and yours. Grant her but her own way for a little while, give her your children, give her the masses of the poor and unlettered, give her the freedmen of the South, let the Roman Propaganda pour out *six hundred thousand gold dollars* each year, for the next decade, shut your eyes to bitter truths, by no means be "alarmed," never be "rash," be not "bigoted," if you handle the matter at all handle it with gloves on, and what shall be the end? *Rome tells us it is but a question of time*—this matter of her political and ecclesiastical supremacy, in the United States—and when her time has come, when that "finger of decay" has touched the ballot-box, the trial by jury, the police system, public education, the liberty of the press, the freedom of the pulpit; when the Empire of the West is trampled in the filth of superstition under that Popery which Austria and Italy are sloughing off, as unworthy of them; think how a race of betrayed and ruined children of freemen, shall wail curses on the head of our infatuated age. Remember the warning of Lafayette, "If the liberties of America are subverted, it will be by Romish priests"—let us say, by *Priests and Nuns.*

APPENDIX.

APPENDIX.

THE "Priest and Nun," while presented in the form of fiction, claims to be based upon facts, and in all its delineations to be true to the life. The authoress has, however, taken full liberty in the grouping and arrangement of her happily-chosen incidents, in order to secure the proper artistic effect; nor has she deemed it expedient to give to any of the incidents (as she could not for obvious reasons give to all of them) actual dates, localities or names. Yet the publishers are fully persuaded that her claim to verity is well founded, and that no one point made by her against the insidious working of the Roman Catholic power in this country, especially in connection with the convent system, is either untruthful or at all exaggerated.

Since the manuscript came into our hands, and while the process of stereotyping has been going forward, we have received additional proofs of its entire truthfulness by many facts which have come to our knowledge, corresponding to and confirmatory of the *most startling* of the statements herein made.

We have become cognizant of several instances of forcible abductions, entirely similar to that of Grace Kemp, in which every sacred obligation of home and kindred has been trampled down, and the natural protectors and defenders of beautiful and accomplished young girls have, by priestly artifice, been made submissive tools to aid in their *imprisonment in convents for conscience' sake:* instances, also, of the *most cruel treatment,* in the convents, of those who have been beguiled to a willing taking of the veil, but who have subsequently seen their error, mourned over their folly and sought release from their vow—treatment which has (in one instance at least) caused lifelong injury to the health of the poor girl who was at length delivered from the convent.

We only wish that we might state these cases, with all their minute details, for the information of the entire Protestant community. But we must, even like our authoress, be restrained from this by the wishes of the parties immediately interested.

We are not so restricted, however, in respect to a most remarkable case which occurred in Louisville, Ky., within a year past, and which is almost the exact counterpart of that of Estelle Wynford, as to the method taken to retain for the convent the great wealth of a young heiress, by actually *swearing away her identity.* This case, as stated in one of the

Louisville daily papers among its passing news items, we give on page 482, and would invite special attention to it.

The case of Mary Ann Smith, who was spirited away from Newark, N. J., on the 24th day of March, 1868, is also open to the public, and an account of it may be readily found in the pamphlet published by Rev. H. Mattison, D. D.; and although we do not claim that this young girl's character has yet been as thoroughly vindicated as we could wish, and are ready to allow much to parental authority as exercised over a minor, we nevertheless boldly assert that, *on their own showing*, the abductors and imprisoners of this girl stand convicted of a very grave offence against that freedom of conscience and personal liberty which ought to be sacred in this land.

In England, even more than in this country, attention has been of late awakened to the glaring abuses perpetrated in convents. Within a few months the Hull Convent case has been adjudicated in the courts, and has excited great interest. We furnish a synopsis of it on page 486, extracted from the foreign correspondence of one of our own weekly religious journals; and we doubt not it will impress all who read it as affording a remarkable *unveiling* of the inner life of those who take the veil.

In addition to these and a few other minor incidents, we have also placed in this Appendix some statistical information, to which we invite attention, as showing what the Roman Catholic Church is doing, and what she aims at in this country. We do not believe she will ever attain her aims, but we believe that "*ceaseless vigilance is the price of liberty.*"

A LAWSUIT FOR A MILLION.

A TWELVE-YEAR-OLD HEIRESS IN DISPUTE—ONE OF THE MOST REMARKABLE CASES ON RECORD—A PHYSICIAN AND A CATHOLIC SCHOOL THE CONTESTANTS.

ONE of the most extraordinary cases on record is now pending before Judge Bruce in the Circuit Court. The facts connected therewith, so far as we have been able to gather them, are as follows:

Dr. Samuel E. McKinley, son of Judge McKinley, formerly Judge of the Supreme Court of the United States, and United States Judge of this circuit, was residing and practicing his profession at New Orleans when that city was captured by the Federal army. He was retained as surgeon for the Confederate sick, and was afterward retained in the United States service. The doctor married a very wealthy heiress, a Miss Morrison, of Louisiana, by whom he has two children—one a boy named James, who is now with him in St. Louis, and the other a little girl, E. J. Lyon McKinley, twelve years of age. His wife dying during the infancy of the girl, the Doctor in 1864 moved to New Albany, Indiana, taking with him his two children. About a year ago last winter, he moved to this city, where he remained till some time in 1867, and becoming desirous of going back to New Orleans to look after his property, left his little daughter at the Ursuline Academy, a Catholic female school in this city, for education, sending her from time to time money to pay her expenses. Before, or about the time of vacation, the Doctor having moved and established himself in St. Louis, requested Judge Taylor to send by Adams Express his little daughter to him, the express company agreeing to undertake the care and custody of the child. When Judge Taylor applied for the child, the Superior of the Academy objected to letting her go till her tuition should be fully paid. The Doctor, on learning this, declared he had sent by mail the full amount, and then came for her himself. His counsel advising him that the Academy could not retain a lien on the child for their money, he sued out a writ of habeas corpus before his Honor Judge Bruce; and this case, as it happens, is the first brought before Judge Bruce since qualifying as our circuit judge. *The Superior of the Academy, answer-*

ing the writ, stated that the girl was named Lizzie Brown; that she was not the Doctor's daughter; that she was fifteen years of age; and that the Doctor was drunken and unfit to control the child. This answer was yesterday adjudged insufficient, and the respondent was required to state the time and the means by which respondent obtained possession of the child—that a mere allegation that the Doctor was not her father was no ground for respondent to retain her. While the Doctor was away, some two weeks ago, it seems that the Superior applied to the County Court to become her guardian, and exhibited, it is claimed, a printed envelope with the name of E. J. Lyon McKinley, in which her father had enclosed money to his daughter—this being the true name. It is also alleged he has letters from the Superior calling her, his daughter, Lyon.

It is further said that she has become a Catholic, contrary to her father's wishes, who is an Episcopalian, and that *she will, at her grandfather's death, become the heiress of more than a million.*

The case coming up yesterday afternoon, and the parties not being ready for trial on account of absent witnesses, it was continued till next Friday at 9 o'clock A. M. The court ruled the answer of the respondent insufficient, and required her to be more explicit.—*Louisville Daily Courier*, Aug. 28, 1868.

INCIDENT IN THE TRIAL OF MR. CHINIQUY.

Two witnesses swore point-blank against Mr. Chiniquy, and it was clear that he must be convicted next day, and, if convicted, sent to the penitentiary. This the reporter of a leading Chicago paper telegraphed, and the news was at once published, as the trial excited much interest. A Roman Catholic who had read the paragraph remarked to his wife, with satisfaction, that they were going to get rid of Chiniquy at last, and mentioned the news.

She said, "If he is convicted on that testimony, it is false."

"How do you know that?" asked her husband.

"Because I and another lady were visiting the niece of such a priest (naming him), and the door of his room was not quite close. He did not know we were there, and we overheard the whole bargain made with these two witnesses, that they were to swear so and so, and to get two hundred acres of land."

"Can you swear to this?" said her husband.

"Certainly."

"Can the other lady swear to it?"

"Undoubtedly."

The gentleman, though a Roman Catholic, loved justice more than the priesthood, and started at once for the night train. He reached the place of trial about two o'clock in the morning, roused Mr. Lincoln, told him to telegraph for the witnesses he named; and Mr. Lincoln, after doing so, came to Mr. Chiniquy's room (who was spending the night on his knees) to tell him that he was all safe.

When these ladies appeared in court, the priest asked what was their business and if they were going to destroy him. They said they would have to tell the truth, but it was he who had destroyed himself. Thereupon there was a consultation, and the prosecution came into court requesting leave to withdraw the charge, saying that further evidence had convinced them of its groundlessness, and offering to pay expenses and apologize to the accused.—*Correspondent of Montreal Witness.*

CONVENT LIFE IN ENGLAND.

EXTRAORDINARY REVELATIONS—PERSECUTION OF A NUN.

EDINBURGH, February 13, 1869.

MESSRS. EDITORS: I have a very remarkable tale to communicate to your readers—a real narrative of facts of our own day, showing the existing convent life in England, brought out during an eight days' trial in a court of justice. These facts are strange indeed.

The case has been eight days before the Court of Queen's Bench in London, and, though still unfinished, has so far produced a profound sensation throughout Great Britain. The complainant is a Miss Saurin, a young lady of good family and of high connections in Ireland. The defendants are a Mrs. Starr, the Mother Superior of the Convent of Our Lady of Mercy, at Hull, in England, and a Mrs. Kennedy, a local Superior in the same establishment. All the parties are Roman Catholics, passionately devoted to their Church. Two of Miss Saurin's sisters are nuns in different Roman Catholic Orders, her brother is a Jesuit priest, her uncle is the head of the Drogheda Convent of the Sisters of Mercy, and she herself, so far back as 1850—contrary to the wishes of her parents, who thought two of their daughters quite enough to be devoted to the service of the Church as nuns—entered the Convent of the Sisters of Mercy, in Bagot street, Dublin, as a postulant. In 1851 she became a novice, and toward the close of the same year she made profession as a regular Sister of the Order of Mercy in the same institution, taking the name of Sister Mary Scholastica Joseph. In accordance with her vow of "poverty," she surrendered to the convent the sum of £300. Mrs. Starr and Mrs. Kennedy were postulants and novices in the convent, and made their professions about the same time—the former taking the name of Sister Mary Josephine; the latter that of Sister Mary Magdalene. All were there, and down till 1857 on the best of terms with each other. In August, 1857, Mrs. Starr left to be Mother Superior of a new convent at Clifford, in Yorkshire; Mrs. Kennedy followed her, and in 1858, at the request of both, Miss Saurin, with the reluctant consent of her parents, joined them. Soon after there was opened another new convent in Hull, over which Mrs. Starr was appointed Mother Superior; in point of fact, Mrs. Starr held the office of Mother Superior in both; and in both Miss Saurin, down till 1864, spent the whole of her time, acting as housekeeper, visiting the sick and taking charge of a morning and evening school. It is necessary to state here that Mrs. Kennedy passed the greater part of her nunship at Hull, acting as a sort of local assistant, and that two other ladies came upon the scene—a Mrs. De Lane and a Mrs. M'Owne, each of whom in turn acted as local assistant to Mrs. Starr at Clifford. The friendly relations of all these parties were not disturbed down till 1860, when it seems Mrs. Starr demanded that Miss Saurin *should tell her what passed between herself and the priest at confessions.* Miss Saurin declined to allow her bosom secrets to be known even to her Superior, believing that to reveal them would be a breach of honor, and that nothing in the vows of "obedience" she had taken required her to divulge them. Mrs. Starr insisted upon knowing the nature of the confessions, and was again refused, the result of course being mutual alienation and dislike. Mrs. Starr, however, was not to be beaten. She would have her sweet revenge. From that time everything that Miss Saurin did was unsatisfactory; punishments and penances were therefore inflicted with a frequency and a persistency which ought to have worn out the soul, if not the body, of an ordinary lady. "Some work had been sent from Hull for me to do," says Miss Saurin, and the Mother Superior "obliged me to cut it out and prepare it on Sundays." The usual time of rising in the convent is half past five o'clock, and the usual time of retiring to bed ten o'clock. Mrs. Starr ordered Miss Saurin to get up about three o'clock in the morning and pursue her work till the latest hour at night. "I went to her cell one night," continued the complainant, "and said, 'Reverend Mother, what in the world am I doing that gives you so much displeasure? I am trying my best to please you and give you satisfaction. If you tell me anything more that I can do, I will try and do it.' She replied, 'I allow you too much liberty, and I am determined to pull you down.'" True to her word, "down" she did pull her. In every variety of petty form and way she thwarted and vexed her, and even when life in the convent had become almost unendurable, and Miss Saurin felt it necessary to write to her parents and friends to have her removed to Dublin, her letters were either not sent, or, when sent, the replies to them were intercepted, portions of them erased, and several of them never handed to her at all. In point of fact all this attempted letter-writing, complaining of grievances and seeking relief was deemed by the amiable Mother Superior and her faithful substitute, Mrs. Kennedy, as *insubordination*, a violation of the vows of obedience, and to be punished accordingly. Let me now give you, from Miss Saurin's evidence, the following exquisite *morceaux* of conventual discipline:

"My mother and brother called upon me about this time. I was teaching in the school, and saw them arrive. I sent a girl from the school to answer the bell. In a few minutes Mrs. M'Owne came to me in the school and ordered me to go to my cell. She told me my mother and brother had come, but that she could not allow me to see them, as Mrs. Starr had given her directions to that effect. It is usual to go after school to the chapel to pay a visit to the sacrament, and in doing so I passed the open door of the reception-room, where my mother and brother were. My mother saw me, and came and embraced me, but as I had not leave to speak to her I passed on as quickly as I could without speaking to her—Mrs. M'Owne following me to my cell. She desired me to close the door of my cell, and said she would send my mother and brother away. I asked her to let me see my mother, because I thought she would not leave without seeing me; but she said she could not, and I closed the door and she went away. She returned in five minutes, saying my mother had brought an order from Mrs. Starr, and I went to my mother at the end of the corridor. My mother clasped me in her arms and exclaimed, 'My child, are they going to make a prisoner of you?' Mrs. M'Owne tried to excuse herself by saying she was obliged by Mrs. Starr to refuse her seeing me."

This is not bad as a specimen; it is nothing, however, to what followed. The crime of letter-writing to her parents and uncle was unpardonable, even after the offence had been confessed and atoned for. Miss Saurin *was compelled to go down on her knees before the whole convent and make a full acknowledgment of her "guilt" in writing letters of complaint to her uncle.* The result of this confession was permission to write *once a year* under the direction of the Mother Superior. But Miss Saurin was severely punished. Though, with the exception of the

Mother Superior, she was the oldest member of the sisterhood attached to the convent, she was placed under subjection to a novice, and *made to do all the menial work* usually allotted to the youngest novices, such as scrubbing the floors, making the beds, and cleaning out the closet. A "distribution of time," also, was prescribed for her—quite an unusual thing in the case of professed nuns; that is to say, every hour of the day had a prescribed duty which she was bound to discharge. What some of these duties were let the complainant herself tell:

"At Hull I had three corridors to sweep and dust every day, and three altars, fourteen stations of the cross, closets, stone hall, two pairs of stairs, the sink and the doors and windows generally. I was also called upon to empty a large dust-box. I had, further, to sweep the walls and do needlework. Several times Mrs. Starr called me from mass and chapel to clean the closet. She had a window in it blocked up, because she said I had gone there to sew on strings and write down what was said. Some of these duties had to be performed in the dark in winter. I was not allowed the extra hour on Saturdays. Frequently I was unable to get the work done on Saturdays, and I had to finish it on Sundays. I had to carry the dust-box across the yard, and was exposed to the children. The Sisters are not allowed to go out on wet days. On one occasion I did go, and I had to hold the box the following Sunday morning in my hand, as a penance, during lecture-time, at the end of the table, in the presence of all the community. I was directed to wear a duster over my head. Mrs. Starr thought I had not sufficiently dusted some chairs in the community-room. She took the duster to put over my head. I told her it was wet. She sent Mrs. Kerr to dry it, and then Mrs. Starr put it over my veil, and I was obliged to wear it all day in the chapel and at meal-times. It was a soiled duster. The corridor was covered with cocoa-matting, and required three to carry it. I was directed to take it into the yard by myself to dust it. It had been swept in the corridor up to that time."

Fine spiritual exercises these for a young lady! Still I have not told you the worst. A piece of calico and a pair of scissors are found in Miss Saurin's cell, contrary to her vows of "poverty." She is remonstrated with, and although she is able to show that she is making a coif for Mrs. Starr herself, she is severely punished. *She is not allowed soap, towels or water;* she gets the washings of the coffee-pots, with the leavings of the plates of the Sisters; she is fed never-endingly on mutton, which she dislikes, and which she is at length necessitated to refuse. Once more let the complainant speak for herself:

"About the 30th of May, 1865, I reached the convent from school about four o'clock. I had a little tea and bread, and then I went to the community-room. In passing Mrs. Starr's room she called me in. Mrs. Kennedy was there. The door was then closed. Mrs. Starr desired me to take off my clothes. I hesitated for a few moments, and then I remembered my vow of obedience. I then took off my veil, habit, cincture and beads. I waited a little while between each, but she hurried me and helped to pull them off, and examined each article. She unhooked a pocket, and pulled it very roughly from me and threw it to Mrs. Kennedy. I asked her to let me have my handkerchief that was in it, as I was crying, and Mrs. Kennedy gave it me. Mrs. Starr then directed me to take off my skirt and stays. I did so, but each article she rudely pulled from me. Each article as it was taken off was examined. I never saw my pocket nor the contents afterward. Mrs. Starr undid my last skirt and examined my person."

The Lord Chief Justice—"Did she convey to you for what purpose?"

Plaintiff—"No, my lord. She dragged the scapular off my neck, and also a small rosary I was wearing. She then threw me back some of my clothes to put on. I put them on, and when dressed I left the room by her orders. My examined-book, which contained entries relative to confession, was in my pocket. The articles produced were taken from my desk, except one examined-book that was in my pocket. About the 1st or 2d of December, 1865, I was sitting at my place in the community-room. Mrs. Starr came into the room, and by her orders I went into the small room adjoining, and in the presence of Mrs. Dawson I had to undress, standing opposite the open door, with the Sisters constantly communicating with Mrs. Starr. My clothes were all taken off except my inside tunic. This occupied considerable time. I was standing all the time, and felt very cold. I put the habit over my shoulders, but Mrs. Starr rudely pulled it off. She told Mrs. Dawson she could not tell how I could stay in the house, and that I might go as soon as I liked."

This last statement, "I might go as soon as I liked," revealed the culmination of Mrs. Starr's iniquity. It turned out that, while all the petty persecutions referred to were going on, the Mother Superior had been secretly holding correspondence with the Bishop with a view to the removal of her victim under circumstances of deep disgrace. Charges which Miss Saurin never saw or heard, and which now turn out to have been utterly untrue, were preferred against her; a mock trial was instituted before the Bishop and a commission, and sentence was passed. The sentence absolved the unhappy girl from her religious vows. The way in which it was communicated to her and the manner in which she received it are best described in her own words. She says:

"Mrs. Starr and Mrs. Kennedy came to my cell about five o'clock on the morning of the 12th of February. Mrs. Starr advanced to my bed and said, 'I want all your religious dress; you are to leave the convent to-day.' Mrs. Kennedy secured the greater part of it, and Mrs. Starr took my rosary and cincture that were at the head of the bed, and part of a secular dress was left for me to wear, which I refused to put on. Previous to this I had written to the Bishop, who, in reply, informed me I should have to leave the convent, and that I should be absolved. Later in the day, about nine o'clock, Mrs. Starr came to me with Mrs. Kennedy and a number of the Sisters. She read to me, as if from a letter, that the Bishop had dispensed me, commuting it for the first ten masses after I received notice, whether I would or not. I was to be got rid of at the shortest possible notice. She said, 'Will you go?' I replied, 'I will not. I would rather die than leave the convent of my own free will; but it pleased God to leave me at her mercy, and she might do as she pleased.' She said, 'I can't put you out.' I said, 'I will die where

I am.' This occurred in my cell, where I was sitting up in a bed. Mrs. Kennedy threatened me with all kinds of vengeance from God and the Bishop. Mrs. Starr checked her. They then all left. Mrs. Starr afterward came to my cell with a secular dress. I refused to put it on, and it was taken away. She came in again with lay Sister Mary Collingwood, and said she could not have me with the Sisters, and that I must go to the bath-room. Mrs. Starr followed me there. I remained there until April. I had no fire allowed me. It was very cold. I was not allowed any religious book. A Sister was with me day and night. The Sisters had plenty of warm clothes and hot-water bottles for their feet. Mrs. Starr took away a piece of carpet I used for warmth. I was in April removed to an attic by direction of Mrs. Kennedy, where I found Mrs. Starr. It was always used as a lumber-room, and it was very dirty. The bed in it was dirty, and I had to use the sheets that had been used by me in the bath-room in the previous February. When I was removed to the attic a Sister slept in the corridor, and a rope was attached to the attic-room door and her bed. A Sister sat at the attic door in the day, and after I had been there a short time I was not permitted to leave it for any purpose. The window was darkened, and there was very little light. I had a soiled blanket and a rug for the bed. The blanket was affected with vermin. I complained, but no change was made. Food was brought to me on a plate. I had to sit on the floor. A chair that was in the room was put to the other side of the room, and I was told not to go there, and I habitually sat on the floor. The lay Sister who had to watch me used to clean the knives and that sort of work in the room. One day, when the weather was warm, the Sisters were changed eighteen times. The room was most offensive. On one occasion six Sisters with bad legs, who used liniments, were there at one time. I was not allowed to leave the room for any purpose whatever. At times I felt as if I had lost my senses. I thought at one time I was dying, and I wrote to my brother Patrick to come to me and to let me know what my beloved parents would have me do. Mrs. Starr and Mrs. Kennedy dictated the greater part of the letter. They told me the Bishop would not let me leave the convent alone. He came over about the 13th of March, and he brought Sir Henry Cooper, an eminent physician, to see me. After that the food and conduct of the officials became worse. I was not allowed to be alone with my physician. Mrs. Kennedy and Mrs. Dawson sat near enough to hear what was said. My brother went out when the doctor came in. He suggested they should leave also, but they refused. The next day my brother came and took me from the convent."

The result of the whole, as might be expected, is the trial instituted by the relatives of the young lady, and now being conducted in the light of day before a British judge and jury. Eight days have already been occupied in taking evidence, and it is believed that at least eight days more will be consumed before a verdict can be obtained. I may state, however, that nothing has yet occurred in the slightest degree to affect Miss Saurin's direct testimony. She was three days under examination, and came out of a most searching cross-examination—in which all kinds of jesuitical insinuations were made as to her life and conduct—utterly unscathed. Her statements were straightforward and consistent throughout, and had the ring of sincerity and honesty about them; while it is too evident that her persecutors, so far as can be judged of the line of conduct pursued by their counsel and the evidence of the Mother Superior, have no defence that will for a moment weigh with a jury of "twelve good men and true." As a specimen of the ingenuity of Rome in trying to damage character when its owner is in peril, let me give you the following from the cross-examination of Miss Saurin:

"I never took a book from any Sister for the purpose of secreting it. I never took another Sister's book for a temporary purpose without permission. I have held business conversation with one of the priests at Hull. I never endeavored to attract his attention on any occasion. I was never in an habitual state of excitement when he came to the convent. I never purposely put myself in his way. Sister Mary was at the school; I never remember being with her in the presence of the priest. I never went on my knees, pulled things out of his hand and entreated him to go with me, in her presence. I have not the least idea of anything that will give a color to such a charge, etc., etc. I never endeavored to make strife between the Mother Superior and the Sisters. I never put the clock back or altered it for my own convenience. We are allowed lights in the cells until ten o'clock, and one night a week a quarter of an hour later. I was never charged with having ends of candles in my cell. We used gas at Hull and at Clifford. I never put a letter in a book for one of the children to get it and take to the post. When refectorian I had to make the tea, but I never poured out a good cup and put it by for myself with buttered toast." (Laughter.)

It is enough to quote a few of these answers to show the nature of the charges trumped up against this poor unfortunate nun.

Next, Mrs. Starr was put upon the stand, and examined in defence of her own conduct. Her testimony consisted simply in a repetition of the petty charges against Miss Saurin, to which the latter, when under cross-examination, gave in nearly every case an emphatic denial. Thus she charged Miss Saurin with being particularly unobservant of the rules of the convent in the matter of poverty and obedience. "She had articles of clothing, such as bits of cotton, by her which she had no right to." "On the occasion of Cardinal Wiseman's visit to the convent, Miss Saurin appropriated a pair of Mrs. Kennedy's shoes without leave. She repeatedly saw Miss Saurin eat out of meal-times! One day she saw her go into the pantry. Witness asked her a question, but she was unable to answer as her mouth was too full! Miss Saurin was so ashamed of herself that she nearly fainted." "When refectorian, Miss Saurin was partial in her distribution of food. She used to give better food to the seniors than to the juniors. Witness thereupon changed the plates, and when they were uncovered, the unfair distribution was made apparent. The seniors had the worst of it that day." "Miss Saurin used too affectionate a tone in her letters to her relations. Her language was not sufficiently restrained! To write to her uncle, though he was a priest, 'My ever dearest uncle,' exceeded the limits of language enjoined upon the witness when she was a novice." "The plaintiff was guilty of other violations of rule. She had gathered unripe gooseberries in the garden! She used a candle to go to bed with in July, and denied it. She washed her clothes on a certain day against general orders. She spoke to strangers when forbidden—among others to the Rev. Mr. Collimere, the chaplain of the convent. Being fond of early rising, Miss Saurin put the clock forward a quarter of an hour."

Such, amid roars of laughter in court, were a number of the heinous transgressions of the poor nun. As nothing worse has so far been proved, I think you may look confidently to a verdict against the defendants.

CALEDONIA.

P. S.—The expectation of our correspondent was well founded. The trial lasted some days longer, and resulted in *a verdict for the plaintiff, with damages of five hundred pounds!* This is a righteous judgment. This convent system—shutting up young women in cells almost like those of a prison, subjecting them to a thousand petty annoyances and persecutions, by which the life is crushed out of their young hearts—cannot stand before the light of day, and is sure not to find much favor whenever its vices and its cruelties are exposed to the honest in-

dignation and the righteous verdict of a British jury.
—EDS. EVAN.

N. Y. Evangelist, March 11, 1869.

REV. DR. CUMMING ON CONVENTS.

THE Rev. Dr. Cumming, London, delivered a lecture in the Scotch National Church on the nature and rules of convent life. The Rev. gentleman, after some introductory remarks, proceeded to place the suicide, the nun and the monk on the same level, in the respect that each from various reasons sought to hide themselves from the world and its turmoils. A convent was a place where no man was allowed to visit except the priest who received confession. There were two hundred and forty convents and thirty monasteries in England, and from seven thousand to ten thousand nuns shut up in these prisons. The queen could send her inspectors to any of our lunatic asylums to see that justice was done, but into those convents where these ladies were shut up no official dared to enter to inform the world what was going on; and it was said, rather than submit to lay inspection, the Roman Catholics would sweep every convent from the land. But, argued the Rev. Doctor, if they were such abodes of bliss, so fragrant with virtue, surely their conductors would court visits from the inspector, that he might tell the world of the joys of the inmates, and induce others to enter. On the contrary, by the Council of Trent the secular arm was invoked to keep the world outside, and to prevent the nun from escaping from her cell under any pretence whatever. The Rev. gentleman proceeded to read a very dreadful curse which was pronounced on any layman who in any way interfered with the seclusion of the nun. He was to be cursed sleeping and waking, from the sole of his foot to the crown of his head. No doubt this curse in part was pronounced on the jury, and particularly on the solicitor-general for his able and eloquent speech in the defence of Miss Saurin.

Dr. Cumming proceeded to read copious extracts from accredited authorities to show the dreadful system and laws by which convents were governed, showing the system was more even to blame than the Mother Superior. According to the discipline as laid down, the Superior was allowed to flog a nun, if not done in the presence of strangers or a novice. Nuns were forbidden to see faults in the Superior, but were to obey her as God, and also obey their confessor, not as man, but as God. What a dreadful system, if this priestcraft were carried out to the extent the Ritualists as well as Catholics desired, to have in every district men who knew the failings, the strong points, the prejudices and the weak points of their flocks! In short, the confessor was enjoined to know him who confessed better than he knew himself. The Doctor next gave a graphic sketch, from Roman Catholic authorities, of the inducements held out to ladies to enter the convent. On the other hand, from the same sources the miseries of the married state; husbands were brutal, and children said to be a perpetual nuisance. He (Dr. Cumming) thought quite differently, for to him the two most beautiful things on earth were young children and flowers. He was afraid there were numbers of ladies being trained for convents by the Ritualists and others. But he would ask such if it were not better even to be living under a bad husband in their home than in a convent under such as Mrs. Starr. Was woman fit to be trusted with such autocratic power as the Mother Superior? Was it an expedient thing for twenty or thirty women to be shut up together from the world, never to see a newspaper, and lead entirely a monotonous life? Such a life was alike as unnatural as useless, and to his (the lecturer's) mind there was more Christianity in a mother's apron than in the nun's veil.—*Advertiser.* [*From N. Y. Obs. April* 8, 1869.]

CONVENT OF THE SACRED HEART.

By Rev. S. M. Campbell, D. D., Rochester, N. Y.

We have an institution with the above designation in Rochester, at which many young ladies from Protestant families are being educated, with the stipulation that their religion will not be in any way interfered with. To my great sorrow, one of the members of my own flock is an inmate of that institution; and as she was recently at home on account of sickness, I gathered the following information concerning the management in the convent.

Protestant girls, as well as Catholics, are forbidden to attend any religious service, even on the Sabbath, outside the convent. Those whose parents reside in the city are made no exception to this rule. They are not allowed to go even where their own parents worship. Their only resource is the convent chapel. Miss T., of my own church, says:

1. "I find it very difficult to practice my own religion. They do not forbid it, but their rules and regulations render it almost impossible. In order to pray in secret and read my Bible by myself, I am obliged daily to disobey the rules. No pupil has a room by herself. About thirty young ladies lodge in the room where I sleep, and we are barely allowed time to undress and get into bed when a 'Sister'

comes through to see that all is right. I get up in the dark, after she has gone through, and kneel down and pray. I manage the case something in the same way in the morning. They seem trying to make us forget our own religion as much as possible. For a time I yielded and gave up my Bible and prayer, but lately I have done as I describe.

2. "Every Sunday they require us to learn a 'Gospel,' and furnish us with Romish Testaments for that purpose. The girls generally use those Testaments, but last Sunday I used my own, and intend to do so hereafter, though they do not seem pleased with it. We are required every day, from half past eleven to twelve, to listen to a lesson on the doctrines of the Catholic Church. The Protestants do not recite or answer questions, but they are required to put away their books, sit round the teacher and listen respectfully to what she says. Her teaching lately has been on purgatory and the distinction between mortal sins and venial sins.

3. "We are required to attend chapel service daily. We come in with long black veils thrown over us, and moving very slowly. On Sunday we have white veils. It seems very solemn, much like a funeral. On the altar are images of the Virgin and of St. Joseph, and we are all required to 'bow down to them.' We all conform to this regulation.

"Since Lent came in, seven pictures have been hung on each side of the chapel, and in coming in we are expected to kneel before each one in turn on our way to the altar while they pray to the Virgin. This is called 'the way to the Cross.' The prayers are mostly for souls in purgatory. *Several of us Protestants respectfully declined kneeling to the pictures, and were reprimanded for it in the chapel.* Then we were taken into a room by ourselves and talked to very severely.

"I have to use great effort to resist these influences. *Two Protestant girls, members of a Presbyterian church in Pennsylvania, go through the whole ceremony.* They have been in the convent some time. One of our Protestants had just bought her some beads, and has great faith in them. She thought she got a clear day not long ago by using them in prayer."

How faithfully the promise not to interfere in any way with their religion is kept with the Protestant young ladies at the Convent of the Sacred Heart, let candid readers of the above statement judge for themselves. How wise it may be to place our daughters at school where the influences are so bad that we feel obliged to exact any such promises, is still an additional question on which I would like to offer something at another time.—*N. Y. Evangelist.*

THE PRIESTS IN NEW YORK.

A FEW months ago the Christian young men of one of our churches resolved to sustain prayer-meetings, one evening in the week, among the poor who literally swarm the tenement-houses of this city, and for this purpose secured two rooms in different localities occupied by Protestants, who gladly assented to such a proposition. These meetings were quietly conducted and well attended, while many conversions rewarded the labors of these workmen of the Master. But Romanism was afraid of hymns and prayers, which might drop some spark of life into the souls of her poor slaves of superstition; and so the landlord was instructed by the priests to forbid the meetings, which was done, for the penalty of disobedience was the expulsion of the family from their room. The same efforts were made, and as successfully, to close the other meeting, but the young men were not discouraged, and a third room was secured with a Protestant family, and here the numbers increased, and the Holy Spirit was poured out upon the disciples thus gathered together. But again the priests became alarmed, the landlady was enjoined to forbid such meetings, and when the evening came not only was the door closed against them, but a *Romish priest* was at the door, insulting the young men, as, surprised, they inquired the reason of this movement against the meeting of prayer.

Now, how long shall Protestants be blind to the startling fact that Romanism is a foe to all which we hold dear in our republican institutions; that she is determined to keep the iron fetters of ignorance and superstition upon the souls of the citizens of this land; and that, had she only the power, she would to-day close every public school, burn every Bible, link together Church and State, and persecute, as bitterly as ever in the Dark Ages, those who dared to think for themselves! Now is the hour to *protest* against that subtle and awful despotism, instead of sleeping on until that "protest" will be attended with war.—*N. Y. Observer*, April 22, 1869.

ROMANISM ON THE RAMPAGE.

A CATHOLIC priest some time since intruded into a Presbyterian mission school in the South-west. His outrageous conduct was severely and deservedly criticised in the *South-Western Presbyterian.* The Catholic organ denied the facts, but they being proved, the priest ventured a public explanation, of which the following is a part:

"Some time ago rumors reached me that the

enemy was insidiously at work establishing a viper's nest in the shape of a Sabbath-school mission in the neighborhood of the Jackson R. R. depôt, for the purpose of carrying on a Protestant propagandism and proselyting institution—soliciting Catholic parents to send their children thereto, and bribing Catholic children to frequent those dens of hypocrisy, lies and deceit, in order to imbibe in that poisoned source those biblical cants and sanctimonious slang belched forth by their authors in Luciferian eructations. Not wishing to act immediately upon the rumors until I would be better informed, four Sundays ago I made a descent upon the den, and there found one of my Catholic children, whom I ordered out of that nest of darkness and irreligion, remarking to one who was a Sabbath-school teacher, or connected therewith, that I would tolerate no one to influence the Catholics of my parish to frequent that haunt of error—that I would allow no wolf to come in the clothing of sheep and make incursions among my flock, without sounding the cry of alarm, and expurgating, with all the might of my moral force, my parish of this imported religious infection."—*N. Y. Evangelist*, July 22, 1869.

AUSTRIA.

A NUN RELEASED AFTER TWENTY YEARS' CONFINEMENT.

VIENNA, July 26.

GREAT excitement was created last week in Cracow by the liberation of a nun confined in a convent twenty years. A popular demonstration on the occasion led to a series of disturbances. The military were called out to restore order, and many arrests were made. The city is now quiet.—*Philadelphia Inquirer*, July 27, 1869.

POWER OF THE CONFESSIONAL.

A WRITER in the *Church of England Quarterly* says: "Let any one consider this subject well. What woman but must quail before the eye of him who has wrung out of her soul secrets with which no man on earth besides is cognizant? who has tortured her spirit to agony till it has forced from her lips words, the very recollection of which withers her heart and burns her cheek with the blush of shame? And what woman who thus quails before the eye of the confessor but must of necessity be already fitted as an instrument for all that he desires to effect in the way of influence with a husband, a brother or a son?

Rome insists upon unquestioning obedience from her children, and she well knows that the first step to it is the loss of self-respect on their part. There is that in every man's heart which he holds in sacred confidence between himself and God—something in the sad experience of every man's individual frailty which can only rightly be told to God, and be told in secret mournings of the spirit, which he alone in his mercy can understand and pity. The moment that another steps in and possesses himself of the secret, the blessed nature of that holy confidence between the soul and God is broken in upon, and he who usurps the place of God becomes the master of the poor penitent. Body, soul and spirit are thenceforth delivered to his will, and are made the instrument by which he works his purpose."

PRESENT ASPECTS OF ROMANISM IN THIS COUNTRY.

HERE, in Protestant America, Catholicism is striding on with a conqueror's tread. The shrewdest minds in the Roman Church have given up the Old World. They see, as well as we, the handwriting on the wall, and all their energies are set upon building up the old empire in the New World. They have hitherto succeeded beyond their best expectations;

how well even facts and figures fail to adequately set forth. In 1800 there were in the United States 1 bishop, 100 priests and about 50,000 laymen; now, the Romanist can point to 44 dioceses, 3 vicariates-apostolic, 45 bishops, 3,795 churches, 2,317 clergymen, 49 ecclesiastical institutions, 29 colleges, 134 schools for girls, 66 asylums, 26 hospitals, and a communion of 4,000,000. In the older States the Catholics are a confessed power of great magnitude. They secure the choicest sites for their buildings, they erect churches at a cost at which Protestants would shudder, they make themselves seen and felt as no other sect can or cares to do. But they do not stop here. The energy of American Romanism is boundless. It outruns the advancing tide of our civilization, so that we learn by experience the truth of the European proverb, "Discover a desert island, and a priest is waiting for you on the shore." It is dotting the Western prairies with churches and convents and religious houses. An article in a recent magazine informs us that an American "saw two years ago, at Rome, a better map of the country west of the Mississippi than he ever saw at home, upon which the line of the Pacific Railroad was traced, with every spot dotted where a settlement would naturally gather, and a conjecture recorded as to its probable importance." The four millions of blacks in the South, just in the transition state from slavery to freedom, susceptible to any influence that comes clothed in the garb of kindness, offer an inviting field, and Romanism is not slow to recognize the fact and turn it to account. A teacher of the American Missionary Association in Texas says that the greatest evil he has to contend with is the Catholic influence at work among the people. A biography of Peter Clavers, a Jesuit missionary, has recently been published, detailing the wonderful sacrifices he made to preach the gospel to the blacks, as a proof that the Catholic Church was the earliest and is the truest friend of the negro.

Perhaps, on the basis of facts like this, the Romanist is not so far wrong in drawing the conclusion which an able writer in the *Catholic World* for October thus expresses: "The question put to us a few years since, with a smile of mixed incredulity and pity, 'Do you believe that this country will ever become Catholic?' is now changed to, '*How soon* do you think it will come to pass?' Soon, very soon," he continues, "we reply, if statistics be true, for it appears by the calculations of a late Protestant writer that the rate of growth of the Catholic religion has been 75 per cent. greater than the ratio of increase of population, while the rate of the increase of Protestantism is 11 per cent. less."

With change of fortune there has come, as might

be expected, a change in the *attitude* of Romanism on this continent. Once it was very well contented with "leave to be;" now, it is the most grasping and defiant of denominationalisms. The enormous influx of emigration and the easy conditions of citizenship have made it a first-class political power in a country where, next tc dollars, votes are omnipotent. It has taken possession of New York City by fifty thousand majority, and, remembering its majority of a thousand in one ward of Boston last autumn, it would not be safe to deny that it is soon to control this city. Indeed, it looks now as if nearly all the cities and large towns of the country were, by naturalizing of voters, to be given over to it. And it is the problem which may be the next to solve in this country, whether the civilizing influence of free institutions will be able to keep pace with the influx of ignorant foreign voters, so as to keep the balance of power on the side of freedom, virtue and good government.

To purchase that vote unscrupulous politicians are willing to pay any price, and those who control it are by no means scant in their demands, always asking and receiving that which will inure to the advancement of Catholicism. In 1866 the Legislature of New York voted for Romish institutions over $124,000, and to like institutions of Protestants and Jews combined, $4000. Between January and July of 1867, New York City granted to Romish institutions $120,000. For two successive years the "City Levy Tax Bill" in New York City has given them $80,000. They hold, by special grant, a lease of land on Fifth avenue, valued at nearly $2,000,000, for ninety-nine years, at a ground-rent of one dollar a year. You say this is New York, but go as far West as Idaho and Colorado, and you find the legislatures of each appropriating $30,000 for Catholic schools. The Catholics themselves are mostly of the poorer laboring classes, but they find themselves in a position to demand, and do demand and receive from the Protestants of America, vast sums to defray the enormous expenses of their growing establishment. They find money for foreign needs, sending as they did last year to the Pope nearly $3,000,000. When legislatures fail them, they search out other ways of bleeding the community. They placard the streets with notices of proposed charities, and call upon all to aid them in building their hospitals and asylums and refuges; and failing in voluntary subscriptions, they bully men with threats of withdrawal of patronage if their demands are not met. And yet every sane man knows, or *ought* to know, that every dollar given to that cause goes as really to the upbuilding of *Romanism* as though he dropped it, with Peter's pence, into the Pope's strong box. But the Catholic wants money, and money he must have, and the money *he gets*, and in such profusion that the Church has always something laid by in store for anticipated wants, till "it has become a question of no small moment as affecting the public interests to what use this vast property, growing so rapidly, is by and by to be put?" In a land where so many public men are vendible commodities, always up to the highest bidder, the gravest changes in the social order are by no means impossible.

The growing aggressiveness of Romanism has been perhaps most distinctly marked in its attempted interference with systems of public education. Commencing with the outbreak in the Boston schools in 1859, there has been ever since a constant clamor for sectarian schools, or at least a banishment of Bible reading and prayer from the list of school exercises. The disgraceful measure of success which has attended this movement is too well known. No scholar now need commit the sin of reading from the Word of God, or joining in the recitation of the prayer which our Lord taught his disciples, if priest or Catholic parent forbid. The Protestant child may be compelled to this exercise—the Romanist is a privileged character and may do as he pleases. The effort is to be continued till all recognition of God is banished from our schools; some of which, in Massachusetts at least, were established for the very purpose of guarding against the wiles of the Papacy—a fact which those who are interested may find by referring to Paper 682 of the Colonial Record.*

Yet, judging of the future from the past, Catholicism will probably carry its point—if not immediately, sooner or later. For they are full believers in the truth of the saying, "Patient waiters are no losers." All the signs of the times point to a day, and that not far distant, when the great bulwark of the Papacy will be free, republican America. I am quite well aware that to some the statement will seem absurd. One who ventures to make it will hardly be credited with the gift of prophecy. But taking the facts as they already are, and the declared intent of Romanism, with things continuing as they are, what more will the supremacy of the Papacy be than the logical result of these acknowledged premises? It is not to

* Extract from Colonial Records, Paper 682: "It being one chief object of yt ould deluder, Satan, to keepe men from the knowledge of ye Scripture, as in former times by keeping ym in an unknowne tongue, so in these lattr times by persuading from ye use of tongues, yt so at least ye true sence and meaning of ye originall might be clouded by false glosses of saint-seeming decievers" (a palpable allusion to the Douai version), "yt learning may not be buried in ye graves of ye fathrs in ye church and commonwealth, ye Lord assisting our endeavours.—It is therefore ordered that every township," etc.

be barred by calling it an impossibility, and styling those who fear it alarmists. . . . . .

But, says the Protestant indifferently and the Catholic sneeringly, "What are you going to do about it?" There is but one answer to be made to both: FIGHT it, everywhere and always—in all lawful ways—with every legitimate weapon. FIGHT it, till Antichrist loses heart and hope. FIGHT it, till it is settled beyond the possibility of reversion that Protestantism is to rule America.—*Extract from a tract on "Romanism Abroad and at Home," published by the American and Foreign Christian Union.*

OUR COMMON SCHOOLS IN DANGER.

A BILL has been introduced into the Assembly at Albany, which, should it become a law, would summarily destroy the present Board of Education and revolutionize all the public schools of the city. . . . .

The ultimate design is to take the education of our children practically out of the control of the Board of Education and place it in the hands of the Romish priests. Even now a large number of the teachers are members of that Church, and we know of at least one of the largest schools in the city with no Protestant instructor, unless it may be the Principal. We are aware that the Board is not responsible for the appointment of teachers. These are made by the School Trustees of the several wards; the Board of Education only having the power, in case of Principals and vice-Principals of the schools, to refuse to confirm the selections made by the ward officers. The hospital and asylum schools, under the charge of Romanists exclusively, are now supported in part by liberal appropriations from the school fund, and the purpose is to demand similar aid for all parish schools, and have these attached to each church. Already nearly every Romish church in the city has its parish school, and what is now wanted is the privilege to take sufficient money out of the public purse to support them. It does not seem possible that any such wicked scheme as this can pass the Legislature, or, if passed, receive the signature of a Governor who has lived in this city and witnessed the beneficent effects of the Common School System among the children of the poor. Still, it will be well for good citizens to aid the Board of Education in the measures they have taken to defeat the plot.—*N. Y. Evangelist*, March 25, 1869.

HOW THEY DO IT.

We referred the other day to an article in the *Educational Monthly*, advocating a division of the school fund among the sects, so as to give Roman Catholics the public money to support their schools. We now understand that the article was written by a Roman Catholic, and himself the editor of another monthly. We thus see the *art* and *science* of Roman Jesuitism: instead of first printing his article in his own periodical, he finds a place for it in an educational magazine, where it appears editorially, and thus the impression is made that it comes from the Protestant world, or, at least, from outside of the Roman Catholic.—*N. Y. Observer*, March 4, 1869.

EDUCATIONAL STATISTICS.

UNDER the Papal rule nine-tenths of the Italian people on an average could neither read nor write. The best figures were gained from Piedmont and Northern Italy; the next best, or rather worst, in Southern Italy; the worst of all in the Roman states. At this present time there are in Naples alone forty thousand children between five and fourteen who are never found in school.

COLLECTIONS FOR THE AMERICAN COLLEGE AT ROME.—The following is a list of the sums contributed by the different Roman Catholic dioceses through which Rev. G. H. Doane has lately traveled in making collections for the American College in Rome: New York, $44,500; St. Louis, $25,487; Baltimore, $21,155; Philadelphia, $16,920; Cincinnati, $12,455; Pittsburg, $10,155.50; Newark, $9,220; Mobile, $5,030; Boston, $5,000; Hartford, $5,000; Cleveland, $5,000; Rochester, $5,000; New Orleans, $1,575; Albany, $1,500; Sundries, $5. Total, $168,002.50.

WEALTH OF THE ROMISH CHURCH.

THE Roman Catholics are acquiring so great an estate in the United States, and acquiring it so rapidly, that it becomes a matter of public concern how they get it, what they do with it, and, especially, what they will do with it by and by, when it shall have become the largest property held in the country by or for an organization. Other organizations usually live from hand to mouth; but somehow the Catholics always contrive to have a little money ahead to invest for the future. The Catholic Church, seven-tenths of whose members are exempt from the income tax because their income is under a thousand dollars a year, is a capitalist, and has the advantage over other organizations which a man has over his fellows who, besides earning his livelihood, has a thousand dollars to operate with. There are spots in the Western country, over which the prairie winds now sweep without obstruction, that will one day be the sites of great cities. A professor of one of our Western colleges saw, two years' ago, at Rome a better map of the country west of the Mississippi than he ever saw at home; upon which the line of the Pacific Railroad was traced, and every spot was dotted where a settlement would naturally gather, and a conjecture recorded as to its probable importance. The Roman Catholics mark those spots, and construct maps upon which not existing towns alone are indicated, but probable towns also. Five hundred dollars judiciously invested in certain localities now will buy land which, in fifty years, or in twenty, may be worth one hundred millions. Thirty-seven years ago the best thousand acres of the site of Chicago could have been bought for a dollar and a quarter an acre; and there is one man now in Chicago who owns a lot worth twenty thousand dollars which he bought of the government for fifteen cents and five-eighths. Now, there are in the Roman Catholic Church men whose business it is to turn such facts to the advantage of the Church, and there is also a systematic provision of money for them to expend for the purpose.

Look at our island of Manhattan! Sixty-seven years ago there were but one or two small Catholic churches upon it. It was not until 1808 that there was such a personage as a Roman Catholic bishop of New York. Run over the diocese now, and what do we find? Churches, 88; chapels attached to institutions, 29; colleges and theological seminaries, 4; academies and select schools, 23; parochial schools, one to nearly every church; charitable asylums and hospitals, 11; religious communities of men, 6; of women, 10. But this enumeration, as every New Yorker knows, conveys no idea of the facts. Everything which the Roman Catholics buy or build is bought or built with two objects in view—duration and growth. Hence massive structures and plenty of land! Wherever on this island, or on the lovely waters near it, you observe a spot upon which nature and circumstances have assembled every charm and every advantage, there the foresight and enterprise of this wonderful organization have placed, or are placing, something enormous and solid with a cross over it. The marble cathedral which is to contain ten thousand persons is going up on the precise spot on the Fifth avenue which will be the very best for the purpose as long as the city stands. Yet when that site was selected, several years ago, in the rocky wilds beyond the cattle-market, no one would have felt its value except a John Jacob Astor or a Roman Catholic Archbishop. This marvelous Church so possesses itself of its members that Catholic priests are as wise and acute and pushing for the Church as the consummate man of business is for his own estate. The Paulist Fathers, when they planted themselves on the Ninth avenue opposite Weehawken, bought a whole block; and thus, for less money than one house-lot will be worth in five years, secured room enough for the expansion of their community and its operations for ten centuries! And there is the Convent of the Sacred Heart, in the upper part of the island—the old Lorillard country-seat; and the great establishment of the Sisters of Charity on the Hudson, where Edwin Forrest built his toy-castle—were ever sites better chosen? Mark, too, the extent of the grounds, the solidity of the buildings, and the forethought and good sense which have presided over all the arrangements.

All these things cost money, though bought and built with most admirable economy. Fifty million dollars' worth of land and buildings the Church probably owns in the diocese of New York; one half of which, perhaps, it acquired by buying land when land was cheap, and keeping it till it has become dear. Protestants will not fail to note the wisdom of this, and to reflect upon the weakness and distracted inefficiency of our mode of doing business. But the question remains: How was the other half of this great estate accumulated in half a century by an organization drawing its revenues chiefly from mechanics, small storekeepers, laborers and servant-girls? Why, in the simplest way possible, and without laying a heavy burden on any one. The glory of the Catholic Church, as we all know, is, that it is the Church of the poor, and in this fact consists its strength as well as its glory.

* * * * * *

The regular revenues of a Catholic church in a city are numerous and large. Here is the Church of St. Stephen's, for example; let us endeavor to estimate its income:

Six-o'clock mass on Sunday morning	$10.00
Seven-o'clock mass " "	25.00
Nine-o'clock " " "	25.00
Sunday-school collection	10.00
High mass at half-past ten	40.00
Vespers	20.00
Six week-day masses, in all	25.00
Total weekly income	$155.00

This is equal to $8,060 for a year. Add to this the rent of 600 pews, at an average of $75 each, and we have an annual revenue of $53,060. The pew-rent, I believe, averages more than this; although the pews stand open to every comer, except at high mass and vespers.

Such is the income. The expenses are not great:

Pastor's salary	$600
Three assistant priests, in all	1,200
Sexton, not more than	1,000
Organist, probably	1,000
Choir, about	4,000
Fire and gas, possibly	1,000
Total expenses	$8,800

This leaves an excess of income over expenditure of $42,260. This excess, except a small annual tax for the archbishop and the general interests of the diocese, is all expended in the parish. Upon most of these new city churches there is a debt which has to be provided for. If the parish is old enough to be out of debt, you may be sure it needs a new or an enlarged church, for which a fund is forming. If its church is sufficient and the parsonage adequate, then you may expect to see the pastor directing the construction of a parochial school-house, large enough to draw off from the overcrowded public schools of the neighborhood the two thousand too many children on their rolls. Or perhaps there is connected with the church a religious community, whose operations are expensive. Thus, by the unstimulated, quiet operation of the system, all our cities will be covered with costly Catholic structures, which will constantly increase in splendor and number.—*Atlantic Monthly, April,* 1868, *Art.* " *Our Roman Catholic Brethren.*"

BENEFACTIONS TO "OUR ESTABLISHED CHURCH" IN NEW YORK.

NOT far from the year 1847 the diligent explorer of our annual statutes will find, almost for the first time, a few donations for charitable purposes quietly stowed away in the depths of the "Act making appropriations for the support of the government" for the current year. Here and there also begin to appear special statutes for like purposes; as, for example, the Act in 1849 (chap. 279), appropriating $9,000 of money raised by general tax to the Hospital of the Sisters of Charity in Buffalo. From this point, however, the honorable rivalry of parties was producing a like result to that which attends the not dissimilar emulation of a public auction. The bids rose one above another with a boldness which possibly was not diminished by the fact that the bidders were offering what did not belong to them. From year to year more and larger benefactions of this class were found necessary to "the support of the government," until in 1866 they had multiplied sufficiently to be collected into a district "Charity Bill," which has been annually enacted ever since as solicitously as if, like the English Mutiny Act, all our liberties depended upon it. At the same time, and by a movement almost precisely parallel, the yearly statute-book has been encumbered annually to a greater degree with the enactments which authorize, the one for the city of New York, the other for the precisely conterminous county, the levy of such sums as the State deems adequate for municipal government, and which prescribe the general objects for which they may be expended. Exactly in like manner there begin to be discovered in these "Tax Levy" bills, considerably less than twenty years ago, the same germs which have fructified so bountifully in the general "Charity Bill" for the State at large. By virtue of the enactment last mentioned the State paid out during the year 1866 for benefactions under religious control, $129,025.49. Of this a Jewish society received $2,484.32; four organizations of the Protestant sects had $2,367.03, while the trifling balance of $124,-174.14 went to the religious purposes of the Establishment. Looking, by way of variety, at the following year for data regarding the strictly municipal gifts for like purposes, we find from the last report of the Comptroller of the city that during 1867 there was paid to Catholic ecclesiastical institutions the sum of near $200,000, aside from what may lie hidden in a vast total of more than a million, of which the details can be found only in the report of the "Department of Public Charities and Correction." While there are other benefactions in the list, hardly any are for objects having even remotely a religious character, and not one for a sectarian object. And if the proportion thus indicated holds good in the State and civic gratuities of 1868, which exceed, we can hardly say by how much, the princely sum of half a million,* it must be conceded that the Church is in a fair way of obtaining its own, with, perhaps, a trifle of what others might lay some claim to.

* * * * *

Sad stories have been hinted from time to time,

* The State Comptroller reports as paid by the State alone last year, to "Orphan Asylums, etc.," $141,328.84, and adds that this sum is exclusive of $201,000 appropriated by the "Charity Bill."

* * * * *

The reports of various charitable institutions to the Comptroller of the State in 1863 show the following valuation of property owned by those named, over and above their indebtedness. There is no reason to believe that any of the institutions has over-estimated its own property:

Roman Catholic Orphan Asylum, Brooklyn	$161,231.43
Roman Catholic Orphan Asylum, New York	235,000.00
St. Joseph's Asylum, New York	127,000.00
Society for the Protection of Roman Catholic Children, New York	205,760.09
St. Mary's Hospital, Rochester	197,912.25

within these few years past, of something like scoundrelism in dealing with and getting rid of vast properties—the ferries, docks, markets and various blocks and tracts of land—on the part of the New York government. It is not for us to sit in judgment upon those functionaries, nor to conjecture how much of the municipal property, so far from having stolen, they have, with the high virtue of those who let not their left hand know what their right hand doeth—who "do good by stealth and blush to find it fame"—quietly devoted to the pious uses of the Church. But the last Comptroller's report contains, with regard to certain of the real estate which yet remains on the island of Manhattan, some interesting avowals, by which the city government is willing to let its light so shine before men that they may see its works and glorify its father, which is—no matter where. In the schedule of city property subject to payment of ground rent (pp. 166–169), we find that the premises on "Fifty-first street and Lexington avenue" are leased to the (Catholic) Nursery and Child's Hospital; that the lease is dated April 1, 1857, is *perpetual*, and for the annual rent of one dollar, which was three years in arrear. That the property on "Eighty-first and Eighty-second streets and Madison avenue" is leased to the "Sisters of Mercy;" that the lease (the date of which is not given) is *perpetual*, and the annual rent one dollar, which, however, had been paid until within two years of the report. That the land on "Fifty-first and Fifty-second streets, Fourth and Fifth avenues," was leased April 1, 1857, to "The Roman Catholic Orphan Asylum," *perpetually,* for the annual rent of one dollar. This sum, however, it is gratifying to observe, has been fully paid to the end of 1867.

Upon some part of this property, or upon another tract held by a like title and upon similar terms, is in course of erection the new St. Patrick's Cathedral, which is intended to be worthy of its proud rank of metropolitan church of this great Commonwealth. From estimates of those competent to appraise land in New York, it appears that these blocks alone are worth not less than $3,000,000. It may be concluded, therefore, that the city would get the worth of this property if it applied every payment upon the principal, asking nothing for interest, in about one million years.

Thus increasingly munificent in their provision for the maintenance of a Church establishment have been the rulers of an American State, during a generation noted for the fiercest onslaughts, in other lands, upon the sacred institutions of antiquity, and in which scoffers have pretended to discover more "spiritual wickedness" than pure spirituality in the "high places" of politics. In so extraordinary a ratio, too, has this devout allotment of the public revenues increased, that what in 1849 was but about $13,000, and that given but grudgingly, is grown to not far from $500,000 in 1868, bestowed with the frank generosity of those who give of others' goods. If some crabbed rustic, the slowness of whose toilsome gains begets a narrow curiosity concerning the manner of disposing of them, or whose sectarian jealousy sets him against the Church of the Commonwealth, shall reckon that this rate of increase, far beyond the increase of the Church, will bring the annual gift to $40,000,000 in 1918, and to $80,000,000 in 1968, we need only smile at his hedge-philosophy. It is quite enough that these benefactions should continue upon the scale they have now reached for a few years longer.

* * * * * *

Nor does the Church longer stand, as once it did, in the attitude (well as the attitude becomes Christ's poor) of a mendicant at the door of the State-house, asking for gratuities toward the support of its separate schools. It has already established by action in the Supreme Court the clear legal right of its orphan asylums, numerous as they are and liberal as they are in the degree of bereavement required for admission to their scholastic privileges, to an equal participation in all moneys raised by taxation for school purposes in the State, in proportion to their number of pupils.*

* * * * * *

It might, perhaps, be worth while, if any one should prefer mere superficial or external signs of supremacy, to notice a few such as may be found in the city of New York itself. Not many a State Church in the present age imposes the test of membership as a condition to hold civil office. The Church in Austria does not; in England it has not for forty years; in France not for eighty. It does not yet in New York. How near it comes to it may be partly guessed by any one who will look over a list of New York elective officers with the discriminating sense of him who "knew the stranger was an American from his name—O'Flaherty." If the inference from nationality should be deemed illusive, because not all Irishmen are Catholics, let it be remembered that the Catholics who are not Irish will far more than make such an error good. Such researches would show a judiciary adorned with the names of Shandley, Conolly, Hogan, and Dennis Quinn, and would lead us into very green fields of nomenclature; but some one else has prepared, from better data than mere names, the following summary of Irish office-holders as they were at the end of 1868:

* *St. Patrick's Orphan Asylum* vs. *Board of Education, Rochester.*

Sheriff,

Register,

Comptroller,

City Chamberlain,

Corporation Counsel,

Police Commissioner,

President of the Croton Board,

Acting Mayor and President of the Board of Aldermen,

President of the Board of Councilmen,

Clerk of the Common Council,

Clerk of the Board of Councilmen,

President of the Board of Supervisors,

Five Justices of the Courts of Record,

All the Civil Justices,

All but two of the Police Justices,

All the Police Court Clerks,

Three out of four Coroners,

Two Members of Congress,

Three out of five State Senators,

Eighteen out of twenty-one Members of Assembly,

Fourteen-nineteenths of the Common Council, and

Eight-tenths of the Supervisors.

Nor would even a tabular statement of office-holders, however complete, fully illustrate the influence of Our Church upon politics, unless it could include also all those non-Catholic officers or candidates, from Justices of the Supreme Court down—or up—who find it to their interest to be liberal contributors to Catholic charities or building funds, or promptly-paying pew-owners in one or more Catholic churches. So far does the Church permit its favorite dogma of justification by works to extend even to those whose words frankly deny the faith.—*Putnam's Magazine*, July, 1869; *Article*, "*Our Established Church.*"

THE DIOCESE OF MASSACHUSETTS.

THE *Pilot* (Roman Catholic) indulges in a little natural pride in the increase of Romanism in the diocese of Boston, which includes, we believe, the whole State of Massachusetts. When it is remembered that the distinguished Cheverus was consecrated bishop no longer ago than 1810, we do not wonder that the *Pilot* congratulates its readers on the progress of its denomination in what it calls "the commercial and intellectual centre of the land of the Puritans." Here are the figures in a nutshell:

There are in the diocese of Boston, the State of Massachusetts, 128 churches, and 8 building; 36 chapels and stations; 155 priests, and 11 ordained since the last report; 88 clerical students; 3 male and 15 female religious institutions; 2 male literary institutions; and 3 female academies; and 13 parochial free schools; aggregate number of pupils, 5,855. Hospitals and orphan asylums, 5 each; and 550 orphans. There are 12 benevolent and charitable institutions, and a Catholic population of over 350,000 in the entire diocese.

The Boston *Watchman* well says, in view of these statistics: "No man, be he preacher or laymen, has a moral right to complain of the progress of Romanism, or any other form of doctrine he considers erroneous or radically wrong, so long as he fails to exert himself to the utmost to propagate what he honestly believes to be the true and the right. Protestants have a long lesson to learn in these respects from Catholic priests and people."—*N. Y. Evangelist,* July 22, 1869.

APPROPRIATIONS FOR ROMANISM BY THE LEGISLATURE OF THE STATE OF NEW YORK FOR THE YEAR 1866.

THE New York Legislature made religious appropriations last year to the amount of $129,029 49. The remarkable fact appears that only $4,855 35 of this sum was for the benefit of Protestant and Hebrew associations, the balance being for Roman Catholic institutions. The following is a partial list:

Evangelical Lutheran, St. John's Orphan Home, Buffalo.	$9 93
Free School of the Academy of the Sacred Heart, Manhattanville..	346 04
Le Cauteuxl, St. Mary's Deaf and Dumb Asylum, Buffalo..	24 62
Orphan Home and Asylum of the Protestant Episcopal Church, New York..	777 59
Protestant Half Orphan Asylum, New York..............	1,304 87
Roman Catholic Orphan Asylum, Brooklyn, 1864........	2,189 21
Roman Catholic Orphan Asylum, Brooklyn, 1865........	2,476 74
Roman Catholic Orphan Asylum, New York..............	4,340 63
Society for the Protection of Destitute Roman Catholic Children, New York..	2,505 71
St. John's Catholic Orphan Asylum, Utica..................	310 52
St. Joseph's Orphan Asylum, New York.....................	1,007 48
St. Joseph's Male Orphan Asylum, Buffalo........	318 90
St. Joseph's German Roman Catholic Orphan Asylum, Rochester..	9 25
St. Mary's Orphan Asylum, Canandaigua.....................	26 21
St. Mary's Boys' Orphan Asylum, Rochester..............	89 40
St. Mary's Orphan Asylum, Dunkirk..........................	423 04
St. Patrick's Female Orphan Asylum, Rochester.........	238 75
St. Vincent's Female Orphan Asylum, Troy...............	180 07
St. Vincent's Orphan Asylum, Albany........................	766 63
St. Vincent's Female Orphan Asylum, Buffalo...	267 62
St. Vincent's Infant Asylum, Buffalo.........................	104 11
St. Vincent's Male Orphan Asylum, Utica..................	213 90
St. Vincent de Paul Orphan Asylum, Syracuse............	345 51
The Church Charity Foundation, Brooklyn, 1864.........	118 42

The Church Charity Foundation, Brooklyn, 1865.........	$156 22
Troy Catholic Male Orphan Asylum......................	448 72
St. Mary's Orphan Asylum, Clifton (special appropriation)......................	500 00
St. Joseph's Male Orphan Asylum, Buffalo (special appropriation)......................	1,000 00
St. Vincent's Male Orphan Asylum, Utica (special appropriation)......................	1,000 00
Buffalo Hospital, Sisters of Charity......................	8,949 84
Buffalo St. Mary's Lying-in Hospital......................	1,646 10
Jews' Hospital and Hebrew Benevolent Society, New York......................	2,484 32
Rochester St. Mary's Hospital......................	8,845 14
Rochester St. Mary's Hospital (additional special appropriation)......................	2,000 00
Buffalo St. Mary's Lying-in Hospital (additional special appropriation)......................	1,000 00
Church of the Immaculate Conception, New York......	1,000 00
St. Mary's Church and School, New York......................	2,000 00
St. Bridget's Church School, New York......................	1,000 00
Special Donation for the Protection of Destitute Roman Catholic Orphan Children......................	78,500 00

—*New York Tribune*, June 1, 1867.

This is *for one year only.*

N. B. Oct. 15, 1869.—Since the first edition was issued, additional information has been received of the remarkable *Cracow nun imprisonment case*, the first telegram respecting which appears on page 512, under date of July 27th. Also, another case of very considerable interest has occurred in Cracow, both which are now appended.

THE HORRORS OF THE INQUISITION REVIVED.

A VOICE from an Austrian tomb reaches us this week, which reveals heartlessness and cruelty such as the old Inquisition could hardly emulate. In the Carmelite convent of Cracow a nun was found, who is alleged to have been shut up for twenty-one years, or since 1848, in a dungeon seven paces long and six wide. That she was in such a place was learned by the officers of the town from a note sent them and written in a fine hand. The officers broke through the nun-keepers, and found the following facts:

In a dark, stinking hole, on a heap of straw, sat, or rather cowered, a naked, wild-grown, half-witted woman, who, at the unusual appearance of light and human beings, dropped her hands and implored piteously, "I am hungry, pity me, give me meat I will be obedient." This dungeon, with its little straw and much filth, and a dish of mouldy potatoes, without fire, bed, table, or even chair, which no sunshine cheered or fire blaze ever warmed, had the inhuman Sisters chosen as the dwelling-place for their should-be companion; there had they imprisoned her year after year since 1848. For twenty-one years did those dreadful Sisters pass that cell, and to none of them had it ever entered to take compassion on their poor victim. And now, half human, half beast, with her body covered with dirt, with her legs shrunk and withered, with her head squalid, diseased, year upon year long unwashed, a terrible being revealed herself, such as Dante himself, with all his powers, could not have depicted or imagined.

It seems as though this could not be true. That such a discovery should be made in 1869 is almost incredible. Yet the facts come too well authenticated to be doubted. A judge visited the convent, and then called the bishop. It is said the bishop was deeply moved, and, turning to the assembled nuns, vehemently reproached them for their inhumanity. "Is this," he said, "what you call love of your neighbor? Furies, not women, that you are, is it thus that you purpose to enter the kingdom of heaven?" The nuns ventured to excuse their conduct, but the bishop would not hear them. "Silence, you wretches!" he exclaimed; "away, out of sight, you who disgrace religion!" The father confessor, Piantkiewicz, an old priest, who was present, dared to observe that the ecclesiastical authorities were aware of this scandal; whereupon the bishop and prelate, Spital, denied his assertion, and at once suspended the father confessor, and also the superioress, who is descended from an old honorable Polish noble family.

The poor nun, whose name is Barbara Ubryk, was asked why she had been immured. She answered, "I have broken the vow of chastity;" but then added, with fearful gesture and a wild spring, "These nuns also are not pure; they are not angels." Then she sprang on the confessor, crying, "Thou beast!" On seeing the sunlight and green grass of the convent garden, she convulsed with extreme joy.

Justice is now following its course, but there are great impediments thrown in the way. The cause may be shipwrecked by the obstacles made by the ecclesiastical authorities in regard to the testimony of nuns. The nuns wear thick veils when examined by the magistrate, to that he cannot sell who is the witness before him. The Concordat is still a cause of entanglement in Austria, but this deplorable incident will clear up the relations of Church and State. "To curse and oppress," one of the Viennese journals observes, "is known at Rome, but there is neither the strength nor the will to free from the most crying abuses." It is said that the immuring of this nun was known even some ten years ago at Cracow, but that the Concordat and the Imperial policy opposed invincible obstacles to inquiry.

The whole case is one of the most horrible which has come to light in years. Yet it is suspected by many that not a few such cases exist in the convents of the old countries, of which nothing has ever been or will be known outside of the convent walls. It is some satisfaction to know that hopes were entertained that by careful nursing the nun so long imprisoned may be restored to sufficient strength to be able to tell the story of her wrongs and sufferings.—*New York Evangelist*, August 19, 1869.

MORE NUNNERY HORRORS.

A LETTER from Cracow says: The religious houses are getting into new difficulties every day, but Cracow seems to be particularly unfortunate in this respect. A miner belonging to the Wieticzka salt mines became attached to a young Jewess, and his love was returned, but her parents would not hear of her union with a Christian, and betrothed her to a member of her own faith. The marriage was fixed for an early day, and in the mean time the young lady was sent to some relations at the village of Kossocice, between Cracow and Wieticzka. About ten days ago a band of from twenty to thirty men, the friends of the rejected lover, appeared in the night at the cottage in which she was staying, surrounded it and carried her off by force. Her family succeeded in tracing her to the nunnery of the Visiterins in Cracow, and applied to the various authorities to procure her release, but without success. Last Wednesday the father of the young lady, whose name is Perlberg, received a letter from her, declaring that she was detained against her will, and begging him to effect her deliverance. As more legitimate means had failed, Perlberg collected a considerable number of his fellow-believers—who were reinforced by numerous Christians, especially Cracow students—and marched to the nunnery. The Lady Superior was intimidated by the appearance of such a formidable army, and, after some parley, admitted the father to an interview with his daughter. The latter declared with many tears that she wished to leave the nunnery at once, but to this the Lady Principal would not consent. Perlberg then called in his forces, released his daughter and carried her off amidst the shouts of the crowd. If ever there was a case in which a man was justified in taking the law into his own hands, it was this. But the fact of its being necessary to have recourse to such means does not cast a very favorable light on the Cracow police or its Church dignitaries.—*New York Observer*, Sept. 16, 1869.

THE END.

www.ingramcontent.com/pod-product-compliance
Lightning Source LLC
LaVergne TN
LVHW021239110826
845150LV00002B/355

* 9 7 8 1 4 2 5 5 6 1 9 9 4 *